# SILVER'S LURE
## ANNE KELLEHER

LUNA™
www.LUNA-Books.com

LUNA™

SILVER'S LURE

ISBN-13: 978-0-373-80237-1
ISBN-10: 0-373-80237-4

Copyright © 2006 by Anne Kelleher

First trade printing: December 2006

Author photo by: Don Goodman

www.LUNA-Books.com

**Printed in U.S.A.**

For Donny.

# Glossary of People and Places

*Meeve*—High Queen of Brynhyvar, Queen of Mochmorna
*Briecru*—her Chief Cowherd
*Morla*—Meeve's twenty-seven-year-old daughter, Deirdre's twin sister
*Bran*—Meeve's fifteen-year-old son
*Lochlan*—Meeve's First Knight, head of the Fiachna
*Connla*—Meeve's older sister and Arch Druid (Ard-Cailleach) of all Brynhyvar

*Catrione*—druid and daughter of Fengus, King of Allovale
*Deirdre*—Meeve's other daughter, druid
*Cwynn*—Meeve's son, raised by his grandfather

*Auberon*—King of Faerie
*Finnavar*—Auberon's mother
*Loriana*—Auberon's daughter
*Tatiana*—Loriana's friend
*Timias/Tiermuid*—Auberon's foster brother

*Macha*—the Goblin Queen

*Brynhyvar*—the Shadowlands, inhabited by mortals and trixies, call khouri-keen by themselves and gremlins by the sidhe
*Ardagh*—central point in Brynhyvar
*Mochmorna, Allovale, Gar and Marraghmourn*—four main provinces of Brynhyvar
*Lacquilea*—country to the south of Brynhyvar
*Eaven Morna*—Meeve's principal residence
*Eaven Avellach*—Fengus's principal residence
*Dalraida, Pentland*—territories lying within Mochmorna and Gar, respectively
*Far Nearing*—peninsula on the eastern shore of Brynhyvar

*White Birch Grove*—druidhouse where Catrione and Deirdre live

*Faerie, TirNa'lugh or the Other World*—otherworldly country bound to Brynhyvar, inhabited by sidhe and goblins

## BEFORE

*Below*

At the bottom of the World, the Hag crouched on the jagged stone lip of her fire pit. Her face was washed with an orange glow by the crackling flames. Her breath whistled between the gaps in her teeth as she chanted, "Now the fire's nice and hot, now's the time to stir the pot. Take the changeling, toss it in, stir it hard and watch it spin." She cackled softly in anticipation. Her claws skittered across the surface of the milky moonstone globe she cradled in the crook of one arm like an infant. "Make the water into stew, season it with something new, hair and bone and blood and skin, once we put the changeling in, boil brew and fire burn and dark to light will then return…" Her voice trailed off, but her words continued to echo off the lichen-lit vault above her.

She was waiting for Herne to bring her the changeling whose birth had turned her from Mother into Hag. The birth of her first offspring, the goblins, had turned her from

Maiden into Mother. Mortals and sidhe had followed, but it was the last birth that signaled a turning of the Wheel in the Worlds above. The mortals, bless them, would react like ants dispossessed of their hill, the sidhe—who alone would know what was happening—would shake their heads at the mortals' antics and the khouri-keen would burrow deep into their dens beneath the surface, only emerging when all was renewed. But the goblins—they would see it as the opportunity it was.

"And why shouldn't they?" she whispered as she worked. Of all her children, she had come to love them best. They were the easiest to satisfy.

She hawked and spat onto the moonstone, and images of the dark, dirt-lined cave swirled through its milky surface. In it, she saw Herne's fire-lit face as he bent over her mountainous belly, and for a moment, she was Mother once again, back in the birth chamber, red skin flushed and wet with sweat, body wracked with birth pangs. They'd both known this infant would be their last in this particular incarnation of reality.

The memory of herself splayed like a spider, arms back, thighs thrown wide flashed through her, even as she saw its image reflected in the globe. Her belly contracted once more in a painful heave, doubling her over, causing her to nearly drop the moonstone. She clutched it close, closed her eyes, and saw against her eyelids her final impression of Herne as he caught the caul-covered infant as it slithered out, slick with blood. Through the translucent whiteness of the membrane, she glimpsed a squirming body covered in matted hair.

One blink, and she'd found herself here in her cavern, skin mottled blue-gray, teeth yellowed and jagged, her stick clenched between contorted fingers.

She set the stick aside and for a while, she was busy. The blood that rolled between her thighs and down her legs dried to a slow drip, then stopped and crusted, falling off in flakes that the thirsty stones absorbed. She filled the cauldron, sorted through the contents of the feathered bags made from the carcasses of the Marrighugh's ravens, summoned up the fire sleeping at the bottom of the fire pit. Finally she turned to her globes that formed the supports on which her cauldron rested.

Besides the cauldron, which was as much a part of her as her own belly, they were her dearest possessions. She cherished and prized them above all else. Originally there had been four, one for each of the primal Elements that made up the Worlds. They had come to her, one by one, when the World was new, and she and Herne were young. With them, she and Herne had created all that was and would ever be.

Now there were only three, the fourth, her favorite, having shattered with such force that it generated a whole new race of beings, each of whom held a piece of the globe. She thought about collecting the pieces of the globe some day, and putting them back together, restoring the fourth globe to its proper place. But that would represent a bigger change than she felt prepared to deal with, and so, while the idea appealed to her, she ignored it for the moment. Some day, though. It amused her to think about it.

She dragged each of the remaining three to the lip of the phosphorescent sea, dipped them into the salty water, then rubbed them clean. When she was finished, she regarded them critically, trying to decide which of the three remaining she liked the best: the black obsidian smoldering with the memory of the fire that had forged it; the lustrous white pearl gleaming pink in the fire pit's glow, or the moonstone, greenish in the reflection of the phosphorescent sea. She lifted the moonstone, regarding the shifting clouds within its depths. Its surface was as changeable as the Air for which it stood, and she thought this one could be her favorite for a while.

She set the moonstone in its place. It formed a triangular support for her cauldron over the pit along with the globes of moonstone and pearl. With the obsidian and the pearl, it formed a triangular support for the cauldron over the pit. With a great heave and a strength that completely belied her appearance, she set the cauldron in its position. She poked her crooked staff below the black kettle's rounded bottom, into the center of the fire, and the flames leaped up. She stuck her stick into the brew and gave it an experimental stir. At once she frowned at the image that came swirling out of the depths. She bent her head to take a closer look, just as the gelatinous sea began to boil.

In the cauldron, the image swirled away as swiftly as it had risen. The Hag lifted her head, squinting across the rocky shore into the green glow that rose off the phosphorescent water, then licked her lips as the tips of Herne's horns broke the surface at last. Water gushed off his broad forehead, cascaded through his black curls like a curtain as his enormous head and shoulders pushed up and out of the sea, revealing the chest and upper arms of a man atop the body of a bull. He strode slowly up the sloping lip, onto the jagged surface of the shore, the razor-sharp edges of the rocks smoothing themselves under his hooves as he approached. His wet tail flicked from side to side, his eyes gleamed red.

His arms were empty.

The Hag withdrew her stick and scurried to the other side of her cauldron. "Where's the changeling? Where've you got it? My cauldron's hungry and wants its head."

Herne folded his arms and wouldn't meet her eyes.

The Hag hissed. "What is it, Father? Where's the changeling? The cauldron's cold and must be fed."

"It'll have to wait a bit."

She tried to catch his eye, but again, he wouldn't look at her. Something dark and ugly uncoiled in her gut, and the Hag took another step closer. "What have you done now, Father?"

"You didn't see him," Herne whispered. "You didn't see him as he was born."

The end of her stick flared red and in disbelief, she watched tears trickle down his face. "Him? That thing is not a him— it's not a child meant to live—it's a changeling for the pot."

"That pot's all you ever care about," Herne thundered. The ground shook, a rock tumbled down and splashed into the sea. In the depths, leviathan shapes shuddered and spun.

The Hag curled both hands tightly around her staff and stood her ground. "That's what I'm supposed to care about— I'm the one who keeps it all turning. You knew what had to be done even before it was born—we both did. Now go and get it, and bring it here. You know what must be done."

"It can wait."

An emotion so foreign the Hag didn't initially recognize

it traced a cold finger down her spine, and she peered up at Herne. The only moment she could compare it to was the moment the pink crystal globe had shattered. It was a moment that was irretrievably different from the moment before it, one that separated time into now and then, before and after. "Wait?" she rasped. Pain lanced through her chest and a sea began to boil deep inside her lungs. "What did you do to the changeling?"

"The sidhe-king took him."

"What?" A fit of coughing overtook her, and she felt a gush of rheumy mucous rise up from somewhere deep inside. She hawked and spat. The gob was flecked with streaks of blood. *Now the fire's nice and hot, now's the time to stir the pot.* The words danced through her mind and she stared up at Herne, wondering if he realized that the fire now burning in her lungs was his fault. "You let it happen, didn't you—you gave it to the sidhe-king, didn't you? Why? Why would you do such a foolish, careless thing? It's not a child—it's a changeling. It's not meant to grow up—it's meant to go in my stew."

"He was so beautiful, Mother," whispered Herne. "You were gone, the moment I pulled him from you. You didn't see… You couldn't see…how different he was…from all the others…all the other changelings…" His voice trailed off, he closed his eyes and shook his head. Then he looked down at his open hands, gazing with something like wonder on his face. "I never saw such a perfect child—his arms and legs so round, so pink. He was like a rose dipped in milk, and his eyes were green, then gray and his head was covered in curls soft as spider silk and black as—" He broke off and turned away, his hands clenching into fists.

"Black as the shit you've landed us in," the Hag screeched. "Blacker than any midnight you've yet to see—have you forgotten Lyonesse?"

"He'll come down to your cauldron sooner or later—everything does." Herne reared back, narrowed eyes flaring red. His chest appeared to broaden and deepen, his head widened so that more than ever he resembled an enormous bull towering over the tiny woman.

The Hag didn't flinch. Another burst of coughing overtook her and this time the phlegm landed next to Herne's foremost hoof. "And how long do you expect me to wait, Father? What will feed my cauldron? What will keep it turning, while this beautiful changeling of yours slithers through the land?"

"I'll bring him myself if he causes trouble."

"He's already caused trouble—I saw it in my cauldron. I didn't understand what I was seeing, but I do now. All Faerie's in uproar— Father, what do you think you've started?"

"I was going to say his hair was black as yours was, Mother." Herne dropped his shoulders and turned away, head bent. "Perhaps I should've brought him here, let you see. You'd understand."

"Of course you should've brought it here. It doesn't belong in the World. It belongs in the cauldron. That's the way it goes—take the changeling, toss it in, stir it hard, watch it spin."

"I couldn't let you do that."

"Bring it here at once."

Herne shook his head. "I can't do that."

"You have to do that."

"It's already too late—they gave him a name."

A name. The first anchor of awareness into one's own flesh

for every being—no matter what sort of being it was—began with a name. A changeling never had a name. It wasn't supposed to live long enough to need one. The disruption she'd glimpsed in the cauldron was a greater rift than she'd realized. "You have to fix this, Father."

"Why can't you just agree to wait a bit? You know he'll end up here eventually like everything else."

The weight of all existence fell upon her like an enormous rock, and for a moment she wondered if she would ever breathe again. Automatically, because it was the only thing she knew to do, the Hag tottered to the cauldron. She dipped her stick into the brew, and the cauldron rolled gently, settling into place onto the three globes. Tentatively, feeling as if the ground beneath her feet might open and swallow them all, she began to stir in a widening figure eight as she frowned into the broth. "This isn't something easily undone, Father. This one's got away from us—gotten itself a name, even. Oh, this is a clever one, indeed. Cauldron only knows what havoc this one will wreak."

The weight was like a black cloak, settling over her as dense as the soupy water lapping against the rocks. It choked her throat, made the words hard to form and turned her voice into a guttural growl. "Round about the circle goes, dark to light and back it flows, now the fire starts to burn, and the brew begins to churn. Gently simmer in the pot, while the changeling-child rots—take it, break it, let it burn, that Hag to Maiden then return." But even as she chanted, even as she bent her back and pulled the stick through the frantically bubbling brew, she knew it was already too late.

## 1
### THEN

*White Birch Druid Grove, Garda Vale*

The trixies were restless and the butter wouldn't churn. Meeve's messenger, one of her elite corps of warriors called the Fiachna, and sorely afflicted with arrogance, had come and gone and Catrione had been glad to see him go. Since dawn, rain had been sluicing off the thatched roofs like water from an overturned bucket, and while at one time, the thought of his wet, uncomfortable journey might've quietly pleased her, this was the first quarter Catrione had ever served as Ard-Cailleach, the head sister of the Grove, and she was too caught up in the turmoil spiraling all around her to give him another thought.

She dodged the widest puddles as she hurried across the chilly yard toward the low stone still-house, but her feet were soon soaking wet, her hems sodden. The oldest cail-leachs, on whom she might've relied for support and advice, had all left for the MidSummer rites at Ardagh, summoned there early to a special conclave by the ArchDruid, Connla. Catrione, being one of the younger sisters and head of the Grove for the quarter was left with the few druids either too old to travel or too young to be called. There were reports of blight spreading across the land, of increasing numbers of unnatural births—two-mouthed fish and six-legged calves—and rumors that goblins were stirring. The queen's messenger didn't say why Meeve wanted her daughter, Deirdre, home. He had not once looked directly at Catrione, nor any of the other druids, and after he left, the serving maid who'd warmed his bed spoke of trouble between the ArchDruid, Connla, and the Queen.

But nothing seemed to account for the fact that knots wouldn't stay tied, fires wouldn't stay lit, water wouldn't boil and bread was slow to rise. Not to mention the trixies, who spilled and spat and quarreled and caused so much aggravation that that very afternoon, she'd banished them to their dens below the Tor shortly after discovering that an entire batch of starter had to be scrapped, leaving the entire Grove with no means of making bread unless the still-wives had more.

Catrione paused under the eave as a huge black raven shrieked at her, then rose and flapped off. Startled, she put her hand on the still-house latch as the old rhyme ran through her mind: *One for sorrow.* The door swung open, seemingly of its own accord. Catrione gasped as three anxious faces materialized out of the stillroom's gloom the moment she put her foot across the threshold, and she wondered if they'd been watching for her.

"Catrione, you have to let us take the child." Bride, the chief still-wife, broad-breasted as a turtledove but sharp-eyed as a hawk, closed one hand on Catrione's wrist and pulled her inside. "Deirdre's child—it's gone too long past its time."

"Sisters," Catrione managed, feeling weak in the knees. Deirdre the High Queen's daughter, once Catrione's best friend among the sisters, had doubly disgraced herself and the Grove. Not only had she lain with a brother outside the sacred rituals, but a few months after he'd been banished, she'd admitted to carrying his child.

Druids lay with each other only as part of sacred ritual, and then only after preparation and precautions against the conception of a child, for such couplings produced danger-ous rogues and other anomalies. This pregnancy had gone long beyond anything normal, and now, having resisted the sisters' arguments that the child should be aborted, Deirdre was approaching three months, at least, past term. The child was still alive and squirming, and Deirdre refused to do anything more to hasten her labor than to drink the mildest of tonics.

Catrione felt as if her legs might give way beneath her, but Bride's clasp seemed to communicate a subtle strength, allowing her to sink onto a long wooden bench.

"You know we must," Bride was repeating. "You must allow it."

Baeve, tall and thin as a wraith, spoke from over Bride's shoulder, as Sora, youngest of the three, shut the door. "You know we're right, Catrione. It's not natural."

Catrione knotted her fingers together over her stained linen apron. "But, sisters—"

"Think of Deirdre," said Sora, all soft voice and hands that fluttered around Catrione's shoulders like shy birds.

"Think of the Queen," said Baeve as Catrione met her eyes.

"It's not good for her," Bride was saying. "And look what's happening here. This is the kind of thing that's happening all over Brynhyvar."

Baeve's expression made Catrione pause. The messenger had gone away, but his parting words were that both Meeve and her sister Connla, the ArchDruid of all Brynhyvar, would be stopping on their way to Ardagh. But even as one side of Catrione wondered why the ArchDruid wasn't at Ardagh already, she recognized that for all their reasons, the women were right. And yet to order the child taken felt like betrayal.

The memory of Tiermuid's words, his voice like sand-washed silk, whispered through her. *Protect her.*

And so Catrione had, not because Deirdre was her dearest friend, the one among all the twenty or so sisters who really did feel like a sister, but because *he'd* asked it of her, Tiermuid, whose black hair fell around his shoulders, lustrous as a woman's, his eyes so faint a blue they were nearly sidhe-green. She and Deirdre were not the only sisters who giggled and blushed when Tiermuid was around, and if Deirdre had been the one to fall completely under his spell, the fire he'd lighted in Catrione smoldered secretly still, tamped down only by long force of hard discipline. To order the child—his child—taken felt like an arrow in her heart.

"We know how much you love Deirdre. We know how hard this has been for you." Bride's face puckered like a dumpling. She pushed wayward wisps of gray hair under her coif and covered Catrione's hands with her own, eyes steady and unwavering. "But we've no choice."

"What will we tell the ArchDruid when she comes, otherwise?"

"What will we tell the Queen? Her knight said she'd stop here herself on her way to Ardagh, didn't he?"

Catrione raised her eyes to the bunches of drying herbs hung along the rafters, the baskets of nuts and berries and seeds. Somewhere amidst all that profusion was the potent combination that would drive the child out at last. A tingle ran up her spine and down her arms. She could've left at Beltane, for her father Fengus, the chieftain-king of Allovale and nearly as powerful in his own right as the High Queen, had been left without a druid in his own house when the last one died. But Deirdre was here, and the child was due, and she'd stayed.

But that wasn't the only reason, Catrione knew, if she was honest with herself as she was required to be at every Dark Moon ritual. Tiermuid might return. The term of his banishment from the Land of a year and a day was nearly completed. She closed her eyes and wished any of the older sisters present, even Eithne, whose tongue was as cutting as her eye was quick to find the least fault. She had maintained all along that the child should be aborted, while Catrione had been careful never to voice an opinion. No wonder they made me Ard-Cailleach, she reflected bitterly. It's a kind of test.

"Please," said Baeve.

Catrione rose, back straight, deliberately shutting at all thoughts of Tiermuid's naked body, slim and white in the moonlight bending over Deirdre's darker flesh. *That way lies madness—look at what's happened to Deirdre.*

"We know you don't want to," Sora said, eyes liquid and large as a doe's, skin nearly as pale and satiny as a sidhe's.

"But we hope you see you must." Bride sat back, folding her arms.

"We have to end this unnatural thing," Baeve put in.

Catrione held up her hands as she heaved a deep sigh. She was druid, she had always been druid, and this desperate striving urgency building in her belly was a result of the Beltane to Solstice ritual abstention from any kind of coupling. The fire kindled at Beltane must be allowed to burn. That's why she was feeling this growing need, every time she thought of Tiermuid. Druids did not love each other. *Not the way you love Tiermuid.* The wicked little whisper made her belly burn. MidSummer was coming, when the bonfires on the Tors would call out the sidhe, and the druids would couple their fill, infusing the land. But until then, the energy had to be suppressed. "Sisters, you've convinced me. What do you want me to do?"

"Go get her," answered Baeve.

"Bring her here," added Bride.

"What if she won't come? What shall I do then?"

"If she won't come, call the men," said Baeve.

"What men?" Catrione blinked.

"The men who'll be waiting outside the door as soon as we call for them," replied Baeve.

Catrione stiffened. So this had been previously planned out. "Did Niona put you up to this?" Niona MaFee, just a few years older than Catrione, and the daughter of a poor shepherd somewhere far to the north, had been jealous of Catrione, the daughter of the chief of Allovale, from the moment Catrione had arrived at the White Birch Grove nearly fourteen years ago. Since Beltane, when Niona had not been among those chosen to accompany the older cail-leachs to Ardagh, she'd grown even more resentful.

The women exchanged glances, and Bride said, "Every-one—even the neighboring chiefs—are talking. Why, just yesterday young Niall of the glen was here, telling us his sheep were sickening and to see if we had a remedy, and Niona happened to be here. Then she went with him while he spoke to Athair Emnoch about his trees—you were with the Queen's messenger."

Catrione's cheeks grew warm. No one had even mentioned the young chief's visit. Her jaw tightened. She balled her hands into fists, determined to keep control, and said, "You want me to do this now?"

"There's a bit of time," said Baeve with a glance at the other two. "We've got to get a few things ready—"

"And you look like you could use a rest," said Sora.

"Why not lie down for a turn of a short glass," said Bride. "I'll send Sora with a cup of something with strength in it when all's ready."

Catrione nodded at each in turn, wondering if this was how her father felt before setting out on a cattle raid. She trudged across the courtyard, listening to the fading sounds of the flurry of activity that began the moment the door-latch clicked shut behind her. Her sandals slapped against the slates, the smell of roasting chicken wafting through the air made her nauseous. The rain had eased but the sky was as leaden as her mood. The low white-washed buildings with their beehives of thatch looked like giant children squatting under rough woven cloaks. The courtyard was deserted and she was glad. She picked up her skirts and ran as another downpour suddenly intensified. Once inside the long dormitory, she stopped before Deirdre's door, fist raised.

She let out a long breath, considering whether to knock or not, whether to try to reason with her friend once again. But she'd had that conversation too many times, and the dull, dead feeling in her gut told her exactly how it would end—Deirdre would refuse, the men would have to be summoned and she, Catrione, would have to go down to the still-house, tired and unprepared. *Don't do that to yourself,* she thought. *Take the time you need to do it right.*

Preparation was everything. If there was anything she'd learned in the last fourteen years it was never attempt anything—healing, ritual or oracle—without properly preparing oneself, one's tools and one's environment. *But, oh, Great Goddess, why can't this child just be born?* The hollow echo of her footsteps was the only answer.

The long corridor stretched before her, the end shrouded in gloom, every closed door on either side a silent reproach. Most of the rooms were unoccupied. The sisterhouse had been built many years ago, and gradually, fewer and fewer sisters and brothers came to stay. All the Groves were far smaller than they used to be, and some had closed completely. Now that so many had gone to Ardagh, there were only a dozen left.

The deeper into the shadows she went, the more the walls around the doors seemed to shimmer and blur. A tingle went down her spine. It was not unheard of that the OtherWorld occasionally intersected with a corridor—any place that wasn't one place or another, or was a conduit between two places, was a possible portal. She felt a shimmer in the air around her and out of the corner of her eye, she thought she saw a narrow pale face and heard the tinkle of a high-pitched laugh. It would do her good, she thought, to seek out the embrace of a sidhe, fleeting as it might be. It would relax her, help her think. Later, she promised herself. *Later I'll slip up on the Tor and find my way to TirNa'lugh. But not now.*

The sense of overlap faded as another shiver, stronger, went down her back. She paused before her own door, hand just over the latch. It stood slightly ajar, and Catrione knew she was always careful to shut it firmly. She looked up and down, but there was no one about.

She pushed it open. Her dog, Bog, was stretched out beside the cold hearth, apparently asleep, and Catrione gasped to see Deirdre, mountainous belly spilling over the armrests, sitting in the chair. Deirdre turned to look at her, beady eyes unnaturally bright in her puffy face. Her cheeks were flushed, but in the gloom, her skin appeared mottled gray and white. A white coif covered her hair. "What're you doing here?" Catrione faltered with a hand on the door.

"We know what they want you to do, Catrione." Her voice was a low rasp.

"It's not what they want me to do." Catrione collected herself as quickly as she could. Deirdre's unblinking stare unnerved her, and she was puzzled that Bog didn't stir. "Deirdre, this can't continue—the child will grow so large, it won't be able to be born. Don't you see—we're all worried about you."

"Why do you want to hurt us?" The final sound was an almost reptilian hiss.

Catrione knelt beside the chair and picked up Deirdre's hand, swallowing revulsion. Deirdre's fingers looked like five fat sausages, her slitted eyes like a pig's. But Catrione forced herself to look into Deirdre's eyes and say, as gently as she could, "No one wants to hurt you. We want to take care of you. We're worried about you, Deirdre. Strange things have been happening lately—"

"My baby is not a strange thing!" Deirdre cried. She pulled her hand away, cradling her vast stomach with both arms. She shut her eyes and tilted her face so that her cheek nearly touched the rounded tops of her enormous breasts, as she murmured in a low horrible croon, "Leave us alone…leave us alone… Why can't you all just leave us alone?"

Revulsion turned into resolve. The others were right. *How could I have been so blind?* she thought desperately, even as she said, "I have left you alone, Deirdre, and I see I was wrong. Please, don't argue with me—the midwives won't give you anything that hasn't been given to hundreds—"

"What they want us to take will kill us—" Again, Deirdre's voice trailed away into a soft hiss as her coif fell off, revealing lank strands of sweat-soaked hair and wide patches of blotchy scalp.

Only druid discipline kept Catrione from recoiling openly. "When did your hair start falling out?"

But Deirdre was on her feet and moving faster than Catrione could've imagined possible. "Leave us alone. Don't bother sending for the men—" There was something in the way she said it that told Catrione she knew what the still-wives had planned. "We won't go with them."

"How did you know—?" whispered Catrione. Deirdre's continued use of the word *we* was ghoulish for some reason.

"It's amazing how delicate an expectant mother's senses can be," Deirdre snapped. She got to her feet, head lowered, ponderous and slow as a boulder slowly gathering momentum. "We know it was you, Catrione. Even *he* never guessed. But we know. And we know something else, too, something you don't think anyone else does. We know who you want. We know who you *need.*" She leaned closer and the wet stench of her body enveloped Catrione in a sickening miasma that made her gag. "You're so blind, Catrione. You don't *see,* and because you can't, you think no one else can, either. Well, you're *wrong.*"

The silent, sudden words struck Catrione like stones pelting her chest. Her jaw dropped, and before Catrione could gather her wits, Deirdre was gone and out the door. *She knows…she knows.* The words pulsed through her brain. *That can't be possible. No one ever knew. Even when she taunted me… I never admitted anything.*

Catrione put one hand on the nearest chair to steady herself, and Bog caught her eye. Forgetting Deirdre, she knelt beside him, one hand on his head. He didn't stir at her touch, didn't open his eyes, didn't thump his great white plume of a tail, and in a moment of awful realization, she knew he was dead. He'd seemed fine all that day, she thought as disbelief descended on her. She tried to remember the last time she'd looked into his deep brown eyes, fondled his silky ears, tried to think what she'd been doing the last time she'd seen him. Her mind was a complete blank, filled with a raven's screech. *One for sorrow,* was all she could think.

*Deirdre. Find her.* The unequivocal command yanked Catrione into the present, galvanizing her. With one last look at Bog's poor limp body, she shut her door, and paused, looking both ways down the empty corridor. *Find her.*

Catrione picked up her skirts and ran down the shadowy corridor toward the rain-shrouded dusk.

*Hardhaven Landing, Far Nearing*

Wind-driven rain slashed against the panes of yellowed horn, and the shutters rattled against the latch as the storm howled around the tower room. In the hearth, a log cracked and split in a shower of sparks, stinging Cwynn's bare legs like a hundred bees, chasing him out of yet another dream of the woman with the honey-blonde hair. Her now-familiar features dispersed into a swirl of color as he came to himself with a start, just in time to wonder briefly who she could possibly be. The girls who caught his eye were usually dark-haired, like Ariene the midwife's daughter, the mother of his sons. He knocked his head against the stone hearth and opened his eyes to see his grandfather, Cermmus, watching beady-eyed from his pillow. "Sorry," he muttered.

"Hard day?"

"Thought it would never end." Cwynn cleared his throat and shook himself awake. The storm had risen fast out of flat water and hazy sun, catching him off guard and farther away from the shore than a one-handed fisherman should be when the weather was bad. Until his feet had actually touched land, Cwynn'd believed it more likely than not he'd find himself feasting in the Summerlands. The sound of off-key singing, followed by loud laughter and catcalls filtered up from the hall, and he remembered there were three strangers in the keep tonight who wore odd-patterned plaids and supple leather doublets with high boots polished to a fine sheen. He'd had no chance to speak to them himself, for Cermmus had left word with every occupant of the house, apparently, that Cwynn was to come to him directly. A whoop from the floor below sounded like Shane, Cwynn's uncle, who, at thirty-five, was only five years older than Cwynn. "I lost the whole day's catch, and the nets—the mast—the boat's going to need a lot of repairs." He held up his hook. "I put a hole in the side." He braced himself.

But to Cwynn's disbelief, Cermmus only shifted under the sheet. "Forget the catch, never mind the boat. There's—"

Cwynn stared. "Never mind?" Was his grandfather not aware there were two more mouths to feed this summer? Duir and Duirmuid, his twin boys, were weaned and hungry. And there were no men in the midwife's house to provide for them. "We needed that catch, Gran-da—the fish aren't running this year like they should. Why, Ruarch was saying—"

"Did you get a look at those strangers down there?"

"I saw them. I figured if there was something about them I needed to know, you'd tell me."

"I was waiting for you to ask."

"No sense wasting your breath, eh?"

The old man nodded, and what lately passed for a smile flickered across his face. Then his expression grew serious and he rose up on one elbow, fumbling beneath his pillow. "Come here, boy. I have something for you." He began to cough, a hard, hacking cough that brought Cwynn to his side, his right hand extended to help him sit up, a clay cup of water awkwardly held in the curved iron hook that had served as his left ever since the accident.

"Drink this, Gran-da," he said.

The old man waved him away. "Don't fret about me, boy." Cermmus cleared his throat, hawked and spit expertly into a metal pot on the other side of the bed. "Here." He held out what looked like a piece of folded yellowed linen. "Take it. It's yours. I should've given it to you before, but after Shane killed your father—"

It was much heavier than Cwynn expected. He unfolded the stiff, yellowed fabric, frowning as he unwrapped the round gold disk. It was about the size of his palm and nearly as thick. A border of intricate knotwork was etched around the edge. He turned it over. It was warm from his grandfather's bed. The delicate spiral reminded him of a seashell, studded here and there with tiny crystals, spinning out from an enormous emerald in the center. "What is this thing?"

"The druids make them. We all had them—I sold mine off for food in the years the fish ran slow. Could have another made if I had the gold for it, which I don't. But I didn't think it wise to bring that one out." Cermmus turned his head and spat into a clay ewer. "Pull that stool closer, boy. I don't want to shout."

"Are you saying this is mine?" Cwynn asked as he obeyed. The acrid scent of a sick man's body blended with wet wool and damp dog and the heavy scent of fish that clung to everything beneath his grandfather's thatched roof.

Cermmus coughed again, and this time he accepted the cup. "I couldn't let your uncle know it was here—especially after…after, well, you know. I was afraid he'd steal it, sell it." His mouth twisted down, and Cwynn knew he was remembering the terrible day ten years ago when his father, Ruadan, had accused Shane, his younger brother and Cwynn's uncle, of lying with his Beltane-wife.

"And what if I did?" Shane had laughed. He was twenty-five then; dark-haired and tanned, strong and agile from a life spent outdoors on the water, much-liked by all the women, whereas Ruadan, more than twelve years Shane's senior, was balding and beginning to wear his age.

Ruadan had lunged across the table, clearly intent on wrapping his hands around his younger brother's throat. Quicker than Cwynn could blink, Shane was on his feet and his knife was buried to its hilt in Ruadan's chest. Cwynn leaped at his uncle, and it had taken six men to pull him off. The druid court at Gar called it self-defense. Shane paid a blood-fine to Cwynn, which really amounted to no more than assigning him a portion of what he expected to inherit from Cermmus, which wasn't much to begin with, and the matter was considered settled.

But Cwynn never trusted his uncle again, and Cermmus had never been quite the same since. The old man shook his hand, dragging Cwynn back to the present. "It's yours. You keep it, now. You keep it safe. Don't lose it."

"So what's this all mean?" He turned the disk over awkwardly, squinting at its markings in the candlelight. The druid script was impossible for anyone without their training to decipher, but he could see that the tiny gems scattered across it clearly had some meaning.

"It's why those men are here," Cermmus said. "It's your birthright, it's your heritage."

"I don't understand." Cwynn squinted at the intricate workmanship.

"That's your mother's line, there. The ancestors from your mother."

At that, Cwynn looked up. This disk clearly indicated the line of a clan rich and well-renowned. "So who's my mother? Great Meeve herself?"

"Aye."

Cwynn guffawed. "All right, Gran-da, why don't you tell me the real story?"

The old man shrugged as a muffled burst of laughter rose from the hall. "That is the real story. The other you were told—well, I guess we told you that to save your father's honor. It were something of a blow, you see—but you believe what you like. You find a druid to tell you what that says, and maybe you'll believe that."

"Meeve the High Queen is really my mother?" Cwynn turned the amulet this way and that, as if changing the direction could somehow snap its meaning into focus. He felt as if the floor beneath his feet had suddenly started to dip and roll like the deck this afternoon.

"She wasn't the High Queen when she bore you—she was years from that, a thin slip of a girl, she was, with a head like flame. Her mother Margraed who was as fine a piece of flesh in her day as Meeve, was High Queen and *she* demanded such a high son-price it would've beggared us. Now Meeve was a pretty girl, and all that, but not worth every thing I had. So I told Margraed we'd take you instead, and that was one time her strategy backfired. You should've seen her face when I looked at her and said 'no.' See, she thought she was going to get her hands on Far Nearing that way—establish a foothold, so to speak. Fooled her good, we did. And when we told you your mother was a Beltane-bride, it wasn't a lie, for that's how it happened you were made."

*Just like my boys,* Cwynn thought. "Why didn't anyone ever tell me?" Cwynn asked. But he thought he could guess the answer. His grandfather was proud like all the people clinging to a precarious existence on the windswept neck.

"Didn't much like Meeve," the old man said. "Didn't much like her mother."

"Those men brought this?" Cwynn peered at the gems. They were set at seemingly random intervals and he realized, in a flash of insight, that they represented places where the line diverged or crossed with another. The disk seemed to whisper to him, teasing him. Even the gold and the gems only seemed to imply that the information they encoded was even more valuable. He had to tear his attention away from it to listen to his grandfather.

"Oh, no, lad, that came with you. Shane was a child himself. He never knew about it, and I never had a reason to take it out before this. Meeve's invited you to a family reunion of sorts, at MidSummer. In Ardagh."

"I can't be going off to Ardagh—MidSummer's less than a fortnight away. The fish are just starting the summer run at last—"

The old man exploded into another coughing fit. A late spring cold had settled in his chest, and nothing the old women did eased it. The fact that he refused to allow Cwynn to ride to the mainland and find a druid didn't help, either. "No, no, there's more to it. Seems she's got a girl in mind for you to wed."

"What?" Cwynn leaned forward, then peered over his shoulder, as if expecting someone to materialize on the spot. "How— Who— What if I were already wed?"

"Well, boy, that's why the men are here, so they say." The

old man hawked and spit again. "Throw another log on, boy. I can't seem to get warm tonight. But Meeve wouldn't much care, I can tell you that. She won't see young Ariene as any impediment, believe—"

"I don't know Ariene would see herself an impediment," Cwynn said softly. The accident that had taken his hand had also taken both her brother and his rival for her affections, and Cwynn was always bothered by the feeling that Ariene believed he'd dispatched Sorley as coldly as Shane had his own brother.

"That's for you to say. You should consider the one Meeve has in mind for you, though. I'm sure you could do a lot worse." He cleared his throat, gesturing for the cup again. When he'd had another long drink, he said, "And it's an interesting knot right there. She's suggesting a match 'twixt you and the daughter of Fengus, chief of Allovale."

Cwynn shrugged. The name meant nothing. "So?"

"If there's anyone Meeve despises, it's Fengus, mostly because he's been hankering after the High King's seat for as long as Meeve's been on it. Ever since she made it clear she wouldn't marry him, he's been trying to drum up rebellion— even tried to drag me into it. Told him I wanted no part of it."

"You don't like Fengus much, either?"

"He's one of those kind who doesn't like no for an answer. He just keeps coming back, hoping to badger the answer he wants out of you. Never much cared for badgers."

"No, you prefer fish, don't you, grandfather?" A blast of wind and another deluge of rain shook the window frame and Cwynn reached over the bedstead and checked the latch as Cermmus pulled his shawl tighter around his shoulders. "So what do you think I should do? Go with them?"

"No, you're meant to stay here until Meeve's escort comes. She's sending your sister and your brother after you. But you can't wait. You have to get out of here."

"Why?"

"Cat's out of the bag. Shane knows who you are."

"He didn't, before?"

Cermmus could only shake his head. Cwynn reached for the basin, held it beneath his grandfather's chin. "'Course not," he answered when he could. "If I didn't tell you, did you think I'd tell him? I don't want you here, boy. It's good Meeve's acknowledged you. But it's better you get out of here. Shane might get it in his head you're worth more dead than alive."

"What do you mean?" Cwynn frowned.

Cermmus met his eyes. "Something happens to you, now that it's out you're Great Meeve's son—what do you suppose your head-price's worth now?"

"What are you talking about?"

The old man leaned over and smacked his head. "Would you get the fog out of that skull and think, boy? Shane arranges to have you murdered—he kills you himself— some day, out on the ocean, say, when there's no one else around to say it wasn't a freak wave come out of nowhere and take you away with it, or mermaid swim out of the water and pull you down with her. You have two sons— Meeve's grandsons—and you're valuable here, aren't you? With no proof of murder—or even any suspicion of one, who do you think will benefit from any head-price Meeve's bound to pay?"

"You really think Shane would do something like that?"

"I know my son. I think Shane is very capable of arranging to have you killed, if he thinks there's something in it for him. Even without a hand, you're yet a queen's son, and you do bring in quite a bit of fish, even so. He'd have no trouble finding three adults to swear to your worth." Their eyes met and the memory of that terrible night rose up unspoken between them.

"So where do you expect me to go?"

Cermmus leaned forward, his voice a rough whisper. "Get yourself to Ardagh. Leave the house tonight—go sleep in the village, at Argael's house if you will. As long as you have that disk, none'll question who you are. And besides, you favor her about the chin." The old man fell back against his pillow, and Cwynn noticed a grayish pallor around his mouth that even the firelight didn't seem to redden. "She can make you a chief in your own right, give you land and cattle—you'll never need to fish again."

"I like to fish."

"Ocean's already taken your hand. How many chances will you give her to take the rest?" The old man rolled on his side. "The life Meeve can set you up in is a better one than this."

"But—but what about this?" Cwynn raised his hook.

"What about it?"

"I thought one couldn't be king—"

"Can't be High King if you're maimed, but you can be chief of finer fields than these."

"But what about my boys? Ariene and her mother? Her aunt?" It was the death of the brother whose loss affected the family most keenly, for he'd been the one to keep his mother and sister and aunt all fed. It was a role Cwynn tried to take on, and though Argael, the mother, appreciated his efforts, it had little effect on Ariene.

Cermmus clutched his arm with surprising strength. "You do what I say, boy—Shane's already gotten away with one murder. You think I'd let my own great-grandsons starve? You have to live long enough to reach Meeve. You do this for them, too, you know." Cermmus gestured to the flagon beside the fire. "Pour me more."

The cup shifted in his hook, and the liquid sloshed as Cwynn struggled to do as asked, a heavy feeling settling in his chest. "I don't like leaving you, Gran-da. What if Shane—"

"I'm not worth as much dead as you are. I've already disinherited him." Cermmus met Cwynn's eyes. "You have to understand something, boy. This changes everything for you. This isn't just about marrying some girl. Meeve's about to hand you a big piece of something, because that's how she does things. She's constantly playing one off against another, and you, my boy, stand to benefit. It's your destiny, after all—you better get yourself in a state to accept it and all it will entail."

Cwynn handed Cermmus the full cup and when the old man had taken a long drink, he said, "What if I don't want it? What if I don't want any part of this destiny of mine, whatever it's to be?"

"Then you're a madman and I don't want any part of you." The old man hawked and spat. "What're you crazy, boy? Spent too long in your boat? This is your chance to solve the problem of Shane for you forever. If Meeve's planning on displaying you to Fengus, she'll have to make sure you've a household of your own, and that includes warriors, real warriors, not these pirate-thugs. What's wrong with you, boy? You mazed?"

Cwynn refilled the cup, set it on the rickety table beside the old man's bed and met his eyes. "I guess I am, a bit. It's not every day you're told something like this, after all. Are you sure that's what you want me to do?"

"You want to stay and wait for Shane to find a chance to kill you, that's up to you. You want to go and claim what's yours, I'll tell them you've gone fishing." With a long sigh, Cermmus settled back against his pillows. His face was wet with sweat in the gloom, but he pulled the blankets higher. "Just can't seem to get warm tonight," he muttered.

Cwynn tucked the amulet into the pouch he wore over his shoulder at his waist then rose to his feet. As he was about to lift the latch, Cermmus spoke again. "Take my plaid with you, boy. It doesn't smell as much like fish as yours."

*He wants me to make a good impression.* Cwynn's throat thickened, and he had a hard time saying, "What will you tell Shane, if he asks where it is?"

"I'll tell him you took it fishing." Cwynn considered whether or not to hug the old man, but Cermmus cleared his throat again, then turned on his side, his back decisively to Cwynn. "Go on now, will you? By the time you dither, twill be dawn." He punched the pillow. "Hope I can sleep."

*He wants to pretend this is just another night.* Cwynn unhooked the plaid from its nail. He shut the door, folded the plaid carefully, and looked at the closed door. "I'll make you proud, Gran-da," he whispered softly.

"Proud doing what?"

Cwynn nearly hit his head on the low-beamed ceiling. Shane was leaning on the wall at the top of the steps, arms crossed over his chest, wearing the self-satisfied smirk he always wore when he was drunk. "Fishing was off today. Told me where I might look tomorrow."

"Old man's relentless, isn't he? What makes him think you'll be able to put a sail up, let alone fish?"

"Storm's already passing," Cwynn answered, feeling trapped.

Shane nodded, listened. The howling wind had quieted, and even the rain had eased. "So it has. Best get to bed then, nephew. First light comes early." He stood aside to let Cwynn pass. Their eyes happened to meet. Shane's lips curved up but the expression in his eyes didn't change. *The old man's right,* Cwynn thought with sudden certainty. Shane would kill him at the first opportunity. But if he left, would his boys be safe? Uneasiness raised the hackles at the back of his neck as he pulled the cloak around himself and slipped out of the keep.

*Eaven Raida, Dalraida*

From the watchtower of Eaven Raida, Morla bit her lip and squinted into the storm clouds scudding across the sky. *Fly away south or west or east, anywhere but here. Just let the sun shine tomorrow—we're dying for warmth, for light,* she prayed. The damp wind whined as if in answer. She pulled her plaid closer around her thin shoulders, and the sound of the fabric flapping around her bony hips drowned out the dull growling of her stomach. It didn't seem to matter that nearly ten months of famine had passed. Her belly still expected food come sundown. She swallowed reflexively, gazing to the south, willing a rider to come through the rocky pass with the news she longed to hear: Meeve, her mother, the great High Queen, had heard her pleas and was sending corn, pigs, men and druids.

But no matter how hard she prayed, how hard she worked,

how many men she sent, no one and nothing came. What was happening, she wondered—why no answer of any kind? No help had come but for the regular payment of her dowry at Samhain and Imbolc. Nothing had come at Beltane. Now the Imbolc supplies were nearly gone, and they'd been forced to eat almost all the seed. If relief of some kind didn't come soon, they'd be forced to eat the last precious grains. The months before the first harvest were always the hungriest time of any year, with last year's stores depleted, the new still in the fields. But a cold damp summer last year had brought blight. Blighted harvest meant certain famine.

At least her son, seven-year-old Fionn, was safe at his fosterage on the Outermost Islands, in the same hall where she herself had been raised. Something had warned her to send him away last summer, a few months early. It was but a few days after he'd left that they'd seen the first signs of blight. It was not the first time Morla was glad her son was far away.

"My lady?"

The old steward, Colm, startled her. When Fionn, her husband, had died in the plague year, he had transferred his loyalties seamlessly. But she was surprised the old steward had made it to the top of the tower. Hunger hit the old ones hard, made them weak and susceptible and the damp weather kept them all huddled lethargically around the smoky fire.

"I don't understand why we've not heard more from my mother," she said, eyes combing the darkening hills, more from habit than out of any real expectation. "I just don't understand—do you suppose our messengers never got through? Did we not send first word back before Samhain?"

She was talking to herself, she realized and the old man was letting her ramble. She turned around to see him leaning against the doorframe, his cloak falling off his shoulders so that his beaked nose and stooped back made him resemble a big bird with broken wings.

"She's always been prompt with your dowry, my lady." He cleared his throat. "Don't fret so." He took a few steps toward her. "We'll get through this—we always have. Our people are tough, you'll see. They're not used to looking for help from the southlanders."

That's not exactly true, she wanted to retort. A flock of crows wheeled around the blighted fields. *At least they aren't vultures.* She'd seen those terrible harbingers of death far too often this past spring. Fear gnawed at her more steadily than a fox through a henhouse, with far more stealth, plaguing her with the vague sense that something terrible had descended on the land. She herself had no druid ability at all, but her twin, Deirdre, had been recognized druid practically in the cradle and every so often, Morla felt a twinge or two of what the cailleachs called a "true knowing." A feeling that she was being suffocated had lately invaded her dreams, and more than anything, Morla wished her mother would send, if nothing else, a druid—a druid to couple with the land, to heal and reinvigorate it. But the last druid house had been deserted nearly two years ago and no others had ever come back. "Mochmorna lies more east than south." She looked steadfastly at the road snaking through the hills and felt him come to stand beside her.

He turned his back deliberately to the battlement and looked at her. "My lady—" He broke off, and she saw his eyes were dark with care and hollow with hunger. He wore the expression that told her he had something to say he didn't think she wanted to hear.

"Say what you will, Colm." Lately, she'd seen a lot of that look.

"What if there's no help anywhere, and we're all that's left?"

Morla stared out over the gray land. Gray land, gray sky, gray stone, gray skin. She didn't want to think about that. Hardly anyone came this far north in winter, and the spring traffic had been slow, too.

"Dalraida's on the edge of things, my lady." He came forward slowly, shoulders hunched against the wind and the few cold drops of rain that stung his cheek. "Things come to us but slowly, they trickle through the passes and filter up from the south. I don't mean to frighten you, or give you any more trouble. It's just that—"

"You want me to understand what we might be facing." Morla met his troubled gaze with a thin, brave smile. Since her husband's death, she had come to love Dalraida and its people, for it was much like the windswept, rocky shores below her foster mother's halls, and they were similar in nature to the hardy souls who clustered there. It had taken her longer to learn to love the sheep, but this winter she mourned as the cold winnowed all but the hardiest of the herds, and she keened with all the other women as the spring lambs sickened.

A flicker of movement on the far horizon caught her eye and she squinted harder. Was that a rider?

"—shadows of war, my lady."

Morla jerked her head around. "What're you talking about, Colm? No one's at war—we're all too weak to fight, and what's there left to fight over?"

The old man clutched his cloak higher under his chin and shrugged. "The old wives say they see the shadows in the fire, in the water." He glanced up. "Even we can see the clouds."

Morla ignored him. It was very hard to see. The road disappeared through a copse of blighted trees and the twilight had nearly fallen. She leaned a little farther over the wall, and just as she was about to give up and return below, she saw a dark dot burst out from beneath the withered branches. The wind whipped the standard he carried, and she was able to glimpse the colors. She pointed into the storm, relief surging through every vein. *Thank you, Great Mother,* Morla thought as she blinked back tears and wondered for a moment who she meant—the goddess or her own mother. Not for nothing was her mother called Great Meeve. "Look there, Colm. See, coming down the hill—do you see the rider? He's bearing my mother's colors."

The old man tottered forward, shoulders bent against the wind, but before he could speak, to Morla's horror, she saw a gang of beggars emerge out of the brush. They bore down on the rider, makeshift weapons raised. "Oh, no," she gasped. With a speed she hadn't known she still possessed, she raced down the steps, voice raised in alarm.

*On the road, Pentand*

*Watch the road ahead.* The rumbled warnings of both Donal, chief of Pentwyr, and Eamus, the graybeard-druid, echoed through Lochlan's mind, as impossible to ignore as the thickening scent of threatening rain. Ever since he left the house of Bran's foster parents, the sky had grown increasingly sullen, and now the misty day was falling down to dusk behind the heavy-leaden clouds. Druid weather—a day not one thing nor yet another, neither foul nor fair, a day easy to get lost in fog or stumble into a nest of outlaws—or any petty chieftain with a grudge and a mind for ransom. Lochlan glanced at the boy on the roan gelding beside him. He was fourteen or maybe fifteen by now, Meeve's youngest child, and he rode with the giddy impatience of a colt run wild.

Bran seemed to know this was something more than an ordinary visit. It was a year earlier than most left their fostering, and the boy appeared to think the druid, Athair Eamus, was responsible in some way. Bran made no secret he was impatient to know what his mother's summons meant. But Lochlan didn't think it his place to tell the boy his mother was dying.

The road disappeared into the looming shadows beneath an arching canopy of trees and the skin at the back of Lochlan's neck began to crawl. He was the First Knight of Meeve's Fiachna, and so far as he knew, the only person in all of Brynhyvar the Queen had trusted with that information. When Meeve announced she was gathering all her children together, he had volunteered to escort the young prince. Lochlan wanted to gauge for himself the temper of the land she was about to leave, and Bran's fosterage was closer to the center of the country, south towards Ardagh. What he'd learned troubled him even more than Meeve's impending death.

*Watch the road ahead.* The old chief, Donal, had gripped Lochlan's upper arm with a strength that had surprised the younger knight. "You show Meeve what I gave you. Those

Lacquileans I hear she's so fond of aren't to be trusted." The day before Lochlan's arrival, a shepherd had come down unexpectedly from the summer pastures, bringing troubling news. A cache of weapons had been discovered in a mountain cave, weapons that bore no resemblance to anything made, as far as Donal or Lochlan knew, in all of Brynhyvar. The shepherd brought a sword, a fletch of arrows and a bow, and it seemed everyone in the keep, from scullery maid to blacksmith, from stable hand to bard, had a thought as to who had hidden them.

But old Donal had no doubts. "It's neither sidhe nor trixies—it's those foreigners who've been paying Meeve such court. They're carving out toe-holds in the wild places, hunkering down and planning to attack us before winter. You mark my words, there'll be slaughter while we sleep." He'd insisted Lochlan take the sword back to show Meeve. Now it was rolled in coarse canvas, tied on the back of Lochlan's saddle. *Watch the road ahead.* An enormous raven alighted on a branch just ahead, cocked a beady eye and stared at both of them, piercing Lochlan's reverie.

"Why'd Mam send for me, Lochlan?" Bran interrupted his thoughts with the same question for the tenth or twelfth time since setting out. "You think it's because Athair Eamus sent word to Aunt Connla? Did Mam say she knows I'm druid? Is that why they want to see me?"

"There're could be any number of reasons, Prince," Lochlan answered, also for the tenth or twelfth time. He watched the bird take flight as they rode beneath its bough, then slid a sideways glance at the boy. He wondered if Meeve even intended to tell him the truth. Calculating as she was flamboyant, Meeve might well decide not to, unless and until the boy himself guessed. "Maybe your mother missed you."

Fortunately Bran accepted that answer and subsided into silence. He reached into his leather pack, withdrew a withered apple and bit into it. "Want one?" he asked, munching hard. Lochlan shook his head, but the boy held out the bag. "I have a bunch in here—Apple Aeffie gave 'em to me."

"Who's Apple Aeffie?" asked Lochlan. Bran appeared ordinary enough—his nut-brown hair curled at the back of his neck and spilled over the none-too-clean collar of a soon-to-be-outgrown tunic, the edges of his sleeves ragged, his leather boots scuffed and crusted with mud. He had no look of a druid about him at all.

"Apple Aeffie's what we call Athair Eamus's cornwife. He used to jump the room with her each Lughnasa. She died last Imbole, but she comes to me in dreams. She tells me stories of who I was before. Do you ever wonder who you were, before?"

"Before what?"

"Before now." Bran chomped on the chewy fruit.

"Before I was what I am? I was a lad much like you, of course. I wasn't a chief's son, but my family's—"

"No, no." Bran swallowed the entire apple, core and all. "I meant before you went to the Summerlands. In your last life—don't you ever wonder?" He licked his fingers, looking at Lochlan expectantly.

*Keep a close eye on the boy. He's more than he seems. And watch the road ahead.* Those were the druid's parting words, spoken when they were already in the saddle. "No, boy, I can't say as I ever have." Lochlan wished there'd been more time to ask the old druid what he meant, but the boy's next words startled him.

"Do you suppose Athair-Da is dying? I know he misses Apple Aeffie."

"Dying?" Lochlan looked more closely at the young prince. The old druid had seemed in fine enough health to him. Athair Eamus wasn't a young man, by any means, but he certainly didn't appear as if the Hag was ready to send him to the Summerlands, either. "What makes you think he's dying?"

The boy shrugged, gazed moodily into the distance. "I don't know—the thought just came to me. You think maybe Mam's planning on sending me to Deirdre's Grove-house? Deirdre's been there a long time. She used to send me things. I'd like to go there. Think Mam means to give me leave to start my training early?"

A flicker of movement out of the corner of Lochlan's eye made him glance in the opposite direction, and when he turned back, he saw that Bran was staring in the same direction.

"Did you see that trixie, too?" he asked.

"What trixie?"

"The one that went darting across that branch and down that trunk—I know you saw it, too—you turned to look at it."

"It was a squirrel, boy."

"No, it wasn't," Bran insisted. "It was a trixie."

Only druids could see the earth elementals, and only druids could control them. Lochlan regarded Bran more closely. Deirdre, one of Bran's older twin sisters, had been born druid, though not much good it had done her. Her disgrace was one reason Meeve wanted nothing to do with druids, Lochlan knew, even though the great queen would not admit it. But Bran himself, as far as Lochlan could tell, lacked all signs of any druid ability. He hair was neither pure white nor shot through with tell-tale silver, his eyes were neither bright blue nor impenetrable brown-black, nor lacked all pigment. He was not, so far as Lochlan had heard, particularly gifted in music-making, nor singing, nor recitation, which were all considered certain signs of druid ability and critical druid skills.

Even his seat on the horse, his hands on the reins, didn't mark him as anything but an adequate horseman. Except for the fact he was Meeve's son, he seemed as ordinary as an old boot. It would certainly be better for the boy if he were, Lochlan thought, listening with only half his attention as Bran chattered on. The druids as a group did not number among Meeve's favorites right now, despite the fact that Meeve's own sister was ArchDruid, or Ard-Cailleach, of all Brynhyvar. As far as Lochlan could discern, Meeve at times appeared deliberately determined to antagonize them.

*He's more than he seems.* The old druid's warning repeated unbidden in his mind. There was something odd about Bran, something difficult to define perhaps, but definitely there. Lochlan tried to remember what Deirdre was like, but he'd not seen her much when she was young.

"Will Deirdre be there? And what about Morla?"

Lochlan stiffened and raised one brow. Druids read thoughts, but only after long training and never without permission. Was it possible this boy could read thoughts without the training? Maybe it was only logical the boy would inquire about his sisters. After all, as far as Lochlan knew, Bran hadn't seen either of his twin sisters since he was a very young child. And neither had Lochlan, for Deirdre stayed at her druid-house, except for a holiday or two at Ardagh, and Morla, the other twin—Morla was long married. Her husband died a year back, a voice reminded him, and he tried unsuccessfully to push all thoughts of Morla out of his mind. He remembered she came home from her fostering a young woman of sixteen, moody and quiet, dark and ripe as the brambleberries that grew along the beach she loved to wander. He might have married her himself if Meeve hadn't tapped his shoulder the Beltane after Morla came home. Fleetingly he remembered the stricken look on the girl's face as her mother had led him out of the hot, smoky hall. *She'd been about to pick me.* The pang of regret that accompanied that realization was unexpectedly deep. "I don't know," was all he said. "They may have work of their own—after all, Morla's married—"

"She's not married anymore," Bran said. "Her husband's gone to the Summerlands."

Startled, Lochlan looked at him harder. "How did you know that?" Dalraida comprised the remote northwestern tip of Brynhyvar. Lochlan found it hard to believe that Morla spent much time sending messages back and forth to Bran. In ten years, she'd never come back once to Meeve's court.

"He came to me last Samhain."

"Fionn? Her husband?"

Bran stared off down the road, as if he could see the shade rising before him. "Said I'd be seeing her soon and asked me to give her a message from him. It was an answer to her question."

"What was the question?"

"Oh, I don't know that. But you see, I've been sort of expecting to see Morla since MidWinter."

Lochlan looked more closely at the boy in the greenish shadows. Meeve had first mentioned bringing Bran home nearly nine full moons ago, just after Samhain. Before he could stop himself, he said, "So what was the answer?"

"No."

"No what?"

"'No' is all the answer he gave me," said Bran. "He told me to tell her that the answer to her question is 'no' and then he vanished."

There was a queer light burning in the boy's eyes, reminding Lochlan of the druid fires flickering around the standing stones up on the Tors while they worked their magic within the stone circles. It was not uncommon for the dead to come uninvoked to the living at Samhain, when the veil to the Summerlands was thinnest. But not common, either, and how could Bran know that Meeve had first mentioned bringing both Bran and Morla home shortly after Samhain, right before MidWinter? The road ahead looked very dark. A chill went down his arms. The druids said the trees were aware, and looking down the road, he could believe it. The trees stood on either side, so evenly spaced, it was hard to imagine how random chance gave rise to such order.

Lochlan glanced at Bran's eager face. It was hard to imagine such an ordinary boy could possess any kind of extraordinary talent at all. *He's not what he appears.* Lochlan shifted in his saddle and flapped the reins. Maybe it wasn't his place to tell the boy his mother was dying, but maybe he should tell the boy the druids weren't high on his mother's list of favored people right now, and that he doubted that any plans she had for Bran included druid training. He cleared his throat. "That's quite an amazing thing, all right."

The boy narrowed his eyes, his expression an exact replica of Meeve's when crossed. "You sound like you don't believe me."

"It's not that I believe or don't believe you, boy. It's not for me to say." Thank the Great Mother, he added silently. "But as for the druids—well, there's something I think you should know. Your mother's been at odds with her sister, your aunt, for months now, and she's not at all happy with her. Nor any druids."

"Because of the blight?"

Lochlan shrugged. Blight was not yet a problem in Eaven Morna. "Blight, goblins, silver—whatever it is, boy, you don't want to be in the middle of it. So, when you meet her, wait to see what she says to you, before you go telling her you feel you're a druid. All right?"

Bran frowned, opened his mouth, then shut it.

"Just remember, she's not just your mother. She's the Queen of all Brynhyvar, the beloved of the land. You listen, and speak when she asks you, not before."

Bran made a face, but said nothing.

Night was falling quickly behind the lowering clouds, far faster than Lochlan had anticipated. He wanted all his wits about him, and the road was getting dark. His shoulders ached from a bad night's sleep. "I say we stop at the next house we come to."

"All right," replied Bran. "That suits me—I'm starved." He caught the reins up in one hand and kicked his heels hard into the horse's flanks. "Let's go," he cried. "I'll race you!" He took off down the road as the old druid's warning echoed once more through Lochlan's mind.

*Watch the road ahead.* "Hold up, boy," cried Lochlan as he touched his own heels to his horse's sides. *Keep a close eye on him.* With an inward groan, he galloped after Bran who charged heedlessly down the darkening road like a stone tumbling down a mountain. "Wait!" he shouted and plunged headlong into the dark green twilight.

The air was oppressive and very wet and the road appeared to curve up the hill, away from the lake. He heard loud trickling and looked up. A run-off brook wound its way down the mountain and across the road. He'd have to cross the water to continue after Bran, who'd rounded the curve, and now was nowhere to be seen. But instinct—or maybe the old druid's words—made Lochlan hesitate. *You've faced Humbrian pirates, the wild men of the Marragh-mourns and the outlaws of Gar and now you're afraid to cross a stream?* The doubt that taunted every warrior whispered through his mind. It wasn't even a stream, really, just a channel that rainwater carved into the hillside. But it was at just such a place that one was most likely to fall into the OtherWorld of TirNa'lugh, where both sidhe and goblins roamed, dangerous to mortals in very different ways, but equal in peril.

*He's more than he appears.* "Bran?" he called. "Bran, wait for me." Cursing Bran beneath his breath, Lochlan spurred his horse forward, and the animal didn't even seem to notice the water crossing the road. Inexplicably, the light began to fade, the shadows deepened. The road took another turn, pitched sharply up a hill. "Bran?" he bellowed at the top of his lungs. "You wait for me!"

The high-pitched yelp that came in answer galvanized Lochlan. He sped around the turn and pulled up straight.

Bran stood spellbound in the center of the road, staring straight ahead at a naked girl bathing on a riverbank that shouldn't have been there. A young moon had already risen in the purple sky, spilling silvery light across the sidhe-girl's shoulders, reflecting off her copper-colored hair with a pale gold glow. Almost black in the shadows, her waist-length hair fell fine as spider silk across her naked breasts and her nipples were pink as quartz and pebbled from the chill of the gurgling brook. She turned this way and that beneath the bending willows, splashing the water all over herself. Droplets gleamed like opals on her shimmering naked flanks, fell like diamonds from her fingertips. A high laugh floated through the trees and Lochlan looked up to see more eyes, more pointed faces and tiptilted breasts peeking through the trees.

"Look, it's mortals." The whisper floated down from somewhere up above, and Lochlan saw the red-haired sidhe turn to Bran, arm extended, smiling as she strode up through the water to the bank. To Lochlan's horror, Bran smiled back and leaned forward, hand outstretched.

"No," Lochlan bellowed. If this was what the old druid had meant, he should've spelled it out for him, not warned him in a riddle so dense it sounded like nothing more than good advice to any traveler. How could they have blundered into TirNa'lugh? Only a druid could take you there, and more important, only a druid could lead you out. There were stories though, of warriors on the brink between life and death, who'd fallen into the OtherWorld, and stayed held captive there by the sidhe. He dug his heels so hard into his horse's side the animal reared and screamed his displeasure, so that Lochlan had to struggle to bring him under control. Bran didn't even appear to notice as his own horse began to dance skittishly beneath him. His eyes remained fastened on the sidhe.

The other sidhe were creeping down the trees now, luminous as fireflies, green eyes glowing in their narrow pointed faces. They were all beautiful, all naked, all with long limbs and flowing hair. He could feel warmth emanating off their skin, even as their unearthly fragrance twined around him like tendrils. He forced himself to concentrate on the feeling of the horse, solid and scratchy and real between his thighs, on the weight of the weapons strapped to his back and his waist, on the feeling of the hair prickling on the back of his neck and not on the aching pressure rising in his groin. "Bran," he said again, this time with even more urgency. He reached over and cuffed the boy's head. "We're not meant to be here, remember? We're on our way back to Eaven Morna, remember? Throw them your apples and they'll let us go. I'm taking you back to your mother, Bran. Remember? Your mother, Meeve. Your mother wants you home. We're going home, Bran—home to Eaven Morna. Home to your mother and Eaven Morna."

"Mother," Bran repeated, his cheeks pale, his eyes wide, beads of sweat rolling down his face. The sidhe were singing now, something soft and low and nearly indistinguishable from the gurgling brook and the whispering of the leaves, but Lochlan could feel it; tempting and wooing and sweet, twining in his hair, trailing down his back like the long slender fingers that even now were reaching down and out of the branches. *If they touch me, I shall be lost,* he thought. But he had to save the boy.

"Give them the apples, Bran, now. Now!" Lochlan cried. He swatted Bran across the shoulder. He helped Bran toss the bag to the sidhe and shook the boy's shoulder. "Home—home to Eaven Morna!"

Drops of sweat big as pearls glimmered on Bran's upper lip as he stared, mesmerized by the naked sidhe. Lochlan felt his own resolve weaken. He leaned over, wrapped the reins around Bran's wrists, slapped the horse on the rump. The gelding leaped forward. They fled down the road and across the border, back into a wind and rainswept dusk where, impossibly, the watchtowers of Eaven Morna twinkled on the horizon.

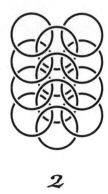

## 2

*Faerie*

"Auberon?" Melisande's soft voice broke the stillness of the summer twilight, taking the King of the sidhe entirely by surprise, penetrating the soft pink fog of dream-weed smoke. His queen seldom attempted the winding climb to his bower at the top of the highest ash of the Forest House because she, unlike almost every other sidhe, was terrified of heights. It was one reason he'd chosen her among all the others to be his Queen. Now she perched in the archway of the bower, quivering only slightly. Her long fair hair, fine as swan's down, feathered around her shoulders, down her back and chest. In the orange glow of the setting sun, it gave the illusion she was covered in white feathers.

*She's begun the change,* he realized, and looked down at his own furred flanks. When the change in both of them was complete, it would be time for their daughter, Loriana, to assume her place as Queen of the sidhe and all the creatures of the Deep Forest. Presuming, of course, that all Faerie wasn't turned into some foul wasteland overrun by goblins. It was beginning to seem like a distinct possibility.

He extended a hand, but she didn't reach for it. Instead she looked at him, not with fear, but suspicion and he realized she was trembling, not with terror, but outrage. "What's wrong, my dear? You look upset."

"Is what your mother told me true?"

Anger flashed through him, but he controlled himself enough to smile tightly and beckon. Finnavar was an interfering old crow who belonged, like the rest of the sidhe who completed the change, in the Deep Forest. "I can't imagine what sort of mischief she's making now. Come sit, my dear. Tell me all about it."

Melisande raised her chin. "Should we call it mischief when it's our daughter's choice that's being bargained away? And if we do, I don't think she's the one making it."

Auberon clenched his teeth. In the midst of everything else, his mother couldn't resist causing trouble. She stubbornly refused to leave the Court, creating an embarrassing situation. It was as if she didn't quite trust him to rule. Despite all his directives to ignore her no one really did. Her instincts both for causing trouble and ferreting out information remained intact. "Let's talk."

"You admit it."

"Beloved, I—"

"Oh, enough. I'm not your beloved." She stalked into the room, anger making her sure-footed. "Is it true you promised Timias that you would ask Loriana to consider choosing him to be her Consort?"

"My dear, you're shaking—there's no need for unpleasantness—"

"Unpleasantness? Auberon, our daughter is not a prize to be awarded or a—a possession to be handed over. How could you listen, let alone agree— He was raised beside you in the nest— If you were mortal, you'd be brothers and such a thing not even considered."

"Melisande." He picked up his pipe. "Don't you understand it's not important? I don't think he's coming back—I never expected he'd be back, to tell you the truth."

"You didn't?"

"Of course not. It was as absurd an idea as I've ever heard—learn druid magic and bring it here to Faerie." He picked up her hands and brought one, then the other to his lips. "Sweet darling queen, it was a way to find something for him to do."

"So what exactly did you agree to?"

Auberon shrugged, picked up his pipe and tapped dried flowers into the bowl. "He asked me if I'd approach Loriana and ask her to consider his suit. It seemed a small enough thing—considering I didn't think I'd ever have to do it. Where was the harm, after all? It made him feel useful, gave him a purpose."

"And what if he does? What if he comes back?"

"You have been talking to my mother, haven't you?"

"Loriana is of an age to consider such things. Look at us, Auberon—you and I are clearly entering our change. When your mother tells me you've made some kind of bargain involving our daughter—"

"Enough, Melisande. There's no bargain involving Loriana

or anyone else. Timias has not been seen in—I've forgotten how long exactly. Maybe you should ask yourself why my mother sees the need to bring it up now?"

"She's concerned. The Wheel's turning—we have to prepare ourselves and everyone else."

The dream-weed hit his head just as she spoke. It elongated her words, separated out the subtle shades of tone and melody, turned the light around her face ethereal and fey. He was captivated by the glints of pale yellow and tender gray in her hair and in her eyes. In all the time he'd known her, he'd never noticed these before. A vein beneath her ear beat a steady tattoo in her throat, in time to that which pulsed up through his feet. The firs stood straight and tall, black against the indigo sky, the drooping branches of the enormous willows all silver by their sides. The first stars had already appeared. A low pounding throbbed through the trees, and the leaves rustled as the branches swayed in time.

A horn rose in the distance, its note pure and piercing as a shaft of morning sun. It stabbed into his awareness, made his ears ring and his head ache.

"Auberon?" Melisande shook his arm. "Did you hear that? That's the alarm. The goblins are rising."

There was a screech in the doorway. Finnavar stood there, looking like an enormous raven cloaked in black feathers, her nose and chin fused into a long shiny beak, her arms folded back. "Where's Loriana?" she croaked. Her beady eyes darted right and left, her feathers gleamed blue in the purplish shadows. "Have you seen her? I've looked everywhere."

What little color there was in Melisande's face drained away. "She's been told not to leave her bower at dusk."

"She's not there now," the old sidhe screeched.

"She has to be," cried Melisande as the dull vibration grew stronger, and from somewhere far away, they heard a faint roaring, growing ever louder as the wind carried it closer.

"She isn't," answered Finnavar. "Follow me." She flapped awkwardly off without another word.

Melisande pulled away from Auberon and rushed out the door, nearly colliding with Ozymandian, the captain of the guard. He scrambled past her, brandishing his spear. "My lord." He sketched a salute, then said, "My lord, you must come. Something's roused the goblins—all of them, apparently—and it seems they're headed this way."

Red steam rose from fire pits of glowing molten rock, seeped from crevices in the floor and hissed from fissures high within the cavernous chambers and passageways that were the realm of Macha, the Goblin Queen. The floors were slick in some places and sticky in others, and the smell of excrement was everywhere. Timias shrank behind an enormous boulder. The air was thick with the steady throb of drums, a sound so constant he sometimes thought it must be coming from inside his own skull. He cocked his head and listened to the squeals and screams and bellows echoing from the chamber, trying to decide if he dared to take the only direct route he knew that led to the surface of Faerie. The druid spell of banishing had finally worn off. He could feel the tattered remnants shredding off him like an old cloak, one thread at a time. He had never expected it to be as effective as it was, for it not only kept him from Shadow—

anywhere at allin Shadow—but it prevented him from returning to Faerie, as well. For a mortal year and a day, he'd been trapped in the strange nether places of the World. He was impatient to return, and he risked a slow death by searching for another way to the Forest House. The effects of the banishment still lingered, preventing him from directly returning to the Forest House.

He'd counted on Macha's halls being silent, the goblins curled up fast asleep, thin and gray as the ghosts of the mortal dead whose flesh they consumed. But something must've happened, he mused, in the time he'd been banished. Somehow they'd gotten a taste of living flesh.

It was possible he might find another way to the surface, but he could just as easily encounter lairs filled with starving hatchlings. If the goblins were this lively, they were certainly copulating. The cloak of shadows, woven with a mortal druid on a Faerie loom, might not fool the goblins. Like a river of velvety water, the cloak flowed out of his hands, vaporous as fog, dense and wet as the Shadowlands themselves, its one edge jagged where Deirdre had ripped it in half. He wrapped it around himself, careful to tuck it well over his face and around his hands. He was more afraid of how he'd smell than anything else. But he had to risk that a wafting scent of Shadow, while alluring, would not be as riveting as the sight of a sidhe scurrying along the perimeter of the cavern.

With a last check to make certain he was completely covered, Timias edged down the widening passageway, careful to keep to the sides where the shadows were thickest and his cloak provided the best cover. But he had not counted on the stench.

The closer he got to the central hall, the stronger it was. It pervaded his nostrils, crept into his skin, insinuated itself into the crevices around his nose, his fingers. It filled his mouth and made him gag. Dizzy, eyes burning, Timias crept along the Hall, trying not to breathe too deeply. It was worse than the foulest cesspit, the fullest charnel pit in Shadow.

Behind him, a noise made him flatten himself against the jagged outcroppings along the wall, and as he watched in horror, he realized the source of the wet trail of slime. It was blood—mortal blood, gelling as it dried. It dripped from the squirming, screaming, struggling bodies of the mortals the goblin raiding party was now dragging along or had slung over their backs. Some struggled and kicked more than others, but one thing was very clear to Timias: They were all still very much alive.

The coppery scent of the blood, the acrid tang of urine and the fetid aroma of feces, bowels opened and bladders spilled filled Timias's senses. Timias waited until the tramp of goblin feet had faded. His eyes were finally adjusting to the reddish light, and he crept, one hand clamped around his nose and mouth.

Macha, the enormous queen, crouched at the peak of her throne, her beady eyes bright in the nightmarish light. She uncoiled and coiled her tail, reflexively, surveying the scene before her. The goblins were all over the hapless humans, tearing them apart in a frenzy of showering blood and ripping flesh. The ragged end of a leg was tossed up toward the queen; she snarled, reached for it and crammed it into her mouth. Red drool spooled down her chest as she chewed and swallowed and grinned. Timias could not look away.

With the same casual ferocity with which she crunched the bones and swallowed them, Macha reached for the nearest male, threw him on the ledge and proceeded to raise and lower her massive body over his, ramming him nearly flat with the force of her thrusts. She bared her fangs and howled, which sent up a chorus of answering screeches. The smoke and the smells and leaping goblin hordes were making Timias dizzy. He pushed himself hard up against the wall, trying to hold on to his bearings as a wave of nausea swept over and through him, nearly dragging him to his knees. He felt his legs begin to buckle and he clutched the cloak hard around himself, even as he tried to lean back. He tried to back up and realized he was prevented by a tail.

His tail.

The cloak floated off his shoulders as he swung around, staring at the shadow that stood in stark outline against the rocks. His shadow. For a moment, Timias wondered if this was some trick of the light, some result of the druids' curse of banishment. But no, he'd been himself in the passageway. He was sure of it. Of course he was. He remembered looking down and being grateful he was wearing boots. Boots. He looked down at his feet, and saw clawed toes bursting through the tips.

Behind him, he heard a hiss and a cackle that was taken up and turned into hoots and shrieks. Timias turned to see the goblins—every one of them, including the queen—looking back at him. And they were laughing. Or what passed as laughter. They were pointing at him, slapping each other on backs and rumps, rolling between the fire pits in unrestrained glee. What was it, he wondered. *What's wrong with me? Why are they all staring? What's so funny?*

And then he looked down at himself and realized that he not only appeared to be a goblin, he alone was wearing clothes. *Am I mad?* he wondered in an instant. But he didn't have time to consider how this transformation had taken place, or why, because the other goblins—*no,* he told himself firmly. *Not other goblins at all. The goblins.* The goblins were creeping closer. Inspiration born of desperation gave him an idea and he knew what he had to do. With a bound, he decided to play the best of it he could. He swaggered out, into the center, gesturing and posturing. He held his maw shut, then bent over and pretended to break wind. Then he began to pull the clothes off, one at a time, throwing them into the assembly. The goblins shrieked and capered and he looked up, into the eyes of the queen.

"I don't know you," she said. Her black forked tongue flicked out and she sniffed, as if teasing out his smell from among all the other odors swirling through the cavern.

He felt as if her eyes were boring into the center of him, seeing him for what he really was, and he felt himself quail. *Don't collapse now, fool,* he told himself. She was intent on looking for weakness, sniffing it out, determining which of all her many subjects she would allow to live. The weak she would kill. He forced himself to stand straighter, even as he noticed how her egg sacs bulged beneath her tail, how clear fluid spilled down the insides of her thighs, pooling around her feet.

Saliva spilled from the corners of his mouth, oozed down his chin. He was alarmed to realize he found the odor as appealing as honey, and he shuddered, appalled by his body's own response.

"Name?" she said, watching him closely enough to kill him in an instant.

Did he have a goblin name, he wondered? The name he'd used among the mortals had simply risen to his lips the first time he was asked. What was he supposed to call himself?

"Name?" she repeated. She took a step closer and the nearest goblins stopped eating or copulating and turned to watch.

What was he expected to say, he wondered? Timias? Tiermuid? He opened his mouth and a bleat came out. The court laughed.

The queen narrowed her eyes and the corners of her maw lifted. He wasn't sure if she was smiling or if she was merely opening her jaws wide enough to bite off his head. "Name?"

"T-T-Tetzu." He heard himself say the word as his goblin tongue tried to form the syllables of his name, either of them.

"Gift?"

"Gift?" Timias repeated, trying to look as if he didn't understand the meaning of the word. What could she possibly want from him?

"Macha likes gifts," she said. She coiled her tail under herself almost daintily and to his surprise, his own nearly naked body responded to the invitation it portended. She leaned closer, sniffing the air around his neck, and he felt his ruff rise.

"Xerruk bring Macha gifts," snarled a voice behind the queen. He handed her a head, the lips still moving, the eyes still aware.

Timias saw his chance. With a speed born of complete and

utter hopelessness, he bolted around the nearest fire pit, racing to the opposite passageway.

But the queen's interest, once roused, was not so easily dissuaded. As he reached the opening, she took off after him and the entire Court followed. Timias pelted up the passage, praying and hoping the sun was out, that the hot light of day would drive the goblins back into their lairs.

Dank air seared his lungs. He imagined he could feel her vicious claws tearing him to shreds, ripping out his throat, and he pumped his arms and legs as fast as he could run. He burst out, into the trees. A few stars twinkled overhead in a pale purple sky. If it was dawn, he had a chance. He raced through the trees, the goblins pursuing him in full force after their queen, howling and shrieking.

The farther he ran, the darker it got, and Timias realized that far from being dawn, which was the worst time of day for the goblins, it was dusk, the best.

The darkness was giving him some advantage, however, for he was able to blend in with the trees. He ducked around the trunk of one enormous oak and slumped against it. He felt his flesh shrivel as it touched the rough-ribbed surface, felt his frame collapse into itself. His tail curled up and under his buttocks and disappeared, his goblin skin softened and gave way to smooth pale skin. Somehow, he wasn't goblin anymore. *I am sidhe. Not mortal, not goblin. Sidhe.* He didn't understand what had happened, but he knew he could never tell anyone. Fooling mortals was one thing, becoming a goblin quite another. Not away from the scent of the others. He sank down, and the horde surged past.

A blast of horns filtered through the trees, and Timias realized the sidhe had been alerted. He wondered if Auberon and his Court realized how close Macha's lair really was. Light flashed above the treetops, limning the sky with brief glimpses of green and blue and gold, fleeting as summer lightning. The sidhe were riding out to confront their foe, armed with their spears and swords of light and their high, piercing horns. A shiver of antici-pation ran down his spine as he got to his feet and crept through the trees, careful not to make any sounds. He heard the trickling of a brook and knew he must be close to the river that ran through Faerie. The Forest House was built of the great trees that grew on either side of it. If he followed the river, he would come to it, sooner or later. The trees were like grim silent sentries as he made his way between them, slipping like a shadow from one to the other. He passed a pool and beside it, saw a piece of shim-mering fabric. He bent and touched it, rubbing it between his fingers. It was woven of spider-silk and it was sticky with a sidhe's pale blood.

He stood up, listening. The goblin rampage had met the warriors of the sidhe and the battle had joined somewhere not far enough away. But nearby, someone was trying very hard not to breathe. He looked up and realized that, of course, any sidhe would've sought refuge in a tree. He'd been in Shadow too long, and then banished from both worlds, he thought bitterly, to have forgotten so much. He hoisted himself into the branches, then paused, squinting into the green darkness. Nothing in the trees could be as dangerous as what was roaming on the ground, he thought as he saw a pair of eyes gleaming back. "Who's that?" he whispered. "Don't be afraid. I won't hurt you."

There was a soft gasp and then another, and a pale face peered out from between the boughs. "Who're you?" she whispered.

"I'm Timias," he answered. "Who're you?"

The girl's mouth dropped open and for a blink, he was afraid her reaction was to his name. She raised her hand and pointed over his shoulder. He turned to see Macha storming out of the trees.

"Did you see that one? That young one?"

"What about the other one? Did you see the other one? I know that one—I've been with *him* before."

The voices of her companions blended into a harmonious chorus as they raced here and there to catch the mortal apples. Loriana, the sidhe-king's daughter, eased herself up and out of the water, heart racing. There was something about the young mortal who'd come crashing so abruptly across the border. He was unlike any other mortal, druid or not, she'd ever met. He was obviously one of the druid-born, of that she had no doubt, for every one of his senses had fully engaged hers. But he smelled so fresh and young, like the first pale shoots of new spring leaves. She shook her damp hair out so that it spread around her shoulders like a silken cloak, while she tried to listen beneath Tatiana and Chrysaliss's chatter.

There was a lambent energy surging through the air like a barely audible hum. The sound of horns was fading but the scent of Shadow lingered and she wondered what brought her father out to hunt. The sidhe didn't hunt at night. It was far too dangerous, for at night, the goblins crept out of their lairs below the Forest. They themselves were disobeying by leaving their bowers at night.

She sniffed, delicately sorting through all the competing scents twining through the Forest. There he was, she thought, catching the barest whiff of the boy, ripe as a sun-warmed acorn. She closed her eyes and inhaled, pulling as much of his essence, of his scent, as far and as deep into herself as she could, until she was certain she could find him again. He made her palms tingle and her toes curl.

"Let's go after them—" Tatiana's hot breath in her ear made Loriana jump. They pressed against her, their bodies damp and cool, and Loriana could feel the need the mortals had roused.

"There was something strange about him," said Chrysaliss as she wrapped an arm around Loriana's waist and combed her fingers through Loriana's wet hair, twining the silky strands around her fingers into long curls. "Don't you think he smelled strange?"

"He didn't smell strange. He smelled young," Loriana whispered. It was already too late to follow, for she could read his essence fading even now, as the breeze dispersed what was left of him in Faerie into the wind.

"Young..." Tatiana drew a deep breath and closed her eyes, leaning her head back into Loriana's shoulder, wearing a wide smile as she savored the last of the boy's scent.

"I'd prefer the other," said Chrysaliss. "The other one—didn't you see him? The one who told the young one to ride?" In the fading dusk, her teeth were very white as she smiled and her eyes were very green. "Do you know who he is? I've seen him on this side of the border more than once or twice—he's the first I'd pick at night, too." The two collapsed on each other in gales of giggles.

Loriana looked up and frowned. The leaves on the trees were quivering and the throb in the air was more palpable. Beneath the branches, the dark pools of shadows began to grow around the trunks. Their bath had been fun, but now it was spoiled somehow and she felt not the slightest desire to get back into the water. "I think we should go home."

"Why?" Tatiana waded out into the center of the water and peered down into the shallow depths. "You know, if the moon would just rise a bit, I think we could—"

"Tatiana, come back." Loriana grabbed Chrysaliss by the wrist, as if to prevent her from doing the same. "Come, let's get out of the water. I think we should go now."

"But why?" Tatiana flung a few drops of water at them both and grinned. "This stream cuts straight through Shadow. We can follow him, we can find him—and the other one, too. Come, what's the harm?"

Beneath Loriana's feet, the ground gave a palpable throb. "What's that?" asked Chrysaliss, looking down. The throb was growing stronger.

Loriana looked up. The leaves shook visibly and the subtle throb had turned into an audible pulse. "It's drums," she whispered. "Goblin drums and they're not just getting louder, they're getting closer."

As if she'd given a signal, a hideous cacophony erupted from somewhere far too close. Chrysaliss wrapped her arms around Loriana, and Tatiana, galvanized, came running out of the water.

The pounding was growing louder. Loriana grabbed for

Tatiana's hand and the three clung to each other. "Which way are they coming?" breathed Tatiana, as they backed up close to the largest of the nearest trees.

The sound was all around them now, shuddering through the ground, rending the air, and Loriana pressed her back against the tree. *Up.* The word filled her mind with urgency and Loriana looked up. The branches above their heads were bending down. "We have to go up," Loriana answered as the ground began to quake beneath their feet.

"They're coming this way," Loriana said. She reached up, into the welcome of the tree, felt the branch twist itself beneath her hands. The other girls scrambled beside her just as the leading edge of the horde ran across the stream.

The screeches and the screams, the trills and the yelps were all part of some discordant language, she realized, but the drums, so wild and so loud, were disorienting as they filled the air.

"Wait—I'm fall—" cried Tatiana, and she did, slipping off the branch and tumbling to the ground below. She landed with a thump, and as Loriana gazed down in horror, Tatiana was caught up by the goblins. With shrieks of glee at their unexpected prize, they dragged her into their midst, tossing her from one to the other as they ran through the trees.

Her screams faded as the horde swept by. "What should we do?" Chrysaliss whispered.

"Stay here," Loriana whispered back. The goblins were galloping under the trees now, scrambling like drunken mortals, heady with the noise and the scents. "We're just going to stay here. And hope they go away."

"Or that someone finds us." As if in reassurance, Loriana

heard faint, frantic blasts of the horns. "Hear that? Father's coming." She squeezed Chrysaliss tight, and the two clung to each other and the trunk of the tree. Loriana pressed her cheek against the papery bark of the ancient birch. But the goblins weren't going away. They roamed back and forth beneath the trees, pausing every now and then to sniff and peer.

"What're they doing?" muttered Chrysaliss. "Why don't they go away?"

"It's like they're…like they're looking for something," Loriana breathed back. The horns sounded louder, and in the far depths of the wood, Loriana thought she saw distant flashes of the sidhe's lych-spears. "Or someone."

"What if they look up?" Chrysaliss whispered. "We should go higher."

Loriana froze. Like her mother, she despised heights. Beside the squat old birch, its boughs interlaced, a graceful ash soared high.

"Come on," Chrysaliss was tugging at her, pulling her off the birch and onto the ash. "Come, we have to get higher— higher where they won't see us—" A clawed hand snaked around her ankle and yanked her down. She disappeared below with a high-pitched scream.

Gasping, Loriana bolted. Across the limbs, light as a wisp, she darted, dashing from branch to branch, following the line of the river that carried her, against all instinct, away from the Forest House. But the horns were louder now, the goblin drums less insistent. She paused to catch her breath in a hollow of a bending willow. The goblin roars were louder, if possible, but she heard the battle trills of the warriors, saw the flashes of light zigzag across the sky like summer lightning. They were fighting somewhere very close, she thought. She curled up as tightly as she could within the hollow, her arms wrapped around her knees, her face tucked down. The sound of her friends' screaming echoed over and over, and she trembled, bit her lip and tried to stop shaking.

But the smell of burning and wafting smoke choked her and, peering cautiously out, she looked around in all directions. Another noise was rising on the wind, a noise only the sidhe and the trees could hear. It was the screaming of a living tree on fire. Loriana's gut twisted and nausea rose in the back of her throat. She staggered, clinging to the trunk of the nearest tree, and felt the pain resonate underneath her hand. They all shared it to some degree; they all felt it. And then someone stepped around a tree, a tall figure, pale as a goblin in the sun, carrying what appeared to be something limp and dead.

At first she thought the figure was her father. *But it can't be Father,* she thought. But the figure had his walk, his stance, his set of shoulders. Not his hair, for Auberon's was as copper as her own, and this man's feathered around his face in coal-black waves, reflecting blue glints in the moonlight. He was mostly naked, but for a pair of torn boots and ragged trews of the kind the mortals wore, and she wondered why he didn't come up into the trees out of harm's way like any reasonable sidhe. Intrigued, she watched him as he passed beneath the willow. Swift as a cat she uncurled herself and crept silently just behind him.

He paused, looked up, and seemed to sense her presence. She darted around the trunk as he hoisted himself into the tree. He turned one way, then another, and their eyes met. In the dark, she saw the green gleam of his. "Who're you?" she whispered.

"I'm Timias," he replied, and the name made her eyes widen.

*This is Timias?* Raised by her grandfather, King Allemande, beside her father Auberon, after his own family was slaughtered, Timias was hardly mentioned by anyone at Court, he'd been gone so long. She'd been still a child when he left. He looked like a pale imitation of her father in the starlight.

"Who're you?"

She opened her mouth to answer, when violent movement in the trees behind him caught her eye. She gasped and pointed over his shoulder as the biggest goblin she had ever seen burst through the trees, running, it seemed, directly at them both.

Timias grabbed her wrist and pulled her up higher into the tree, but not before the goblin spotted them. As the goblin leaped for them both, Loriana saw her mother and a dozen or more mounted sidhe come riding into the clearing. As the sidhe raised their weapons, Loriana clung to Timias's hand. "What is that thing?"

"That's Macha, their queen," he answered. "The sidhe have a king—the goblins have a queen."

The enormous queen reared up and around, dwarfing the warriors on their dainty white horses.

"And that's my mother," Loriana said. She tried to see past him but he wouldn't let her.

"We have to run," he said. "Now!"

He dragged Loriana stumbling and weeping through the trees. At last he paused. "I'm sorry if I hurt you."

"That was my mother," she whispered, wiping her face. "Leading the warriors, that was my mother."

She heard the soft intake of his breath. For a long moment, they sat in silence in the dark. Then he said, "You're Auberon's daughter, aren't you?"

She raised her eyes to his. He was staring at her almost the way a goblin would and for a moment she felt a prickle of fear. *Don't be silly,* she told herself. *He saved your life.* "Yes," she said. "I'm Loriana."

She expected him to say something, but he ducked his head and said, "We can go lower now, I think."

Instinctively, she clung to his hand. The palm was wet, the skin was fleshy, but he held her strongly, firmly and she was comforted enough to let him lead her. She could see the lights, hear the shouts of the Court.

"What were you doing out there?" Timias was asking her.

Her lower lip trembled as she looked up at him. "We were bathing," she said.

"Did no one warn you to stay out of the wood?"

"Of course they did," said Loriana. "The wood, not the bathing pool by the river."

He took her by the elbow and pointed. "Look—we cross that stream, we're there."

She took a deep breath, forcing herself to follow his voice, to cling to his hand. Her grandmother had nothing good to say of Timias, her father spoke of him seldom if at all. But he'd come back just at the right moment. She thought of her mother and her friends and the other warriors and tears filled her eyes. She followed him blindly, and stumbled against him, not realizing that he'd stopped, for no apparent reason, in the middle of the path.

"What is it—" she began as she peered around him, but the words stopped in her throat. She gulped, blinked, and blinked again, as if she could clear away the nightmarish scene spread before her. The banks of the little stream were pocked with blackened grass, and on it, creatures that oozed whitish substances flopped miserably about. She looked up at the holly tree beside her, wondering why she felt nothing at all from the tree, and realized the tree, and all the others around it, was dead, the berries dull and black amidst the waxy gray leaves. "What did this?" she whispered. "Do you know what happened here?"

To her surprise, Timias nodded, his mouth a straight grim line. "This is what happens when silver falls into Faerie."

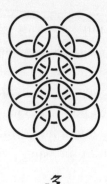

## 3

*White Birch Druid Grove*

"Deirdre?" Catrione called. She barged into the courtyard, heedless of the rain sluicing off the edges of the roofs in solid sheets. She glanced frantically around in all directions. How was it possible Deirdre could've vanished so fast? She looked back down the corridor but saw nothing. She decided to check each room once more when she heard her title called.

"Cailleach!" She looked up to see Sora scampering across the puddles, skirts kilted high. When she caught sight of Catrione, she paused beneath a dripping overhang and beckoned frantically. "Catrione—a troop of warriors has just come, with a message for you."

"From the Queen?"

"From your father."

*Now what?* she wondered with a sinking heart. She beckoned to Sora. "My father can wait. I need you to help me look for Deirdre." Tersely, she explained what had happened. "Deirdre ran right past me, but I was behind her—she couldn't have made it down the corridor in her state. So you take that side and I'll take this one and we'll look in every room. She must be hiding in one."

But a search yielded nothing. Sora twisted her hands in her apron and looked down the corridor to the end, where the door swung open in the wind. "You should go talk to the men, Catrione."

Catrione bit her lip, calculating the chances of Deirdre climbing out a window in her condition. It was exactly the sort of thing the other girl was capable of doing…before. But now, bloated and swollen and clumsy as Deirdre was, surely such a feat was impossible. Then out of the corner of her eye, Catrione thought she saw a flicker of movement near the door. She bolted down the dormitory corridor, but by the time she stuck her head out, the entire yard appeared deserted. Catrione cocked her head, listening carefully before she answered as softly as she could, "She's been eavesdropping, apparently. She somehow knew exactly what we're about." *Not to mention, she scarcely looked human.* Catrione suppressed that thought with a shudder and took Sora's arm. "You go back to Bride and tell her what happened and I'll go see what this message is from my father."

Sora nodded and Catrione hurried away. She was halfway there when she realized that in addition to her soaking sandals and bedraggled hem, she'd not stopped to wash her face or comb her hair or change into a fresh coif and clean apron. There was no help for it, she reckoned as she turned the corner into the outer courtyard where she was startled to see, in the light of the brightly burning torches, six or seven horses milling among unfamiliar men who nonetheless were wearing a very familiar plaid. Now what, indeed.

"Lady Cat?"

In the hall, she recognized at once the grizzled warrior who respectfully touched her forearm as she lingered on the threshold, her eyes adjusting to the smoky gloom. "Tully?" Catrione clasped her hand over his and turned her cheek up for a swift kiss. Tulluagh, her father's weapons-master, was his dearest, most trusted friend. Fengus-Da never let Tully out of his sight for long. As the men crowded around the central hearth, shaking off their wet plaids, holding out their hands to the flames, Catrione glanced around, more confused than ever. There were too many for just a message, she thought. "What're you doing here? Is something wrong?"

Tully shuffled his feet, frowning down at her with furrowed eyes the color of the watery sky. "Fengus-Da sent me to fetch you home, my lady."

"Why? What's wrong?" Catrione stared up at the old warrior.

Tully sighed heavily. He turned his back on the others and glanced over his shoulder. "May I have a word in private with you, Callie Cat?"

"Is it my grandmother? Is she sick?"

Tully put a hand under her elbow and drew her to a shadowy corner, out of the way of the servants scurrying to wait upon the newcomers. "It's your grandmother, aye, but she's not sick—well, not in the manner of dying-sick, anyway."

"How sick, then, Tully?" Catrione stared up at him. "What's this about?" She spoke softly but with enough of a hint of druid-skill that her words seemed to resonate in the air around him.

The old man's eyes were steady as he stared back. "Don't try those druid-tricks on me, Callie Cat. It's like this. Since the season turned, your grandmother's been plaguing him. First she started barging into his council meetings, into his practices, his games, even into his hunts. Then she started begging, tearing her clothes, pulling her hair out, moaning and groaning all the day—"

"About what?" Catrione stared up at the old man. Maybe the world really was turning upside down.

"He thinks she's gone mad, Callie Cat, because all she'll say is you're not safe, and then she gibbers and howls and no one can get through to her until the fit passes. We can have you there before MidSummer if we leave by day after tomorrow."

"Tully, I can't leave." Her Sight revealed gray mist, indicating hidden information. Immediately she was wary. "I'm Ard-Cailleach of the Grove this quarter. When I decided not to go home at Beltane, the charge was handed on to me. So till Lughnasa, Tully, I can't leave, and certainly not now. Things are—unsettled."

"Unsettled, you say? You don't know the half." Tully glanced over his shoulder, then stooped and spoke almost directly into her ear. "I don't want to scare you. To tell you the truth, I was hoping I'd come and find you gone to Ardagh. Then I could've gone home and told him you were out of harm's way."

"What are you talking about, Tully? No place is safer than a druid-grove."

"Callie Cat, do you think I'd be here for just an old woman's ravings?"

Catrione narrowed her eyes. This sounded more like it. "So now what's that trouble-making father of mine—"

"Your father's not the one starting trouble."

"Then who is?"

"There've been sightings of strangers in the high, remote places, and things found—weapons, clothes, equipment— all of foreign make. He thinks it's the Lacquileans that Meeve's so fond of, coming over the Marraghmourns a few at a time, hiding out, waiting for some signal, putting out rumors of goblins to keep people afraid."

"The ArchDruid's called a convening—"

"Maybe she should consider the possibility that there are no goblins but someone who wants everyone to think so. Your father's worried about you here. He thinks the deep forests provide too much cover, and these woods could be riddled with them even now. He's afraid they'll have no respect for druids, Callie Cat."

Catrione took a deep breath. "This is all news to me, Tully. We've heard rumors of goblins in the southern mountains. In Allovale, now the druids are gone, are the charnel pits emptying? Are the goblins being fed?"

"Aye, as far as I know. The old woman tend such matters now. But, Callie Cat, this isn't about goblins, it's about war."

"I think what you're really saying is Fengus-Da is going to war, and he wants me out of it. Isn't that it?"

"No. He means to confront Meeve at MidSummer and raise the issue with the chiefs, but he's not intending to go to war. He says you and all the sisters, all the brothers here are welcome at Eaven Avellach."

Catrione blinked, her mind racing rapidly. From no druids, to an entire groveful—not as many as Meeve could muster out of Eaven Morna, of course, but impressive enough if they all crowded into the audience hall at Eaven

Avellach. Outward show was everything. So was Tully's visit motivated by real concern, or simply her father's attempt to co-opt the White Birch Grove's support, whether they meant to give it or not? "Maybe he's right, Tully." This wasn't something she could decide in a blink. "But in the meanwhile, I can't go anywhere, because among everything else that's happened today, one of our sisters is—"

"Is definitely missing."

Catrione jumped. Tall, stern, as composed as Catrione felt frazzled, Niona stood at her elbow, as unsmiling and unwelcome as Marrighugh, the bloodthirsty battle-goddess of war, who was already, apparently, awake and marching across the land. Niona had come in with the servers who were now passing trays of oat cakes and tall flagons of light mead, and despite all the frustrations of the day, she somehow managed to look as cool and calm as a cailleach was supposed to look, her apron spotlessly white, her coif perfectly arranged over her smooth hair. Beside her, Catrione felt like a small girl caught masquerading in her mother's robes. "A word with you, if you will, Cailleach?" Niona nodded a quick smile to Tully, but the expression in her eyes was grim.

"Please, Sir Tully, eat and drink," Catrione said. "We'll speak more when you're refreshed." With a tug of his forelock, Tully seized the nearest flagon, and as he tilted his head back, she followed Niona a few lengths away, her wet soles squeaking audibly. "Have they found her?"

Niona shook her head. "Not yet. I've taken the liberty of calling up the brothers and we're starting a systematic search—it's everyone's guess she's hiding somewhere inside these walls. We'll find her—sooner or later she'll get hungry."

"Catrione, dear?" Baeve approached and met Catrione's eyes with uncharacteristic softness.

"What is it, Baeve?" asked Niona.

"Yes?" Catrione replied, controlling her urge to elbow Niona aside.

But Baeve ignored Niona entirely. "My dear." She looked directly at Catrione. "About Bog."

"Bog." She'd nearly forgotten him. She bit her lip to keep the sob that rose in her throat from escaping as she remembered his limp body lying on the hearth rug.

"You told Sora that Deirdre was waiting for you?" When Catrione nodded, Baeve continued, "She'd time, then—"

"Time to do what," interrupted Niona.

But again Baeve ignored her and spoke softly, gently, to Catrione. "It seems his neck was broken, child. Someone killed him."

Niona made a horrified sound, and Catrione covered her face with both hands. "Are you saying Deirdre killed him?" Niona asked.

Catrione's mind reeled. "We…we don't know for sure Deirdre killed Bog," she heard herself say weakly.

At that Niona rounded on her. "Come now, Catrione. We all know you love Deirdre, but you have to face facts. Who else was in your room? Who else would have reason to do such a thing?"

The possibility that Deirdre, once her best friend and confidante, was capable of killing an animal that would never have harmed her sickened Catrione. But Deirdre never showed any compunction about killing anything if it needed to be done. She was as capable of squashing a moth in the woolens as she was wringing a hen's neck for dinner. Catrione saw Deirdre's strong hands wrapped around a squawking chicken's throat and deliberately squelched the memory. *Even if she were capable, that doesn't mean she did it.*

"I don't think it was Deirdre who killed Bog," Baeve said softly.

"Then who do you think it was?" Niona cocked her head.

"I think that thing inside her has some kind of hold," Baeve answered.

Niona's brows shot up. "You mean you think it's the child?" She made a little noise of derision, but Baeve wouldn't be cowed.

"I've been catching babies here for over forty years, Sister Niona, and this is the most unnatural thing I've ever seen in all my time. I've had babies go past their dates—oh, long past, a month or more. But they die, they don't survive. And their mothers are sickened, but they don't start to look anything like that thing that Deirdre's become." She looked at Catrione. "I asked Sora to check the Mem'brances—"

"Those old barks are half crumbled to pieces—" began Niona.

Catrione cut her off. "Sister, make sure there's someone in the kitchen at all times. There are lots of places to hide."

Niona shut her mouth with an audible snap and marched away, back straight, shoulders rigid.

"Have patience," murmured Baeve, then jerked a thumb over her shoulder at the men. "What's this about?"

"They're from my father—he wants all of us to leave the Grove and go to Eaven Avellach."

"Well, now. We can hardly do that, until we find Deirdre." She patted Catrione's arm.

"What do you think Sora will find in the Mem'brances? Anything of use?"

Baeve shrugged. "I'm not sure, to tell you the truth. With our luck today, I'm half-afraid we'll find the very one we need long crumbled into dust. But anything is worth a try, isn't it?"

"It's worth a try if it helps us find Deirdre."

"We'll find her. You'll see."

And what if we don't? a cautionary voice whispered in a corner of Catrione's mind, sending a shiver of fear through her. *Don't be ridiculous,* Catrione told herself immediately. *Of course we'll find her. We have to find her. She can't possibly have gone very far.*

*Hardhaven village, Far Nearing*

Cwynn paused before Argael's door, hand raised to knock. The rain had eased, but the wind was still blowing hard off the ocean. The windows were shuttered, the door was firmly closed. White smoke belched in fitful drifts from the chimney. He imagined everyone inside was sleeping by this time, for this was the kind of weather that even in summer, drove most to bed. His children, Duir and Duirmuid, were surely sleeping by now. At least, he supposed they'd be asleep. In the two years since their birth, he'd never shared a roof with them at night.

He drew a deep breath and was about to turn away when the door opened abruptly. Argael herself stepped through the door, buckets in hand, an apron tied around her waist, a shawl wrapped over her shoulders. She gasped and stifled a cry as she nearly collided with him. "Cwynn daRuadan. Great Mother, is that you?"

"I-I'm sorry, Argael." Cwynn stepped back awkwardly, into Eoch. The mare whickered and stamped her displeasure.

"What're you doing here?" Argael was a broad-boned woman, her face pale in the grayish light. Wisps of the iron gray hair that had once been as dark as her daughter's, peeked out from under her linen nightcap. "Is everything all right up at the keep? Is your grandfather—?"

"He's fine." Cwynn hesitated. "It's me. I'm off— Leaving, me and Eoch—"

"Where're you going?" Argael set her buckets down and raised her chin. She was nearly as tall as Cwynn and she'd never lost that aura of being bigger than he was despite his greater size.

He glanced over his shoulder. He should've slept in his boat, then left without saying anything, for he couldn't tell Argael anything but the truth. "I'm going to Ardagh."

"And you're leaving in the middle of the night?" For a moment she looked at him as if she didn't believe him, and then she jerked her head toward the door. "Come inside." When he'd followed her into the small house, she kicked the door shut and set the buckets on the floor, then regarded him with crossed arms and narrowed eyes. "Now. Tell me what this is all about?"

"Gran-da gave me this." He pulled the disc from beneath his shirt, where it nestled warmly against his skin. He lifted the heavy leather cord over his head and let it dangle before her, standing silent while she examined it.

"This is yours?"

"That's what Gran-da said."

Argael raised her eyebrows and regarded him with a penetrating look in her faded blue eyes. "Your mother's line?" When he nodded, she sighed. "That explains a lot, I suppose." She handed it back to him.

"Like what?"

She shrugged. "Like why Ariene can't keep her hands off you come Beltane every year. Some part of her recognizes something in you even if you don't see it in yourself. You're a prince of the land, Cwynn. Your roots are in people who married the land itself. There's a lot of druid blood in your line." She fell silent, as if thinking, and then said, "But why're you leaving now? It looks to storm all night."

"Gran-da didn't think it was safe for me to stay." He hesitated, then said, "Shane, you know."

"Ah." She drew a deep breath, then wiped her hands on her apron. "The boys are sleeping in the loft. You're welcome to join them as long as you take the edge." Her face softened. "I never much cared for Shane, either." She nodded to the dark passageway that led to the back of the house. "I'll be back in a trice—I just want water for the night." She nodded at the barrels set out to catch the rain, then looked at him appraisingly. "Have you had your supper yet?"

It surprised him to realize the answer was no. He shook his head and she snorted softly.

"No wonder you're forever drifting off—it's that druid blood that's all through your mother's side." She picked up her buckets. "Go on back and have a seat. Ariene got a mess of clams this morning—there's chowder in the pot."

He went, feeling as if there was something else he wanted

to say. He passed through the shadowy kitchen, startling Argael's sister, Asgre, who was bending over the fire, covering up the coals. If her face was thin and gray and sour as week-old milk, her voice was as sharp as new cheese. "Argael," she shrieked, brandishing her poker over her head. "Ariene! Sound the alarm—we're being attacked!"

"Callie Asgre, it's only me." Cwynn held up his hand. "I-I came to see the boys."

"Strange time to come calling, don't you think?" she snorted as Ariene, in a homespun nightgown and a bright red shawl slipped in behind Cwynn.

"A very strange time, indeed," Ariene said. "What's wrong?"

"Asgre, it's all right," Argael said from the doorway. She handed a bucket to Ariene and set the other down on the chest beside the door. "She won't believe me when I say she's going blind. Asgre, this is Cwynn. He's but come to spend the night with his lads before he takes off on a journey. I've told you for weeks now you can't see, you silly hen. Put that poker down."

"Where're you going?" Ariene cocked her head.

"Go put the bucket down before you spill it," her mother said. "Here, Cwynn, sit. The man's hungry. He's not had his supper. Let him eat."

"They don't feed you anymore up at the keep, then?" murmured Ariene as she strolled out of the room. Her eyes met Cwynn's, her lips curled up in a half smile that didn't reach her eyes. She blamed him for the loss of her brother and Sorley, Cwynn's rival for her affections, but her grief didn't stop her from choosing him again last Beltane, though afterward, she claimed to be under the influence of the goddess and not entirely in her own mind.

"I'd no time to eat."

"Why?" she asked at once, her dark eyes shifting from Cwynn to her mother. "What's wrong? What's going on?"

"He's a guest, Ariene," Asgre said sharply, surprising Cwynn. "He's to eat before he answers."

"I'll explain," Cwynn mumbled as he was hustled to the place beside the fire. A dish of clams in milky broth, on top of a hunk of brown bread, was placed on his lap and a spoon thrust into his hand. Before he could dip the spoon in, however, the dish was momentarily whisked off his lap and a square of homespun linen laid across his knees.

"There you are," said Argael, smiling. She handed him back the dish. "Eat, now."

"Quickly," said Ariene.

Aware of the scrutiny, Cwynn gulped the food in between telling his story once more. Finally he handed his plate to Argael and waved it away when she would've filled it again. "That was plenty. Good, too," he added.

"Come see your sons," said Ariene. She got up off the backless stool, her nightshift blousing around her body like a sail. She led him through a low doorway on the opposite side of the kitchen, into a storeroom. "Be careful, now, they're up in the loft." She pointed to a ladder.

Cwynn fumbled his way between the baskets piled with provisions, the bunches of hanging herbs, the sacks of meal and barrels of ale. He felt for the rickety ladder and tested his weight, then carefully climbed up just high enough to see two dark downy heads nestled together on one pillow in the evening twilight, their little faces round and tan on the sunbleached linen. A pang went through him. There was no doubt they were his, conceived on one of those wild Beltane nights he'd shared with Ariene, in the bower he'd made in a cave underneath the cliffs. Beltane was the source of all the trouble, he thought. He'd left Ariene alone, once she'd made it clear she preferred Sorley. But why then, did she keep choosing him each Beltane?

One of the twins sighed and turned on his side, hand beneath his cheek, and the other followed, their little bodies cupped together beneath the woolen blanket and patched quilt. He tucked the quilts higher beneath the little chins, and realized he had no idea which one was Duir and which Duirmuid. He touched the top of each head in turn, fingered identical black curls. "Stay safe," he whispered. "Grow strong." He leaned over to kiss each one in turn, and as he did so, the nearest twin awoke. His eyes widened, his mouth gaped and he started to scream, high-pitched, piercing wails that immediately woke the other twin.

"Hush now, hush, hush," cried Cwynn as the children screamed. The women rushed in from the kitchen. One twin cowered, while the other launched himself straight at Cwynn, small fists flailing. "Hey, now! No, stop that!" Cwynn was forced to throw up both arms to defend himself. Already rickety, the rung he was standing on cracked beneath his boots, and he fell into a pile a whirling skirts and swirling night-shawls. Somehow, Argael got them all untangled. She pushed Cwynn in the direction of the door, called, "It's all right, boys, auntie's coming up first," as she boosted Asgre up the ladder.

Ariene was standing by the fire in the kitchen, arms crossed over her breasts. Cwynn entered, feeling even more foolish and out of place than before. *It was a mistake to come here,* he thought. *I should've gone down to sleep in the boat.* He made as if to pick up his pack, but she stopped him with a swift touch on his arm. "It's all right, Cwynn, that wasn't your fault—I should've gone up first, woken them for you. I'm sorry." She nodded at his pack. "Where're you going?"

He nodded at the door. "I'll go sleep in the boat—it'll be easier in the morning—"

"To do what? Catch your death?"

"Ariene, I shouldn't have come." He tried to think of something else to say, for the tension was palpable between them. It tied his tongue and stopped anything but the truth from running through his head. *I wanted so badly to love you.* He spread his hands helplessly, for those words didn't seem to make much sense.

"Of course, you should've come, Cwynn. You've every right to know the boys—soon they'll be old enough to fish with you. They should know their father."

He narrowed his eyes. She sounded conciliatory, even friendly.

She nodded at the door that led down to the beach. "Will you walk with me? The rain's stopped."

"All right," he said. From the loft, he could hear Argael crooning to the children. He wished either she or even Asgre would come in and break this awkwardness he felt filling the room.

Ariene held the door open. He hesitated, then followed her down to the beach. The sand was wet and the rocks were slippery, but she didn't stop until she reached the water's edge. She let the ocean lap at her toes, her shawl flapping around her in the wind. The wind lifted her hair, blowing it in little tendrils around her pale face.

"Are you sure you want to be out here?"

"I wanted to talk to you." She glanced out to sea, then turned to look up at him. He was shocked to see tears like tiny pearls limning the edges of her dark eyes. "There's part of me that's telling me to keep my mouth shut. And then there's part of me that needs to say it anyway."

"If it's your truth you should speak it." Cwynn shuffled his boots in the sand. From here, the keep looked like a giant mound of boulders, topped with thatch, a bigger version of the cottages clinging to the shore. The windows all glowed brightly, though, and he hoped it meant that Shane intended to drink long into the night. Thunder rumbled and a bolt of jagged lightning forked across the horizon from sky to sea. "But speak it quick—the storm's not over yet. This is just a lull."

"The boys are getting older now—they're lads now, not babies, anymore—soon they'll be men at the rate they're growing."

"Ariene." He touched her shoulder. "You didn't bring me down to the water in the middle of a storm to tell me the boys are growing, did you?"

She gave a short little laugh. "No." She shook her head. "No, of course not." She pressed her lips together, took a deep breath, then said, "I wanted to tell you I've been thinking. That the boys need a man, they need their father. The sea took Sorley, and it's not giving him back. My boys and I—we're a burden on my mother, though she'll never say—"

"Ariene, my Gran-da will keep you fed, you know that. Since when has any suffered in this village more than any other?"

Ariene shook her head and looked down at the waves rushing to cover her toes with white foam. "I don't know how to say this, Cwynn. It's coming out all wrong—"

"What is?" he asked gently. The wind was picking up again, the waves were swelling as he watched.

"I heard what you came to tell us, and I realized—" Again she broke off, her eyes fixed on the storm clouds massing on the horizon.

"What?" He touched a finger under her chin and was stunned to see that she was crying. "What's wrong, Ariene? What is it?"

"After I heard your story, I realized I can't say what I decided, what I've been thinking, what I wanted to tell you. Because now, no matter what I say, you won't believe me. You'll think it has to do with that you're a queen's son—the High Queen's son, at that, and even if you can't be High King, well—you'll still be a great chief. And you'll always wonder if what I had to say was because of what you told us tonight."

"What did you want to tell me?"

She actually blushed. "I wanted to tell you I've been thinking—the boys need a father, and—"

"Sorley's not coming back." He took a deep breath. Part of him did want to take her in his arms and part of him remembered every year on the morning after Beltane when she'd run away, sometimes before he himself was awake. "But I will." He wrapped his arms around himself against the wind as sporadic raindrops stung his face. "I will come back." He touched her arm. "We should go back inside. I can't lie to you, Ariene, there's part of me that—you were so mean when all I wanted—" He broke off. What was the point of telling her this? She was still the mother of his sons, no matter what else happened. And whatever else was to happen between the two of them had to wait while he took this unexpected turn.

"Ah, look, Ariene. Maybe you won't like me as a chief," he said, trying to lighten her mood. "Maybe you'd rather I smelled of fish than horse or cow." She eyed him, like a mare about to bolt. "But we used to be friends, you and I, before Sorley came between us. Maybe when I come back, we could go back to being friends. And see what happens next Beltane."

"Ariene! Ariene!" Argael called from the back door. "Come inside, the two of you—don't you see those clouds?"

As if on cue, the rain dropped out of the sky in a sudden sheet of water, drenching them to the skin almost instantaneously. For a moment, they stared at each other. Want, pure as the water and raging as the sea jolted through him. He stared at the outlines of her ample breasts thrusting through the sodden clinging fabric, topped by hard peaks. He could think of nothing but ripping the nightgown off her shoulders and suckling till they were both satisfied. Instead, he raised his cloak over both their heads and they ran together back to the house, where Argael handed both of them dry linen towels, clucking and fussing like a hen. Ariene strode purposefully through the kitchen, pausing only long enough to take a towel from her mother's hands, then disappeared through the doorway into the dark front room.

Argael gave him a questioning look, but he only shrugged. He understood Ariene's dilemma. Part of him wanted to believe her, that she, too, had finally sensed the connection he had always felt with her. But so much more of him was wary, hurt, suspicious that he was merely being used, especially now she knew what he stood to gain.

So he covered his head with the towel and dripped onto the mat in front of the door while Argael said, "I'll get you a tunic and trews that were Aedwyr's, Cwynn. There's some in the chest in the storeroom. They may be a bit tight, but they'll be dry."

"And you take my bed," Ariene said, strolling back. She had changed into another, drier tunic, this one with long sleeves, tied high at the throat with a blue ribbon. Even her feet were encased in thick socks. She dragged a bone comb through her damp curls, deliberately avoiding his eyes. "I'll sleep in the loft with the boys."

"I can stay on the hearth, Argael," said Cwynn. "I don't mind—"

"Ah, but I do. That's my place." The midwife smiled and pointed him to the front of the house. "There's something about storms and midnight that seems to bring babies. A night like this, I'm almost sure to be called. Just go up the steps off the front room. She's got a little nook fixed under the eave, right opposite Asgre."

"I wanted to talk to you, Argael—about Shane—that's why I came here, you see. It wasn't just the boys or a place to sleep—"

She stopped him with a quick pat on his cheek. "We'll talk in the morning." She held his eyes in a long look. "You rest now. You have a long ride ahead."

The front of the house was dank and chill and very dark and Cwynn stumbled more than once in the unfamiliar room. He managed to find his way up the steps and saw it was more of a nest than a bed. Ariene had a mattress and a couple of old quilts and a pillow that smelled like her. He lay down, listening to the rain pelting so hard on the roof, it sounded as if it wished it could pound its way through. The window beside it rattled in the wind, and now and then, a rain drop spat in his face. With a sigh, he turned on his side, pulled up a quilt and burrowed his face in her scent.

It occurred to him that Ariene might come to him in the night, and he wondered what he would do if she did. Pride said reject her. *But I'm not sure I could,* he thought as he inhaled a great breath of her musky odor that immediately conjured the dark circles of her nipples jutting against the rain-soaked linen. She'd always made it clear she preferred Sorley. And now…he thought about what his grandfather said, about what Meeve could give him. *You'll be a chief in your own right, boy, of far grander fields than these.*

Then there was the woman with the honey-blonde hair, who'd been coming to him in dreams, both day and night now, since the turning of the year. Was she part of this new future that now stretched out before him? But already, it seemed, this future had raised a barrier between him and everything he thought of as home, including the mother of his sons.

*Eaven Raida, Dalraida*

The knight died at midnight without ever waking up. That he was a knight of Meeve's Fiachna was obvious by the raven feathers he wore in his hair, in the tattoos twining his forearms and chest, in the pattern of his plaid and the crests on his sword. But he carried no written message. Morla rocked back on her heels beside the cooling corpse, her mind turning rapidly as she watched the old women begin to prepare the body for the charnel pits.

There was on him no hint as to what news he might've been bringing. If they'd had a druid, they might've been able to follow his spirit into the Summerlands, where it most likely lingered still, on the edges. But they had no druid, and the time of year wasn't conducive to contacting the dead, either. So she was left to guess.

She paced the room as the old women worked, watching them peel off the rest of the knight's clothing. The man's big body was heavily muscled, without an ounce of excess flesh. But he looked well fed, thought Morla, as she moved in for a closer look. She crossed her arms over her own bony chest and surveyed the dead knight stretched out before her as if she were assessing a side of beef. She looked at the corded, muscled forearms, the now-flaccid chest. He looked very well fed. On a whim, she opened his mouth and probed his teeth. They were white and strong and they didn't move against her finger, like hers did against her tongue.

He was very well fed, indeed.

She backed away, splashed water from a ewer into a basin and washed her hands. She looked up to see Colm watching her from the door. "This man doesn't look like he's starving."

One of the old women cackled beside the bed. "This one doesn't look like he missed a meal a day in his life. Would you look at the length of his legs?"

"That's not his legs you're pointing at, Moira. Have some respect for the dead, will you?"

The women snickered. Sickened, Morla pushed past Colm into the corridor that led to the main hall, where the rest of the household huddled. She paused on the threshold and gazed over the lumpy shapes stretched out around the smoldering hearths. Most were already asleep. The rain had started up again, and the fires hissed and steamed. Somewhere a child called out and a woman hastened to hush him. A surge of pity swept through her for this dwindling flock of souls who depended on her. She heard Colm's sandals tapping an uneven tattoo across the stones as he hurried to her side. "My lady, the sergeant—"

"There's only one thing to do, Colm," she said, as if he hadn't spoken.

"What's that, my lady?"

"The knight's horse—it was unharmed?" In the orange rushlight, Colm's face was very thin, the cheekbones prominent, skin stretched tight across his forehead. She felt as old and as tired as he looked.

"The sergeant of the guard wishes to speak to you, my lady. I think you should hear what he has to say. This thing you're thinking to do—it's dangerous out there, my lady. You saw those brigands—"

"Those weren't brigands, Colm. They were starving people. They won't bother me. I'll take an escort—I'll ride under a white flag and Mother's colors—"

"Ride where?"

"Where else? To Mother, wherever she is. I suspect that's either Ardagh or Eaven Morna. I suppose I'll find out."

"And how do you expect to find her? Get on the knight's horse and tell him?"

In spite of the situation, Morla had to grin. "That's exactly what I intend to do. The horses of the Fiachna are trained to find their way home. Wherever he came from, they'll give me a fresh ride, and tell me if Mother's at Eaven Morna or somewhere else."

"But, my lady—"

"It's the only way, Colm. Clearly that knight was from my mother. What else is there to do?"

"The roads aren't safe, my lady. You saw that yourself."

"Then I'll take guards with me." She shook her head and shrugged. "If I set out at dawn, and ride straight through, I should be at Eaven Morna in four, maybe five days." Morla wrapped her arms around herself, ignoring the maelstrom of emotion that name raised deep within. "It's been ten years since I've been back."

"Do you think that's why Meeve's forgot us, lady?"

Despite the lateness of the hour, the leaden weight of hunger in her belly and of fatigue in her head, Morla choked back a laugh. "Oh no, Colm, you've never met my mother, have you? Believe me, I don't think she's noticed I've been gone."

*Eaven Morna, Mochmorna*

"Please tell me what I've just heard isn't true." Connla, ArchDruid of all Brynhyvar raised her chin and squared her shoulders as she stared up at Meeve across the food-laden board. Thunder rumbled in the distance and a flash of lightning flickered through the hall. She clenched her oak staff of office in her left fist and held her right arm against her side, trying to quell the palsy that shook it whenever she was in the grip of strong emotion. She wasn't quite sure she could believe that she finally had proof of her suspicions: Meeve was stealing sacred silver. It should never have been able to happen, thought Connla. The earth elementals, the khouri-keen, should never have allowed such a thing, but she knew in her bones that somehow, it had.

The hall was crowded with Meeve's warriors and neighboring chiefs. No one was ever turned away from Meeve's table, no matter how high or low, rich or poor. Her bounty was part of her power. The humid air reeked of sweaty men and greasy meat, but Connla ignored everything, even as she was jostled nearly off her feet by a servant scurrying by with a basket piled high with rounds of cheese. The bard's voice rose in a mournful wail, and Connla silenced him with one ferocious stare. "Well? Do you mean to answer me, sister? Or must I wait by the gatehouse, like a beggar after crusts of news?"

Meeve lowered her jeweled goblet, tossed back her fabled, though slightly faded, red mane beneath her thin circlet of braided gold and copper, and licked her fingers. "Depends on what you've heard. I'm having a hard time believing what I've just heard, I know that much."

Pain shot up and down Connla's arm, from her shoulder to her wrist, but Meeve's blatant insolence only fueled her resolve not to show weakness. "Is it true your knights have taken the silver from Hawthorn Grove at Garn?"

"They haven't stolen it, you old crow. That druid-house was abandoned to blight so long ago the roof was caving it. Would you have preferred they'd left it there?" Meeve held out her goblet to her cup-bearer and nodded at the end of the table. "We've all had news today, it seems. I had a few messages myself, thanks to Ronalbain and Fahrwyr." She raised her brimming goblet again in the direction of two mud-splattered men who crouched over the long board, hunks of stringy meat clutched in both hands. There was a look on Meeve's face Connla couldn't quite read as she stared harder at her sister, deliberately opening her druid Sight. A gray veil of mist appeared between them, and Connla realized Meeve was hiding something.

Connla glanced around the table at the reddened, grease-stained faces, and spoke beneath the raucous laughter that followed some half-witted remark. "May I speak to you alone?"

Meeve only belched and waved an airy hand. "Why don't you come eat? Come, sit…you, Turnoch, and you, Dougal, move aside, make room for Callie Connla." Even before the sentence was completely out of her mouth, the men began to shift, benches began to scrape across the wooden planks of the raised dais. Meeve nodded. "There you are—go sit. Let's eat and drink like civilized people, and then we'll talk."

"You'll be too drunk to talk soon." The silver chalice and blade of her office clanked against Connla's thigh as she hoisted her robes above her knees and hauled herself onto the dais, waving away hands that would've helped her. She leaned as far over the board as the piled platters would permit and stared directly into her younger sister's eyes. Another peal of thunder rolled through the room, echoing in the high rafters. The storm was moving closer. "I need to talk to you now. Alone."

"Now?"

Connla glanced at the warriors leaning on either side of Meeve, at the guards lined up along the wall. Sweat began to gather under her armpits as a sense of spiraling disaster, of something very dangerous coming closer, almost riding on the edge of the storm, began to grow. She shoved the feeling away and concentrated on Meeve. "Yes, now. Unless you'd like to discuss this in front of everyone?"

Meeve belched again. "You're not the only one with something to say, sister. If I were you, I'd take the time to fortify myself first."

"Am I to understand that as a threat?" Connla narrowed her eyes. "You don't know what you're doing, sister. You don't know what balances you're upsetting—no one would dare to touch that silver but those Lacquilean robbers you've let loose upon the land."

"Well, now, sister. That's hardly diplomatic of you, considering I'm expecting a delegation from this person or persons who call themselves the Voice of the city, whatever that means. I thought to do you a favor—"

"A favor? You take our silver to appease foreigners, bargain it away and call it a favor?"

"Is silver all you're worried about, Connla?" Meeve put her goblet down with a thump and leaned forward with a clink of twisted gold and copper bracelets.

"Of course silver isn't all I'm worried about. That silver was guarded by the khouri-keen—your knights should not have been able to find that silver, let alone take it away. There's far more at stake—"

"Then I should think you'd better be off to Ardagh, don't you? If there is some sort of problem with those creatures, the silver's safer with the Fiachna than it was in that burned-out grove."

"Will it be here when I return? Or will robbers have somehow snatched it away from the Fiachna, or will pirates have managed to sail all the way into Lake Killcarrick and raid the druid-house at Killcairn?"

"You still blame me for that?" Meeve hiccupped softly, her golden brown eyes hollow in the torchlight. Lightning flashed, accompanied by a sharp crackle and a sudden blast of cold wet air. Torches whipped out in long plumes of white smoke, casting shadows on Meeve's face. Buffeted on all sides as warriors and servants scattered to bolt the shutters against the rising winds, Connla could only stare in disbelief at the undeniable ring of tiny white flames wreathing Meeve's face.

"What're you about, Meeve—" Connla began, but her question faltered and died on her lips as rain splattered on the roof, then settled into a fast, steady drumming. *So that's what Meeve doesn't want us to see,* she thought. *That's what Meeve doesn't want me to know.* "Why didn't you tell me you were dying?"

Meeve knocked over her goblet, spilling purple wine across her white linen and cloth of gold. With a curse coarse enough for the stable, Meeve pushed back her chair and rose. "You come with me. *Sister.*" The last word was a snarl that sounded anything but sisterly.

Perhaps it was the hard pounding of the rain that contributed to Connla's sense of ripping through some layer of reality as she followed Meeve across the crowded floor, eyes riveted on Meeve's rigid back as if she were the only other person in the room. The only person who mattered, Connla thought, and out of the corner of her eye, against the kaleidoscopic background, Briecru, Meeve's chief Cowherd, stood out, his rich gold chains and red mustaches vivid against the shifting shadows forming around him like a cloak, so that it seemed he stood in a pool of black. The idea that Briecru could betray Meeve bolted through her mind, just as Meeve pulled her into the small antechamber to one side of the hall, her fingers clamped like a vise around Connla's upper arm.

Meeve slammed the door, then wiped her hand ostentatiously on the thigh of her trews and made a face. "Faugh, Connla, must you wear all that wool? You not only sound like a crow, you reek like a dead one."

"Better like a dead crow than a living thrall." Connla met the wall of Meeve's anger. She was still partially in that hazy state between the two worlds where she could see the flames flickering around Meeve's face, but she was too angry not to retaliate. "Is that what you need my silver for, sister? For the perfume you've taken to wearing?"

"I should slap you for that."

"Why didn't you tell me you were dying, Meeve?"

Meeve snorted and shook her head. "You druids tell us we're all dying, some of us sooner than others is all. I don't want your pity, Connla, and I don't want your help." Black anger surged around Meeve like a cloak, cutting off Connla's Sight.

Stung, Connla could only blink. "But I—I don't understand. Surely, sister, there's something that can be done—"

"Oh, spare me." Meeve sank down in the wide chair on one side of the fire and leaned back against the linen-covered cushions, then held out a scroll. "It's what killed Mother. I've all the same symptoms—the rashes that come and go, the aches, the sweats, the flesh falling off my bones. There was nothing to be done for her and I know there's nothing to be done for me. If you were really concerned, you'd mind your own affairs so I wouldn't have to. Do you have any idea who sent the message Ronalbain brought? He's the one who brought the most distressing news, I think."

"And what's that?" Connla raised her chin. Meeve's words pelted her like windblown acorns.

"He brought me a message from Deirdre, who—though I find it hard to believe—is yet still with child. Can you explain that, as well as why my daughter's begging me to rescue her?"

"Rescue her? From what?" Connla faltered a little and tightened her hand on her staff. Deirdre, one of Meeve's twin daughters, was a gifted druid who had been under Connla's guardianship since her arrival at the White Birch Grove at the age of seven.

"Maybe if you'd paid more attention to your duty, this disgraceful situation would never have occurred. But when it did, I told you to take care of it. Now it seems that not only did you not address it when it could've been easily eliminated, Deirdre's now in such a state she thinks her sisters are trying to kill her. Are they?"

Connla tried to breathe through the grip of the palsy that shook her arm. "No one would kill Deirdre."

"What about the child?"

"The child's an unnatural—"

"Then it should've been taken care of long ago," Meeve replied. She tapped her finger on the arm of her chair. "I had a message from Morla. They need a druid desperately there, for it seems there's blight in Dalraida and no druids."

"I sent a druid last Lughnas—"

"One? You sent one, out of all who crowd us to the roof here, Connla?"

Connla watched the spectral death lights dance around Meeve's face. She had lost weight, Connla realized, her skin was jaundiced. *She looks just like Mother, in the months before she died.* Even the uisce-argoid, the silver-charged water the druids distilled as their most potent remedy, could only slow the disease's inevitable progress, not cure it. "That's not fair, Meeve," Connla said, appalled. "The brothers and sisters are not mine to command—Dalraida's sent no druids to the mother-groves…there're few who're willing to go that far. I had nothing—"

"You have everything to do with it—you're the Ard-Cailleach, the ArchDruid of all Brynhyvar, are you not? If you've nothing to do with it, all those titles mean nothing, too." With a contemptuous glance over her shoulder, Meeve rose and swept to the window, where the rain spattered on the horn pane. "I won't leave this land anything less than settled and at peace."

Feeling slapped, Connla opened her mouth, then shut it. She knew what Meeve implied. One's status in the Summerlands was dependent upon how well one was regarded by those left behind, and Connla had no doubt Meeve intended to be remembered as the greatest queen who'd ever reigned. Meeve's strategy had always been simple: she perceived every man in Brynhyvar as a suitor, every warrior a potential knight. No other queen in all of Brynhyvar had ever so identified herself as the love, as the wife, of the Land, and no other in all its history had ever roused such passions, inspired such loyalties and spawned such rivalries.

Great Meeve, she was called, even by her enemies; Red Meeve, for the color of her hair; Glad Meeve, for the bounty of her thighs she spread so willingly; Gold Meeve, for the treasure she dispensed with a generous hand. But Connla had sometimes wondered what would happen when youth and vigor inevitably decayed. "You can't buy your peace or your place in the Summerlands with druid silver, Meeve." The dancing lights were back now as Meeve paced to the fire and stood over it, warming her bone-thin hands. Meeve's face had a ghastly pallor, the color of a day-old corpse. She's dying quickly, Connla realized. And Meeve was right about Deirdre, who was more than two months overdue. How could whoever was Ard-Cailleach of the grove not have taken matters in hand? Connla had been so concentrated on Meeve and her machinations she'd forgotten her responsibility to her own sisters, her own blood.

An implacable sense of an impending presence filled her, but she shook it off, sure it was merely the sense of Meeve's approaching death. Meeve would be dead by Imbolc—the energy she usually emanated had diminished alarmingly now that Connla had seen beyond Meeve's own carefully constructed pretense. There was no point in continuing to antagonize her. She drew a deep breath. "I believe you want to leave the land at peace."

"Then go do your work, Connla. And leave me to finish mine."

At the door, Connla paused. There'd been no resolution

about the silver. "I'll expect the inventory of the Hawthorn Grove to match the inventory of that silver in the rolls at Ardagh."

Meeve cocked her head and pursed her lips. "You know, Connla, one might think you care more about your silver than you do for Deirdre or anything else. I'm starting to think that what people say is true."

Stung, Connla stiffened and tightened her grip on her staff until her knuckles turned white. "And what do they say, the people? And which people, exactly, do you mean?"

"You need look for them no farther than these wards and halls, sister. They say that the druids care only for their dreams, for the pleasures of the sidhe, that they dally on the Tors while the Land grows cold and the trees die. They say the druids are losing their power. They say the druids are dying out, and as they go, the land dies with it." Meeve shrugged and arched one brow. "And given that you've preferred to stay here and make trouble while there's reports of blight and rumors of goblins and now my daughter—your own niece—believes her life to be in danger, I wonder if what they say might be true."

Connla bit back the hard retort that sprang to her lips. *Have mercy,* she told herself. *Have mercy. Meeve's dying and there's more at stake than what anyone thinks of druidry.* "All right, Meeve. I'll do as you suggest. Doubtless your dying has had some affect upon the land. You should've told me sooner." She turned to leave and then remembered the other piece of news she'd had that day. "I'll plan on stopping to see Bran on my way through Pent—"

"Don't bother—I've already sent for him."

"He's on his way here?"

"As we speak." Meeve narrowed her eyes. "I sent Lochlan after him two nights ago. What's this sudden interest in Bran? He's none of your concern—he's not druid."

"He very well could be. I had a message from Athair Eamus."

"Oh, come. He's never shown even the least sign—"

"According to Athair Eamus, Bran appears to be a very strong rogue."

Meeve stared at Connla, then snorted. "You expect me to believe that?"

"Why should you not believe it?"

"Because Bran was duller than Morla as a baby, if that's possible. He was happy with his rocks and shells for hours, lining them all up in row after row. He didn't even start to talk until well after he was weaned. No one's ever—"

"According to Athair Eamus, he's showing signs. He'll be here soon? I'll wait."

"Oh, no, you won't. Let me be clear." Meeve advanced on her, bright eyes fixed in her flushed face. "I don't want you here, Connla. I don't want any of you here. I want you to pack up—all of you—and take yourselves off to Ardagh or TirNa'lugh or wherever you will. The blight, the goblins— these are your province. If you'd do something to ease my passing, you settle this land before I die."

Connla stared at Meeve, anger surging through her, blinding all vestiges of her druid-sight. Her whole arm twitched a frantic tattoo against her side, and she gritted her teeth, striving for control. "Watch your back, sister," she blurted before she could stop herself. "Briecru—"

"Oh, enough," Meeve waved her hand in dismissal, a look

of disgust on her face, and before Connla could continue, the door opened and a young page peered in.

"Great Queen? Lord Lochlan's been spotted on the causeway—at least, we think it's Lord Lochlan—in this rain it's hard to see."

"Lochlan?" said Meeve. "How could that be? Is he alone?" She glanced over her shoulder at Connla. "He must've turned back—"

"He's got someone with him—someone riding one of your own roans."

Connla limped forward. "Pentland's a full three days' ride from here, Meeve—even if he got there by now, they could only have just left. You think it's only coincidence they arrived here on the edge of a storm?"

For a long moment Meeve stared at her, then turned to the page and said, "Set the watch for my son— Open the gates—have mead and blankets waiting. Tell them to draw hot baths and set fresh clothes warming. Go on now." When the page had gone, she looked at Connla. "And you, too. I'll order horses saddled and waiting. As soon as the weather breaks, I want you all on your way."

In disbelief Connla gripped Meeve's arm. "I don't think you understand what you could be dealing with, Meeve. This is all beyond your ken—it's beyond mine, if that really is Lochlan and Bran. How'd they get here in less than half the time it should've taken?"

Meeve stalked past her, and for a moment, Connla thought she might simply walk out of the room without replying. But with her hand on the latch, she said, "I'll watch him and if he shows signs, as you say, I'll send word."

Connla put a hand on Meeve's shoulder and was struck by how thin it felt beneath the sumptuous silk tunic. "You send me the boy, Meeve. Promise me, or I won't leave. That boy shows any sign at all of being druid, and you send him to me. To Ardagh, at once."

Meeve looked pointedly at Connla's hand, then said, "Fine. Now allow me to go greet my son."

"I'll see you at MidSummer, Meeve, and I'll expect a full accounting of every dram of silver," she managed to finish as Meeve shut the door with a hollow slam that reverberated through every one of Connla's aching bones.

She couldn't just depart the castle, she thought. She couldn't just leave Bran here, unguarded, untended. What to do, what to do, she wondered, gnawing on her lower lip, rubbing her right arm. Then she thought of the trixies in their hive under the Tor. She'd set them to mind him, she thought. That should divert their attention, and as long as he was here, they'd ground his magic so that he'd not slip into the OtherWorld by accident and be lost. Whether or not he'd be able to cope with them—well, they didn't call them trixies for nothing. She'd set it as sort of a test for him, she thought as she limped out of the room, her old bones aching from the damp. If he wasn't druid, he wouldn't see them, wouldn't be aware of them and, at best, would find their attentions a source of puzzlement and perplexity. On the other hand, a small voice cautioned, if he is druid, they can make his life a living torment. But that, she decided, was a risk she would have to take.

# 4

*Faerie*

"So you see, Auberon, if we bring the crystals here, we won't need the druids—we won't even need mortals. Faerie will belong to us in a way it never did before. We'll be able to make it everything—anything—we want it to be." Timias sat back and noticed that the sky above the Forest House was slowly turning pink. He watched Auberon's face, searching for some sign the stricken king had understood, or even heard what he'd said, for he asked no questions, made no response at all.

Timias waited and wondered what the king would do or say if he knew that Timias was indirectly responsible for not only the queen's death, but all the others, as well. A furrow had appeared between Auberon's brows, his shoulders drooped, and he looked more like a stag than ever. The change was on him—soon Loriana would be Queen. Timias leaned forward and decided to try again. "I know it all sounds unexpected. But ask me anything, I can explain. We can use the khouri-keen, Auberon, just the way the druids do."

"The what? I thought we were talking about gremlins."

"We were—that's the name the druids use—it's the name they use for themselves. We can call them anything you like."

Auberon stroked the fine brown down that had appeared on his face. "This isn't what I expected."

"But, Auberon, isn't that why you sent me to the mortals? To learn druid magic? Those goblins last night—what if there's more?" And there were, Timias knew. But he couldn't say how he knew, or even that he knew, for that might betray the fact that the forest's devastation and the death of Auberon's Queen were his fault.

Auberon stalked to the single window. He leaned on the frame and gazed down into the Hall, where the sidhe were preparing a pyre to mourn the passing of the Queen. "We have to do something. No one in this Court—except possibly Loriana—understands more how important it is we prevent last night from ever happening again. But you have to admit, what you propose is most…most…irregular. I expected some kind of tree magic, not this talk of bringing a new kind of creature into Faerie—"

"You sent me to learn druid magic," Timias replied. "Just because the old word *drui* means *tree,* doesn't mean that's where their magic comes from. It's not the trees that gives mortal magic the stability that ours doesn't have, it's the gremlins, the khouri-keen. Don't you understand, Auberon? The gremlins are the secret, not the trees. We won't need druids to ground our magic in if we have the gremlins."

Auberon sighed. "I don't know about this, Timias. This opens a whole new—"

"How could it be what you expected? Auberon, I don't understand. You send me into Shadow, charge me with something no sidhe has ever attempted, and now that I've done as you asked, you're shocked it's not what you thought it would be? Of course it's different—the mortals are as different from us as water from air, as fire from water. The goblins are growing stronger. What if they rampage again tonight?"

"I know you've done an astonishing thing, Timias." Auberon clapped one hand on Timias's shoulder and grasped his hand with the other. "I know your knowledge, what you've brought us—but today…now…" He attempted a thin smile that made his face look pinched in half. His eyes were hollow, as if the life had been blown out of them. "We'll talk more later."

It was clearly a dismissal. But as he turned to leave, Timias said, "What about our bargain, Auberon?"

"Timias, that bargain was made long ago—you can scarcely expect—"

"Loriana's ripe to choose a Consort, isn't she?"

"Soon. There are others for her to consider, of course— what I say may not matter." Auberon refused to meet his eyes, and in that instant, Timias understood that Auberon had never thought he'd see him again, and it wasn't so much his ideas that shocked the king as his return. *That's what Auberon really hadn't expected,* Timias thought.

"You didn't think I'd come back, did you? You never thought you'd have to keep the bargain, did you, Auberon?"

"Is that all you're concerned about, Timias? Whether or

not I'll keep to my bargain?" Auberon's voice was low and savage. "My daughter's lost her mother, Faerie's lost its queen and I have lost over fifty of my most valiant fighters. We don't even know what set the goblins off last night—that was no ordinary hunting party, that was a—a frenzy of some kind. And that stinking, poisonous mess. It's clear we're in the midst of some great turning of the Wheel. No one disagrees we need to do something. I'm just not sure what you suggest is the answer. This druid magic's not—"

"Our magic? Come, Auberon, you knew it was different."

"What about the blight in Shadow? The trees there are sick—there're places we no longer go. What if by using druid magic, we invite the same infection?"

"Then the sooner we create a kind of barrier between ourselves and Shadow the better off we'll be. And we will not only be able to control the goblins, but we'll be able to keep silver out of Faerie, too."

"You'll have to explain all this to the council, Timias. I can't agree to something like this without discussing it further. What would we do with these creatures? Even the druids find them hard to control, do they not? Perhaps we'd only trade one evil for another."

Timias flexed his hands into fists. He wanted to leap at Auberon's throat but Auberon would think he'd been infected by his time in Shadow and might even banish him again. Then where would he go? Back to the miserably cold caverns he'd just managed to crawl out of? So he restrained himself, even as resentment burned in his bones.

Why should the king understand what this knowledge had cost him? Auberon hadn't experienced the long, uncomfortable nights when the scent of sleeping mortals twined around him like a rope, coarse and irritating and arousing all at once; the tedious days of dull, back-breaking work. No sidhe had ever attempted to pass as mortal for more than perhaps a moment or two—long enough only to lure the particularly enchanting one, or to beg from the especially kind. Timias had done the impossible. He had lived and slept and worked among the mortals right under the noses of the most sensitive of druids, and no one had known. He'd even incurred their wrath by experimenting with druid magic, using it in a way no one else had ever tried, to create the cloak of shadows. The cloak of shadows he'd lost so cavalierly in Macha's hall.

"I've called a convening," Auberon was saying. "Tell the council all you've told me. I've not said no." And then he was gone, in the manner of all the sidhe, who could appear to be by one's side at one moment and then vanish in the next.

Timias sank onto the window seat, a hollow feeling in his chest and nausea in the pit of his stomach. He could well imagine the way his brother's Council would greet his suggestion. Without Auberon's support and endorsement, the sidhe would laugh. They probably wouldn't laugh if they knew he could turn into a goblin, however.

Through the latticed floor, he could see into the hall below, where the sidhe flitted in and around and among the trees like shining orbs of light. He wondered what they would do to him if they knew that he was what had set the goblins off last night. He suspected that the druids' punishment would be mild in comparison. All his life, he'd been the strange one, the odd one, the one that was different from all the rest. He'd gone and done the thing not one of them could do, and he wasn't going to get anything from it at all—not even, apparently, gratitude.

He heard a rustling in the woven branches above his head and raised his eyes. "You can come down now, Loriana." He took a deep breath of the fragrance that betrayed her, an unmistakable combination of roses and night-blooming jasmine. It had seared itself into his consciousness as he had led her back through the trees. One of the ivy-laced branches trembled. "Come, Loriana, I promise I won't tell." A pair of bright green eyes peered through a gap in the tightly woven vines and the branches shook more violently. He heard a rustling and in a flash, she appeared at the doorway, her bright hair gleaming as the daylight brightened. He was acutely conscious of the way her gaze lingered on him, as if she was memorizing his every feature. "Are you looking for your father?"

"I was looking for you." Her forthrightness took him aback. She raised her chin. "You look surprised."

"I thought you'd be downstairs, princess, with everyone else."

She looked down, and for a moment, she looked just like the very young child he recalled. "I'm very sad about Mother, about my friends. But everyone blames me. They all say it's my fault."

"Ah." She was wearing a wispy garment made of spider silk, and around her waist she wore a belt of woven honeysuckle vine, just like the scrap he'd found beside the pool, and it was difficult to keep his eyes on her face. "So you weren't supposed to be out there, were you?"

She shook her head. "My father won't even look at me. But I wanted to thank you for saving my life. I know I wouldn't have survived if you hadn't come along. And it's not your fault Mother died, either, no matter what Grandmother says."

"Finnavar blames me?" How was it still possible she was here? wondered Timias. She'd made his life a waking nightmare, as the mortals said. The least he'd hoped for from his banishment was to return and find her gone. "She's still here?"

"She says she won't leave because she's worried about what's happening."

Timias took a long look at the princess before him. Her eyes were a brilliant shade of green, her skin flawless as a pearl. But it was her hair that was her great beauty, her hair that even in her childhood set her apart from the other sidhe. It glowed rich and red as fire, coppery and orange in the twilight and like pale spun gold beneath the moon. Her fragrance entwined him, more potent than Auberon's dream-weed. "I don't want you to think I'm angry with your father, princess." He wondered why he felt it necessary to tell her so. "I just don't want what happened last night to happen again."

"I don't think my father wants it to happen again, either." Loriana said. "I know I don't. What is this bargain you spoke of?"

The air between them hummed with a palpable tension. Timias cleared his throat, trying to think of what to tell her. It had been one thing to ask for something, it was quite another to have it standing before you. "Perhaps I'd be wrong to hold your father to something he clearly never believed he'd have to keep."

"What do you mean?" Loriana frowned. "What was your bargain?"

"He didn't believe I'd come back."

"You came back to save me," Loriana said. As if she were afraid she'd said too much, she shut her mouth audibly. She hesitated for just a moment, and then she was gone, leaving him stunned, his mind whirling with possibilities he had never dared imagine before.

Loriana fled, heart beating like a hummingbird's wings. What everyone said about him was true, but not in the way they said it. There was something different, something strange about Timias. But it wasn't just the way he looked or the intense way he stared at her. He reminded her of the young mortal who'd burst through the border with such raw and rampant power. *That's how he's different,* she thought. *He's got that same sense about him.* Maybe that's what her grandmother meant when she said Timias was dangerous. When their eyes met, she'd felt a jolt of energy so intense it took her breath away.

She slipped through the trees. In the hall, a few of the sidhe had already begun to sing and their voices followed her, calling for their late queen to return. The leaves rustled softly all around her. Part of her wanted to go there, to seek the comfort of her kindred. But part of her knew she'd be greeted by stares and whispers. It wasn't just the loss of the queen they blamed her for—it was Chrysaliss and Tatiana and all the warriors, too. *And it is my fault,* she thought miserably. "How can I ever be queen after this?" she muttered to herself.

"It's not your fault, Loriana," Finnavar's voice was a harsh whisper from the branch just above.

Loriana gasped and looked up. "Grandmother? Is that you? Are you following me?"

"Someone has to keep an eye on you, Loriana. Your father's not thinking clearly, that's obvious. Come up here and talk to me."

Loriana made her way through the branches and saw why Finnavar had chosen that particular perch. The branches were covered with thick green moss, creating a private sitting space. Loriana nestled into it while Finnavar balanced beside her. "First of all, you're not responsible for what happened last night. You were wrong to leave your bower, when you'd been forbidden. But no one could've known—no one expected—it wasn't your fault." She made a little noise, between a sniff and a caw. "If anyone's to blame, it's Timias."

"But why, grandmother? If it weren't for him—"

"Rather convenient that, isn't it? The night the goblins rampage, he happens to show up just in time to save the princess? Where was he coming from, that's what I'd like to know? He's not been in Shadow, he's not been here. So where could he have been? Maybe no one else cares enough to ask those questions but I do. And so should your father."

"He told Father he got into trouble with the druids, and when they banished him from the land, he couldn't get back to Faerie, either. He's been trying to come home for a year and a day." Timias hadn't exactly said below and between what, Loriana thought. "He said he had a lot of time to think about things—things he learned from the druids."

"Your father would do well to forget Timias ever came back."

"But, Grandmother, why? If Grandfather loved him—"

"Your grandfather loved him the way you love a pretty pebble you might find lying in a stream or under a tree."

"So the story is true, then? He really did find Timias under a tree, in the woods? And there were animals fighting over him—about to eat him?"

"Ha. Is that how the story goes now? Allemande told me he found him in a cave. At least, that's what he said happened. He was out hunting one night—oh yes, don't look surprised. We could hunt at night, then, for the goblins were thin wormy things, kept well pacified by the druids. I'll never forget the morning he brought him home. The sun had just risen and I had gone to bathe. And Allemande came to me, carrying something that looked like a bulging white worm."

Her grandmother's voice faded into a harsh whisper, and Loriana wrinkled her nose. "It really looked like a worm?"

"Until I got close. And then I saw it was a child, a newborn child still in its caul. It was squirming—a piece of it had already come away from its face, or it might've suffocated. Allemande said he'd heard its cries coming from the cave. He called back his hounds and crawled inside and found it."

"The child—that was Timias?"

"That's the name Allemande gave it. I was glad I had no part in that at least."

"But why didn't you like Timias? Wasn't he just a baby?"

"He didn't smell right, for one thing. In fact, he never smelled like anything at all. He didn't feel right, either— slippery, somehow, as if his flesh could slide off him at any time. And he was never quite where you expected him to be. I wanted as little to do with him as possible and insisted on bearing Auberon. That was my mistake."

"But why, Grandmother?"

Finnavar reached out with one curved yellow nail and gently tucked an errant curl behind Loriana's ear. "Because things come in their time, child. Like the seasons, like the turning of the Wheel—some things cannot be called into being before their time and some should not. I forced something into being that wasn't quite ripe—and look at him. Auberon's not the sort of king Faerie needs now. Why do you think I stay? I know the mistake was really mine."

"What sort of king does it need?"

"Oh, child." Finnavar shook her head. "It needs a queen. Already your father's time is passing—if the goblins don't get him, he'll have Changed by MidWinter, if not before, and all of Faerie will be yours, to win or lose."

"Win or lose? What do you mean?"

"Every time the Wheel turns—for example, when a monarch dies and a new one rises, or an old season passes and a new one begins—there's the possibility that everything that exists will collapse and go down into chaos, into the Cauldron. That's what the druids would say. It used to be we could trust them to manage things, but these days…we must look for another way. I resisted the Change with everything I had. I was afraid Auberon wouldn't be equal to the task."

"Isn't that why Timias wanted to go to Shadow? Learn the druid magic?"

"Forget Timias. He's not important. You and I—the once and future queens of Faerie—we will work our own magic."

"How? What kind of magic?"

Finnavar's smile stretched wider and her lips cracked and began to flake away. When her mouth came back together, it resembled a beak even more than before. "Old druid magic. The kind the druids themselves forget."

More confused than ever, Loriana glanced over her shoulder, almost wishing someone would come along and shoo her down to the Court. But most of the others were already there and this spot was well secluded. "Grandmother, I don't understand. Isn't druid magic what Father—"

"That's what he doesn't understand," Finnavar shrieked. "A druid isn't something one can learn to be—a druid is something one's born. A druid isn't someone who understands how to use those miserable mud-creatures—a druid is someone the trees remember. That's what's gone wrong in Shadow, and that's what the druids there themselves don't understand. The blight is wiping out the memory of the trees. And so we must find a druid. A druid the trees in Faerie remember."

Despite her confusion, her fear and her grief, Loriana laughed in disbelief. "But there're fewer and fewer druids at all in Shadow, everyone says. So where do we find a druid like that?"

"You met one on the road last night."

"H-how—" Loriana's jaw dropped.

"I can smell him on you—yes, he's *that* strong." Finnavar unfolded her twisted frame. She was more birdlike, her speech more garbled with every passing moment, and Loriana realized soon she might not be able to understand her grandmother at all. She had been resisting the change, and now, it was almost impossible. "I happened to notice him one day when I was crossing back and forth after Timias. I always took time to have a look around. One never can be sure what mortals might be doing next."

"You've seen that boy before? The one who just—who just burst over the border?"

"That very one."

"How do you know him? You've seen him before? Met him?"

"I didn't so much meet him as find him. I went looking for him, you see. Something as strange as Timias, I thought should have an echo somewhere in Shadow. Sooner or later, something or someone was bound to show up. And sure enough, someone did. His name's Bran. And, not surprisingly, he's the son of the High Queen—the dying High Queen. Can you see how it all fits together, Loriana? Echoes and overlays, spiraling around? What happens in Shadow reverberates in Faerie, what happens in Faerie is repeated over and over again in Shadow until the energies wear themselves out. So I knew there had to be someone like Timias. Someone different. He's very young, just a boy, but strong— Oh, he's strong! He just needs… He needs to be awakened."

"How? What do you mean?"

"We sidhe are born aware and knowing of our magic. But mortals take a while—they have to learn and grow, and finally, they need one of us to light the spark, to kindle the knowing. So you see—we need him, he needs you."

"But he's so young—I thought it took most druids years—"

"He's what they call a rogue, child, a druid who comes suddenly into the full flower of his or her power, without the understanding and the discipline necessary to focus it. If any mortal ever made an impression on the trees of Faerie, it would be a rogue like that one." Finnavar fixed her beady eyes on Loriana. "Come, child. If your father can't bring himself to act, we must."

"Where are we going, Grandmother?" Loriana scrambled off the bough after Finnavar, who seemed to actually fly through the trees. "Grandmother, where are you taking me?"

"Into Shadow, of course, child."

"But, why?"

"To fetch the boy, of course."

"And then what?"

But Finnavar was so far ahead that the answer that filtered back to Loriana scarcely made sense: "To see if he remembers the trees."


In his bower, Timias stroked the clay pipe Auberon had left behind and tried to decide what to do. *What to do? Maybe you should decide who you are or what you are,* the insidious little voice whispered through his skull, making it difficult to plan his next move. *You didn't really think the king was going to listen to you, did you?*

Why hadn't he seen through Auberon's plan? It wasn't so much a plan, of course, as an opportunity that he'd presented to the king himself. You were an embarrassment, he thought. Once Allemande went into the Deep Forest, there was no place for Timias at the Faerie Court. There was no suggestion he could be king. The throne belonged to Allemande's son. Auberon had no use for him. He had tolerated Timias's presence for the sake of his father. When Timias offered to go to Shadow, of course Auberon had agreed.

Of course he'd agreed to present Timias as a potential

consort to Loriana. *He'd've promised anything. He never thought you were coming back.* The mourning song of the sidhe was rising higher now, and it grated on his nerves, for it reminded him he had two things to conceal—the first that he was the one who'd started the goblins rampaging, and the second, that he himself apparently was able to metamorphose into goblin form. He wasn't quite sure what to think of that but he was quite certain it wouldn't be met with approval.

He remembered what Finnavar always claimed—that he didn't so much blend in among the mortals as become one. Everyone laughed, dismissing her comment as wit, but Timias had always recognized how uncomfortably close she came to the truth. So was he sidhe or mortal or goblin or some curious combination of all three? And how could that have happened? What combination of parents could possibly explain who, or what, he was?

Whatever he was, the druid banishing had been effective in both worlds. Now he was back, in the world he had always thought of as his home. He wanted to stay here, in this green and pleasant land, with Loriana and all the sidhe. *This is where I belong*, he thought. This was where all his happiest memories were, of Allemande and the long days in his sunny Court. *This is where I want to be. And if they wouldn't let me stay because of what I can become…I just won't let on.*

He could keep secrets. And maybe if he convinced Loriana that his plan would work…maybe it wouldn't matter what Auberon thought. How to make her understand, then, that the magic of the sidhe would be enhanced by the magic of the khouri-keen, made stable and permanent in a way nothing in Faerie had ever been before? How to make her see what her father could not?

He stroked his chin. Unlike his chin in Shadow, his skin was smooth and beardless. His appearance was something else that was going to set him apart, he thought. All the other sidhe of Auberon's generation were showing signs of changing. But as far as he could discern, in pools of still water and polished crystal mirrors, his appearance hadn't altered at all. It was as if he'd exchanged one set of clothing for another.

If only he hadn't lost the cloak of shadows, Timias thought. That was an artifact created out of a blend of both magics, something real and tactile, with substance and weight. If he hadn't lost it, he could've shown Auberon and the Council—and Loriana, too—that a direct blending of sidhe and mortal magic could result in something stable, something lasting.

He remembered the motion of Deirdre's fingers, weaving form and weight and substance into the dark and slippery strands of shadow, mimicking the motion of their hips as he drove the magic into her. The cloak would've been a perfect illustration, something the sidhe could understand far more readily than all his wordy explanations of concepts that didn't really exist in Faerie. There was only one thing to do. He'd have to go back to the druid-house and either find Deirdre's piece of the cloak or find a druid to make him a new one. He could get the Khouri crystals, too, from the Chapter house, and show her those, as well. As the sun rose over Faerie, Timias found he was able to cross into Shadow just as he had hoped. He headed once more for the White Birch Grove.

*5*

*Eaven Morna*

The trixies were relentless and the fire wouldn't burn. At least not the one in the charcoal brazier where Bran swatted over a finger-length of ore. It was demeaning the way the Master Smith refused to believe it was trixies that kept smothering the fire with their dirty little feet or dousing it with their smelly piss. He, Bran, was apparently the only one with a drop of druid blood left in the whole of Eaven Morna. No one else admitted seeing them, and even the charm Apple Aeffie had taught him only worked for a few minutes at best.

"Tricksie trixies, run away quick—here I come with a big, fat stick. Here I come with a big long bone, so run away, trixies, run away home." He gritted his teeth and swatted at them with all his might. He didn't understand why his mother had set him to this torment. He'd expected to be welcomed and congratulated on his marvelous abilities, maybe even have a song made about him, and then sent to start his druid schooling. But instead of special attention, he'd returned to find all the druids gone and himself shunted aside in favor of a lot of foreign strangers who reeked of foreign spice, consigned to this forge he very quickly decided to hate, not the least because it was infested with trixies.

They scurried under the benches and into the walls, disappearing into the dark crevices so that only the gleam of their liquid eyes was visible, while he picked up the hammer and bent over the anvil once more. It was bad enough he'd been left to hammer out the slag in this minuscule piece of metal, heating the iron over and over and over, tap-tap-tapping away for what seemed like hours without respite so that his legs began to ache, his shoulders began to cramp and his eyes began to sting. The air was muggy in the forge, the day overcast. Sweat poured down his sides and trickled down his ears, winding down his back in long itchy rivulets. And the trixies. The trixies were merciless in their torment.

They not only played with the fire, they pinched his ankles and tickled his toes, blew in his ear and pulled his hair. At last he could bear it no longer. "Enough!" he cried. He waved his arms as if to fend off a swarm of bothersome flies and whipped off his apron, flinging it around the room. Curse Deirdre to the Summerlands—she was the reason he was chained to this horrible labor and Connla wasn't here. The rumors were rampant through the castle she'd gotten herself with some unnatural child by another druid, a child that by all reports she'd carried far too long.

*We have to keep you busy, your aunt said.* Meeve's voice damning him echoed over and over as the trixies bolted for cover. One managed to set his apron on fire with a piece of flaming coal, just as the oldest of the apprentices, Liam, rounded the corner, trundling a wheelbarrow of fresh charcoal.

"Herne's balls, Bran, what're you doing?" Liam dropped the wheelbarrow and grabbed a bucket of water as Bran danced around, swatting at the flames with his hands. Liam threw the water full on Bran, thoroughly soaking his lower half.

Bran spun around, face flaming redder than the coals, which were now glowing perfectly. Blue fire leapt out of the brazier, as the trixies—invisible to Liam—blew on it. "I was just—I'm just— It's the trixies, I'm telling you. They're everywhere."

"Will you watch that fire?" Liam continued. Bran ducked out of the way just as Liam threw the bucket of water at an errant flame that had apparently jumped out of the brazier by itself. "You've got to get that head of yours out of your backside. I told them not to leave you alone. Next you'll be telling me it's the trixies keeping you from getting work done, right?" He paused and shook his head as Bran nodded eagerly.

"That's exactly what I'm telling you. They're everywhere."

The older boy glanced over his shoulder, put the bucket down and advanced a few steps into the forge. "Look, Bran," he began, "I wouldn't talk about the druid thing too loudly. No one here thinks very much of them, you know, from the Queen on down. You might not like the work, but for the time being, we're stuck with you. No one much likes having you around. You're a danger to everyone—look at where you laid your hammer, you moon-mazed calf." He gestured at the fire, and Bran turned in horror to see a pair of trixies had dragged his hammer so that the handle lay across the coals. It was beginning to smoke and the handle had already turned black. The trixies were dancing over it, jumping from side to side in such a way they created a draft that fanned the flames.

"Get away from that," Bran yelped. He pulled the hammer out of the fire and plunged the handle into the nearby vat of water. The flames were leaping higher now, borne aloft by the trixies who were tossing sparks back and forth like tiny balls of flame. "You have to believe me. They're all over the place—this forge is infested—"

"The only thing this forge's infested with are lazy 'prentices," rumbled Mordram the Master Smith from behind. "Look at the mess this place's in while you two stand and shake your jaws." He cuffed the back of Bran's head with the edge of hand as thick as a slab of ham. "Get to work, the pair of you—now!"

Bran's jaw dropped as he looked beyond Mordram's bulk, and saw, to his horror, that the trixies had systematically stripped one wall of all its implements. Hammers and tongs of varying sizes now lay scattered around the forge in haphazard piles. It would take hours to replace the implements. Hours and hours and he was already tired and soaking wet. "I can't work like this," he shouted. "And I won't!"

He threw the apron down and bolted out of the forge, past Liam who tried to restrain him, past the wagons and the piles of scrap metal, broken weapons and untouched ore. He charged out of the smithy yard, into the outer courtyard of his mother's keep and paused for just a moment, breathing hard and thinking fast. Who was going to help him get rid of the trixies, now that all the druids were gone? *Mother's just going to have to find me one,* he thought as he stormed off, ignoring all the shouts behind him. He dashed into the enormous central courtyard and paused, momentarily disoriented by the choreographed confusion all around him. He was jostled and pushed, brushed and almost backed into. As he jumped out of the way of a heavy cart that had been jerked over the paving stones by a recalcitrant mule, a hard grip fell on his shoulder and he was spun around, nearly off his feet.

Strong hands righted him and relief washed over him in a floodtide as he stared up into Lochlan's puzzled eyes. "Is that you they want, boy?" Bran tried to wiggle out of Lochlan's grasp, but the big knight held him hard. "Be still, now. What's wrong?" The expression on Lochlan's face offered no hope, but his eyes were kind.

"Tell them, please tell them— You've got to tell them—"

"Slow down, boy, tell them what?"

"That I'm not mazed, and I'm not being disobedient deliberately, and I do see trixies!" Bran finished just as the Master Smith, accompanied by Liam and another apprentice stormed across the courtyard. He struggled beneath the knight's hand as the master approached. "Please!"

"There you are, you wretched laggard. And thanks to you for catching him, Sir Lochlan. This one's slipperier than an eel and quicker than a trout." He grabbed Bran's ear and yanked. "Now you come with me—"

But Lochlan put a hand on the smith's wrist. "Master Smith."

The smith dropped Bran's ear as if it burned and turned to Lochlan with an expression bordering on disbelief. "My lord knight? You interfere?"

"I think you should listen to what he says." Lochlan let go of Bran. "Tell him."

"He won't believe me and he'll beat me."

"You've no call to beat a lad for telling the truth."

"And you've no call to interfere, my lord." The smith folded his arms over his massive chest and lowered his head like a bull about to charge. "No one tells me how to handle my 'prentices, and no one's ever complained the way this one—"

But Lochlan shook his head. "Hold right there, Master Smith. This lad's been put into your charge, that's true. But he's not been 'prenticed to you, not as far as I think his mother believes. I was there when she brought him to see you. There was no talk of apprenticeship. She asked you to keep him busy. Not kill him." Lochlan leaned closer and from that moment on, Bran knew he'd follow Lochlan blindly into battle, or anywhere else, in fact, he might care to lead. "Easy now, Master Mordram. Meeve's got all those guests—she has her hands full—"

"And we don't? Or need the extra work this one's caused?" Mordram raised his chin and took a belligerent step in Lochlan's direction with all the swagger of a man who knew exactly how valuable he was. "You want him kept busy? Then have the lad shovel out the stables, or peel potatoes, or chop wood. You want him to learn to be a smith—you send him back to me." With a disgusted look at Bran, he tapped Liam on the shoulder. "Come on, lad. Let's get that smithy set to rights."

"Wait—" Lochlan began. He looked down at Bran and shook his head. "You know every druid must earn a 'prentice's letter in blacksmithing. Aye." He nodded when Bran's jaw dropped. "No one ever told you, hmm?" He scratched his head. "All right, boy. You might as well come with—"

A line of trixies had appeared underneath the nearest wagon. They blew kisses, made faces, stuck out their tongues, winked and wiggled their fingers. Bran stared down at them, horrified. It didn't matter where he went, he realized. They were all around him, everywhere. And it didn't matter who he told. No one else could see them, and no one else believed him. With a shriek of exasperation, Bran bolted. He ran across the courtyard and through the opposite gate, and he kept running, despite Lochlan's shouts. Soon, he realized he was lost.

He halted, breathing hard. He was in some sort of enclosure. All the walls were high sandstone, all the doors carved and wooden and closed. Barrels of what appeared to be provisions were stacked neatly against two walls. A low open arch was set in a third wall. He had no idea how to find his way back to the main courtyard, let alone his mother's rooms.

A sudden chill raised a ripple of gooseflesh across his arms and he dismissed it. There was no reason to be afraid of anything here, he thought, in the very center of his mother's keep. He peered through the archway and saw that it led to an enclosed orchard of rows of fruit trees.

A scent filled the orchard, sweet and earthy and wet, and the light filtering through the trees had a greenish cast that reminded him of the road from Pentland. It was very quiet and very warm and the air was very still. He glanced over his shoulder. From the adjoining courtyard, he heard shouts and curses, the rumble of wagon wheels and the clatter of something being unloaded. He must be somewhere near the kitchens, he realized as a strong scent of baking bread wafted past his nose. He had no idea how to find Meeve. But the orchard beckoned, the rows of quiet trees tempted. He was so tired. Roused at the crack of dawn, forced to work harder than he'd ever worked in his life hauling ore and coal, then expected to shovel and lift and hammer until he was nearly dizzy, who could blame him if he needed a nap? He glanced over his shoulder. He heard footsteps and the rumble of barrels trundled over stones coming closer. He dodged into the orchard.

The afternoon air had weight. It made his eyes heavy, his limbs like lead. He stumbled down the path, yawning. He noticed a rounded hollow at the base of a stumpy apple tree, its gnarled limbs already clustered with hard green fruit. His eyes filled with tears as he remembered Apple Aeffie's ample lap as she leaned against her favorite tree and sang and shelled peas or picked through berries or beans.

A few minutes curled up beneath the tree couldn't hurt, he thought, as he yawned hugely once again. He slumped down beside the trunk. The base was covered in thick moss that smelled slightly sweet, just like Apple Aeffie. He drew a deep breath, curled on his side, his cheek pillowed on his hand. He glanced up into the tree and thought he saw a trixie watching him. He jerked upright, saw it was just a big black bird, a raven or a crow, watching him. The lassitude overtook him again, and his head felt heavy on his neck. He lay back down. "Tricksie trixies, run away quick, here I come with my big fat stick…tricksie trixies run away home, here I come with my big long bone." *I'll just rest here a minute or two,* he thought, even as he wondered fleetingly what kind of bone. He closed his eyes and almost immediately, fell fast asleep.

"Look at him—he's sleeping," Loriana breathed. She twined her long fingers around the trunk of the apple tree and leaned down, her nostrils flared. She could feel her grandmother watching from higher in the tree. Below her, Bran's eyes slid closed. She crept down another limb, listening intently as his ragged breathing steadied and deepened. She could feel his mind, open and dreaming, the energy within him banked but palpable. He was very quickly sound asleep, one hand curled beneath his face, the other tucked between his thighs. His young limbs were tan and very smooth. He was so beautiful her breath caught in her throat. Before she could stop herself, she reached out and stroked his face with the tips of her fingers. It was then she noticed that his cheeks were tufted with fine brown down. All her senses were inflamed, every part of her alive. She reached out with a trembling hand and touched the rough silk of his nut-brown hair falling across his thick brown brows.

"Be careful, Loriana, don't wake him yet," rasped Finnavar.

But Loriana was entranced. She leaned down again, daring to trace the curve of his jaw, and a hissing and spitting erupted from underneath the apple tree. She gasped and startled back onto a higher bough as half a dozen leathery little faces peered out of knolls and between the roots of the tree. "Get away from him," cried one, its gravely little voice as harsh against her ears as metal over stone.

More crept up and out of the ground, ears twitching, flat noses sniffing, their eyes huge and round. "Look, there they are," one cried.

"A sidhe—a sidhe—look, two of them," shouted another, so loudly Loriana wondered why the boy did not wake.

There were dozens of them now, all converging around the sleeping boy. "Get away from him," a third hissed, baring his stumpy teeth.

"Grandmother," cried Loriana. "What are these things?"

"Nasty creatures," replied Finnavar. She plummeted down from her branch, wings extended widely, and the trixies scampered out of reach. "They're gremlins, that's what they are. The mortals call them trixies. They call themselves khouri-keen. And all of them have the same name. Get away from him— get back from him—we want him. We found him first."

"You can't have him," wheezed a fourth.

"Unless you want us, too." A fifth smiled up at Loriana, then dared to rub its filthy little head on her thigh. "She smells so good," he whispered to the others and Loriana shuddered and withdrew up the tree.

"The grand callie told us the shining ones would come," murmured still another.

"He's ours and we don't have to share," said one, who stood on tiptoes, the tips of his ears quivering, his huge eyes wide and round as dark wet moons.

"What do you mean, he's yours?" shrieked Finnavar, circling low. "We found him first—he's ours."

"He's ours—the callie gave him to us."

"We mind him."

"We watch him."

"We help him."

From every side the voices rose, but Finnavar didn't

flinch. She landed on the lowest branch and cocked her head. "What callie? What druid?"

"The big druid," they replied in unison. They smelled wet but their skins were leathery, like a snake's, and their eyes were beady and huge.

"There's no druids here now," Loriana shouted down from her perch, but to her surprise, Finnavar only rose and circled. The creatures jumped onto to Bran's chest and began to wave and spit and hiss.

"Come, Loriana," screeched Finnavar. "There has to be another way."

Beside the tree, Bran lay oblivious, a hint of a smile curving his soft pink lips. Loriana ached to kiss them. But there was no help for it. Her grandmother was gone. She stepped back over the border, leaving the gremlins dancing on the sleeping boy's chest.

"Now what?" she asked the moment she was across. Finnavar was perched on a log, daintily stripping the flesh from a fish. She shook her head and pretended not to be disgusted when her grandmother offered her a stringy red slice.

"There's only one thing to do," said Finnavar as she spat the last of the bones into the river. "I'll go find the druid—"

"How will you do that? How will you know which one?"

"There's only one druid who'd have the audacity to do that—only one I can think of, that is."

"Who?"

"She's quite well known in Faerie, for she's been Arch-Druid in Shadow for years and years now—forever as the mortals would count time, I think. This working has her scent all over it. Mortal magic leaves a trail, a residue. You know that scent you find so irresistible about the boy? Every working he ever does will have something of that odor about it, Loriana. Remember that. Now. I'm going off to find this big callie, find out why she did it, and see if there's a way to convince her to undo it."

"What about the boy? What if he wakes up—"

"Stay and watch him, then. But keep your distance. Those gremlins would love to get their dirty little hands all over you." Then she was gone, without further explanation, in a blur of black feathers and a rush of cool air, leaving Loriana open-mouthed and dismayed.

*Eavan Morna*

Night was falling, but the rain had mercifully stopped and when the sergeant suggested they stop by the ford of a stream for the night, Connla was more than willing to agree. They made camp beneath a stand of oaks. A few of the druids grumbled sacrilege, but Connla wearily dismissed them. She was tired, she thought, as she crouched over the measly fire, attempting to warm her stiff joints. Since the night on the Tor when she'd bound the trixies to Bran, she'd not been able to get warm. It was as if part of the cold wet earth she'd lain on had permeated her very skin. She pressed her cold fingers to her clammy face and blew on them, rocking back and forth in her shawl. A tap on her shoulder roused her.

"Cailleach." Duirnoch, the bony athair who'd helped her bind the trixies to Bran stood there, his hands knotted together between his sleeves, double thicknesses of cloaks draped around his shoulders. She wasn't the only one who felt invaded by the damp. "We think you should see this."

"Eh?" she asked, not understanding at first.

He beckoned and gestured, and finally she understood he wanted her to come. She rose heavily to her feet, settling her shawls into place. "What's this about, athair?"

"Just come."

He led her through the wood to a track. It led up the hill and down to the river. "Well?" In the dark, it was hard to see.

"This way."

The smell of rotting meat wafted on the breeze, and Connla wrinkled her nose. "What's that?"

"You'll see." He took her arm. "Watch your step."

At the top of the hill the path opened up to a small clearing and a little hut. Firelight flickered inside. "There's someone there?" she asked.

"No, that's Athair Tam. We found this place when we were down by the water's edge. We noticed the path, decided to see where it led. This must've been a woodsman's cottage—a woodsman and his wife."

The smell of death was thick in the air, suffocating the closer she got. She peered inside, and the other druid turned and held his lantern higher. "Callie Connla, we thought you should see this."

A slaughterhouse was cleaner, she reflected as she gazed around the blood-splattered walls, the floor flecked and stained with clots and gobs of flesh. "It's goblins," she said. She turned away and tottered to a stump, then sat down heavily, taking great gulps of the fresher, cleaner air. She covered her face with her hands then looked up at the men. "Get the sergeant. Rouse the others. What was I thinking when I agreed to stop here for the night?"

"This place?" Tam glanced. "You know this place?"

"This is near the place last year where the silver went into the water, remember? At the solstice? They couldn't get all of it out, because the water is so cold and so deep. I guess what I was afraid would happen did happen. But why wasn't there a ward put on this place?"

The athairs glanced at each other and Tam said, "I'll go fetch the sergeant."

The leaves in the forest whispered and rustled and Connla felt the hair rise on the back of her neck.

"You think they could come back?" Duirnoch whispered.

Connla snorted softly. "Of course they could. These people have been dead and gone awhile and there's more remains scattered through the yard and down the path than two bodies would justify, even two bodies torn to shreds. The silver burned a hole in the border and water is the surest conduit from here to TirNa'lugh. The goblins are using this as a track—they come out of the river, hunting, and bring their prey back this way."

"What's all this about, Callie?" The sergeant sounded as sour as he looked at having been dragged from his warm spot by the fire. He was surrounded by five or six grumbling soldiers.

"Show them what you showed me," she said.

But instead of coming directly back and agreeing, the men tramped in and out, around and over the clearing a dozen times, pointing and gesturing, shrugging and arguing. Finally Duirnoch came to squat beside her stump. "What's going on?" she asked, frowning. The sky overhead was clear and the moon was very bright. Fair weather, at last. She was sick of rain. If she'd seen her last rainy day, she'd be glad.

"They don't agree with us it's goblins."

"What?"

He shrugged and shook his head. "They seem to think there's a human hand behind it…that it was made to look like—"

"Do they understand those things could come back at any time between now and dawn? Do they understand we have to take what small precautions we can?" She looked around. "We have only moonlight and starlight. Go call the others. Let these soldiers dither all they will. Something has to be done—" She stood up.

"And it will be done, Cailleach. Just sit down and rest yourself. My men and I will see—" said a voice behind her.

Connla spun around to confront the sergeant. "You and your men are blind—you don't know what you're looking at—"

"With all due respect, Cailleach, I could say the same of you. You believe this was done by goblins and so that's what you see."

"But there're signs—"

"Have you ever seen a battle, or cleaned one up?"

Stung, she shook her head.

"Then sit down and let my soldiers work."

He turned on his heel and stalked away and Duirnoch let out a long low breath. "And just who does he think he's talking to, and how does he think he can speak—"

"He thinks he's talking to a greedy old woman and her greedy young servant, Duirnoch," Connla replied flatly, staring after the sergeant as he bawled out order after order. "That's the brush Meeve's tarred us with, don't you see?"

"It isn't right that he dismiss us so—"

"It's what my sister did." Connla pressed her mouth shut. Patience, she told herself. Patience and this would all be sorted out when they reached Ardagh. Assuming, of course, they lived to reach it. *Great Mother, don't let me think that way,* she told herself. "Summon the others, Duirnoch. Let's do what we can. It may not be much, but…well, who knows? Maybe the sergeant and his men are right."

In the end, they were able to weave a weak caul of watery light. It wasn't much, but it was more than Connla had expected, and she was able to close her eyes when exhaustion finally overtook her. *It only needs last till dawn,* she told herself sleepily as she snuggled between Bronwythe and Nialla.

A spray of warm droplets woke her. She opened her eyes and heard screaming and an odd gurgling sound near her ear. She turned her head and watched Nialla's eyes go blank. And then Connla realized that the liquid she'd felt was blood—Nialla's blood. She heard shouting, running footsteps, and she twisted her neck to look.

A wide metal blade thudded into her neck, severing skin, gristle and bone in one horrific swoop. In the moment that her head tumbled off her shoulders, Connla realized that there were indeed those who killed just as savagely as any goblin.

*On the road to Ardagh*

In his dream, Bran was lying with his head in Apple Aeffie's lap, staring up at a blue sky through the leafy branches of a flowering apple tree. She stroked his hair with her work-roughened hand and hummed a little tune.

"Apple Aeffie, it isn't anything like I thought it would be." They seemed to be in the middle of an extended conversation.

"It never is, boy. The Hag keeps things stirred up enough that it's never the same thing twice. And just when you think you have the lesson learned— Ha, it's then she throws a new one at you." She patted his cheek. "Have an apple."

"That can't be the answer to everything," he said. He sat up and looked around. They were sitting beneath an apple tree, but they weren't in any orchard. Instead, they were in a warm sunny place surrounded by what appeared to be hundreds or thousands of trees stretching out in all directions. "Apple Aeffie, what is this place?"

"This is the place between all the other places, you might say. It's easy to get here if you know how, but impossible to find if you don't know where to look."

"That's why there's nothing here but trees?"

She chuckled. "Nothing but trees, boy? I suppose that's how it looks. This is where the magic happens. Right here—in the in-between. This is where the power in is, Bran. Remember that."

"In the trees?"

She nodded as she sighed. "You used to know that. A long time ago. That's why I've come, you see. To help you remember all that you've forgot."

"Forgot what?" he whispered.

"There isn't much time, child. Things are happening faster than even the Hag can control. Now, just shut your eyes. Shut your eyes, and let yourself remember."

He closed his eyes and saw a dark void stretching out before him, but he felt Apple Aeffie holding his hand. As if from very far away, he heard the skirl of an ancient pipe and smelled burning heather on the wind. He opened his eyes and stared down the long rows of trees, into the far and distant past. He saw himself in a life similar to this one, but older and bigger, stronger and wiser—druid, warrior, then king, called upon to do the thing that no one else could do. It had cost him his life. But it hadn't mattered, because his daughters and his sons and their mothers, his sisters and their children had all lived and Brynhyvar had been left stronger, better, than it had been before. "I do remember," he whispered. "I *do*. Will I remember this when I wake up?"

She shook her head. "It doesn't work that way, Bran. But what you can remember, what you should remember, what you *will* remember, is that in the end, you always come back here. Here to the trees, who remember everything." The old woman smiled and cupped his chin with a hand so smooth and pink, it felt as if she'd never done an hour's work. "Remember Bran. Before there were trixies, there were trees."

Another voice was coming from very far away. "Wake up, boy. Come on, wake up." The voice came again, this time accompanied by a rough kick that jolted him out of the most pleasant dream. The details instantly vanished, leaving him with an impression of luminous light on his skin beneath a sky of brilliant blue.

Bran opened his eyes with a groan, and met the brown eyes of a girl wearing a dirty apron over her tunic. Her stringy brown hair hung lank over her shoulders, and she had a basket under her arm. The basket was filled with onions.

"Wake up," she said, and she kicked him again. "You'll make it bad for the rest of us. Wake up."

"Enough, enough—I'm awake." He sat up and scrabbled away as Apple Aeffie's presence faded with the dream. He felt sore all over, as if he'd been trampled on. Maybe sleeping on the ground did that. With a start, he realized he was naked, his clothes tossed in all directions. *Blasted trixies, can't I escape them even when I sleep?* he thought as he made a grab for his breeches. He backed away, trying to cover himself.

The girl was looking at him curiously. She was about his age, he saw, her face freckled and tanned, her long hair streaked all shades from light brown to lightest blond. He was still swept up in the dream, the experience, or whatever it was, for he was overly aware, all of a sudden, of the way her breasts filled out her homespun bodice, of the lush swell of her hips as she bent over him with a disgusted expression. Her sleeves were rolled up past her elbows, and her forearms were muscled and tanned. "Are you all right? You look sick. Are you sick? Why'd you take off all your clothes?" She turned her head suddenly and coughed.

"Are you?" he whispered. The world felt like it was settling around him like a heavy cloak.

"Of course not. What's wrong with you?" She was backing away from him and he blinked, hard, and shook his head to clear away that sense of being carried away.

He got to his feet, reached for his shirt, wondered where his boots were. "I—I just got lost in here. I'm new, I don't really know my way—"

"And so you thought you'd take a nap?" She was looking

at him as if she clearly didn't believe him. "I think you're just looking for a way to avoid Cook."

"I'm not a scullion," he replied, horrified that she should think him one of the servants. "I'm Bran."

But the name didn't seem to mean anything to her at all, for she only shrugged and looked over her shoulder before she said, "I'm Lys, and I've never seen you before."

"I told you I only arrived the other day. I'm Bran," he said again. "Can you just tell me how to get to the queen's bower?"

"And what do you want with the queen?" she asked, her hand on her hip, her expression changing from curiosity to disbelief.

"Lys?" An older woman's voice floated through the orchard. "Lys? Are you in the orchard? Cook needs those onions now!"

"She's my mother," Bran replied. He looked around. The light was brighter than he'd remembered it, the daylight full and intense. He glanced up and the sky was cloudless and blue, the sun warm and yellow.

Lys laughed. "Of course she is. And I'm her sister. Everyone says her son's a fisherman from Far Nearing. You don't look like a fisherman to me, either."

"What time of day is it?" he asked. It was pointless to argue with her when he was so hungry.

"Almost noon," she answered.

"Almost?" he repeated. Hadn't it been late in the afternoon when he'd fallen asleep? If he'd slept a whole day through no wonder he was hungry. He rubbed his eyes again.

"Lys!" The summons came again, more impatient this time. "Come on, boy. It's coming down to time for dinner—

cooks needs all the help they can get and the still-mistress would beat you raw if she found you in her orchard."

"I'm not a scullion," he protested as he scrambled to his feet and took off after Lys. But in the kitchen yard, before he could ask her which way to find his mother, he saw Mordram the Master Smith, gesturing and arguing, and he tried to dodge behind a wheelbarrow piled high with sacks of grain, but Lys shoved him so that he tripped and fell. His foot caught in a spoke and the pile collapsed. The blacksmith, along with everyone else, turned to stare in his direction.

"Well, there you are at last, you laggard. Disappear on me, will you? Make a fool of me before the Court, will you? Do you know we've been looking for you for a night and a day?" The blacksmith strode over, grabbed Bran by the ear and dragged him out of the kitchen, swearing loudly, Bran twisting and kicking in his pincerous grip.

"I see you're right, boy," laughed Lys, as she stepped aside to let him pass. "You're not a scullion at all, are you?"

"I'm not a blacksmith, either," he shouted after her.

"You got that right, maidy," Mordram shouted over his shoulder as he dragged Bran under the archway.

"Let me go," cried Bran, kicking and struggling. "I'm not going—I'm not going until—"

"Master Mordram." A tall shadow blocked the path. "Bran, where've you been? Do you know the fit you've caused your mother? Master Mordram, I see you found him. His mother will be pleased with that."

Bran tumbled to the cobblestones as Mordram let him go, sprawling at the knight's feet in an undignified heap. "Lochlan, did you talk to my mother? Did you tell her?" Out of the corner of his eye he saw a trixie clearly dart across the path. It turned, bent, and blew a puff of stink in his direction, then ran off toward the forge.

Lochlan picked him up by the scruff of the neck as if he were a puppy, gave him a shake and stood him on his feet. "Aye, Bran, I spoke to your mother—and she spoke to Master Mordram here and—" He broke off. Lochlan looked tired. There was a dark haze of beard on his chin, dark circles beneath his eyes. He reeked of mead and sweat and something else. He held up a hand to Mordram. "Just wait." He pulled Bran to one side, put an arm around his shoulder and said, "Running away is no way to solve anything but it's a very good way to get yourself whipped. I can intervene now—once—you're not his apprentice, after all. But—"

"Lochlan, I didn't run away," Bran said, bewildered. "I was asleep under the tree—I guess no one saw me but—"

"You've been asleep?" Lochlan raised one eyebrow. "You mean to tell me that you've been asleep the whole time we've been looking for you? Bran, they about tore the place apart—" He broke off and ran a hand through his tousled hair.

Bran nodded, scratched his head. "I wasn't trying to run away. I just wanted to get away from those miserable trixies. They're making my life a torment. Please, Lochlan. You have to believe me." A crowd was gathering, and he wondered, briefly, what a knight of the Fiachna was doing in the kitchens.

Lochlan narrowed his eyes. "Do you realize how long you've been asleep? You went missing yesterday afternoon."

"Yesterday?" Bran's jaw dropped as Mordram reached for his upper arm.

"Come on, boy. I won't beat you. Your mother made it clear." He looked at Lochlan. "It's nice she lets you up for air long enough to check on her whelp."

Beyond the blacksmith and the knight, Bran saw Lys watching. He felt his cheeks burn at the blacksmith's insult, and he felt his cheeks flame. But Lochlan only smiled and shrugged. "Go on with him, boy. Do your best to do his bidding. There's a revel tonight. You'll like that."

"You come with me or the only part of the revel you'll attend is the part where they clean it all up." But at least the smith was gentle as he pulled Bran through the snickering crowd.

*Eaven Morna*

Finnavar, in the form of a raven, swooped low over the burning embers. She tried to alight in several places, but the heat drove her back. She circled low as she dared, searching the blackened remains. Melted puddles of blackened silver pooled on more than half the bodies and even she recognized the pattern on the tattered remnants of charred cloth. It was unmistakably the plaid of Mochmorna. Someone had slaughtered the druids of Mochmorna. With a shriek that would've been a curse, she rose with a flap that fanned the flames, heading back to Loriana and Faerie with the news that the druid who'd woven the spell so effectively to Bran was dead and in the Summerlands, well out of the reach of Finnavar or any other sidhe.

# 6

The sun was a thin red crescent barely above the horizon's rim when Argael nudged Cwynn awake. "I'll be in the kitchen," she said.

For a moment, he lay staring up at the shingles overhead, trying to remember where he was. The light was blue, the air heavy with damp and the smell of mildew. The ocean was louder, too. Then he got up and pulled on the dry clothes Argael had left him.

In the kitchen, she handed him a mug of warm cider and a hunk of cheese. "I packed some food for you—salt fish and bacon and a few of last year's apples. It's not much but should see you to the nearest crossroads."

He swallowed the cider and set the mug down. "You know I'm worried about Shane and the twins."

"I was thinking last night." She uncovered a bowl of dough and frowned into it. "That's odd. Hmm." She frowned, poked it with an experimental finger and shook her head.

"Bread didn't rise." She put the bowl aside and wiped her fingers. "I was thinking I could send them across the bay, to my sister. She married a herder over there. Ariene and the boys would do well on fresh goats' milk, I think." She handed him his grandfather's plaid, all dry. "Ariene's upset you're leaving. There's been talk, you know, of banning the Beltane practices, to avoid this sort of thing. Without a druid to sort it out, bad feelings linger. Sometimes I think Ariene's too much like her own father. What she doesn't understand, she fears. But you go on and don't you worry. I'll make sure those boys are safe. And another thing," she said, as he wrapped the plaid around himself.

"What?" he asked.

"You should speak to the druids about your hand. They've magic, you know. They can make you something much better than this hook." He met her eyes, gray as the light now strengthening through the clouds. "Ariene's always had feelings for you, Cwynn."

"It's just she liked Sorley better," he said. He pulled his arm away. "I didn't mean to scare the boys."

She patted his cheek. "You're a good lad, Cwynn. Now don't lose that disk, whatever you do."

Cwynn led Eoch out of the stable and down the path that led out of the village. He gathered up Eoch's reins and nodded a last farewell, then made his way down the rocky path where the shells lay heaped in piles with seaweed and driftwood churned up from last night's storm. *Red sky at morning; wise sailors, take warning.* The sea still looked choppy, sullen storm clouds still piled along the gray horizon. He remembered last night's narrow escape and thanked the Great Mother, with the customary wish he might live to return the favor.

Be careful what you wish for. The silent voice that ran through his mind had something of Cermmus's bite but it wasn't quite Cermmus. He turned to take a last look at the keep over his shoulder as he slipped past the gatehouse. From inside, he could hear the guard snoring. At this hour, even the gulls were quiet. A thin thread of white smoke drifted from the direction of the kitchens. The smell of fish was strong in the heavy salt air.

At the stone bridge over the estuary, he hesitated. The hair on the back of his neck rose and he sniffed, but all he could smell was fish. There were stories told around the fires at night that long ago a goblin had taken up residence beneath the bridge. It had hunted with impunity until a druid was summoned and the goblin was chased back to the bowels of TirNa'lugh where it belonged. The stories had terrified Cwynn the child, and even now, he never approached the bridge without caution. He'd left his skiff tied up to the dock, and now he realized that the configuration of boats was not the same as it had been the night before.

The horse pawed the ground, impatient to be off. She tossed her head and nuzzled his face. He slipped an old carrot out of his pocket and fed it to her. To his right, the tide was low, and the sandbars beckoned seductively in the middle of the bay. Theoretically, it was possible, if treacherous, to cross to the mainland. But the sandbars could be illusive, the channel deeper in places than it frequently appeared. Distances were deceptive, too. Movement caught his eye, and far out on the sandbars, he thought he saw a big white dog with a plume for a tail bounding toward the beach.

Startled, he peered more closely, and the dog seemed to disappear. "Trick of the light," he muttered and slipped the mare an apple. Eoch's big liquid eyes met his with a calm he could not share. "Just wait here."

He peered down the wide beach. A few of the boats were missing. He wondered if that many had been lost in the storm, then noticed the fresh footsteps across the sand. A chill went down his back and he tried to dismiss it.

*Shane knows who you are, now, lad. You're worth more dead than alive.* Cwynn had no doubt Shane had overheard their conversation. But there was nothing to say Shane was the one who'd taken the boats, either. Cwynn chided himself as he swung up into the saddle. So his uncle had killed his father in a fit of rage. Such things happened; the druid court had seemed to think it of scarcely any consequence. He patted the dagger he wore at his waist for the reassurance only it gave. He gathered the reins and touched his knees to the mare's sides.

But by the time they'd crossed the bridge, every instinct was screaming not to take the road that disappeared beneath the scrubby pines, the only road leading to the mainland. Between here and the mainland, he thought, as he slowed the horse, there were plenty of places where it was easy to beach a boat and lie in wait. He wished he'd had the presence of mind to count the number of boats missing, or the number of sets of footprints. It was entirely possible, however, there were other dangers up ahead that had nothing to do with Shane.

He glanced to his right and saw that the white dog was not at all an illusion, for it was running back and forth, splashing in and out of the shallows, kicking up wet sand. It stopped when it caught sight of him, barked and wagged its tail. Eoch pricked up her ears and Cwynn patted her neck. "You think we should head that way, hmm?"

He glanced at his saddle roll. There wasn't much to weigh the mare down. Whether to risk it at all, that was the question, for the sandbars were deceptive and even at low tide, there were waters deep enough to drown the unsuspecting. On the other hand, Eoch could swim so well the old women called her a sea-mare, a horse with the blood of the ancient lost land of Lyonesse running in her veins.

The dog had reached the beach. He ran in circles, barked again, wagged his tail and headed out toward the water. There was no doubt at all in Cwynn's mind the dog wanted him to follow. "What do you say, Eoch? Shall we go with him? Make a run for it?"

She tossed her head back and whinnied a response he could only assume was yes. "But can we outrun the tide, do you think?"

She pawed the ground and stared straight ahead, her nostrils slightly flared. With a shrug, he touched her sides, and she leaped forward, eager and ready. The dog barked joyously and took off. The first arrow sang past his ear as they broke past the estuary. Cwynn glanced over his shoulder as a second arrow whistled overhead and landed with a splash a few lengths away. It was Shane—Shane and maybe five or six of his gang. The water was deeper now, almost up to the mare's knees, and he urged her on as another arrow splashed into the water just beyond her rump. She gathered herself up and leaped onto the next sandbar, and he was about to turn in one direction when the dog suddenly leaped in front of him, forcing him to turn and head out toward what looked like deeper water. Another arrow whistled passed his ear and he bent low, urging her on, but Eoch needed no encouragement. She seemed to understand the danger as well as he did.

Nervously he glanced over his shoulder. The dog was just ahead now, barking and bounding, and Cwynn realized the dog was leading them across sandbars underwater, guiding them through the shallows, across places where in less than a footstep in either direction, the bottom dropped steeply.

One of their pursuers had already foundered in the deeper water. But Shane, curse him to the Summerlands, was gaining. Cwynn pressed his knees into the horse's side and she leaped ahead, the white dog bounding just a few lengths ahead. A dagger thudded into his calf, and he cried out, yanked the blade out, turned and hurled it back at Shane. It splashed harmlessly into the water.

The white dog had doubled back, somehow, and now stood planted in front of Shane's horse, barking ferociously, baring its teeth. Shane whipped his sword out and swung at the dog, and Cwynn plunged ahead, the cold water numbing the pain in his leg. Another arrow whistled into the shallows, and Eoch spooked, stumbling into shoulder-high water.

Her eyes opened wide, her hoof flailed and he was thrown off the saddle. Cwynn rolled into the water, floundered for a second, then kicked and pushed his way to the surface. Eoch thrashed in the water, her eyes rolled back in her head in absolute terror. Even though he knew he risked his own life, he took a deep breath, then dove beneath the surface. Her leg was stuck between two rocks, but her other hooves flailed in the water. He broke the surface, gasped for air, then dove down again in time to see a pair of pale white hands shift the rocks around the horse. As the horse kicked and righted herself, a creature with a pale white face and bloodless lips peered out of the sand-swirled water. She tugged the gold disk off his neck with one swift jerk, then disappeared. The burning in his chest forced Cwynn to surface. As he filled his lungs with a fresh draught of air, he thought he saw a silver tail break the waves with a flip before it disappeared. Frantically, he felt at his chest but the disk was gone. Eoch was free, swimming strongly once more, heading directly toward the opposite shore. The sandbars around them seemed to be shrinking at an alarmingly fast rate.

The rising tide and the white dog had driven his pursuers back. Even Shane had given up the chase and was now picking his way back. Not a turn of the glass from home, thought Cwynn, and already he was wet, cold and had lost his disk. One thing at least was certain. He couldn't go back.

There was nothing to prevent Shane from following him to Allovale. Cwynn sighed as he stared at the mainland rising dark and forbidding in front of him, a solid block of forest behind the fishing villages clustered up and down the coast. Had he really seen what he thought he'd seen? The fishwives told stories about the beautiful creatures who lived below the waves, who lured unlucky fishermen to their deaths below the water. They loved beautiful jewels and bright objects of all sorts. The salt water had clouded his eyes, and the dog seemed to have disappeared again, too. When he looked back over his shoulder, all he saw was the flat surface of the bay, shining opaque silver in the sullen morning and he forced himself to concentrate on reaching the opposite beach.

The white dog was running up and down the headland, wagging its tail when Cwynn splashed ashore, leading Eoch by the bridle. The water was up to his thighs, and the horse's mane and tail were stiff with salt water, but at least they'd managed to outrun their pursuers.

Cwynn estimated he had perhaps one turn of a long glass to lose himself somewhere on the mainland, but Eoch was already exhausted from the swim. Hopefully, Shane would be forced to wait until the entire channel was navigable by boat, and then come after him. The dog barked, one short woof. Cwynn looked up, but at just that moment, the sun broke through the clouds, and the dog appeared to vanish. Cwynn grabbed for the reins as a sharp series of barks rang out. Eoch nosed him as Cwynn squinted into the mist.

The white dog was now perched on the headland above the beach. The dog gave three sharp, short barks, trotted off, looked over its shoulder and trotted back, wagging its tail. It repeated the same sequence. Cwynn glanced over his shoulder. The tide was rushing in now, the sandbars all swallowed by the gray rushing water. Maybe he'd less time than he thought. The dog barked again with more urgency. *Follow me,* it seemed to be saying. *Follow me.*

"What do you say, Eoch?" Cwynn murmured as the dog bounded off into the treeline. The horse trotted in the dog's direction, catching Cwynn off guard so that he dropped the bridle. "Wait," he cried, stumbling on the sand. "Just wait." The horse paused long enough to let him grab the reins and swing back into the saddle. He glanced at the water once more, thinking of the pale creature beneath the waves. Eoch cantered after the dog, who seemed to have vanished once again into thin air. A mermaid and a fey dog, he thought. What next?

Around the bend, at the nearest village—or what was left of it—he had his answer.

The small collection of cottages clustered on either side of the dusty road leading down from the cliffs was still some distance away when Eoch whinnied and balked. Cwynn slid out of the saddle, peering up ahead. Although the sun was above the trees, there were no signs of activity. No smoke rose from squat chimneys, no chickens scratched, no children played. Then the breeze shifted and a wave of stench, almost as tangible as the waves crashing on the beach, engulfed him. A stench so nauseating it brought tears to his eyes and his breakfast up his gullet. He fell to his knees and vomited. When he was spent, he wiped his face with the back of his arm and rinsed the foul taste from his mouth with a swig from his water-skin.

Eoch tossed her head, whickering displeasure. She planted her hooves squarely on the ground, refusing to move.

"It's not my choice, either, Eoch, but there's no way around it." He pulled out his fishing knife, the one with the serrated blade, and grabbed the reins, wrapping them tightly around his fist. "Let's go."

But there wasn't much to see, only splashes of blood, a few feet, still shod. Eoch tossed her head from side to side. The stench was so thick it was palpable. Doors were pulled off their hinges, shutters torn from window frames. Fishing spears lay scattered, ends coated in thick purplish blood and clumps of offal. Cwynn swallowed hard, clutching his dagger. It was hard to imagine who could've attacked with such savagery. And why, he wondered, looking around. Fishing nets hung undisturbed, barrels full of yesterday's catch still lined up and full.

"Who could've done this?" he said aloud.

A goblin staggered out of the cottage, tall as a man, flesh mottled white and gray, the handle of a pitchfork wavering out of its back. Eoch reared up, front legs flailing, and a second goblin tottered out from behind the cottage.

Cwynn struggled to get the horse under control, but she bucked and reared. A hoof caught Cwynn in the chest and he was knocked backwards, landing flat on his back. The world turned black momentarily and when his vision cleared, the goblin with the pitchfork was bending over him. Cwynn rolled out of the way just in time to avoid a swipe of clumsy claws, but the goblin lunged after him, arms extended, yellowish slime spooling down its maw.

From out of nowhere, the white dog leaped at the goblin with enough force to push it well away from Cwynn. He tried to draw his dagger while the dog went straight for the goblin's throat. The dog's gleaming teeth sank into goblin flesh and, for the blink of an eye, Cwynn was sure he saw the goblin's claws pass directly through the dog. But that wasn't possible, he thought. A vicious swipe that took the skin off his arm made him forget the dog. The goblin raised his arms and launched itself at him; Cwynn raised his hook and buried it in the goblin's chest. The goblin turned its head, and nearly bit Cwynn's neck. He fell on top of the goblin and for a moment they rolled. And then the dog was there, snarling and snapping.

Cwynn extricated his hook in the same moment the dog crunched down on the goblin's throat, severing it to the bone. Cwynn backed away, chest heaving, sweat rolling down his face in great drops. A stinking gobbet of goblin flesh hung on his hook and he flung it away. The dog trotted over, wagging its tail, nudging him with its nose. It bounded a few lengths down the road, turned, and barked. Eoch whickered and pawed the ground and Cwynn got to his feet, dusting himself off. "All right," he breathed. "All right. You know how to get to Meeve, dog?"

The animal sat down on the road, threw back its head and howled.

As the hair rose on the back of Cwynn's arms, he swung up into the saddle. "All right, boy. You're that sure? Lead on."

"She tricked us," grumbled Otherself to Khouri. "She tricked us, we know she did, she did, she did."

"We know she tricked us," Khouri replied, hissing under his breath. Otherself had been complaining all the way down the Tor, across the field and under the postern gate to the kitchen gardens. But Otherself had better stop, because beneath the exquisitely sensitive soles of his feet, Khouri could feel the ground starting to resonate with the dull thump of human footsteps. They had not settled down till very, very late, and now, very, very early, they were all beginning to stir. "But we mustn't be caught, mustn't be seen."

"Tricked us," Otherself said again. Khouri elbowed him in the belly as a yawning druid came around the corner, heading in the direction of the laundries, then pulled Otherself beneath a stone bench. "Tricked us."

"Be quiet," Khouri said through clenched teeth as he peered around the bench leg. It was always that way with the druids. They had ways of explaining that made it easy to believe they were always right and a khouri-kan usually wrong. But this time, if they were caught, they would truly be in trouble. The cailleach had not been in a good mood yesterday, and he doubted enough time had passed for her mood to have changed much.

Khouri had misgivings the moment the Otherselves dragged him out of his den, bent on locating the source of that glorious fragrance that pervaded the depths of the Tor. It was completely impossible to deny the lure of that smell, wet as new-turned earth, green as spring grass, captivating as sunlight through crystal. It gave him shivers just to remember the feeling of it on his head, and he put his hand on top of his head, between his ears and rubbed the spot. He sniffed his hand as another druid swished by. As the tap of her sandals faded, he stuck his head out from beneath the stone bench, and pulled Otherself out from under it. "Come," he mouthed, pointing toward the door. "That way."

Glancing in both directions, and then over the bench, they darted into the long vestibule that led to the kitchen. He could hear the scullions stirring, could hear the splash of water from the pump on the other side of the wall. Along one wall, sacks of meal and strings of onions hung, along with baskets of mayberries and barrels of potatoes from the cellars. They scurried behind a barrel and made their way behind the supplies into the main room of the kitchen. A yawning scullion nearly stepped on his tail, and they darted under a table just in time. "Apples," Khouri whispered.

"Apples and oat-cakes," echoed Otherself.

No butter—the dairy's too far. He glanced at Otherself as the unbidden thought ran through his mind. Otherself hadn't spoken. Otherself wasn't thinking about butter. Otherself was probably thinking the corridor smelled like old ashes and cold oats, and about how Khouri and all the Otherselves were blamed whenever anything went wrong. But even as a wave of resentment rippled through him, doubling his resolve not to be caught, Khouri recognized the dim presence of Something Else—something that wasn't Other. The delicate hair on the tips of his ears stiffened, his skin shriveled as if with cold.

Otherself shivered visibly as he edged along the wall, sniffing delicately. He reached a barrel in the corner. His eyes lit up and he jumped for the rim, missed and tried again. "Found apples! Found apples! Apples in here!"

Just then, a door in the far wall opposite the hearth swung open without warning. Otherself tumbled to the floor and scrambled behind the apple barrel. Khouri motioned for him to be quiet. A woman with a linen coif wrapped around her hair accompanied by two yawning boys walked in, all carrying buckets. They put the buckets on the table, and at least a dozen more humans, all men, ranging in age from young to old, all carrying long walking sticks, entered the kitchen. One plopped down on the bench beside the apple barrel, another scraped his muddy boots on the stone nearest

Khouri. They'd missed their opportunity, he thought miserably. From now till midnight, or maybe even later, the kitchen wouldn't be deserted. Otherself peered around the barrel and Khouri gestured frantically for him to stay hidden. He wriggled as best as he could into the crack in the stone, listening intently to the conversation.

"Maybe that handsome athair who was here, Tiermuid, came back and took her away," one young boy piped up.

An uncomfortable silence fell at once, and someone else said, "Don't mention that name, boy. Even in jest. What happened wasn't funny."

"Maybe she got taken into TirNa'lugh," another said with an awkward laugh.

"Aye, that's it," someone else chimed. "She's not lost out on the moors—she got taken into TirNa'lugh."

She? Khouri froze. Across the space between them, he met Otherself's eyes, and they shared the same thought. The men with the funny smell they didn't recognize were talking about the pale white druid with the bloated belly who hid beneath the Tor. She had not only tricked them, she'd lied to them.

*What are we to do? We're not even supposed to be outside the Tor. Maybe we should run. We'll be in terrible trouble.*

*Only if you're caught.* Hard as a hammer, the alien awareness smashed through his mind, accompanied by a razor edge of stinging pain. It felt like something had…attached itself, almost, and Khouri swept his hand across the back of his head. His knees buckled from the pain and he watched Otherself do the same, simultaneously. Whatever he felt, Otherself felt it, too.

The kitchen door opened again, and the cailleach who'd

sent them all to their dens stepped over the threshold, looking gray as her robe in the bright morning light. But despite the droop in her shoulders, and the dark circles beneath her eyes, she strode up to the table, rapped her knuckles on the surface, and began to pepper the men with questions.

From behind the apple barrel, Otherself waved, and Khouri clamped both hands over his mouth, ears twitching frantically. Now that a druid was here, they had to be doubly careful to not be detected. Already, he could hear the cailleach sniffing. He dared to take a peek, and saw her holding up her hand. Everyone was sniffing now, turning this way and that, snorting and peering under tables and in corners.

Khouri motioned to Otherself, trying to make him understand he should slip into a crevice, a crack, anything in the wall. The cailleach was moving now, eyes closed, face raised.

"Look, I see it—there it is—" A young druid boy's high voice rang out and to Khouri's absolute horror, Otherself bolted out from behind the barrel, heading directly toward Khouri's hiding spot. With a sinking heart, Khouri knew Otherself would never make it. He covered his eyes and curled as small as he could make himself, even as the triumphant cry rang out. Before he could wriggle any farther, a heavy hand smashed down on his arm, and grimy fingers closed around his neck.

"Got him!" The boy turned, triumphant, the limp khouri trapped beneath his hand.

"Be careful with him," Catrione cried. The khouri-keen, tough and wiry in some ways, were easily bruised.

The boy had landed on the khouri-kan's arm. The khouri kicked and spit and hissed and tried to bite and claw. She grabbed the linen towel one of the cooks handed her and gingerly wrapped the creature in it, swaddling it securely. "There's never only one. Keep looking. I'm sure there's at least three or four more. Now," she said, turning her attention to the captive on her lap. "Who called you out of your den, little friend?"

The others clustered close around her, oohing and aahing at the creature most of them only ever glimpsed out of the corner of an eye. The khouri-kan shut his eyes and turned his face away from the bright shafts of sunlight now streaming into the kitchen from the windows on either side of the chimney. "It burns, it burns…" He spat and struggled.

Carefully Catrione sank down on a bench, blocking the bright light with her own body . "There, is that better? I told you not to come out until you were summoned. Did someone call for you? Why'd you leave? Where're Otherselves?" But nothing she said seemed to get through to him. He twisted and struggled and seemed to be in such pain, she frowned. "Relax," she murmured. "Relax. I'm not going to hurt you. I just want to know what brought you out."

"It burns, it burns!" He screeched like a cat in heat. His face contorted and his limbs stiffened, his back straight as the pokers that suddenly clattered to the floor beside the hearth.

"What's wrong?" Catrione frowned, wary of being tricked into letting the creature go. "Nothing's burning you—"

"Arrrrgh!" screeched the creature, and from under the bench, a second trixie rolled into view, writhing and twisting. Everyone jumped. "What's wrong with them,

Callie?" asked one of the scullions, dodging out of the khouri's way.

"Get another towel," said Catrione, wondering if every khouri under the Tor was similarly affected.

"They seem to be in some kind of terrible pain—you think that's why they're out?" asked one of the cooks, broad hands on broad hips, round face creased.

"If this is what drove them out, where're the rest of them?" Catrione replied. She rubbed the little creature's back and both khouri-keen only howled louder. "It could be one of their tricks."

"That's why they call 'em trixies, right?" put in another boy.

A shadow fell across Catrione's shoulders. "Cailleach, we've checked the chapter-house. The khouri-crystals are missing."

Catrione looked up into Niona's icy gaze but ignored her. She reached out with the Sight, seeking the invisible essence in the core of the creature, and slammed into a wall of pain so ferocious it sent her reeling back. That pain was no trick. As she gasped audibly, the creature's face worked, his tongue twisting out of his mouth, but the only noise that escaped his tortured throat was a ghastly rasp.

"Can you let me past it, Khouri?" she whispered. "Khouri, please, let me help. Let me past it." But this time, the pain like a wall of flame completely encompassed the creature's essence. Beads of sweat popped out on her forehead and the khouri-keen writhed and wailed in obvious agony. Driven back once more, into the safety of her own self, Catrione could only stare with the other onlookers as both creatures gasped once more, and then crumbled into fine powder.

Catrione gasped as the towel went limp and a shower of dust poured onto the floor. "Someone—someone crushed a crystal."

"Two," said Niona.

For a long, long moment there was silence while everyone—druid or not—stared helplessly at each other. Catrione raised her head. "We never checked the Tor, did we?" She stared up at Niona. "We all assumed she couldn't climb the hill." Catrione stood up. "Don't you see? That's where she's gone. Somehow she got in and out of the chapter-house without anyone seeing her."

"She could never fit in the trixie dens," said one of the cooks. "How could she—"

"She's at the top," Catrione replied. "In the chamber under the Tor." She gestured to the men. "Where else could she be? No wonder we haven't been able to find her—she's not needed food or drink or anything else. With the crystals, she has the khouri-keen to do her bidding." She looked from face to face. In the unforgiving light, the men looked tired and drawn, their clothing stained with sweat and grass, their boots caked with mud.

The door suddenly slammed and she looked up to see Athair Emnoch striding toward her, a young boy in tow. "Cailleach?" he called. "Ard-Cailleach?"

Now what? Catrione wondered as the searchers parted to let them through. The boy was wearing the plaid of one of the neighboring clans. There was blood across his forehead and his plaid was slashed to shreds along one side. "What is it?" What else could possibly go wrong? she wondered.

"This lad—you have to hear him out. He brings terrible bad news."

"What is it, boy?" asked Niona, and for once, Catrione didn't bother to step in.

"Cailleach, goblins," he stuttered, looking wide-eyed around the white-washed walls, the vaulted ceiling. "Goblins—goblins came last night—they came crawling right out of the burn."

"Oh, come now, lad, goblins?" cut in one of the searchers.

"What makes you think it was goblins?" asked another. "We were crawling all over the heath last night. We saw no goblins."

"Well, we saw their big bug eyes, their white, leathery hides and long tails," the boy said, chin raised. "We held them off with fire through the night, and toward dawn they left. I'm the quickest runner and my da sent me to tell you."

Goblins. Then Tully's heavy hand fell on the boy's shoulder and spun him around. The warrior squatted down in front of him. "Now, see here, boy, are you sure it wasn't men pretending to be goblins? How're you sure?"

"They left their scat on my shoe," the boy replied in his high treble and pointed down, sticking his boot up practically in the knight's nose.

A chuckle went around the kitchen. The knight scowled. "Easy enough to get that stuff in any charnel pit, lad. What's your name?"

"Tamkin, they call me. My da's Big Tom the Miller. And he don't make mistakes."

"All right, child." Catrione cut off Tully's next question. "Sir Tully, you and your knights believe you're such experts, why not take this boy home after he's breakfasted and bring us back your considered opinion? And as for the rest of us—" she paused as a sigh went around the room "—we'll go up to the Tor." She remembered Baeve's words. *The most unnatural thing I've seen in over forty years.* Over forty years. "Cailleach Niona, would you please make sure everyone has equipment?"

"Where're you off to?"

"I want to see if I can make any sense of those old tree scrolls."

Niona snorted. "In The Mem'brances of Trees? There's nothing in those old scratchings about trixies. Why—"

"I'm not going to see what it says about trixies. I want to see what it says about unnatural children."

"The only thing that even comes close is that nonsense about a child who can't be slain by hand of woman, hand of man."

"Yes," replied Catrione. "And I'm afraid that that's exactly what Deirdre's child is."

7

Long before the watchtowers of Eaven Morna were visible above the treeline, Morla smelled the fire pits full of roasting meat. Her mouth watered and her belly rumbled. With any luck, she might go to bed full three nights in a row. Custom and honor demanded a guest eat before anyone else, and so Morla had, for the first time in a long time, eaten her fill at every stop.

As she crested the top of the hill, she heard the muted shouts of the riders on the playing fields echoing off the shallow hills. She wiped a splatter of mud off her cheek as the memory of herself on those fields flashed through her mind, charging across the flats after the round pig's bladder, swinging her long curved stave over her head. She'd been good at those sorts of games, if nothing else. It was on those playing fields she'd first noticed Lochlan. Her heart contracted unexpectedly at the memory.

He'd been but newly knighted, a warrior not yet in his prime, but strong and eager in the way of the best of the young men who clustered around Meeve like bees after honey. She remembered the way his blond hair, darkened to brown by his sweat, whipped around his face, nearly blinding him, jeopardizing their victory. She'd ripped a streamer off the sleeve of the nearest lady and had handed it to him, not as a favor, but as a mop. Their first laugh had been shared at the look on the startled lady's face.

Morla flapped the reins and tried not to think about how Meeve had tapped his shoulder the following Beltane before Morla could. She'd hated her mother's court from the day she'd returned from her fostering on the Outermost Isles to that cold dawn more than ten years ago when she'd left as a bride bound for her husband's holdings. No matter that Fionn had turned out to be a kind, generous man, just a few years older than she, straight and fair as his name implied; a bit quiet, his conversation mostly limited to the complexities of raising sheep. Her mother knew all about him, of course, but Meeve was too busy celebrating Morla's marriage with Fionn's father to think such details important enough to share with her daughter. Morla supposed it was just as well the groom had not accompanied his father. Meeve would probably have bedded him, too, if she hadn't already. Morla had wondered, more times than she liked, if her husband had bedded her mother, but she'd never summoned up the courage to ask. Or maybe she just hadn't wanted to know.

A gust of wind brought the smell of seaweed from the swampy flats along the coast, and another memory burst through her mind, of the beach at low tide, the waterline heaped with brackish seaweed thick with tiny shells, of herself perched on one of the huge rocks overlooking the sea, arms wrapped around her knees, staring into the horizon until she was sure she could see into the Other-World. The beach below the cliffs of Eaven Morna had been the only place she'd felt at home.

Meeve's court, whether at Eaven Morna, Ardagh or anywhere else, was nothing like the spare life Morla had become familiar with, carved out by the fisher-chiefs of the Outermost Isles, whose halls, perched high on the windy cliffs, were always vulnerable to the raids of Humbrian pirates. Meeve's court was extravagant; Meeve herself flamboyant and rowdy. She was always ready to take a new man to her bed, never concerned about whose man he might otherwise be.

Morla had felt like a misfit from the first day of her return. She wasn't good at word games, she couldn't play an instrument, she knew no poetry except the rough songs of the fisherfolk. Her hair was a nondescript brown. She lacked Meeve's high color in her cheeks. Long-limbed like Meeve, her body was sturdier and lent itself more to trews and tunics than the elaborately embroidered bodices heavy with jewels her mother's ladies favored. She knew over a hundred ways to prepare twenty different fish, a fact Meeve never failed to mention with a laugh and a knee slap. The only bright spot had been her friendship with Lochlan. Despite knowing next to nothing about her mother's choice of a groom and Dalraida's dismal reputation, Morla'd been glad to leave.

It had been ten years since she'd been back. She bent low over the horse's neck and tried not to remember the tide of humiliation she'd felt watching Meeve lead Lochlan, already flushed and panting like a hungry dog at the honor of being chosen by the great queen, out of the keep. Instead Morla focused on the torches winking from the tops of the towers and across the upper edge of the outer curtain wall. Then the wind shifted direction and her plaid flapped in her face. The banners of both Mochmorna and Brynhyvar fluttered proudly in the wind, announcing to anyone who might have cared that Great Meeve was in residence.

From high atop the gatehouse, a shout went up, more torches flaring in a long line across the battlements. Men pointed down. They'd seen her. She wondered, fleetingly, if any would recognize her and again Lochlan's face intruded like an unruly hound's. Ten years was a long time in the life of one of her mother's knights. Meeve tended to wear out even the most vigorous. The bards even sang songs of the ones said to have died of exhaustion. Surely he wasn't still there.

Morla slowed the horse as the great keep loomed closer. Her stomach clenched painfully and she wasn't sure if it were anticipation of meeting Lochlan or the realization that even as poverty ground away at the lives of all in Dalraida, Meeve lived in luxury. The burnished torches were set in sconces that looked like gold, the walls were in fine repair and everyone along the walls and at the base had the relaxed, happy air of satisfaction that only bellies filled regularly and often ever had.

She pulled the horse to a stop at the gatehouse, and a guard stepped out, squinting up at her in torchlight that burned so brightly the shadows on the ground and on the walls were nearly dark as those at noon. "Your name, Cailleach?"

Morla swept the plaid off her head, wondering if the hard

life in the uplands of Dalraida had been as cruel as that. She noticed the suppleness of the leather, the polished glint of the pike blades, the fat, round rumps of the horses led in and out. No creature had gone hungry here in a long time.

"Cailleach?" he repeated. "Your business?"

The doughy aroma of baking bread wafted from the kitchens and her mouth watered. In her haste, out of habit, she'd picked up the plaid she'd grown use to wearing, but that most likely was unfamiliar to all at Eaven Morna. "I'm Morla," she replied. "Morla MaMeeve," she repeated, when she saw the name meant nothing to him. "Morla, the High Queen's daughter?"

He stared at her blankly until another guard, this one a grizzled older man with a sergeant's stripe across his chest, poked him in the back with the butt of a spear and elbowed him in the ribs. "You dunderhead, this is Morla, the princess. One of Meeve's lasses—it's been a long time, hasn't it, lassie?" he finished, peering up at her in the flickering glare.

"It has, Fornaught," she answered, pleased—amazed, even—that she remembered his name. She slid off her gelding, and as her stiff muscles protested, a flicker of color and the sudden flap of a gaudy banner caught her eye—red, a white so pure it looked blue in the shadows and an indigo so intense, she recognized it by the descriptions of it alone. Made only one place in the world, the city-state of Lacquilea, from ingredients expensive and rare, it was known to cost a queen's ransom. Fat tassels of braided silk in all three colors embellished the polished wooden pole, which was chased in gold and topped with a gold replica of some kind of bird of prey. The crest on the white portion was Meeve's.

*Great Goddess, how many cattle did that cost her?* she wondered, looking around. More gold flashed in the torch-light, and she saw the courtyard teemed not only with Meeve's knights, but also with unfamiliar, dark-skinned warriors dressed in unfamiliar garb, throwing dice and drinking from Meeve's deepest goblets, laughing and talking in a language she did not know. Meeve was entertaining foreign guests.

She almost stumbled as she dismounted, and Fornaught reached to steady her. "Come on, girl, I'll take you to your mother."

But before she could move, from out of nowhere, a long body thudded into her so that she nearly fell, but for the pair of strong sweaty arms that wrapped around her in a bear's embrace. "Morla? Is that my sister? Morla, you haven't changed a bit."

"Bran?" she whispered, as she steadied herself. She had never expected her younger brother to be here. Thirteen years younger than she, he should be still in the last year or so of his fostering. But he was fumbling at his neckline, and from under the sweaty, stained layers of linen and leather, he withdrew a dazzlingly white seashell on a leather cord, souvenir of the last day they'd spent together on the beaches below Eaven Morna. "Look, Morla, I've kept it all these years."

Fornaught tapped Bran's shoulder. "Master Bran, shouldn't you be at your shoeing?"

Bran glanced over his shoulder, a pout curling his full red lips, but ignored Fornaught otherwise. "Morla, I'm so happy to see you."

Her throat thickened as she stared at Bran. At fourteen,

he was maybe an inch or two taller than she, skinny as a newborn calf. His hair, once as yellow and downy as new flax, had darkened to a sun-streaked nut brown. There was almost nothing left of the baby he'd been but the expression in his dancing eyes. Meeve's court had been tolerable until Bran had gone away for fostering. "Come, I'll take you—" He tugged at her arm, exuberant as a puppy.

"Hold, Bran," she said. "Let me look at you—I never thought you'd be here. Did you give your foster mother so much trouble she sent you back a year early?"

"Ha, Mam sent for me, but I've scarcely seen her. Maybe now that you're here, she'll listen to me—I've not seen her in days—"

Foreboding flickered as Morla wondered why Meeve would send for both of them. Before she could ask anything, Fornaught coughed pointedly and stamped his spear. "Young master, you've caused more than enough trouble already with Master Mordram, don't you think? Now that Morla's here, you don't want to give him an excuse to work you late, do you? Off with you now."

"Come see me later, all right? You look for me in the forge?"

"I'll look for you in the forge," she replied. "You go now—I don't want you getting into trouble on my account, all right?" With another sulky pout, Bran slunk off.

"I'll see you later," called Morla. She turned to Fornaught. "What do you mean, he's caused trouble?"

"Oh, he ran off a couple days ago. Caused a lot of ruckus—had to turn the castle upside down looking for him. Looked high and low and they didn't find him till two days later, almost." Fornaught shrugged. "He's a typical lad who's not happy being set to real work. Come with me, now."

She felt like a puppy trotting in his wake, and heard her name whispered over and over, lifted up and rolled through the crowd like a curiosity. They entered the first ward and Morla gasped. Surely no house of TirNa'lugh could blaze as brightly. Light shone from every window, illuminating the fountained courtyard, the wide swaths of carefully tended cobbles. She felt the weight of many eyes. The scent of baking bread and roasting meat filled the space, and her mouth watered.

"Come," said Fornaught, leading her past a fountain from which dark purple wine flowed. There was a crowd clustered around it, filling goblets, dipping into baskets filled with fruit and cheese. They were laughing and drinking and toasting each other and they turned to stare. She glanced down, realizing suddenly how shabby and worn her clothes looked compared to the tunics and kirtles all around her. With every step, the realization that her mother's court lived in luxury while she and her people toiled in abject poverty, their plight mostly overlooked, fanned the anger the sight of the silk banners and golden torches had ignited. She found it hard to breathe, but Fornaught seemed not to notice. He led her across the courtyard, into the long wooden arcade branching off the main hall that led to her mother's private apartments. The corridor was deserted, but at the far end, the warriors stood with crossed spears in front of the closed doors.

As they entered, the doors swung open, and a fat, red-faced man leaned out and beckoned.

"Ah, that's good," said Fornaught. "Looks like Meeve's still within."

The polished breastplates, the oiled leathers on the guards made Morla ever more painfully aware of her worn leather trews, her sweat-stained shirt, her thin doublet, her frayed plaid, as he led her down the corridor. She recognized Briecru, Meeve's former First Knight as she stepped across the threshold into a room more sumptuous than anything she'd ever seen in her life. Her muddy boots sank into the thick pile of a carpet woven in such intricate patterns of red and blue her eyes couldn't quite focus on it. In front of the hearth, huge tasseled cushions were piled beside a white cloth, on which lay abandoned the remains of a feast so lavish, it could've fed half a village in Dalraida. A whole roast goose lay breast up, one leg torn from its carcass, a gold handled knife stuck carelessly in its crisp brown breast next to platters of fish, a ham and a haunch of meat, baskets of bread and crumbled cakes, bowls of berries and the tiny, sweet grapes that grew along the coast. It was more food in one place than Morla had seen since last year's harvest was brought in. Saliva filled her mouth and her stomach rumbled ominously.

Briecru's first words puzzled her. "Great Herne, couldn't you have found one a bit younger? Where's she from—up in the hill country?" He regarded her with a wrinkled nose and a furrowed forehead. He'd grown fat, Morla saw, his belly bulging over his belt, his mustache long and lustrous as a gold fox's tail. Dangling from his belt was the bull's tail that signified the office of Chief Cowherd. He had indeed come up in the world and he didn't look as if he'd ever set foot in a byre in his life.

"Briecru? You look like a merchant."

But he didn't seem to have heard her. He only gripped her upper arm, and said, "Pinch your cheeks and bite your lips to put some color in them—let's hope Her Majesty's too drunk—"

Through the partially opened door of Meeve's bedroom, Morla heard her mother's throaty laugh. "Send her in, whatever she looks like, Briecru."

"We can put a sack over her head—that's not the end we care about," shouted another voice, a male voice.

Fornaught's eyes widened and he grabbed unsuccessfully for Morla's arm, as she, not understanding, allowed Briecru to propel her through the opened door. She gasped as she stepped across the threshold. The room was in gloom, the windows opened to catch the cool salt breezes off the sea, and the bed was a rumpled pile of skins and furs and sheets, on which three tangled bodies uncoiled audibly. Morla's jaw dropped at the sight of her mother entwined with a tall, dark-skinned stranger and a tanned knight with tangled brown hair tumbling around his shoulders.

Lochlan, she thought as her eyes swept helplessly down the length of his muscled torso to the dark nest at the base of his rampant red phallus.

Meeve turned with a toss of her faded red hair and a look like the Marrighugh. "By the Great Mother herself, girl, is that you, Morla?"

She met Meeve's startled eyes, ignoring the gasps and

sputters of Meeve's bedmates. "Hello, Mother." In a kind of daze, she spun on her heel and slammed the door behind her.

"Ah, Morla, I didn't recognize you…" Briecru began, but she simply stormed passed him.

"Morla," Fornaught reached for her as Meeve appeared on the threshold, wrapped in an assortment of furs and sheets.

She looked at Morla in the outer corridor. "Come with me." She spoke over her shoulder to Briecru as she started up the spiral steps that led to the roof. "You're a fool, Briecru. Calm the ambassador. I think he's taken some sort of fit."

The air had cooled considerably, and the draft had a chill that cut through Morla's damp leather. A gust slapped the fabric of the pennants in her face and she slapped them away.

Meeve leaned against a battlement, gazing out over the sea, her mouth pinched down at the corners. "Well, daughter. Your sense of timing, as usual, leaves something to be desired. But I'm sorry you had to witness that. We were…playing a game the ambassador suggested—a foreign game—and expecting—"

"Someone else." Morla felt dizzy. "Judging from the message, I thought someone was dying."

An odd expression crossed Meeve's face. "Are you cold? Here, have a fur—yes, here you are, take it." Meeve never took no for an answer. She tucked the dark brown fur around Morla's shoulders, smoothing it over her braids. "There, that's pretty on you—you should keep it."

Impatiently, Morla pushed her mother's hand away. "I don't need a new fur, Mother. What is it you want?"

"Always so direct, aren't you? You might go further, Morla, if you could learn to be a bit more subtle. Not to mention courteous." Morla flushed as Meeve continued, "But since we're being blunt, I'm dying, Morla."

"What?" Morla stared at her mother's thin white face, her wild red hair whipped by the wind, skin white as a ghost's against the dark furs, certain she could not have heard correctly. "What did you say?"

"I'm dying, Morla," Meeve repeated, as if she expected that to explain everything.

"Of what? Who says? Are you sure?"

"We're all dying, Morla, some of us faster than others, that's all." Despite her light patter and teasing tone, the words rang hollow and false. But the hard look on Meeve's face, the hollow, hunted light in her eyes, confused Morla. "That's why I sent for you. I need your help."

Help from me? thought Morla. She thought of her thin, pale people, of their scrawny herds scratching out an existence on fields pocked with blight, and wondered what kind of help Meeve could possibly want from her. "What about the druids, Mother? Surely they're the ones—"

"The druids." Meeve's mouth twisted down and she waved a dismissive hand. "I've had enough of druids— they're all so busy gazing into the OtherWorld they've forgotten that this one changes. For more than twenty years, I've ruled this land, not Connla, nor any other druid, much as they like to hold themselves above the rest of us. And now, when we're facing near certain war, they tell me I'm to abandon my policies simply because it doesn't suit theirs. Well. They've their own affairs to mind, from Deirdre disgracing herself—"

"What's happened to Deirdre?"

"Thank the goddess you've not heard."

"Dalraida's remote—we don't hear much of anything." But an accounting might be in order, thought Morla. *My people starve and Mother nibbles goose.* Her dowry, paid in annual installments, was supposed to reflect a percentage of the fluctuating wealth of Mochmorna, in order to allow that some years' harvests were better, cattle and sheep more fertile. In all the ten years, the amounts never varied. Yet Meeve's fortunes had surely, indisputably, increased. Morla turned to look at Meeve with new eyes, even as she wondered how to broach the subject while Meeve continued her tirade.

"But not only has she disgraced the entire sisterhood, but she's conceived some kind of monster, by all reports. Three months past its time, or nearly, and it's still not yet born."

"How's that possible?" asked Morla.

"Who knows?" Meeve shrugged. "Connla doesn't."

Morla took a single step forward, her elbow grazing the roughened, salt-pitted stone. "What is it you want of me, Mother?"

"I want you to go to Far Nearing—"

"What for?" Morla blurted. If Meeve had told her to go to the moon, she wouldn't have been more surprised.

"Just listen." Meeve's voice was somewhere between a growl and a hiss. "I'll not be able to hide my condition sooner or later—"

"You've not told anyone?"

"I've told my First Knight. But only because he guessed. You probably don't remember him, though he was here before you were married, I think. His name's Lochlan. Lochlan of

Glenrae." Meeve cleared her throat, then turned her head and spat a thick wad of greenish phlegm onto the cobblestones.

"Don't tell me you've taken up cudwort, Mother?" Morla looked down, wrinkling her nose more to cover her shock than in actual disbelief.

"It helps the pain." Meeve answered. "Now. Fengus— you remember Fengus, don't you? Chief of Allovale? Itching to be High King for as long as I've been High Queen?" When Morla nodded, she continued, "I've decided that much as I despise him, I'm going to offer Fengus the ultimate in peace offerings."

"You mean to marry him?"

"No, not me. I intend to offer him a marriage between his daughter—his only daughter, from what I understand—and your brother, at MidSummer and turn his Lughnasa competition into a betrothal feast."

"Bran? He's but a boy— How can you even—"

"Not Bran." Meeve looked out into the night, pulled her black furs close to her throat. "Your other brother."

"What other brother?" Morla took a step back, feeling the hard edge of the stone butt into her back. It steadied her, as did the cold lick of the wet wind. "A foster brother?"

"No," replied Meeve. "Your brother I bore when I was fourteen. His father…his father couldn't pay my bride-price, let alone a child-price. And there were other reasons my mother would not see a dowry paid to that part of the world, and so the boy was sent to live with his father and grandfather as soon as he was weaned."

"And he's been there all these years?"

Meeve shrugged. "I sent messengers to make sure he was

alive—they'll be expecting you. And you'll like Far Nearing, Morla—lots of fish, you know."

Morla felt her cheeks grow warm, but she only said, "You want me to bring him here?"

"I want you to bring him to Ardagh. We'll introduce him to Fengus's daughter there. At Lughnasa, we'll announce the wedding for MidWinter. I always think of winter as the best time for weddings—all those long dark nights."

Stunned, Morla heard herself say, "But the only daughter I remember Fengus having is a druid—she's of the same sisterhouse as Deirdre, isn't she? What if she doesn't want to give up that life? And—" she paused "—am I to understand you mean to make this brother of mine king of Mochmorna?"

Meeve's bare arm snaked out from beneath her furs and she cupped Morla's chin in one cold hand. "Morla, nothing's settled—"

Morla blinked. She felt as if the air had been punched out of her lungs. Druid blood ran strong in Meeve's line. She had always believed that her mother's title would one day be hers. She was, after all, the oldest daughter.

"Nothing's settled, at all. But you know the decisions I make affect far more people than just you and I. My decisions affect the Land."

The Land. Morla gazed out into the darkening twilight, tears pricking at her eyelids, the fur suddenly hot and somehow dirty. The damp salt air felt cleaner. This is what it meant to Meeve to be High Queen. Everything she did, from the men she bedded, to the famous feasts she hosted, to the gold she dispensed, was calculated in terms of its benefit to the land. Meeve would give Morla's birthright to an utter stranger if she believed that by doing so, the land and the people would be strengthened. Deep inside Morla recoiled. *Maybe you don't want to be Queen after all,* ran silently through her mind. She'd spent all this time believing that her time in Dalraida was a test of her abilities, not a life sentence. "Why send me?" Morla managed.

For a fleeting moment, Meeve's eyes softened. "Because I trust you, daughter." Then she said, "And you're not a druid."

That was the real reason. A wave of grief and longing swept over her as a sudden gust of wind brought the clean tang of salt and the ocean's endless dull roar, reminding her of the smell of her foster mother's spare, half-timbered hall, snug against even the strongest of icy blasts. Everything about Eaven Morna she thought she loved were all the things that reminded her of Hulsa's snug hall. No wonder the place had never really felt like home. Now it felt, however, as if she'd stepped through a portal, into some upside-down, inside-out OtherWorld, even stranger than TirNa'lugh. Suddenly she couldn't wait to be away. "All right, I'll go," she said, "On one condition—two actually."

"And what's that," Meeve bridled.

"You have to send a druid into Dalraida—more than one—as many as you can. The blight's spreading there. The people are starving. They need a druid to heal the land, and they need corn to eat, until the land is healed."

Meeve's eyes narrowed. *Surely she can't say no,* thought Morla, bracing herself for one of Meeve's clever answers that was neither a yes nor a no.

But Meeve surprised her. "Curse Connla to the belly of the Hag." She spat another wad of cudwort over the battlement and turned back to Morla. "I'll do what I can. Corn I have— Druids—" she broke off and shook her head as she stared out into the night. "I packed them all off to Ardagh. I'll see if one can be found." She gathered her furs to her throat. "One more thing, Morla." Meeve paused by the steps, her hand on the railing, the other twined in her furs. "I want you to take Bran with you."

"Why?" Surprised, Morla cocked her head. Under the circumstances, she'd have thought Meeve would want her youngest child close.

"I want you to get him away. It seems the old athair in Pentland filled his head with druid nonsense." Meeve's lips quirked down. "He's making himself the laughingstock of the keep—claiming to see trixies, disappearing for days as if he'd gone to the OtherWorld—"

"What if he did?"

"He'd better stop it," Meeve spat back. "I've had enough of druids. They don't do any good—" She broke off. "Bran won't give you any trouble. He was always your favorite brother, no?"

*Bran's my only brother,* Morla thought, biting her lip.

"In ten years, I've asked nothing of you, have I? Sent what you needed? Gave you seed and corn and cattle?"

*You sent me what was mine,* Morla nearly said, but she bit back the words in time. The best way to understand what Meeve was planning was to do exactly what her mother asked. There was no reason for her to return immediately, so long as she sent back supplies. Her absence, in fact, meant one less mouth to feed. And on the road, with Bran, maybe she could forget what she'd seen just now. Lochlan? she thought, as her jaw dropped and the image of his naked torso rose before her unbidden. "I said I'd go," she said, stumbling over the words. "As long as you send corn tomorrow to Dalraida."

It wasn't until Meeve had disappeared down the black hole of the staircase that Morla remembered they'd been expecting someone. Another woman. Her mother had been in bed with two men—one of whom was Lochlan—and they awaited another woman. She wondered what sort of diplomacy her mother thought to practice.

In the gloom of Meeve's bedchamber, Lochlan finished lacing his tunic and pulled on his boots. Of all the women in the world, Morla was the last he'd expected to walk through the door at that precise moment. He was certain she recognized him.

The door swung open and Meeve stalked in, face angular as a cat's, her bone-white arms stippled with gooseflesh. "You all right?"

He nodded. "And you?"

She walked over to the hearth with an unreadable expression on her face, threw back half a goblet of mead, swallowed hard then said, "I want you to escort Morla."

At first he wasn't sure he'd heard correctly. He was the only one, to his knowledge, at the entire Court who knew the truth. He'd expected to stay by her side, especially with the Lacquilean ambassador here. "Are you sure?"

Her brows rose, almost comically, and he nearly laughed

aloud. "The last thing I want is you coddling me like a broody hen. Do you understand?"

"But I've brought you hard proof the rumors are true. I don't want to leave now—who knows what they're capable of doing, the double-dealing sons of pigs?"

Meeve eyed him up and down and a grin flickered across her face. "There's no need to insult pigs. We all love ham and bacon." Then her expression hardened. "Lochlan, I don't think you understand. I don't want you here. I want you in the country, being my eyes and ears."

"What did the ambassador say when you showed him the sword?"

"I haven't shown it to him. He's only going to deny it, Lochlan. He'll acknowledge it's of his people's make, and then shrug and have nothing further to say. My goal isn't to eradicate these people from this land, Lochlan. I don't have time left to do that. All I can do is leave a land strong and unified. The fight is up to those I leave behind. And the land is in danger—there is trouble and turmoil all over. So who else can I trust with my children?"

"Do you remember Morla's last Beltane here?"

"I remember it." Meeve's eyes were fixed on the fire. She slumped down into her chair and swung her feet up onto the stool.

"Then, Meeve—" he hesitated. In all the years he'd known her, he'd never asked the question "—was it goddess who made you choose me? Or was there another reason?"

Meeve filled her goblet, took a long drink and smacked her lips. Then she looked at him squarely. "It was goddess and god who made me queen, who married me to the land

and sanctified my rule. Fionn in Dalraida came looking for a wife for his son. I needed Morla married to young Fionn, not here, carrying a child got on her by a god. I saw the way she looked at you. I saw the way you looked back."

"So you intervened."

"I made a decision to make my daughter a queen. Ten years later, I've no intention of apologizing for it. So you'll take Morla to Far Nearing, fetch Cwynn and go on to Ardagh. Oh, and take Bran with you—he's causing nothing but trouble and I can't afford to be distracted right now. I'll see you all at MidSummer."

"Connla told me she put a ward on Bran to keep him safe," he said. "What if it doesn't protect him on the road? How am I to keep him safe from the sidhe?"

"And when did Connla tell you this?"

"She was waiting for me in the stable-yard when I rode in. She told me you'd quarreled."

"Ah." Meeve paused, then said, "Well, if you've fear of any ability Bran might manifest beyond an uncommon recalcitrance, stay at druid-houses." She looked directly at Lochlan, and their eyes met. "The sooner you leave for Far Nearing, the sooner you can be at Ardagh."

There was something about the way she sprawled across the bench, long fingers laced, huge eyes glittering, that reminded him unpleasantly of a spider. "Does Morla know I'm to escort her?"

"No," Meeve said evenly. "Do you think she remembers you?"

He hesitated. *I'd like to think she does.* But he wasn't ready to be as brutally honest as Meeve. "I suppose it's not likely."

He picked up his sword-belt and buckled it on. "Things are bad in Dalraida?"

Meeve looked up at him. "How'd you know?"

How could anyone fail to notice, he thought, Morla's frayed plaid, her bony face? "I noticed she looked thin."

Sounds of revelry were beginning to filter up from the lower levels of the keep. "Go on," said Meeve. "I have to dress."

With a bow, Lochlan opened the door and collided directly into Morla.

"Sweet goddess." She recoiled when he would've taken her arm.

"I'm sorry," he muttered, stung for some reason he didn't understand.

The air crackled between them. Morla moved to one side as he stepped to the same side and for a moment they were locked in an awkward back-and-forth two-step, during which time he saw just how gaunt she was. "I'm to escort you," he said. "To Far Nearing."

Her eyes grew wide as a startled doe's and she hissed, a sound that didn't convey any kind of pleasure. She looked as if she might say something, but all she did was dart, deer-like, down the steps.

Morla reeled down the corridor, heart pounding audibly. Was the Hag laughing at her? How was it possible that the first time she'd seen Lochlan in ten years he was naked, in her mother's bed, and the second time, he informed her he was escorting her halfway across Brynhyvar and back? She tried to keep sight of the serving woman who was leading her to her room, but the shock made her dizzy and disori-

ented, and Morla found herself in a narrow passage somewhere off the main corridor.

She turned around, but the woman was nowhere to be
seen and the corridor was completely deserted, even though
she could hear distant laughter, and the smell of baking
bread wafted strongly from one direction. She must've taken
a wrong turn, for this was clearly a passage that led to the
kitchens. There was nothing to do but to retrace her steps
and hope that her guide realized she was lost and turned
back to find her.

But tired and unnerved as she was, Morla found the laby-
rinthine maze that wound through Meeve's keep beyond
her ability to navigate. She found herself in totally unfamiliar territory, stumbling into a stable-yard stacked high with
barrels and chests of every size, and apparently reserved for
the use of the foreign guests. Four or five sat clustered
around benches, engaged in some sort of dice-throwing
game. Almost as one, though, they turned and smiled at her.
The two closest leaped to their feet, gesturing and motion-
ing her to join them. She shook her head, stepping backward, squarely into the chest of a huge soldier, his black
braids arranged in neat rows all over his head. He caught her
by the shoulder and spoke to her in halting Brynnish, while
the others guffawed to each other. "You? Encipio send?"

"No one sent me," she replied, shaking off his hand.

But he only wrapped his palm behind her head and tried
to pull her toward him, white teeth flashing. "Encipio, no?
Then, Bree-crew? Bree-crew?"

"Leave me be," she cried. Morla squirmed away, and the
man let her go. She heard hoots and catcalls following as she

dashed back through what she hoped was a corridor leading to the main hall. As she rounded the first corner, however, she collided with a fur-lined robe and velvet-covered chest. Two hands steadied her when she would've fallen, and she stared up into the florid and mustached face of Briecru. Bree-crew, she thought, his duties as Chief Cowherd apparently included those of Chief Procurer. "Lord Briecru—I'm lost. Can you help me find my way back?"

"Of course I can, princess, but whatever are you doing here?" He glanced over her shoulder, back down the way she'd come, almost as if he expected to see someone. "How'd you come to be here?"

"I've no idea," she said. "I was following the woman sent to show me my rooms—the next thing I know I was wandering around back here. Aren't we near the kitchens? Where's everyone gone?"

"The revel's already begun," he said. "That's why these halls are empty. Come." The smile on his face was bland as a sullen sea. "Let's get you away from those ruffians down there."

"What kind of people are these, Briecru? They looked at me as if I were a piece of meat."

Briecru sighed as he motioned for her to follow him through a side arch. "Here, princess, this is a shortcut." He waited until they turned a corner, then said, "You're right, princess. The ways of Lacquilea are not like ours at all—the men all seem to have difficulty understanding how a woman might rule men. It makes them doubly difficult for your mother to deal with."

"She seemed to be getting along with the ambassador just fine."

Briecru shot her a glance and she was gratified to see he looked embarrassed. "Princess, I beg your forgiveness for the misunderstanding. Surely, you realize we were not expecting you—"

"You didn't know my mother sent for me?" The expression that passed across his face was as unreadable as a cloudless sky. "She told you I was coming?"

"We knew you were on your way," he answered in such a way that made her wonder if he really did or not. "But your arrival was not expected."

"I could see Mam had other things to think about."

He made a noncommittal little noise that might have been construed as an assent and Morla wondered why it was she found herself listening so intently to every nuance. It was because there were so few, she realized. He was like a blank slate, his impersonal pleasantries and conversation as smooth as new-milked cream, as thin as yesterday's buttermilk. He was not at all as she remembered. And then she did remember. Briecru had been First Knight of Meeve's Fiachna when she'd arrived from her fostering. He occupied the place that Lochlan did now. At the end of his term, Meeve had not taken him as her Beltane-husband for a year and a day as had been her custom. Instead, she'd made him her Chief Cowherd, effectively putting him out to pasture. Morla had been married by that time, but the story had filtered as far as Dalraida.

Briecru could not refuse. He'd no lands, no herds, being the fifth or sixth son of a very small chieftain somewhere on the coast of Gar. And so he'd accepted what amounted to public humiliation, stepping aside in favor of other men.

Meeve didn't see it that way, of course. Morla had known from the first exactly how her mother saw it. Meeve believed she'd identified something unique in Briecru, something that suited him, in her estimation, for the role she wanted him to play.

In a few moments, he'd led her up two flights of curving stairs and paused with her before a door. "Here you are, princess." He appeared to hesitate.

"What is it, Briecru?"

He glanced both directions down the deserted corridor. "I'm not sure what your mother told you, Morla, but you know, she's not well."

Had Meeve not said no one knew but Lochlan? Though it certainly made sense Briecru would know—he was nearly as intimate with her as her knights—a strong intuition warned Morla to choose her words with care. "I'm glad I have an opportunity to ease her, then," she answered and pushed against the door.

He understood the dismissal at once and bowed. "I'll send a maid up with water for you directly, princess. Do come down and join the revel when you're ready." With another bland quirk of his lips, he was gone.

Morla pushed open the door and found herself in a pleasant-enough room, with a wide bed and a chest and a chair beneath the window. Her window looked directly down into the courtyard where the dancing was just beginning. A game was in progress, some sort of a wagering game that involved drinking and coin tossing into the pool in the center of the courtyard. She looked up as a few raindrops spattered on the glass pane. The lowering clouds and darkening dusk didn't faze the crowds, who surged, then parted, as an enormous roasted ox was wheeled in on a cart hauled by six men.

Meeve had found a place on the ambassador's lap, who'd recovered sufficiently from the shock of Morla's arrival to don a Brynnish tunic embellished with intricate knotwork studded with tiny gems, his full black beard combed and oiled and spilling over his broad chest and large belly. Meeve took her jewel-studded goblet from her cup-bearer, pinched the boy's ripe young cheek, then raised the goblet in a toast.

Morla glanced away, through the crowd. Briecru was standing on a stone landing, halfway down a stone staircase that led directly into the courtyard, staring up at her through the glass. His gaze made her feel uneasy and she stepped back, out of his sight. She dodged behind a curtain, her eyes fixed on her mother. Morla's jaw dropped. The ambassador wasn't holding a goblet—he was holding a chalice, a druid chalice, made unmistakably of silver. Could Meeve have taken it from the Heather Grove's storehouse? No, Morla decided, surely not. Druid silver was protected by special wards and spells. No one touched druid silver.

The crowd was shouting at Meeve, encouraging her to drain the goblet to the dregs. She grinned in response, then tilted her head back. The crowd roared encouragement as Meeve's throat worked. At last she sat up, belched and overturned the goblet to show it was empty.

Then another cheer rang out as a white-aproned cook stepped up to the ox and began to carve huge slabs off its side. Meeve was kissing the ambassador now, and he was greedily sucking the wine off her tongue. No, Morla told herself again. Meeve would not have taken the chalices from the Grove. But something told Morla that she had, and she understood why Meeve sent Connla and the other druids away. Morla stepped back, troubled, and turned away, even as she felt Briecru's gaze following her into the room.

Beneath the overhang, Briecru watched as Morla disappeared into the shadows of her room. The musky scent of Meeve's perfume still filled his nostrils, and from his vantage point, her red-gold mane of curls spilling down her back gleamed in the flaring orange torchlight. Her linen gown was heavily embroidered in gold and silver thread. Unguent stained her lips and cheeks and she appeared almost healthy. Meeve believed herself to be sick of the same creeping cancer that had killed her mother and all her aunts and she assumed herself to have at least another year or more. But Briecru was confident she'd be gone by MidWinter. The poison was doing its work. He bowed as she caught his eye, applauding in the direction of the fountain.

Meeve's engineers had rigged it so that purple wine splashed out of the spigots embedded in the rocks above the fountain. The wine flowed down the rocks, mingling with the fresh water bubbling up from the underground spring at the fountain's base. A crowd holding goblets to catch the wine had gathered. Some simply scooped up liquid and stood slurping it in great gulps, while others called for more goblets. Baskets of soft white bread and huge wheels of hard cheese were passing through the crowd, and in a corner, a young bard—a mere stripling—began to warble. Meeve put every other chief in Brynhyvar to shame with the richness of her feasts. It could have been a ritual day—the only thing absent were the druids in their capes of beaten silver.

He heard a footstep and the rustle of the silk hangings on either side of the doorway. Someone had come to stand behind him. "There's going to be a shortfall in the next few shipments," he murmured. "Please tell your master."

"Oh?" Encipio Sulpanus, secretary and interpreter for the ambassador, Diodorian Lussius, crossed his arms over his chest. Briecru noticed he was careful to stay out of sight of the merrymakers in the courtyard.

"Morla's back. Meeve will be paying attention for the next month or two—I won't be able to send the full shipment until the first harvest is in, and maybe not till the second—"

His voice was suddenly choked off in midsentence as the Lacquilean dragged him by the neck through the open doorway behind the curtain. "We've a bargain, Brynman," Sulpanus hissed in his ear, his black beard tickling the edge of Briecru's earlobe; the edge of something sharp poked into his back and Briecru stifled a little cry. "I don't care where you take the grain from." He poked the sharp point into Briecru's rib again, and Briecru jerked against the other's hairy forearm. "We can find another, you know. This land's crawling with would-be traitors."

With a muffled curse, Briecru wrestled himself free. "How dare you—" he sputtered as Sulpanus sheathed his knife. "You won't soon find someone who has Meeve's ear the way I do."

"You won't soon find someone who can deliver the means to kill her, either." Sulpanus's breath was hot in Breicru's ear.

"That poison's not exactly working as quickly as you said

it would, either—look at her—at this rate she'll still be here next summer." He gestured to the courtyard, where Meeve was sharing a bowl of wine with Diodorian. It was silver, he saw, and so big the two could drink from it together. They looked like pigs dipping into a trough, he thought, as he stared for a moment, transfixed by the image of the queen of all Brynhyvar lapping up the wine audibly, her upper lip stained dark and purple as goblin gore. She disgusted him.

"Give her more."

"How can she possibly be encouraged to wear more—she reeks like a Humbrian whore as it is."

"Tell her the ambassador especially enjoys the scent of her perfume." Sulpanus's eyes met Briecru's evenly, and he touched the hilt of his knife in a gesture as significant as it was small. "Be sure to tell her I said so, too."

Meeve was highly susceptible to compliments of every kind, but Briecru doubted even Meeve could be induced to put on more than she wore already. She had once or twice complained that the scent of it interfered with the taste of her mead. "Even so, it'll take time—"

"Then stop coddling her. Get her blood stirred up—put some pressure on her. The poison's weakened her—she'd never live to fight a war."

Briecru glanced down into the courtyard, where Meeve was engaged in a drinking game with three of the Fiachna, who were lined up below her on a wooden dais. "She's doing everything in her power to prevent—"

"Surely there's something you know to do, something that might even be construed as a misunderstanding, but against which a real hothead might react?" Sulpanus's voice was smooth as fresh-risen cream, and he was no more a real secretary and interpreter than he, Briecru, actually herded cows.

Briecru opened his mouth, then happened to glance up and once again saw Morla's pale face pressed against the glass, dark eyes fastened directly on her mother. There was an opportunity he'd overlooked. He looked back to Sulpanus. The man had disappeared, and not even a curtain moved to suggest that he'd ever been anything but alone on the balcony. He'd recognized the hunger in her eyes even before he'd recognized her. He knew exactly how lean the shipments had been going to Dalraida, because Meeve's fatal flaw was that once she delegated something, she forgot about it. An alliance with Morla might work to his benefit even before Meeve was dead.

*Something against which a real hothead might react...* The land was full of hotheads, hotheads always ready to nurse a grievance and look for ways to create new ones. However, not many had the resources to challenge Meeve. There was really only one—Fengus of Allovale. He and Meeve had chased each other around and around Brynhyvar, fighting over anything and everything from breeding rights to pasture lands, from tributes to ferry fees. Once convinced she was dying, however, Meeve had decided peace with Fengus should be achieved at all costs. This did not mean that every kinsman and woman in Meeve's considerable kin-holds agreed. There was a wedge here, he knew. It was simply a question of finding a way to thrust it in.

Morla had backed away from the window once more. Lean and hungry Morla—he remembered the last communication from her detailed the death of her bull and asked her mother to send new bull-calves. Fengus-Da possessed a legendary bull, the Black Bull of Avellach. He smiled as it occurred to him just what to do to set Fengus raging across the land and collapse Meeve's fragile peace. He smiled as the people drank a toast to Meeve, and he was quite certain that Morla, if she watched, did not drink.

*8*

"Should we keep digging, Cailleach?" Athair Emnoch leaned on his shovel and mopped his brow as Catrione trudged up the Tor. The other diggers paused and looked at her expectantly. The day was not at all overcast and the worst weather appeared over, but it was hot, and the sun was strong. "The more we dig, the more there is to dig—it's as if the earth itself's resisting."

Catrione put her hands on her hips and looked around the Tor. No one appeared to have made any significant progress at all. "I suppose that's exactly what's happening, Athair. All right. We can't outdig the khouri-keen." As the men set their shovels down with sighs and stretches, Catrione scanned the landscape stretching out around the Tor. The ragged line of people struggling up the road toward the Grove had increased to a steady stream as news of the goblin attack had swept across the countryside. *Where's Tully when I need him?*

Athair Emnoch came to stand beside her. "So what now?"

She glanced over her shoulder at him, trying to gauge his expression. His face, like his voice, was carefully blank, but his eyes followed the refugees to the camp rapidly forming outside their gates. She wrapped her arms around herself and shook her head. "I've sent ravens to the druids at Ardagh, and to any left at Eaven Morna. Meeve's knight said Connla was still there." She drew a deep breath. Everyone looked as tired and dirty as she felt. "Tell the others—clean up, rest for a bit. There's a lot of frightened people down there, and we're needed."

Niona came striding over, her shovel on her shoulder. "Was there anything of use in the Mem'brances, sister? Anything at all of any use?"

Catrione bit her lip. She wanted very much to tell her, yes, that the scraps and scrolls of bark contained the answers. "I don't know yet. I want to talk to the still-wives. They spend more time working with the scrolls than any of us. As I said to Athair here, I've sent ravens to Ardagh and Eaven Morna asking for help."

"And in the meantime?"

"In the meantime—in the meantime, we'll try to make some sort of order out of the chaos building in our court-yard. Take some time to rest, though. All of you." She raised her voice and looked at each digger in turn. "We'll convene later, at supper." A cloud of dust on the road drew her attention. It disgorged a familiar-looking troop of horses and riders. Tully was back from his expedition. "Now I need to go speak to Sir Tully." Before anyone could speak, she strode down the Tor, feeling as if Niona's eyes bored into her back.

She found Tully in the stables. "It's hard to tell," he began. "There's no—"

"Then we must assume that Fengus-Da's wrong, at least

in this instance, and prepare for goblins." Catrione shook her head. "Tully, there's no point in you hanging around. I can't go with you. I can't leave now."

"Your father's orders were to bring you home." Tully folded his mouth into a hard thin line and folded his arms across his chest.

A seed of suspicion stirred to life as she stared up at the grizzled warrior, so carefully cloaked against her druid Sight in gray mist. *He's hiding something,* she thought. "What haven't you told me, Tully?" She stretched her mind deliberately, expanding her awareness beyond her physical limits, delicately probing the surface of all the knights present, slipping across their minds like the brush of a butterfly. Tully was prepared and therefore nearly impossible to easily penetrate. But close enough, she sensed a rough patch of energy, indicating that someone was holding something else back. Like information. She applied an extra touch of pressure and in the stall to their right, a young knight popped up over the wall.

"There's the man you are to marry," he said. The words tumbled out like coins and he clapped his hands over his mouth.

Catrione stared at him. "A man I am to marry?" She looked back at Tully. "Is this true?"

Slowly Tully nodded, even as he spoke over his shoulder through gritted teeth. "Haven't I told you again and again to keep your head empty around a druid? Any druid?"

"I have no time for Father's games, Tully. You go back and tell him that."

"These aren't games, Catrione. He's worried about you, about the land."

"Who is this man he wants me to renounce all my vows for and marry?"

"Meeve's oldest son."

"Deirdre's little brother? Bran? He's a child. He can't be more than ten—"

"There's another one, apparently. One no one bothered about—he was off on Far Nearing, somewhere. But Meeve's decided to bother about him now. And your father thinks its a way to wed two great parts of Brynhyvar into one. You see, Callie Cat, what you don't understand is he and Meeve agree for once."

*The world has turned upside down.* Catrione blinked. Reality had taken on a slippery, slimy feeling, as if the strands that held all things in place were in danger of simply dissolving into nothing.

*Don't you ever wonder if someday a man will come...* Deirdre's voice whispered through her mind, and for a moment she was thirteen. *Don't you ever wonder if someday a man will come and make you want to leave forever?* Tiermuid had come and made them both want to stay. What if he comes back? whispered the voice of the demon who lived under her skin. Catrione pressed her hands to her temples to block out the interweaving whispers. "I will not leave, Tully."

"Then we're staying. Don't worry about feeding us—we can take care of ourselves and provide for others, too. But Fengus-Da wants you safe. I do, too." He looked around at others, who peered over the stalls, clustered in the aisle. "We all do. And since we don't dare kidnap you...there's not much else to do."

For a moment, despite everything, she was tempted to

laugh. She opened her mouth and a soft voice whispered through her mind: Father. Catrione looked around, turned her head. Father? she wondered. *Father's coming.* "Tully, did you say my father's coming?"

He shook his head, looking puzzled. "No, my lady. I said we were staying here."

*Father's coming.* The voice was less than a sigh. "All right, Tully. Of course you can stay. I—I have work to do." She hurried back to the still-house, head cocked, all her druid senses opened. A gray void stretched out before her Sight, a mostly empty landscape populated here and there by an occasional shimmer. *Father's coming. Did you ever think there's a man you are to marry?* The words echoed through her in Deirdre's voice, reverberating up and down her spine until she clamped her hands over her ears and stamped her foot. "Enough!" she cried. She opened her eyes to see a courtyard full of refugees watching her. Her gaze was drawn to the Tor. As a monstrous possibility occurred to her, she picked up her skirts and ran to the still-house, where Baeve and Bride were pounding out decoctions. They looked up when she entered and Baeve put down her pestle. "What's wrong, Catrione?"

"We have to look at those barks again—the Mem'brances— That child, Deirdre's child. I think Tiermuid's coming back, and all those references to the child who can't be slain by the hand of woman or man… I think…I think Deirdre's child— I think it's the child foretold." Her breathing was coming in great gasps, her heart was pounding against her chest.

"Now, child, now. Catrione—sit down. You're all flushed— get her some water, dear," said Bride to Sora.

They pulled her onto the long bench, pressed a goblet filled with herb-scented water in her hands. Baeve watched her drink, then took the cup from her shaking hands. "I heard it," Catrione said. She looked at each woman in turn. "I know I did. It said, 'Father's coming.'"

"Your father?" asked Bride.

"No—no, the child's father—Tiermuid. I think he's coming back—and I think that child—that child—" She gripped Baeve's hands. "You said it yourself. In forty years, it's the most unnatural thing you've ever seen. Look at Deirdre. Not only is she turning into something hideous, she's doing things—how could she possibly have gotten into the Tor, even made it up to the top? She snuck in and out of the chapter-house and took the khouri-crystals. I don't think we've time to wait for a raven to fly back from Ardagh. Please—you know herb-lore better than I, better than any of us. Please, let's all look?"

Bride and Baeve exchanged glances. "Sora, fetch the barks," said Baeve.

"All of them?" Sora asked.

"All of them," replied Catrione.

Cwynn wasn't sure when it occurred to him that there was something strange about the white dog. It could've been the way Eoch followed after him, trotting docile at his heels as a puppy. Or perhaps it was the fact that they'd been traveling for hours and he hadn't seen the dog lift its leg once. As if in answer, the dog trotted off to the roadside, sniffed around a boulder and a stump, then lifted its leg. He turned around to look at Cwynn as if to say, "Is this what you expected?"

Cwynn narrowed his eyes, but the dog merely trotted on. He sighed and settled into the saddle and wondered if the dog really did know where it was going. The few travelers he'd passed had all agreed, however, that he was on the road that eventually led to Ardagh. Every one pointed west and nodded. The dog just bounded on and on.

The light was warm and tinged with gold, and the rolling green hills were dotted with red sweeps of clover and white heather and purple sage. A light wind was on his back, and the red-clay road seemed to rise to meet his feet. From time to time, they passed white cottages where men and women sat tending their fires, singing and joking and telling tales. No one seemed to do any work at all, nor did there seem to be work that needed doing. Everything seemed tidy and clean and very, very bright. Everyone seemed very happy. They all nodded and smiled and pointed him on his way.

On the road he met an old woman carrying a basket of the reddest and most fragrant apples he'd ever seen. They had obviously just come from the tree for most had fresh green leaves still attached to their stems. She smiled at him and held the basket up for him, indicating he should choose one. The sun turned her white hair silver. Her eyes were blue and freckles dotted across her nose and her teeth were very white.

On Far Nearing, he mused, the apples were barely recognizable as fruit. Could the climate on the mainland be that different? "Where'd you get these apples?" he asked.

"Over there." She pointed to rolling hills covered in apple trees extending far as the horizon, all laden so heavily with fruit, their branches bowed to the ground. "Take one, if you like. And when you see Bruss, tell him Apple Aeffie said hello."

Without thinking, Cwynn reached into the basket and plucked one. It was warm in his hand and he could almost feel the juice in it, rich and ripe, bursting against the red-and-green speckled skin. It made his mouth water, his tongue itch to taste it. "What kind of apple is this?" he asked, but the old woman had disappeared. The dog whined and woofed heavily. Eoch took off, forcing him to run to catch up with her. He tucked the apple into his bag and ran.

They rounded a bend in the road, and he could've sworn the sun was suddenly on the other side of the sky. The countryside was distinctly different, too, from the broad meadow land through which they'd journeyed—the road steeper, rockier. From somewhere nearby, he heard the splash of water and looked down and saw a brook tumbling down the side. He looked back and realized he was looking back at an entirely different landscape. The forests rose all around them, dark and forbidding in the twilight. The gently rolling hills, the warm light, was gone.

In the sky, the first stars were beginning to twinkle. He had the feeling he'd rushed not only through space, but time, as well. He slid off Eoch and looked around. The white dog ran back and forth, whining. Beside him Eoch whinnied, nosed his neck. Her soft nose, the barest edge of her teeth grazed his skin, her hot breath blasted down his back, grounding him as his head spun and the fog rushed in around him like a cloak. A curious light was gleaming over the hills, a pure white radiance that glowed like a pearl above the treetops. He had never seen anything like it before. He wondered where he was and how he'd got here and if perhaps, ahead lay Ardagh.

"Is that it, boy?" he said to the dog. "Is that Ardagh up ahead?"

The dog only barked joyously and ran off down the road. Eoch neighed and took off after him at breakneck speed, forcing Cwynn to jump on and cling to the reins as best he could.

The buildings of the White Birch Grove were just visible through the trees when Timias stepped across the twilit border from Faerie into Shadow and frowned at what he sensed. He could feel his shape shifting, feel flesh settling around his frame like a slightly different suit of clothes. You don't pretend to be a mortal—you become one. *Just like you became a goblin. What would Finnavar think of that?* Never mind what she'd think, or Auberon, or even Loriana, he thought as he steadied himself beneath a tree. He wasn't sure what he thought or felt about it. The flesh felt slippery on his bones, like an unfamiliar set of clothing.

He looked down at himself. He was still naked. If he could get into the laundry, he might have a chance of filching some clothing, but without so much as a cloak, he had little hope of blending in enough to slip through even a side gate. Then he saw that there were people all around the gates, and camped on either side of the road. What was going on? he wondered as he eased as quietly as possible through the underbrush. For the most part, they appeared to be farmers and shepherds, all members of the local clans. Then he re-membered the mortals the goblins had been feasting on and realized that these people fled either rumored or real attacks.

An unattended wagon yielded tunic, plaid and trews.

Timias finished tying a makeshift belt around his waist when he heard the voice clearly for the very first time. *Father.* Timias jerked up and looked around. It was as faint as the brush of a butterfly's wing, fragile as the tip of a dragonfly's tail, yet compelling as the bleating of a new lamb. *Father... Father...Father, are you coming?*

Mesmerized, Timias turned in the direction of the Tor, away from the buildings and the people.

*Father?* The voice came again, this time tinged with joy.

*You know me,* Timias thought. His heart began to pound against his mortal chest as a rush of exultation so pure it took his breath away surged through him.

*Father!*

Timias felt dizzy. He reached out, grabbed the nearest tree and sank to the ground. The ground beneath him felt as if it were tingling, sending up pins and needles into his spine. Was it possible the magic he and Deirdre made had created a child? A child conceived as the cloak of shadows was woven? Amazed and overwhelmed, Timias fell back against the trunk.

*I'm mortal,* he thought, raising his hands before his face, examining the broken, dirty nails, the newly forming scab across his knuckles, the red bump of an insect bite. Mortals and sidhe can't mate. He touched his cheeks, felt the rough prickle of his beard. So what was he? he wondered once again. What kind of creature was he? Goblin, mortal or sidhe? Or some strange hybrid of them all, all of them and none of them? *But I have a child,* he thought. *I have a child. A child, who knows me.* Cautiously, lest he overwhelm the infant consciousness, he tried to send an answer out as a test. *Child?*

Faster than a hawk plummeting from the sky, a response returned, at once joyous and demanding, echoing in his skull like the ringing of a great bell. *Here…here…here. HERE.*

This was the last thing he'd expected. There was a child, he thought, his mind twirling and spinning, even as he set off in the direction of the Tor, forgetting the mortal and the horse, stunned to realize that the magic had created life. He and Deirdre, in the coupling that created the cloak, had conceived a child. The druids and the sidhe coupled on the hillsides and in the green-wood had never conceived children of each other. While he and Deirdre…had done not only the unthinkable, but the impossible.

Finnavar, may she burn in the belly of the Hag, was right. He wasn't really like the other sidhe—he wasn't like other mortals. But for the first time, he didn't care. An image filled his mind, claustrophobic, hot and wet, and he felt the weight of ages worth of dirt pressing in all around him. *HERE, FATHER…. HELP… HERE!*

The plaintive cry galvanized him, breaking through the shock. He took off in the direction of the Tor, ready to confront whatever threatened his child.

9

"This is it," Catrione whispered. The air within the still-house was stifling as the four women huddled over the birch-bark scrolls, trying to make sense of the etched glyphs. "The child who can't be slain by the hand of woman or of man…" She ran her finger along the line. "Once in every full revolution of the Wheel…the last child is born to the Mother and Herne heralding a period of confusion and discord and turmoil, until the child…" Her voice trailed off. "The rest… The scratchings are so faint. This isn't the symbol for death."

"Isn't that the symbol for balance?" asked Sora.

"That would fit the general sense of it," said Baeve. She looked around. "I'd say I'm ready for some balance in the midst of all this chaos."

Catrione scanned the bark scrolls. "Ah. Maybe it's this. Every time the Great Wheel turns, everything gets shaken up again, like pieces of a puzzle. When the pieces spill out, how they land is how they are. In other words, if we're not careful, every time this happens, there's always a chance the goblins could end up in control." She tapped her finger on the bark and a piece cracked beneath her nail. "Oh!" she cried.

"Careful, they're that fragile," said Bride, shaking her head. "Why don't the khouri-keen know this?"

"This suggests that we're not powerless—we can choose one thing over another, depending on what we're willing to give up…what we're willing to risk." She peered down at the bark, wondering what that might mean for each of them. Deirdre risked everything, willingly, and had paid a terrible price, was paying it still. *It could've been me,* she thought. *Or Sora, or any of us, really.* She looked down at the scroll again, but there was nothing more. "Part's missing. See here how it ends and then— nothing? This next one's about mead-making."

"But what about this child? This child that can't be killed by the hand of woman or of man?" asked Baeve. "Clearly it can't be part of anything good—isn't there anything we can do?"

"Well, there is something," whispered Sora. "I wanted to show it to you, Catrione, because when you came in, it was the first thing I thought of. This part—this part here—" She fumbled through the fragile scrolls. "This part speaks of following the trees into the ground—through the roots. Some say the ancient druids were able to travel this way across great distances, otherwise impossible."

"And how're we to do it?" sniffed Bride.

"It describes the way." Sora handed Catrione a scroll. "I've always wanted to try it, but I was afraid."

Catrione raised her eyes to the others. "Maybe Deirdre wasn't afraid. Maybe this explains how she was able to move in and out and up to the Tor."

"Tiermuid was in here a lot," Sora whispered. Her face flushed deep scarlet. "Maybe I should've told you before."

"He was? When?" Bride began to sputter. "You never said a—"

"Hush now," Baeve said, patting the other woman's hand. "Everyone is free to read them."

"But no one ever does. Didn't it occur to you, child, there was something strange about that?"

Sora hung her head, twisting her hands together miserably.

*He had her under his spell, too. Maybe it was all of us—not just me, not just Deirdre. Maybe all of us were affected.* Something twisted in Catrione's gut, like a snake coiling and uncoiling. She stood up and patted Sora's hands. "What does it matter, now, Bride? Who knows what he thought he was doing, or why he was doing it. Come, let's see if there's something in this scroll we can put to use. Maybe we can get inside the Tor, see what's going on, and try to figure out how to get the khouri-crystals back. It doesn't matter now, Sora, what you did or didn't do, or who you didn't tell. Let's just hope that anything Deirdre or Tiermuid understood enough to use, we can, too."

The white dog raced across the meadow, heading directly for the line of trees that ringed the lower level of the Tor. It rose above the treetops, the highest peak for leagues and leagues, topped by the double circle of standing stones. Cwynn squinted into the gathering twilight. He had no idea where he was but he was quite sure the community built beside the Tor wasn't Ardagh. He had no idea how close he was to Ardagh, or even how far he'd traveled that day. For a moment, he was tempted to take the road that led to the main gates of the community. But the dog was so insistent, stopping and barking at him every few moments, making it clear he was expected to follow, and Eoch seemed to have no will to obey him, even when he tugged at the reins a few times. She whinnied and knickered and flatly refused.

*All right, all right,* he thought, and relaxed into the saddle, letting the horse have her way. *But where in the name of Herne are you taking me?* A footpath wound up the Tor, but he could also see shallow steps, cut into the turf and reinforced with stones and wooden beams. They led directly to what looked like a hollow. The shadows were long; it looked like a navel set into the hill. The white dog paused halfway up the steps, ears alert, hackles raised. Cwynn frowned. He had reached the base of the Tor. The trees were all white birches. He swung out of the saddle and tied the reins to one of them. "You stay down here," he told her. He patted her on the neck and her liquid eye found his in the dusk.

He followed the dog up the steps, hand on the hilt of his dagger, surveying the scene that spread out below him. The leafy crown of trees gave way to a partial view of the thatched roofs of the druid community that clustered near the base, chimneys that drifted white smoke and the smells of cooking oats. The place seemed bustling with activity and suddenly, with an unexpected pang, he thought of home, of Argael and Ariene and the dish of buttery clams. His mouth watered and the dog growled.

Cwynn looked up. The dog seemed on full alert, its tail low and tense, ears back. Cwynn looked around, but the Tor appeared deserted. *Everyone's at dinner,* he thought, and his stomach rumbled again. The dog growled. The sky overhead was turning deep purple. The stars were beginning to shine. Cwynn paused and surveyed the trees, but nothing seemed to move beneath or within their branches. "I don't think there's anything there, boy, but Eoch." He looked over his shoulder at the dog. The dog was at the top of the Tor, wagging its tail, pawing at the ground. "How do you do that?" he asked aloud. But he knew he wasn't getting any answer. He bounded up the rest of the stone steps.

A lot of feet had tramped up and down the Tor that day, he thought, for there were gouges in the thick turf and places that appeared as if someone had tried to dig shallow holes. He paused, considering the dimple in the Tor. It was filled in with rocks, through which he got a whiff of something rotten. The dog woofed once.

"I'm coming," Cwynn answered. The ground shuddered, as if an enormous beast beneath the ground turned over in its sleep. He lost his footing on the steps and fell to his knees and then on to his face, and his hook sank deep into the soft turf. The dog was growling, hackles raised, pawing at the ground above him. There was something coming, thought Cwynn, something the dog's afraid of. It took him a moment to wrestle his hook out of the grass. The sky was darker now, the last lavender fading in the west.

The dog was a white blur. Cwynn scrambled up as quickly as he could, cursing the uneven holes, the rough patches, that made for difficult footing in the dark. By the time he reached the summit, he was covered from his hips down in smears of mud and bits of grass. The dog was behind the farthest stone, he saw, frantically pawing at the ground.

When Cwynn bent to examine what the dog was digging at, he saw a rusted iron ring. Further clearing of the sod revealed rotted wooden slats. "It's a door, isn't it?" he muttered to the dog, who was clearly patrolling the top of the Tor, whining and prancing.

Cwynn bent and tried to pull it up. He peered through the rotting slats, wishing he had some sort of light. A foul odor drifted up, the same as that which seeped through the rocks on the other side. As he tried to push aside a piece of wood, it crumbled in his hand. The dog threw back its head and howled. "You want me to go down there, boy, don't you?"

The dog was beside him, nudging him, nosing him, whining and licking his hand, his arm, any part of Cwynn he could touch. With a sigh, Cwynn shattered the rotted wood. It crumbled and split and splintered. A shallow set of steps led down. "Down there, eh?" The miasma sifting up gagged him. It was impossible to see how far down the steps led. "Let's see if there's another way, boy." But the dog butted up against his legs, surprising him, so that he lost his footing and tumbled down the slippery stone steps. His eyes slowly adjusted but the shadows were so thick it was nearly impossible to see anything at all. From the top of the steps, the dog woofed twice.

"I'm fine." Cwynn picked himself up. His hook was stuck once again, this time between two stones, and the leather straps that held it in place were caught on a jagged piece of rock. "Hey, aren't you coming down here, too?" The dog turned its back deliberately and growled at something—or someone—Cwynn couldn't see. Cwynn wrenched his hook into place, wondering what he was doing here and how he was getting out. From above, the dog growled menacingly. The putrid stench was growing stronger all around him. He thought he heard a noise, like a groan, and the earth seemed to shift all around him. He squinted into the dark.

A thousand eyes looked back.

Cwynn gasped, then eased forward. There had to be hundreds of scrawny, skinny creatures, with huge ears and eyes, all whispering, all centered around something that lay in the center of the open space. It had a bald spotted head, and the eyes that turned to stare at him might have been human, but they burned with an unnatural light, like an animal's, in the gloom. It's belly was enormously distended. The thing opened its mouth and the ground beneath his feet vibrated to the low moan that issued from its mouth. The creatures chattered like locusts. The thing shrieked, and two arms flailed, and Cwynn saw, to his disgust, that they ended in two small human hands. "Help me," it…she…mouthed.

But Cwynn couldn't move. He stood there, as with a jerk and the sound of wet cloth rending, the creature's midsection began to rip apart. Something white and wet as a maggot squirmed out. It had a sectioned body that ended in a double-pointed tail. With feet, he noticed. Human feet. Ten toes. It had nubs for arms, too, that ended in perfect little hands, just below its head.

Two huge eyes swiveled around and fixed on Cwynn where he stood, scarcely able to comprehend what he witnessed. From the other side of the room, he heard a hiss, and a snake raised its head. The writhing creature looked up at him with human eyes, and its rosebud mouth opened, but not in a newborn's cry. "You're not Father," it hissed.

"You're not a thing meant to live," Cwynn replied without thinking. He raised his hook and with one fast swipe, buried it in the thing's chest, ripping the wriggling body almost in two as he gutted it, like a fish. Green and purple slime spilled out, drenching him, but the creature's eyes burned into his, fixing.

The rocks all around began to shift and from far away, he heard the dog begin to howl. The rocks tumbled, a mass of boulders to the side and in the round entrance, Cwynn saw a figure outlined, a figure that was tall and seemed to have a goblin's tail. "I'll kill you, mortal," it cried, as it leaped at Cwynn.

Blinded by the image of the maggot-thing's eyes seared into his, Cwynn tried to turn and run. But his forehead collided with a wooden beam, and the world went black as he felt two hands close around his neck.

Catrione closed her eyes as she leaned against the white birch that gave the Grove its name. The bark was smooth and green against her skin, the saturated ground chilly. She felt the familiar uncoiling of energy deep in her belly as her power woke in anticipation of the magical work. But this wasn't quite like anything else she'd attempted. According to what Sara could discern, she was going to give herself— body, mind, spirit and heart—to the tree.

She tasted sweat as she drew the heavy air into her lungs. Tingling spread down her spine, down her arms, down her legs as she pressed her back against the tree. The cold sank deep in the sinews under her skin, turning her bones to long lengths of lead. *By Alder, Ash and Aspen Trees, Birch and Beech and Rowan three. Hazel, Holly, Elder, Vine, Yew and Apple, Oak to bind…* The names of the trees spooled out unbidden. She leaned her head against the trunk, felt her hair tumble down her naked back. She drew her knees up to her chest, wrapped her arms around her legs. She could feel Sora and Baeve and Bride, all breathing, all chanting.

She felt a tremor in the tree and felt something reach up, through the ground, into her tail bone, a jolt of energy so intense she gasped. Her eyes popped open. She wasn't in the Grove any longer. The light was an even gray. All around her, the forest rose, arching branches intertwined so far above her head she could not see the sky. She realized abruptly she had somehow changed form. Her elongated body moved across the leaf-encrusted floor like a wave's over water. The flash of a too-large mouse across her too-low field of vision and the forked flick of a black tongue confirmed her suspicion. She was a snake.

A tremor of revulsion shot through her. She forced herself to focus on her own breath, to look through Snake's eyes and hear with Snake's ears. This was too easy. *I didn't do this on my own,* she thought, struggling to retain her human command of language. *I am the adder of the mountain, the serpent of the river.* As Snake, she could pass both goblin and sidhe without any fear at all and she could go places she could not in human form. With a final sigh, she surrendered herself and all her senses to the sinuous motion of Snake.

She flowed across brush and leaves and fallen logs as gracefully as a dark, meandering stream. A crevice at a fork in the roots of a huge tree beckoned and as she moved closer, she saw that the tree was an oak, for the ground around it was littered with acorns.

*Eat one.* The idea was not so much a thought as a command that came from somewhere outside herself.

Experimentally, Catrione licked one and a sensation exploded along the length of her entire body, something that included the scent and taste and smell of the leafy loam, as well as something else so alien and strange to her human perceptions she had no words to give it. She could only allow it to move over and through her. The opening gaped seductively as she swallowed the acorn.

Even as Snake, Catrione hesitated to enter the black crevice, for she hated dark confined places. But Snake's consciousness was strong in her now, the acorn burning a trail down the inside of her throat that seemed to extend all the way to her tail. She found herself nosing into a moist world she'd never imagined. The roots of the tree scratched pleasantly all down the long length of her spine, the dirt was drier and spongier and warmer than the chillier air. The warmth invigorated her, and she plunged deeper and deeper, giving herself up to the transformation, allowing it to overtake her in a way she'd never experienced before. *Show me,* she thought, with the last of language. *Show me what I need to know. Show me what I need to see.*

Snake delved on, nosing through the soil as the scent of moisture intensified and the low vibration in the soil increased. She had reached an underground stream. Hissing, she followed the stream bed deeper into the subterranean night.

The atmosphere turned heavy and oppressive, even as the sense of crushing weight above and around her eased. Catrione probed the air with her forked tongue, and information began to pour in, settling into the crevices of her skin, sinking into Snake's spine like molten metal poured directly onto living flesh. She was in an open space now, black as pitch. She sensed, rather than saw, the beating of what felt like hundreds of hearts beating all together, against which two others beat in separate counterpoint.

One sound was a slow tortured throb accompanied by a harsh rasp. The other sounded like a galloping horse, and the pounding had a meaning, evocative as distant thunder and as vague. *Faah-THER...Faah-THER...Faah-THER...* A face, a human face with bright blue eyes locked into hers and she was swept into a swirling pattern of gray and blue and green and yellow. The colors wound around her in double helix patterns and she realized each color had shape and texture—that gray was slippery and fluid as silk, that yellow was jagged and itched like wool. Green curled in on itself like parsley, and blue rippled like feathered fronds. *There's a man you are to marry. This was the man.*

*How can this be what I need to know or see?* she thought, horrified. The shock of it wrenched her out and down, into a dark well of black, where soft voices echoed over and over: *Come back, druid. Come back, druid.* But the words didn't seem to mean anything and Catrione was content to float.

*Catrione. Wake up, Catrione, wake up.* As if from very far away, Catrione heard her name being called. *Wake up, Catrione.* "Wake up, Catrione, wake up."

Catrione opened her eyes, flicked her tongue across her bottom lip. She was lying on her side, curled around the tree, her feet practically touching the top of her head. Someone touched her legs and she reacted like a serpent, hissing, writhing. A papery hand slapped her cheek gently, and a woman with faded eyes looked deep into hers. Sunlight poured down through the branches. It was clearly no longer evening. And then Catrione realized the screams she heard were coming from her own mouth.

Timias had not expected the white dog. It confronted him halfway up the Tor, ears back, tail low, teeth exposed in a steady snarl. The animal was clearly intent on preventing him from moving any higher. He grabbed a long stick and tried to beat it out of the way, but the dog was too fast. He rushed it behind a leafy branch, even as the Voice increased in intensity.

*FA-THER…FA-THER…FA-THER…HELP HELP…*

In desperation, Timias rushed at the animal, and thought he might've passed through it. But he had no time to consider whether or not he actually had, for the Voice was screaming now, a high-pitched wordless cry. He bolted up the Tor, undeterred by the dog who followed, nipping at his heels.

The rocks blocking the entrance of the SunBirth Chamber tumbled as he approached and he heard the chittering of a hundred or more khouri-keen. Deidre must have all the trixies in the grove up here, he thought as he ducked his head, coughing and choking in the smothering dust. The khouri-keen's eyes reflected green and the sound rose hysterically.

In the center of the floor, something that looked like a giant husk or seed pod lay splayed, split down the middle. The tall figure bending over it turned, ichor dripping from the end of one arm, and Timias saw the thing that had been his child, the monster Deirdre had become. As the khouri-keen trembled and moaned, Timias cried out, "I'll kill you, mortal." He leaped for his throat, tried to run. He hit his head on the low ceiling. He went limp as Timias closed his hands around the mortal's neck, and gave it a hard wrench to be sure.

The wretched dog began to howl, long, wild yelps of alarm. The odor that rose from the corpses was worse than Macha's lair. Aghast, he edged forward. The moon had risen at last above the trees, and now streamed down into the newly exposed entrance. The thing that had been his child lay, white and round and ghastly as a filleted slug, staring up with vacant human eyes. The thing that had been Deirdre lay beneath it, her body like dry sheaves of paper. Outside, faint and far away, he heard shouts and cries in response to the dog. They were coming, he thought. And if they found him here... He glanced over his shoulder. He'd no doubt what they'd do if they found him here with this—these monsters.

The khouri-keen were creeping closer to the bodies, eyes bulging, hissing, reaching for them with outstretched hands. It disgusted Timias and he reached down, threw the nearest of the creatures as hard as he could against the chamber wall. "Leave them be!"

"The crystals," hissed the creatures, in wide-eyed unison. "Give us our crystals."

Timias looked down. So that's how she did it, he realized. He reached down, fumbled with the body. Beneath it, he found the leather pouch that held the crystals. The khouri-keen gasped and screamed and would've rushed on Timias, but he gave the bag a vicious shake and held it high above their reach. "Stay in your dens until I call you," he said, just as the tops of the first heads came up the Tor. He slipped down the opposite side of the Tor and disappeared over the border.

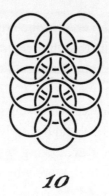

## 10

A blast of fresh air tickled the back of Bran's neck, ruffled his matted curls. He shifted gingerly in his hiding spot, trying not to disturb the ragged saddle blanket that covered him. The trixies had retreated to haunt the kitchens as the revel drew near, and the atmosphere within the busy forge was beginning to calm at last. This was the rare quiet hour, when the apprentices had finished their day's drudgery, and the masters took their ease among the Court. Every muscle in his body ached, from his neck all the way down his back across his shoulders and down his arms. He'd sneaked in here after seeing Morla. He couldn't bear the thought of any more of the backbreaking, unending work.

Morla was coming for him. He'd stay here, hidden, till she came, blessedly alone, blessedly unbedeviled. He huddled deeper into his straw-lined niche and willed himself invisible.

In the shadowy gloom, the purple light filtered through gaps in the overhang sheltering half the yard. Piles of equipment, stacked barrels and parked wagons blended and merged into the black forms of crouching goblins. He sighed and shut his eyes, and thus he felt, rather than saw, the change in the way the light glimmered over and around the empty yard.

For a moment, he froze, wondering if it were possible to cross the border into TirNa'lugh simply by sitting still, and then he dismissed that idea as being completely absurd. No one could get to TirNa'lugh merely by willing it.

Footsteps came around the corner, and several pairs of bony hairy legs crossed his line of vision as a gaggle of chattering apprentices shambled by on their way to their quarters and food. Bran dared another peek as they faded into the dusk, reassured that he remained firmly in the mortal world. A few stars twinkled overhead but the western sky was still streaked red and orange. He was settling into another position, this one less cramped, when he thought he heard the song. Faint and faraway as the stars, it teased his ears with a silvery ripple here, a soft trill there. A scent drifted beneath his nostrils, sweeter than roses, lighter than mist. Gooseflesh rose on his arms, and all his senses felt preternaturally aroused. The hair lifted on the top of his head, and he froze.

"Look, there she is—I told you I smelled her." It was a trixie voice, and Bran's eyes widened. Through a rip in the fabric, he peered as best he could, but his angle of vision was limited by the sides of the barrels, the wheels of the wagon.

"I see her."

"There she is."

"The Faerie-girl, the Faerie-girl…"

Bran froze as their rough little growls rose in a chorus that a less-sensitive mortal might have mistaken for croaking frogs. "Look, I see her—there, there—"

Bran peered up and around the pile of hay. The trixies had unerringly appeared to know where he was, for their backs were to him, and they filled all available perches as they confronted something apparently outside his line of vision.

"Take him, take him, Faerie-girl," some of the nasty little creatures were saying, "and take us, too. Take us, take us, too."

As if a candle had been extinguished, the light diminished, losing its opalescent glow. The trixies jumped and hissed and spit and waved their arms. One by one, then by twos and threes, they disappeared into the cracks of the paving stones, and Bran knew they'd gone after whatever had found him. He wondered if it were maybe the girl from the pool. He unfolded his cramped limbs and got to his feet, glancing cautiously all around. The smells of cooking meat and wafting bread made his mouth water. It was more likely he'd find Morla at the revel, he decided as hunger overwhelmed him.

Led by the scent, he found his way to the courtyard before the great hall. It was crowded, as usual, for it pleased Meeve to see her people eat. Bran hung around the edges, watching from the periphery as Meeve traded barbs with the ambassador, sending all those around her into paroxysms of laughter that rippled across the crowd. Some had already begun to dance to the tunes the fiddlers and the drummers were practicing. Goblets were being passed through the crowd, and he found one shoved in his hand by the very same serving girl who'd found him beneath the tree. As their eyes locked in surprised recognition, she laughed and pinched his cheek. "Drink up, blacksmith boy who's-not-a-scullion."

"I'm not a blacksmith, either," he retorted.

"You're way too scrawny to be much of anything at all." She turned and was lost in the press of the throng.

Bran gulped from the goblet. It was some dark red southern vintage, for he fancied he could taste the hot relentless sun, the tang of acrid soil. It made him a little dizzy, and he clutched the goblet until its rough surface dug into his palm. But there was another taste in it, too, and with a start, he realized that somehow, Meeve had made the sacred fountain flow red wine.

How is that possible? he wondered as he threaded his way through the throng to take a closer look. The wine was having a greater affect on him than he'd anticipated, for the ground appeared to be rising up to meet his feet, then falling away beneath his sole as he tried to lurch his way across the stones.

"Hey, now! Watch where you're grabbing!" A woman gave him a push and he stumbled back, reeling against the stone walls. Clinging to the wall for support, he eased around the periphery, edging closer to the fountain. *That's a sacred spring,* he thought. *Do they know what they're doing?*

Goblet after goblet, mug after mug, was filled and passed back, but as far as he could tell, no one else seemed as affected as he was. He sank to his haunches, feeling a cold sweat break out on his forehead. In desperation, he took another sip. Perhaps I need to eat, he thought, as he watched a basket of bread pass through the crowd. He set the goblet on the ground and stood up, biting his lip and clenching his fists. He managed to swipe a piece of cheese off a tray, then staggered back to the wall. But the food seemed to have no appeal for him, and the odour even nauseated him. *But I love this cheese,* he thought. The cheese of Eaven Morna was legendary, for the brine in which it was washed and the caves in which it was aged. But it was making him sick now, he thought, and he set it down beside the goblet and leaned his head back against the wall, watching through the crowd for Morla.

They were tossing coins into the pool now, he saw, as if from a very great distance and he wondered, as he watched, if that were truly a good idea. Nothing was supposed to fall into sacred springs, and nothing was to be tossed in without the proper blessing, the proper wards. Every child old enough to stand knew that. It was one of the first things drilled into every Brynnish child's head from the time he or she could toddle. Droplets from the spring splashed out, raised by something thrown in by a page who perched among the rocks. Bran frowned, for he could clearly see the trixies scurrying up and down the wet rocks, turning somersaults, even biting and pinching the hapless page's ears. The page couldn't see them of course, but he swatted at them anyway, cursing all blackflies to the belly of the Hag. Then he paused, his attention clearly diverted by something in the pool. "Look," he shouted, pointing down. "There's someone in there—there's someone looking back at me."

No one but Bran seemed to notice. Bran watched, dizzy, but fascinated, as the page lost his balance and toppled into the water, raising a wave of water that lapped the edges of the pool, raising little shrieks and growls of displeasure, bringing Meeve off the ambassador's lap.

The moon had risen, Bran noticed, as the crowd shifted and parted and moved in front of him, blending into a kaleidoscopic pattern that lacked all resemblance to any reality he'd ever experienced. He pushed his head back against the stones, hoping that the pain of the sharp edges digging into his scalp would help him stay grounded.

"Look, there *is* someone in there," cried a woman.

"Get the boy out," shouted another.

"There's no one in there," scoffed a third. "It's but a trick of the light."

"Nonsense," answered the first. "Didn't you see the splash?"

The voices rose and fell in an excited babble, separating and blending into subtle skeins of sound, forming harmonies that somehow matched the visions unfolding before his eyes, but had no resemblance to any language he understood. He found the goblet and gulped more wine, and in that moment, understood what he was drinking, what the foreign taste in the wine was—the water of the sacred spring.

The trixies danced like sparks against the swirling backdrop that in some rational corner of his mind he understood was unfolding in a quite normal fashion. He just had to wait until the effects of the water wore off. He took a deep breath, aware that the page was being dragged up and over the lip of the pool. Droplets landed on his cheek, cold and hard as disks of ice, sharp enough to flay open his skin. He wished with all his might some druid might materialize out of the mist.

But the next time he opened his eyes, he was lying on a mossy green bank beside a rock-lined pool and a girl with huge green eyes and long dark hair knelt over him. "Hello, boy."

He didn't just hear her words. He felt them, smelled them, propelled by the urgent pleading in her eyes. "W-who are you?" he whispered. Sweat broke out all over his body and he scuttled backward on all fours. "And where is this place?"

The girl smiled and looked up, where the sky was an impossibly cerulean blue. "This is Faerie. You call it TirNa'lugh."

"How'd I get here? And what happened to the trixies?"

"They'll come and find you, I suppose. But they don't much like water, so for a while, we're safe."

"If this is TirNa'lugh, what about the goblins?" Bran looked around. Part of him was frightened and apprehensive, but another part of him felt as if he'd been reborn, as if his blood had somehow turned to foam and was running through his veins in streams of light.

"Silly boy. We don't have to worry about them during the day." She leaned forward, smiling at him as if she'd like to eat him and Bran found himself both fascinated and repelled. "Is your name Bran?"

"How'd you know that?"

"My grandmother's been watching you. She says you're 'special.'"

"She does?" For some reason, he thought of Apple Aeffie in his dream.

"Oh, yes. I think you're special, too."

"Who are you?" he whispered, staring at her mouth. Her teeth were like even little pearls.

"My name's Loriana. I've been keeping watch on you while my grandmother looks for the druid who put the word on you."

He startled upright, moved a few inches back.

"The one that keeps the gremlins on you. Can't you feel it?"

Bran stopped.

He could, now that she mentioned it. "How do I get it off?"

"The druid who put it on you has to take it off."

"How do you know who did it?"

"Every druid had his own essence… We can sense it—we know it. I can feel yours on you."

"You—you can? No one else does?"

She moved a few inches closer, sinuous as a cat. "What can you expect from water-logged mortals?"

"Water-logged?" The term was so apt he burst out laughing. "That's exactly it, isn't it? And some are pretty muddy, too."

Her laughter joined with his as she moved to sit beside him, her shoulder close enough to touch his. He felt a ripple of gooseflesh spread across his body. "I know you're druid, but you're not quite…awake yet." She touched his face with the tips of her fingers, ran her hand down his cheek and through his hair.

"I'm not?"

She shook her head, leaned in close enough so that he felt her breath, warm and sweet on his face. "No," she whispered. "Not yet." She picked up his palm then traced the tip of his finger down the center of each of his. With each stroke he felt a line of fire drawn from his finger tip into the center of his palm.

*I can do magic,* he thought.

With a groan he reached for her as her mouth closed down on his, and a warm tide of pleasure surged through him. Her arms reached up, around his neck, drawing him down beside the pool, onto the thick green moss. His back touched the moss and sensations exploded up and down his spine, into his head, where images began to unspool of himself and Meeve and Morla. I see it, he thought as her tongue pushed against his, twining over and around. Colors exploded in his mind as sensation upon sensation cascaded through him.

"Here he is—look we found him—him and that Faerie girl!"

The shrieks and screeches seared like a brand into Bran's brain. What felt like a hundred tiny hands pried him loose and dragged him, writhing and screaming, back to the pool. They plunged into the depths, and Bran kicked and struggled as the water closed over his head, filled his nose and made him gag and choke and struggle. A murky orb of light filled his vision just before the world went dark.

The next thing he heard was his name. "Bran!" Morla shouted.

In a daze he rolled over flat on his back to stare up at the spider-webbed pile of barrels beside the fountain. Straw stabbed at his back. He was lying naked in a patch of yellow sunlight, and he judged it midmorning or later. He had never been so grateful to see anyone in his life, even though he was immediately embarrassed and it was clear she was furious.

"Look at you. Have you no shame?" She pressed her lips together and shook her head. She was wearing a new riding outfit, with a brand-new plaid and her boots had been polished to a high sheen. She put her hands on her hips. "What exactly were you doing last night, little brother? I looked for you at the forge and among the prentices, but no one had seen you since noon yesterday. No wonder they call you a lazy wastrel."

He looked down at himself and flushed, scrabbling back,

feeling frantically all around for his clothes. He couldn't remember how he'd come to shed his clothes. Or why.

"Have a go with the sidhe, did you, lad?" It was one of the grooms, leading yet another saddled horse with a saddle roll strapped to its back, and saddle bags on its flanks. His eyes danced.

Bran felt himself flush scarlet. "Morla, I've been in Tir-Na'lugh. Morla—" He grabbed for her hand. "Morla, you have to help me get back there. I can find out what to do— I think I see it—"

Morla shook her head, hands on her hips. He saw she was dressed for traveling, although Mochmorna's plaid and not her Dalraida's was knotted over her shoulder and held in place by an enormous copper brooch. "Go make yourself presentable. You're coming with me."

"Where we going?" Bran's heart leaped. Was it possible his mother had heard his agony at last? "Are we going to Ardagh?"

"Eventually. Aye. First we're going to Far Nearing."

She turned on her heel, but before she disappeared into the growing crowd, he called, "What's in Far Nearing?"

"Family," she replied, her voice swallowed by the stones, by the voices of the knights. "We've got a brother there named Cwynn."

"Family?" he repeated, stumbling into his breeches. A huge hand came down on the back of his neck, and he looked up to see Lochlan shaking his head.

"Go on now, Bran, get yourself into some semblance of order. No one's in a mood for nonsense—we'd hoped to be on the road hours ago."

Bran blinked. He sensed the man was implying he, Bran, was to blame, but he didn't understand why. "It's not my fault."

"It is your fault. You've had us looking for you since dawn. You've got to stop this running away, Bran," Lochlan answered. "This is no way to settle things, no way to get what you want. I'm not just telling you this for your own good, Bran. I'm telling you so you'll understand I'll have none of it on the road. I'm responsible for getting you safe to Ardagh. Do you understand me?"

Stunned, Bran could only stare. Lochlan stifled a curse. "What ails you, lad? You mazed?"

Bran nodded. What else could it be? Lochlan expelled a great sigh. "Go on, boy—go splash cold water on yourself. Tell Cook to give you something to eat. Are you all right?"

Bran nodded again. The feeling was diminishing rapidly, leaving him feeling hollow and light.

"Go on, then." Lochlan pushed him, but gently, and Bran felt a little comforted. He looked back over his shoulder and saw the big knight watching him until he rounded the corner.

On the road, Morla was still angry. Bran wasn't sure why, and he wasn't sure at whom, but he could feel the emotion emanating off her in waves of heat, burning around something she carried deep inside. It interfered with his recollections of all he'd experienced in TirNa'lugh.

He looked at her and remembered the message he was supposed to give her from her husband, but he didn't dare. He felt sick and weak, as if his skin were stretched tight as a drum over his bones, thin as a horn pane, brittle as a shell, as if his body were hollow and he might collapse upon himself. But he had to find a way back over the border.

Besides, although Morla answered his initial questions regarding their destination with a brusque "yes" or "no," once they reached the main road, she made it very clear she was in no mood for any kind of chatter. She especially ignored the Fiachna, who bantered back and forth between themselves and tried to include the two of them. She caught Bran, once or twice, eyeing her, and the second time, she snarled, "Get out of my head."

He jerked upright in the saddle, startled out of the reverie the horse's motion had lulled him into. He hadn't been in Morla's head—had he? He'd been thinking about her, that was true…but… He thought back, to the last few minutes or so, trying to remember what he'd been thinking.

"Get out of my head," she said again, and this time, she smacked his upper arm hard enough to sting.

*What is she talking about?* he thought in a moment of pure, sheer panic. I've no idea what I'm doing. His pulse began to race and he found he had to concentrate very hard on his breathing. He felt too…too thin, somehow, as if his skin were as fragile as a butterfly's wings. He glanced at Morla, wishing he were young enough to fling himself into her arms and bury his head on her shoulder as he remembered doing when he was small. Morla immediately turned her head and glared at him. He cringed, glanced away, jerked on the reins accidentally and the horse tossed its head in objection. *What's wrong with me?* The back of his throat felt dry, his head was spinning, he felt hollow and weak. He glanced at Lochlan, who met his eyes and said mildly, "Anyone give you anything to eat?"

Bran looked up at the big knight. "Bread and honey before we left."

"That's not enough." The knight reached behind his saddle and rummaged around in his saddlebag. Finally he held out a little wrinkled apple. "Here. Eat this. You look like you're about to blow away. Most find they've a prodigious appetite after a round with a sidhe."

Bran accepted the apple gingerly, hesitant to bite into it. It was from last year's harvest, a hard, pathetically shriveled thing, its flesh like leathery pulp. But its concentrated sweetness exploded on his tongue, thick and rich and nourishing, and before he knew it, he was licking at the core. "It wasn't like anything else—"

"More or less like a dream than the other night on the road?" Lochlan stared straight ahead with a frown as if he didn't like what he was seeing.

"Both." Bran licked each finger in turn. "I wish Mam hadn't sent all the druids away. Why'd she do it, Lochlan? Why'd she not at least leave one for me? I need to get back there, Lochlan. I need to talk to that sidhe I met there, the one who pulled me in. There're things she showed me, things I know—"

Lochlan held up his hand. "There's a druid-house not far up the road. We'll stop there. Maybe someone there can help you, Bran." He dropped his eyes, then said, "Your mother's got a lot on her mind these days." Lochlan shut his mouth, just as Bran sensed his mind slide over something, something Lochlan didn't want Bran to know. He glanced over at Murdo. "You got any salt meat in that saddle bag of yourn?"

Silently, Murdo handed over a strip and it was all Bran could do not to cram the entire thing down his gullet in two enormous bites.

"Don't choke now, boy," said Lochlan. "There's a Grove a few leagues ahead, maybe another three or four turns of a short glass. You can hang in till then, can't you, boy? Sure you can. Chew the salt meat nice and slow. It'll give you something to hang on to, like."

"See, it's not the crossing in that's hard, lad," put in Murdo unexpectedly. "It's getting out. We've all of us been there, one way or another."

"You have?" Bran glanced at from knight to knight. "Why?"

"The druids take you there to heal, if you're lucky."

"That's what's kept you alive, isn't it, Murdo?" Urien hooted. "You're lucky."

"Better lucky than pretty," Murdo retorted as Lochlan guffawed.

Bran grinned then glanced at Morla. She was riding a few paces ahead of everyone else, shoulders rigid. He remembered when he was very young talking about the beautiful people who came and watched him sleep. He remembered laughing at the antics of the trixies chasing each other behind the walls. Morla had believed him, he'd always thought. Now he wasn't so sure. Maybe she'd only been pretending. No one else had known they were there. He remembered a few times laughing aloud at things no one else in the room could see. Only Athair Eamus seemed to understand. But all his other experiences were as much like this one as the lick of candle-flame to a Beltane bonfire. The sidhe had kindled it, and now the heat made his teeth itch, his skin tingle. He could feel colors and see feelings.

Morla's anger was like a hot simmering pot on the back of a fire, the kind that was easy to forget about, easy for others to ignore, the kind that could explode unexpectedly—like the kettle that had blinded his old nurse. "Morla?" he ventured. When she looked at him, he said, "Why are we going to Far Nearing?"

She glanced from Lochlan to Murdo. "To get our brother, Cwynn. Don't you remember? I explained all this before."

Fog swirled through his head, clogging his ability to string thoughts and words together into coherent sentences and forms. As he tried to find the words to tell her that no, he really didn't remember, Lochlan cantered up to Morla on the other side and touched her forearm fleetingly. "Will you ride up a ways ahead with me?"

"For what?" asked Morla as Bran struggled to express himself. But the expression on her face stopped the words in his throat, as did the unmistakable shimmer of a silver cord that appeared to bind itself around the two of them. They'd been bound since birth, he realized, in a sudden flash of insight so intense he didn't think to question how he knew.

"To speak about the journey." Lochlan's jaw was tight, and his shoulders and rigid back conveyed a volume more than the short words.

Morla turned a wary eye on Bran. "Are you all right?"

A pale pink light appeared to flow from behind her, toward him, enveloping him in a gentle sensation that inexplicably soothed him. "I'm fine," he managed. "You go on. Talk to Lochlan."

With a wary look, Morla jogged on ahead after Lochlan, leaving Bran to stare in awe at the fountaining rainbow of emotions that blazed ever brighter the closer she got to the big knight.

"Now what? What's wrong?" Morla caught up with Lochlan and hoped her face did not change as their eyes met. Every time she looked at him, she saw one of two things— his naked body in Meeve's bed and the look on his face as Meeve led him away that long-ago Beltane.

"Nothing's wrong. I wanted to talk to you about Bran."

"My mother said he's been causing trouble." Morla glanced over her shoulder. Bran didn't seem to notice. He was cramming the last of the salt meat in his mouth, and Urien was handing over another apple. "Great Herne, he's eating like he's never seen food before. What ails him?"

"He's been in TirNa'lugh," replied Lochlan. "Or so close to it, he might as well have been there. Haven't you ever noticed how hungry the druids all are after they come out of there?"

"I don't have much to do with druids." Morla raised her chin. Rituals were fine for those who fed regularly, but nothing the druids did seemed to affect the blight anywhere as far as she could see. "There've not been any in Dalraida since…" The last Beltane before the fever took Fionn, she thought. She remembered how proud he'd been of the bower he'd made—for her, of course, since there was no question of her choosing anyone else. She was too aware of how he'd feel if she chose another.

"Well, I have, and it leaves you famished. Every time I've

come out of there, I've felt like a whole ox would only make a good start."

Morla looked at him in surprise. "I didn't know druids called on warriors that often."

"They don't as a rule," Lochlan answered. "But if you're wounded, they take you there to heal, if you're lucky."

"If you're lucky?"

"If you're lucky." He gazed into the distance, smiling wistfully. "With a druid to guide you in and out, TirNa'lugh's a wonderful place—a place of light and rest and healing. But it takes something from them." He glanced back over his shoulder. "I think that's what ails him."

"What makes you so sure he's really druid?"

"Maybe you've not heard. When I was bringing him from Pentland to Eavan Morna, he led us right into TirNa'lugh, easy as a knife cutting through soft cheese. You wouldn't even think the border had been there. He may not look like a druid, but both Athair Eamus and Cailleach Connla told me to watch him."

She looked at him steadily, wondering if he told the truth. He had no reason to lie. "If you were really there, how'd you get out?"

"I told him to ride for home, to ride to Meeve. Gave him something to hook on to, I suppose, for he had us at the gates of Eavan Morna in less than a blink of an eye. Connla warned Meeve before she left, but all Meeve would do is agree to have him watched. And she set him in the smithy because Connla told her hard work would be good for him."

"Why's my mother so angry at the druids? Because she's dying, and they can't help her?"

"She told you, then, did she?"

Morla glanced over her shoulder again. "You don't think Bran knows?"

"No one knows, but you and me. And Connla, because she guessed."

"And Briecru."

"Really?" That seemed to get his attention in an entirely new way, for suddenly he turned and looked at her.

"That's not surprising, is it?"

He didn't answer her at once. "No, it's not. But I'm sure she's not yet told the boy."

"And you're saying we shouldn't, either?"

"Well, what do you think?" Lochlan glanced over his shoulder and nodded at Morla to do the same.

Bran was staring at some point just above his head, his mouth slightly open, his eyes wide. "Look at him," Morla murmured. "He looks completely mazed. Why didn't Mam let Connla have him?"

"She blames Connla for the blight, among other things. And considering what's happened to Deirdre, your mother was loathe to hand over another child, I suppose."

"Is that really how she sees it?" Morla could not keep the bitterness out of her tone, and Lochlan raised his brow.

"What are you insinuating, Morla?"

"My mother keeps a very grand style, Lochlan." Morla stared straight ahead. "The blight's hit Dalraida hard." She glanced at him sideways. "But she throws gold and copper and silver around like trinkets, and kills cattle on a whim. I walked in past a spread that would've fed a family in Dalraida for a week. And it wasn't even dinner."

"She's been entertaining the ambassador," Lochlan said.

"If you think anyone outside a day's ride of Eaven Morna eats like that, you're mazed as my brother." The expression he'd worn as her mother claimed him on that long-ago Beltane flashed before Morla as their eyes met and she felt a pang in her gut. She looked back over her shoulder at the other three knights, Urien, Murdo and Ongus. Her mother had plenty of everything. Why had she chosen Lochlan, the one in all of Eaven Morna Morla had considered a friend? For the first time, it occurred to Morla that Meeve had had a motive. But all she could bring herself to say was, "Maybe we should send Bran on to Ardagh."

"That's what I was thinking."

Their eyes met and Morla felt that shock of connection she'd always felt with him. Fleetingly Morla wondered what might have happened if he'd gone with her that night instead. "What do you suggest? Divide in two groups?" She wondered why the thought of being separated from him seemed to open a hole in her gut.

"I say we go to Ardagh first—take Bran to Connla, and then go on to Far Nearing. I just don't like the idea of dragging him all over the country. There's too many opportunities for—for accidents."

"Why don't you just take him to Ardagh and I'll go to Far Nearing?"

"I can't do that," he replied.

"Why not?"

"I swore to Meeve I'd see you safely to Far Nearing and back. I can't let either of you out of my sight." He looked directly at her.

How commendable. She bit the sarcasm back as their eyes met. Heat surged through her, forcing her to lower her eyes and look away as the breath caught in her throat. *What's wrong with me?* she wondered. I can't possibly still care. We were never more than friends and riding partners. She tightened her hands on her reins and forced herself to stare at the road ahead, as Lochlan continued, "We'll keep to the high roads— no shortcuts through dark valleys and such—and we'll stay at druid-houses as long as he's with us. That'll be safest for him, I think. And us. We don't want to find ourselves lost in the OtherWorld—Bran's not headed any place he knows."

"What do you mean?"

"In order to find your way out of TirNa'lugh, you have to have an anchor in this world—whether a trixie or another druid, or at least some very clear and potent desire to go someplace else. But even then, even then, the druids say, the chance you won't come out is still greater than the chance you will."

"You seem to know a lot about it."

Their eyes met and again, sensation fluttered through her. But he didn't answer, because Bran came riding up. "How much farther are we going before we stop?"

Morla glanced at Lochlan. "There's been a change of plans, Bran. In light of what Sir Lochlan tells me, it seems we're better off to stop at Ardagh first. We'll leave you with the druids, and—"

"Really, Morla?" To her amazement, his eyes brimmed with tears. "Really?"

"Yes, of course." Pity for him overwhelmed her. What was her mother thinking, to bring the boy away from all he knew, then to set him in the forge a full year before any other? If what everyone—but Meeve, apparently—suspected were true, he deserved to be treated far better than he'd been.

Lochlan reached across Morla and punched Bran gently on the shoulder. "Buck up, boy. Just three or four turns of a short glass, right?"

The others had somehow fallen behind and for the moment, the three of them were alone, Morla flanked by Bran on one side, and Lochlan on the other. Was this something like what Bran felt, she wondered, this constant, steady assault on her senses, so that she felt stretched and taut as a too-tight harp string? She was so aware of him she could smell the sweat steaming from his pores. She glanced at Lochlan. He was looking at her so intensely, she thought he might burn a hole through her.

She felt a little dizzy. To cover her confusion, she uncorked her water flask and took such a deep drink, the water spilled down her chin, down her neck and trickled between her breasts. She saw him glance down, then away. *You wanted me as much as I wanted you then. I know you did,* she thought.

*Why did you disappear afterwards?* she wanted to ask, but the words stopped in her mouth, dry as an old sponge washed up on the sand. She knew why he'd gone with Meeve, because of course, he had no choice. It was afterward, when he had nothing to do with her, that hurt. She had been too proud then to seek him out. She let go of the breath she hadn't realized she was holding. And now, more than ever, he was Meeve's.

The others trotted up and Bran whooped off. Lochlan

made a face, uttered an oath, and took off after him. "Oh, no, you don't, boy," he cried as he galloped after Bran. "You wait up there, you hear? We don't want you leading us—"

He broke off in midsentence, just as Morla and the others rounded the curve to see both Lochlan and Bran halted before what appeared to be the gatehouse of a druid grove.

"I didn't know the druid-house was quite so close," Ongus said as they reined in abruptly.

The knights exchanged glances and Bran nosed his horse up beside Morla.

"I don't remember this house even being here," said Urien.

Before anyone could answer, an old man doddered out of the gatehouse. He wore a filthy gray robe that might've once been white, and clutched a knobby staff. "Who're you?" he demanded, glaring first at Lochlan, and then at the rest in turn. "What d'you want?"

"Travelers, athair-da," Lochlan replied. "We're on our way to Far Nearing on Queen's business, and we've a young lad with us who's a bit mazed. He could use a druid—"

"There's no one here." The old man waved his staff in the direction of the road, and Bran had the distinct impression he could accidentally on purpose strike one of the horses. "You're best to keep going down the road, until you come to the lake. There's another house beside the lake. But you'd better hurry if you hope to make it there by dark."

"But what's happening here?" blurted out Bran. His face grew pale as he gazed at the walls, and Morla glanced up and down them herself. Ivy clung in heavy clumps to the wall. His breathing changed and he wrinkled his nose. "What's that smell?"

Morla sniffed. A smell vaguely dank, like laundry left damp too long, hung heavy in the still air.

"Something happened here—something's happening here now," Bran was insisting. He turned to Lochlan, voice high and pleading. "I can smell it—there's something happening here."

"Who told you anything happened here, boy?" demanded the old man. "Nothing's happened here. They all up and left."

"Where'd they go?" asked Murdo. He eased off his saddle, then shook the gates. He nudged Lochlan in the ribs as the old man waved his staff toward the road. Lochlan tried them himself, stepped away, looked up at the walls, clearly assessing.

"They went to Ardagh, of course—where else would they be? I think you all look a bit mazed." He squinted up at Bran. "Who're you, boy? I know your kind. I've seen your kind before. Didn't think there were any left, to tell you the truth."

"What do you mean, his kind?" asked Morla, nosing her horse forward, understanding the implicit threat in the way in which the old man waved his staff.

"You know, there's one thing I don't understand," Lochlan interrupted before the old man could answer. "If they all up and left, why are the gates bolted from within?"

"I don't think we should go in there," said Morla. "I know that smell." She glanced at each knight in turn. "That's blight. Isn't it, old man? This place should've been torched." She looked up at the walls, but they were so thickly covered with ivy they would not easily burn.

"You go on, all of you. Just leave." The old man turned away, shaking his head, muttering.

Bran's face was pale, his eyes huge. In the murky light, he

looked very young and very scared. She looked up, expecting to see clouds covering the sun, but the sky was mostly clear. Still, she could've sworn the light had darkened just as they'd approached the gatehouse. She shifted uneasily in her saddle. She couldn't see anything, couldn't hear anything, but something was telling her to put her heels to her horse and ride as far and as fast as the beast would carry her.

"They're still in there," whispered Bran. He tilted his head. The knights glanced at each other, and Bran looked back over his shoulder at each of them in turn. "They've been in there since it started. Can't you hear them?"

Morla slapped her gloves against her hands. "Listen to me. I know this smell. It's blight. If the druids barred themselves inside, they did it for a reason. We should send help back, but—" She broke off.

"I can hear them in there, and they're screaming for help, Morla," Bran whispered. Sweat was rolling down the sides of his face in great drops. "Please?"

Morla bit back a curse.

"The gates are barred from the inside, my lady." Murdo rattled the gates. "See? There has to be someone inside."

The old man limped forward, clinging to his staff, his bulbous nose and grizzled cheeks flushed nearly purple. "Here now, don't be doing that. The callies and a'dares don't want any folk disturbing the Grove whilst they're gone—"

"They're not gone—I can hear them calling," Bran said again.

*When was the last time you had a man?* The thought intruded out of nowhere and Morla blinked. Beltane last, she thought, and suddenly it was that Beltane so very long ago and she was watching Lochlan as Meeve led him out of the wall, a look of triumph on her face. The memory stabbed through her, made her gasp, so that Lochlan looked at her strangely.

*What's wrong with me?* she wondered. And then she remembered. The blight didn't just kill your body. It affected the mind. Suddenly everywhere she looked she saw a pair of strong shoulders, muscled thighs, a broad back. "We have to leave. You all don't understand. It's playing tricks on us, it makes us think things are there that aren't." She planted herself in front of the gates. "Come on, all of you. We'll send help back. But there's nothing we can do here."

Bran was staring at the gates, his fists balled. He stumbled a little as he reached the ground, eyes fixed on the gates as if he would burn his way in. Sweat beaded his forehead and pearled above his upper lip. "Please, oh, please," he was murmuring, and she realized with a chill he was repeating what he heard. "We are wanted, Morla, oh, we are. They're calling out to us. Please, Lochlan, Murdo—"

"I hear it, too," put in Murdo.

"Bran, you have to believe me—" she began, but before she could protest further, the knights moved quickly.

The old man waved his staff and cried, "Those gates are warded—"

But the wood was rotted and any ward placed on the gates had rotted along with the wood. The blades cut through the iron bar on the inside like knives through soft butter. They kicked and pushed the splintered gates aside.

Morla put a hand on Bran's arm. "Look, Bran, I know you

can see and hear things the rest of us can't, but I've seen blight and I know how dangerous it is."

"Morla, they're in some kind of trouble. How we can leave them in there?" Bran's face was white. "You wait here if you want."

Lochlan met Morla's eyes, and in spite of her fear, she noticed at once how blue his eyes were, how the hair curled at his nape and the strong cords in his neck ran from chin to chest. *It's the blight*, she thought. *It's only the blight. When was the last time you lay with a man?* She felt sweat run down her back, down her sides and he said, "We'll be right back."

The old man shook his head, muttering, and Morla turned to him. "How long ago did they bolt themselves in?" Morla asked. "And what did you mean when you said my brother was one of them? One of who? A druid?"

The old man paused and met her eyes. "Of course he's druid. Any fool could see that. I mean he's a rogue druid. He's got that written all over him, too."

"What do you mean, a rogue druid? What's that?"

The old man rolled his eyes. "They don't teach anyone anything anymore, do they?"

From inside the court, she heard the unmistakable sounds of retching, and she didn't wait for the old man to finish his answer. She sped into the courtyard to see Bran on his knees, vomiting on the cobblestones. Dust lay on abandoned items, spiders' webs were thick in corners and the place smelled like moldy laundry. "Bran? Are you all right?" She whipped a small flask off her hip and pulled the cork off, then dampened a linen square. She waited till he finished retching, then handed it to him. "Here." She looked at Lochlan, which was difficult, for the intense blue in his eyes, the breadth of his chest, even the hairs on the back of the hand that gripped the sword made her knees weak with need. "This is blight. It's not good for him to be here."

"I hear something now, too, chief. Coming from around there." One of the other knights was gesturing with his sword. He turned back to Lochlan, brow raised. "What should we do?"

"Leave," pleaded Morla. "Let's leave now."

"I can hear them," Bran wailed, pressing his hands flat against his temples. "Please," his voice dropped to a whisper. "Please, we have to help them."

"What do you want us to do, chief?" another repeated.

"Bran," Morla said, smoothing back his hair, "This place is making you sick."

His face contorted as he swung around on her and for a moment she was afraid he was going to wrap his hands around her throat. "Don't you understand they need my help? They want my help." With a sound that was something between a scream of rage and a cry for help, Bran staggered to his feet and stumbled off at a full run before anyone could stop him.

"Go after him," cried Morla. The whole scene had taken on an air of unreality, as if crossing the threshold had let them into a different world all together. They rounded the corner of the main building and stopped so abruptly, Morla crashed into Lochlan. As their bodies made contact, she was acutely—preternaturally—aware of his solid strength. She felt a burst of heat between her legs strong enough to make her knees buckle. When their eyes met as he turned to make sure she was all right, she knew she blushed and his expression changed from concern to confusion.

Then she forgot everything as Lochlan moved aside. Morla gasped. The grove, small as it was, had been beautiful once, she saw that immediately; the trees arranged around a central ring of stones. Care had been taken to accommodate each tree's shape and color, so that light-barked birch stood out against the darker holly; slim ash behind fat pines, oaks like sentries on either side of the opening.

But otherwise, the grove was hideous. Cancerous sores covered even the straightest of the oaks and the ashes, the bark of the alders bubbled and wept yellowish slime. The hollies were all black. But the apple tree was the worst, for bloated apples hung like living drops of blood, bright red and pulsing, as if comprised of beating hearts. A subtle smell of rot pervaded the air. It was the worst case of blight she'd ever seen. "Bran?" called Morla. "Bran, come out of there at once."

"I found them!" The answer drifted out, his voice high-pitched and excited. "I found them!"

"Get him out of there," Murdo whispered. "She's right." The other knights followed where he pointed. "Look."

"Great Hag," murmured Morla as she realized the growths that appeared to distort the trunks of the trees were vaguely human in outline and shape, that they moved and that it was their body fluids that ran down the scabrous bark that covered the trees. "Get him out of there," she hissed. "What are you waiting for? Get him out of there." She drew her own long dagger, and started forward, but Lochlan held her back.

"You wait here," he said, running past her. A hot wave of desire exploded through her, leaving her breathless and dizzy. As her head reeled and she tried to steady herself, she glanced at one of the trees, a beech, where a pale face peered. The eyes flickered and opened and stared and Morla looked deep into agonized depths. Help me, it mouthed.

She heard a high-pitched scream, and then another and then Lochlan, followed by Murdo, ran out of the grove, crying, "Let's go, let's go!"

Behind Lochlan, she saw another knight, Ongus, perhaps, trip and fall, and she saw that his legs were bound around with roots. Someone pushed Bran out of the grove, and Morla saw his hands were covered in dirt and blood. From the center of the enclosure, black, oily smoke was billowing, carrying a rank stench on the wind, and on it, she could hear high-pitched wails and an eerie screeching keen that raised the hair on the back of her neck.

The old gatekeeper rushed out of his gatehouse, waving his staff, shouting at them. Lochlan slung Bran over the back of his horse, then leaped into his own saddle. "Let's go," he cried. "Old man, take a horse and ride with us."

The fire had spread with amazing swiftness, leaping across the enclosure as if it pursued them. She could hear the knights screaming. "What about—" she turned to Lochlan with a horrified look. A wall of flame ten men high roared up and over the walls, engulfing the roof of the gatehouse in a solid sheet of fire.

Lochlan reached over and slapped Bran's horse. As the beast leaped forward and took off down the road, Morla touched her heels to her own horse's sides and sped off after them both, the flames and the stench and the screams fading only gradually.

Bran woke up propped against a tree. He opened his eyes into Lochlan's, who was stirring something that smelled delicious in an iron pot hanging over a fire pit. "There you are, boy. We weren't sure you were coming back. How d'you feel?"

"Like someone tried to scrape the skin off my body," he replied. He tried to sit up, but had to lie back as his head began to spin. "What happened? Where are we?" They were in a clearing, in a campsite, surrounded by the stones of what looked like a tumbled-down foundation and rotting wood. "What is this place?"

Lochlan glanced around with a shrug, then lifted the spoon to his lips and carefully tasted. "I think this used to be a druid-house. The lake is just down that path through the trees."

Bran tried to stand but dizziness overtook him before he reached his knees. He sank back down, feeling stiff and sore all over, as if he'd fallen from a great height. He looked around. Rotting wood timbers, shards of pottery and rubble were piled to one side, but one of the ancient fire pits was still in use. Someone had erected a rough kind of shelter against the weather. He rubbed his head and saw only Murdo and Bedwyr. "Where's everyone else?"

"You don't remember what happened?"

Lochlan gave him a hard look. Bran shook his head, suddenly very worried. "Where's Morla? Is she still angry with me?"

Lochlan's expression was grim. "Angry with you? It's thanks to her you're alive."

"I don't remember a thing." Bran stared at the knight in disbelief. "I—I remember we were riding, and Morla was angry."

"We came to a grove." Lochlan paused, then said, "It'd been overrun with blight. You—you got ensnared by it." Lochlan nodded in the direction of the path leading to the lake. "Go find her. She'll be glad to see you're all right. She went down to the lake when we started setting up camp. Tell her food's ready."

Bran hesitated. He wanted to ask more questions, but Lochlan nodded toward the lake. "Go on, boy. Go find her."

He obeyed with a questioning glance over his shoulder. His head throbbed, the backs of his hands were bloody and scrapped. His whole body ached. Once again, Morla had saved him. He remembered all the hours on the beach they spent together when he was very small. She wasn't pretty in the same way as Meeve, but her eyes were big and dark and her hair was black and fine as spider silk. He remembered how it blew around her face while she watched him dig the sand with a small spade stolen from the gardeners.

He remembered listening to the voices that murmured from the water, from the rocks, from the sand. Morla would stare out over the water. He remembered the day he learned that she couldn't hear the voices, too. It made him sad to think that she missed so much. Suddenly he remembered the day she went away, the day she'd given him the white shell he still wore around his neck. Reflexively, he reached for it, to reassure himself, and felt comforted when his fingers touched its cool round surface. He'd missed Morla for a long time.

He found her sitting on a rock, gazing out over the rough surface of the lake, so deep in thought she did not hear his approach until he stood beside her. Twilight filled the air— beyond the lake, the jagged tree-covered hills of the Forest of Gar stretched all the way to the sea. The choppy water gave him an eerie feeling, as if the waves were churned up by creatures moving beneath the surface, and he wondered how deep this lake of Killcarrick was. The sun had gone below the trees, and the black water was broken by little waves crashing over the tops of the rocks that lay below the surface. "Hello, Morla."

She jumped a good handspan in the air. "Great Herne, Bran," she said faintly, face flushed, straight brows creased. A series of expressions rippled across her face like the breeze on the lake, troubled, then startled, then angry. "Don't sneak up on me like that." She turned back to the water with a soft sigh.

"I'm sorry." He waited, uncertain what to say. "Lochlan sent me to find you—"

"Lochlan? What'd he want?" An unreadable expression flickered across her face.

"It's time to eat."

"Oh." She kept her eyes on the water.

He stood his ground, sensing that, like the rocks below the surface, something lay beneath Morla's silence. He decided to take a chance. "Why're you so angry, Morla?"

"I begged everyone not to go in there. But no one would listen."

He watched her face closely, sensing coiled tension tamped down so deeply he wondered if she was even aware of its existence. It was like a huge lake of fire burning deep inside her.

She whipped around, glaring. "Stop that. Stop that now. Hasn't anyone ever told you not to invade someone's head like that?"

"Like what?"

For a long moment, Morla was silent, even while the look in her dark eyes kept him rooted into place. "You almost got us all killed, Bran. You have to get control of these things you can do— You have to learn how to judge what to act on, and—"

He shook his head, frantically blinking back the tears that filled his eyes. "You don't understand, Morla. I don't even remember what you're talking about. I don't remember stopping at a druid-house, or even—" He broke off, balling his fists in frustration. "I don't even know what you mean when you say I'm in your head—I'm just thinking about you—I'm not trying to be in your head."

Her expression was unreadable. "Does Mother know you're like this? Connla?"

"I thought I was going to Ardagh with Aunt Connla. But then Mother changed her mind."

"You know why?"

Bran looked over his shoulder. "Lochlan says Mam wants nothing more to do with them. I guess that's why she's angry with me. I'm not—I'm not what she wants me to be."

Morla nodded. "That might be true, but that's not why she sent the druids away. All the reasons I've heard have got nothing to do with you."

Bran took a deep breath. All his memories of Morla were

bathed in golden light, washed with the scent of the sand and the ocean. He could trust her, he decided. "Morla," he began, then glanced over his shoulder up the path, "I have a message for you."

"From who?" She cocked her head. "Lochlan?"

"No, this is a message from Fionn. Fionn, your husband?"

"Fionn's dead, Bran. Don't tease me like that."

"I know he's dead. He came to me last Samhain. He told me to tell you the answer to your question was no."

"What question?"

"He seemed to think you'd know." Far out on the water, he thought he saw something round—like a head—break the surface. Just a wave, he told himself, forcing his attention back to Morla.

She was staring out over the water but he didn't think she was really looking at anything. A tear glistened on her cheek. "How—how did this happen?"

"I don't know, really. All I know is last Samhain, I looked up, and there he was. He told me who he was and said I should tell you the answer to your question is no. And he said I'd be seeing you soon." Bran squinted at the shadows that appeared to move beneath the water.

Morla let out a long breath, then wiped her eyes. "Well. Maybe you are. I guess it's as well we've decided to take you to Ardagh."

Something moving in the water caught his eye. The air blowing off the lake was as foul as the stench of a charnel pit.

Morla jumped off the rock and pulled her plaid around herself. "Eh, what's that smell? We're not going to be able to stay here if the lake's going to give up that kind of stink. Come on, let's go see if we can still smell it back—"

But Bran was certain that now he could see something moving across the water, a long line of white approaching the shore. A curious kind of shimmer was growing in the air. He knew that smell, too, he realized. It was indeed the very same stench that clung to Athair Eamon after he'd been to the charnel pits. "Morla." Bran grabbed her forearm. "Run."

"What's wrong—?" she began. She took one look over her shoulder and vaulted up the path. But the goblins were quicker than any goblins he'd ever heard of. Bran whipped out a dagger and sank it into the goblin, just as Lochlan crashed through the underbrush, riding his chestnut war-horse, swinging his broadsword over his head with one hand as he grabbed for Morla with the other. Lochlan reached for Morla and hauled her into the saddle, as another goblin raked its claws down her thigh. The horse reared and wheeled and screamed, its front hooves flailing as the goblins swarmed into the clearing. But before Lochlan could grab Bran, just as two goblins reached for him, a huge black raven grasped Bran's shoulders in her talons and pulled him into TirNa'lugh.

## 11

Timias staggered down the Tor, the heavy air thick in his throat, conflicting emotions engulfing him like a cloak. Like the cloak of shadows he'd forgotten all about, he thought, clutching the crystal pouch tightly. Mortals were clamoring up the hillside, crying for more light, more men, more druids. What would they think when they discovered that malformed creature?

He knew exactly what they would think, he told himself as he stumbled into the wood, heading for the border. A parade of torches led up the Tor, and the shouts were muted now, but he could guess what they were saying. They would blame him, call him a monster.

*Isn't that what you are?* a quiet voice whispered silently. *Who wouldn't call you a monster? What would the sidhe do to you, if they knew you could turn into a goblin? What would the druids do?*

Banishment would be mild.

But what if it was their fault? He stopped short, one foot in Shadow, the other raised, and without thinking, he found himself in that place between the worlds in which he'd been forced to spend so much of his exile. Banished by the druids and unable to return to the sidhe, he'd had time to think about his next steps. As he sank down onto the thick green moss beneath the spreading branches of an enormous oak, the idea that occurred to him made him cold all over. He fumbled with the leather pouch that held the crystals, pulled out a handful and shook them gently. Pale pink and warm, they pulsated in his palm. What if it were these things? he wondered. The druids were the first to admit they didn't really understand the limits of the khouri-keen, and they struggled to maintain control over them.

So maybe his…his… His mind struggled to find a word that described and defined how he felt. Maybe his new ability was a result of what the druids had done to him. As he remembered what happened to his child, and Deirdre, too, rage suffused his thoughts, turning to a tangled swirl of anger and grief and fear. The sidhe would never let him live in Faerie with them if they knew he could turn into a goblin—they'd believe him a monster, as well. And if the Court ever heard about this unfortunate birth… Finnavar, that black-hearted old crow, would make it her business to find it out and to broadcast as far and wide through Faerie as her wings could reach.

He hefted the crystals from hand to hand, trying to impose some order on the chaos that choked his thoughts. What had he gained from his time in Shadow? What had the druids taught him, and what had he figured out on his own?

The first thing he'd learned was that these crystals—at least one of them—were necessary for almost all the workings the druids did, other than the fertility rituals they performed with the sidhe. The second was that there was some power inherent in the crystal's that was unlike anything else in either Faerie or Shadow. And the third was that even the druids didn't know where the crystals came from.

Answers from the khouri-keen varied, according to mood and whim and weather. But maybe there was a way to ferret out what they knew. Maybe they hadn't been asked a question for which they had an answer. He put the stones in the pouch with the others, tightened the string and shook it hard enough to make the crystals knock audibly against each other. "Khouri-keen," he said with a will and an intention fueled by shock and anger. He held the pouch between his palms, concentrating on the center. "Here. *Now.*"

Another hard shake of the pouch and above the rattle of the crystals, he heard the first "Ow!," saw the first flash of big eyes in the branches overhead. A dozen or more scampered out from behind and around and out from between the spreading roots or from hollows in the trunk.

"Where are we?"

"What is this place?"

"Can we stay?"

He sat silent, with a tight hold on the pouch, watching them run and caper and jump and sniff. When one dared to blow in his ear, he gave the bag a vicious shake and the khouri-keen, all hundred or so of them, tumbled from whatever or wherever they'd perched with shrieks and flailing limbs and widespread eyes and ears. The offending trixie hurtled to the ground and landed on its side. As he writhed in pain, Timias observed impassively. Then he raised the bag as hard as he could. "Enough!" he cried. "Be still—sit where I can see you, all of you."

Warily, they crept around him, forming a semicircle of bright eyes and batlike ears, twitching noses and spindly limbs. "You're the Keeper now?" one whispered, and the question was taken up through the entire throng.

"Yes," Timias said. "I'm the Keeper and you obey me."

"Khouri like this place," one piped up and the others nodded and chattered in agreement. "Khouri stay?"

"Maybe," Timias answered. He gave the bag another vicious shake and watched as they all crumpled against each other, tossed like leaves in a strong wind. "If you do as I say, maybe I'll let you come back."

They liked that. They nodded and their long tails flicked above their heads. They were like little goblin creatures, he thought with distaste, and he hated them suddenly. "But if you want to come back, you have to do as I say."

"Say what you want Khouri to do," they chorused.

They were like insects, he thought, with one mind in many bodies. It was well established that the more difficult a magical task, the more khouri-keen were needed to accomplish it. What if that's how their minds work, too? he wondered. "I want you to think," he said. "I want you to think about the crystals." The khouri-keen themselves didn't seem to know the real connection. "You don't know where they came from, you don't know what they are. And if they were yours, you should know that, shouldn't you? But what if they aren't yours?" he muttered to himself. He reached into the pouch and felt the lambent energy within the stones, felt the latent life pulse against his skin. The power was in the crystals. In the khouri-keen…

Almost by accident, two edges of two separate stones clicked together like pieces of a puzzle. He felt the two fragments slide together so perfectly that he was able to remove the two still locked. He held the crystals up, felt in the pouch, withdrew another piece and tried to put it together. Another try and another, yielded no match, but a fifth slid into the first two like a key into a lock. A collective moan rose through the khouri-keen, rippling like the wind. They shut their eyes and curled their toes, sighing in what could only be acute pleasure. "You like that," he mused. He rubbed the edges of the crystals together, slowly, caressingly.

He slumped down, stroking the crystals together, and considered while the khouri-keen—the gremlins, he corrected himself—quivered in obvious pleasure. He was sidhe, he told himself and he would use the word of the sidhe, not the mortals. The gremlins acted and thought and behaved as one being. He held up the three interlocking crystals. They fit together so seamlessly it was obvious they were once part of the same stone. And then it came to him. He sat up so fast, he knocked his head against the tree.

The crystals were part of one crystal. And the khouri-keen—the gremlins—they were all parts of a single consciousness, in the same sort of way. "So maybe its not that Khouri made the crystals," he muttered. "Maybe the crystals made Khouri." The crystals began to pulsate in his palm. "Khouri," he began. The intensity of their gaze was tangible. He closed his fingers around the crystals, and felt them beat against the inside of his fist like a living heart. Originally there'd been just one crystal, he could feel the truth of it pushing against his awareness. The druids had always assumed the gremlins had found the crystals. The idea that the crystals themselves had somehow created the gremlins never occurred to the druids. Or maybe this was something even the trees didn't remember.

And where could such an object come from? he wondered. What kind of crystal possessed that kind of power? The trees certainly didn't remember such an event—he had looked all through the Mem'brances, as the druids called them. But the Mem'brances stopped abruptly, and it was said that with the coming of the khouri-keen, the druids stopped harvesting the rings of bark that recorded the memories of the trees. What kind of crystal could have shattered with such force and such rupture that an entire race would switch from one kind of magic to another?

Tree magic was undeniably long and slow and difficult to learn compared with managing the khouri-keen; what the gremlins lacked in self-control, they made up for in swift-ness of manifestation, making tree magic far less attractive to the druids. In all the time he'd been in Shadow, he'd only deciphered a small bit. But maybe, it occurred to him, the trees remembered the crystal in its original state...so was there any mention of some kind of powerful crystal?

He wracked his memory, trying to recall. But the only mention of any kind of stones were the four globes the Hag's cauldron rested on, representing each of the four elements. This wasn't arcane information—everyone knew that there was one of obsidian for fire, pearl for water, moonstone for air and stone for earth. Stone for earth, he mused. But what if it was crystal, not stone? If one of the Hag's globes had shattered, might it not be powerful enough to create a race of beings inextricably linked to itself?

"Khouri," he began again. "When the crystal made Khouri—" He hoped that at least was the right way to phrase the question. "When the crystal made Khouri, where was it?" He held his breath and waited.

There was a long silence. "Far below," one piped up.

"Far within," another said.

"Far away," wailed a third.

"Long ago," whispered a fourth.

"Can you show me where?" Timias leaned forward, chills running up and down his spine. He cupped the three crystals protectively in his upraised fist.

"Maybe," one whispered.

"Perhaps," said another.

"Not yet," muttered a third.

"Why not?" Timias frowned.

"Not enough to know the way," answered a fourth.

Not enough gremlins. Timias sat back, thinking furiously. Everyone—even the waterlogged—knew that the greater the magical working intended, the more crystals required. The greatest concentration of crystals, therefore, was at Ardagh, where they were kept buried under the central altar, with wardings to prevent the gremlins from taking them. But maybe not these gremlins here, he mused. Not if these gremlins were acting under the order of a druid, who understood the ward. The gremlin dens formed the first line of magical defense, in fact, because the goblins couldn't cross a gremlin field, for some unknown reason. But if the gremlins were gone, if the crystals themselves that stabilized and bound all the magic were removed, the way into Ardagh, the seat of druid power and the central point in all of Brynhyvar, would be open to Macha and her horde. Timias smiled and leaned forward. "Let's play a game, shall we?"

"Game?"

"Khouri likes games."

"Khouri loves games."

"Can Khouri all play?"

"Of course," Timias answered smoothly. "Of course, all of you will play. I want you to find all the chambers under all the Tors—run there as fast as you can and gather up all the crystals, as many as you can, and bring them here, to me, with all the Otherselves, as many as you can find."

"All?"

"Many?"

"All Otherselves?"

"It's the crystals, more than anything," he said. "Of course bring Otherselves—bring them all with the crystals, right back here. And wait." He gave the pouch a little shake. "Wait for me, do you understand?"

"Khouri understands Keeper," they whispered. "Khouri understands."

The druids would come after him, he knew, once they realized the crystals were missing. They might be heading into Faerie already, though he doubted they'd move that quickly. It wasn't enough to take the crystals—he had to prevent the druids from coming after them. This time of year they were all massing in one place. Even Ardagh wouldn't be invulnerable to an attack by flesh-crazed goblins—especially an Ardagh robbed of its gremlins and their power. And destroying the druids would prevent them from coming into Faerie armed with silver and taking the crystals back.

"Go on, then. Bring them here, as many as you can—all the crystals, all the khouri-keen."

To his amazement, they converged on him, falling at his feet, kneeling and kissing his hands, ankles, his hair, anything they could reach. He swatted and kicked them away, and they tumbled back, big eyes riveted on him with raw adoration. "Go!" he cried.

"We knew this day would come," they cried, swarming over the border into Shadow, arms overhead, capering and jumping and dancing. "We knew this day would come!"

Timias sat a moment longer, feeling the weight and the warmth of the crystals through the pouch, considering. Once the druids were eliminated as a threat, what then? How to harness the power in these creatures so that Loriana would accept their presence in Faerie was a problem he hadn't yet solved. He got to his feet, tied the pouch to his belt and removed all the rest of his clothing. He headed down to the caves where the goblins lived, confident he could draw on the power of the crystals to shift his form at will.

Bran was dreaming. The dream began when an enormous raven swooped him up and away from the goblins, into the trees and over the border into a sunlit realm of spreading oaks and warm, moss-covered rocks. He had to be dreaming, he decided, because giant black ravens didn't swoop down and yank people away from goblins. Yet his shoulders were still sore from the raven's talons digging painfully into his flesh. He sat up and looked around. The light was curiously intense, the colors sharply defined and incandescent, as if the leaves, the moss, the trees themselves, were lit somehow, from within.

"Hello, Bran."

The soft voice made him jump. He turned to see Loriana sitting on the ground beside a trickling fountain. "Wh-where am I?"

She smiled, looking up and around as if seeing the place, like him, for the first time. "This is the Deep Forest of Faerie. Most mortals never come here."

"How did I get here?"

"My grandmother brought us both here. She wanted us to be safe."

"From what?"

"Bad things. Like goblins, who never come this deep into the wood." She was beside him, and he hadn't seen her move.

"Why don't you just stay here, then?"

"All the real magic's on the border of things. Don't worry. We're safe here for now." She smelled sweeter than the lavender, her skin smooth as cream mixed with honey. She was tiny and delicate beside him, fine-boned as a humming-bird, her golden red hair as lush as silk, turned by the sunlight into the color of fire. He felt himself grow hot and hard, felt his skin flush red. Her breasts brushed his arm as she picked up his hand and clasped it between both of hers.

"Loriana—" He pulled away from her, afraid and breath-less and wanting all at once. Words tumbled out of his mouth. "The other night, when we were together, I started to see things when you kissed me—parts of things that didn't make sense and I wondered what it was supposed to mean, but then on the road—"

She was staring at him with her big green eyes in a way that made it very hard to think clearly. "Then on the road," he said as the memory of those tortured trees, the dying druids, sobered him. "We came upon a grove, filled with sick and dying trees."

"The trees are dying here, too. The trees around the Forest House—those people threw silver in the spring, and the poison spread. Father's doing all he can, but he's afraid if the goblins come— He's afraid if the goblins come again, the trees will not stand." She bit her lip and blinked away the tears. "Grandmother wants us to stay here till she comes for us."

He looked around. Above him, the boughs of the trees were lacy against the blue, blue sky. The moss was thicker than the richest carpet in his mother's house, and Loriana was more beautiful than any human girl he had ever met. "Isn't there anything we can do to help?"

"I hope so."

"What do you mean?" he asked, not understanding, even when she traced a single finger down the curve of his cheek to his lips. "How—"

She pressed her finger against his lips. "Shh. Don't you understand? You have to listen."

"Listen to wh—" As he tried to ask to whom or what he was supposed to listen, she pressed her lips on his open mouth and twined her tongue in his.

Pleasure, hot as fire, pure as cold air, jolted through his entire body as her arms went around his neck. He lost his balance and fell back on the velvety ground. Suddenly he wanted nothing more than to feel that moss against his skin. She was already slipping her hands under his shirt, and the fabric felt gross and thick and far too heavy. With a quick jerk he pulled it off and over his head and turned to face her. She picked up his hands and drew them to her breasts, placed his thumbs deliberately over her nipples. He felt dizzy and his vision clouded.

"Lie back," she whispered directly into his hair. The heat of her breath went straight down his spine, into his groin, and under him. In the ground beneath him, he felt something stir. Many somethings, in fact, like tiny feet.

"Wh-what is that?" he asked, alarmed. The sensation was like ants crawling on his skin, but through the moss, as if they never broke the surface of the ground.

"It's the trees," she said, raising her eyes, looking up and around. "It's the trees—waking up and knowing you as their own. Lie back and let them have you, like I'll let you have me." She moved on top of him, then, so that his phallus was positioned between her thighs, her breasts over his chest. Gently she slid down. Below the moss, he felt the sensation increase, so that he felt himself suspended between two places and two persons. For the longest moment he could ever remember, he stared into her eyes as she enveloped him, took him deep into herself, even as deep within the ground, the great trees all around him pushed up, invading some deeper, even more intimate awareness with a force all their own. Helpless to resist, he surrendered to them all and felt the memories of the trees flood into him, searing into his consciousness like a flood of pure hot light. *I can do this,* he thought. *I can heal the trees.*

* * *

Bran opened his eyes. Apple Aeffie was sitting beside him and Loriana was curled on her side, snoring ever so slightly, her hand pillowed on her cheek. "Apple Aeffie!" he cried. "What're you doing here?"

"Be careful what you wish for, boy. Be careful who you trust here. The sidhe never give without taking. Make sure you understand what they intend to take from you before you give your gifts away."

"I don't understand." Bran frowned. He glanced down at Loriana. He knew he was dreaming, and yet, he also knew that this was all happening. His skin felt thinner, his bones lighter, his blood once again felt light as foam.

"That's the trouble," Apple Aeffie said, and then she was gone.

"Hello, Bran." Again, he jumped. Loriana was looking up at him with those long green eyes, smiling sleepily. She sat up beside him. "Who were you talking to?"

"An old friend," he said, trying to remember what she'd told him. *Be careful what you wish for. Be careful who you trust.* But how could he not trust this small, sweet creature, whose face and form were more perfect than any he'd ever seen?

Loriana smiled up at him. Her head was pillowed on the crook of her arm, and with the other hand, she reached out and traced the line of his arm all the way from his shoulder to his wrist, raising gooseflesh. Then she picked up his hand, brought it to her lips and sucked each fingertip in turn. "Come back," she whispered, drawing him back beside her. "Come back."

She cupped his face in both her hands and brought his

mouth down to hers, guided him between her thighs. "More," she whispered.

She raised her hips and he slid into her. Apple Aeffie's words echoed through his mind: *The sidhe never give without taking.* His spine tingled, his blood seemed to boil in his veins. He felt as if something had ignited deep inside him, a new need that demanded to be fed, a need that only Loriana could fulfill. The flame rose higher and hotter, drove him harder and faster, spurring him into her faster and surer than before. She lay back, thighs drawn up, knees bent wide and spread, arms wide, her eyes closed, fragrant and pliant as a lily. *Be careful what you give away. Be careful who you trust.*

The words drifted through his mind, their meaning lost in the driving rhythm of the motion of his thighs pumping into Loriana's. He felt a curious warmth seeping all through him, a gentle lassitude creeping out from his core, and even as he felt his climax build, even as he felt the pressure in his loins reach the breaking point, he felt something else flow out of himself, something that left him feeling very weak and very sleepy. He collapsed almost on top of her, and shut his eyes, falling at once into a deep and dreamless sleep.

The harsh cry of a raven woke him up. He looked up to see the big bird circling above the trees, Loriana standing up, eyes shielded from the sun with one hand over her forehead.

"What's that?" he asked sleepily, wondering if maybe he was dreaming again.

"Come," she said. She held out her hand and pulled him up, dizzy, sick and weak. "We have to go back."

"Go back?" he asked, trying to stand upright. "Go back where? To Shadow?" He should go back, he thought. That's what Lochlan had said, wasn't it? That a mortal shouldn't stay too long in TirNa'lugh? He tried to remember but there was so much swirling around in his head—pictures and phrases, songs and faces, all blurring and blending together. *This isn't good,* he thought.

She tugged on his hand harder and, helpless to resist, he stumbled after her, head spinning. When he noticed that the berries on the holly trees had begun to glow a soft red, he thought maybe he was dreaming once again.

The smell of fresh mortal saturated the heavy air within the caverns beneath the river, a wet miasma at once tantalizing and obscene. Timias scuttled along the uneven passage, the bag that held the khouri-crystals firmly tucked beneath his tail, trying to give his senses time to adjust.

He hesitated in the opening. Thousands and thousands of eggs lay piled on the edges of the cavern, heaped on boulders, wobbled in niches on the walls. Corpses, fresh and bleeding, lay piled amid stacks of discarded, broken bones. Females leaped from partner to partner, copulating furiously at every turn. He clutched the bag of khouri-crystals tighter, and dared to raise his eyes to the queen's throne where Macha crouched at its apex, gnawing what looked like a woman's leg.

She raised her head, sniffed experimentally. Yellow slime drooled from her jaws as she chewed, swallowed, then ran her black forked tongue over her maw. She tipped her head back, noisily sucking out the marrow from the bone, but her eyes roved across her court in his general direction. He wondered if she could smell him, and hoped she'd be too satiated to try to run him down again. Limp bodies of goblin males sprawled on the various levels of her throne, some headless, some with their torsos ripped open. Goblins were known to kill their mates and the queen was obviously no exception.

Nauseated, Timias raised his eyes to the vaulted space above her throne, and felt his gorge rise. His knees buckled, and he nearly dropped the pouch as his tail snaked out to hold his balance. In the niches above the throne, the heads of sidhe stared sightlessly into space. They were new, he saw, and to his complete dismay, he recognized Auberon's.

*Auberon,* he thought, and the air rushed from his lungs as if he'd been punched. If his adopted brother was there, what about Loriana? Frantically, he scanned the rows of heads, many not more than skulls with hair attached and didn't see her, even if, with a sick feeling in the pit of his stomach, he recognized many more of Auberon's court. Was it already too late? he wondered. Had the goblins won? With nothing to stop them or even hold them back, had they simply over-whelmed the sidhe? He tightened his hold on the crystals. He could do this, he thought. If there was just a little more time… He edged into the room, hoping a female wouldn't grab him. It was too bad the normal border crossings might leave him open to attack from the mortals.

If he could send the goblins off to feast on the druids of Ardagh, he might at least have time to learn what happened to the sidhe. But that would mean engaging Macha, and he wasn't sure he could do that and survive. Maybe you should just go back to the MotherWood, he told himself. Maybe that would be a better idea. With the crystals, with the gremlins, he could wreak havoc on the mortals to his heart's content from the safety of Faerie….assuming Faerie was a safe place. *If I use the goblins against the druids, I can use the crystals against the goblins,* he decided. *And the sidhe would be the most powerful of all.* With his heart beating audibly, he crept along the edge, trying to avoid all notice by the howling, capering goblins.

He was almost there when he felt an arm go around his waist and he was flung onto the rock floor with a hard crack to his skull. The female was on him before his vision cleared, forcing his double-pronged phallus into the tight aperture between her thighs. But unlike anything he'd ever experienced with a mortal or sidhe, the fluid burned as it poured over him, scalding his flesh like fire. He tried to squirm away, but her tail snaked out from under her, wrapping itself around one ankle. She dragged him back and tried to flip him over, but he kicked up, flailing at her with his tail.

Suddenly, Macha was there. She threw the other female off him, reached down, and picked him up by the ruff, her huge jaws snapping in his face. "I know you. Tetzu."

"Great Queen." In any language at all, the words were the same. Timias crouched, tucking his tail under, rolling up his ruff. He felt her stare on him, even as the forked tip of her tongue touched his head, his ruff, his bowed spine.

She snarled softly as her eyes flared red in the shadows. He could smell the fluid spilling from her egg sacs. If she climbed on top of him, he thought, he would die. "Great Queen," he rasped. "The way to Ardagh—the way to Ardagh is free of egg-eaters." He hoped the khouri-keen had kept their word. They were about to be well rewarded if they had. And if not… He closed his claws around the pouch. "Ardagh—where the druids gather to find a way to yoke our flesh."

He had her attention. She shifted her position, snarled again and the goblins quieted infinitesimally. She reached out her long forked tongue and licked his head. "You have been to Ardagh... I smell Shadow on you... Taste it, too..."

"If there is power in living flesh," he stammered, "imagine the power in magic living flesh."

Her eyes flared red and in one swift blur of movement she was on him, pushing him back, splaying him wide, riding him like something from a nightmare. Her burning, oozing flesh closed over his, her foul breath blasted in his face as she rocked above him, forcing his seed up and out and into her egg sacs, draining him dry. He tightened his tail around the khouri-crystals and hoped he was right. *ARDAGH*, he thought with every ounce of intention he could summon, even as Macha drew him in, and he felt the churning in his belly start to burn. *AR-DAGH*, he thought again, wrapping his tail as tightly as possible around the pouch as if he would draw it up and into himself. *ARR-DAAGH*.

"Ar-Dagh!" screamed Macha as she pumped the dregs of his seed from his belly. "AR-DAGH!"

She straightened enough to allow him to roll, then crawl, then stagger out of the way. At last he allowed himself to collapse against the wall, his head churning, his body feeling flayed. The queen began to dance, jumping across the goblins, between the teetering piles of eggs, rousing the goblins out of their sun-and-blood-induced stupor. As the goblin horde took up the chant, and the drums began to beat, Timias saw his chance to escape.

## 12

"Catrione? Catrione?"

Catrione opened her eyes into Niona's, her mind still too meshed with Snake's to speak. She darted the tip of her tongue along her lower lip, her eyes from side to side, desperately seeking to maintain the connection to that other consciousness.

"Catrione?" Niona slapped her cheek lightly. "Come out of it, Catrione. Come back." Niona snapped her fingers. "Hand me that piece of white-sage." She waved the burning leaf under Catrione's nose and this time Catrione heard voices babbling outside her room. She was lying in her bed in the dormitory and from the slant of the sun, it appeared to be the middle of the day.

Catrione stared up at her. "What's happening? How long was I—" *Wherever I was.* Her tongue felt short and thick in her mouth, not sinuous and slender as it had just a moment or two ago. She tried to sit up, but the room spun, and she fell back heavily onto her pillows.

Baeve pressed forward, a steaming goblet in her hand.

"Here, dear, have a sip of this first. Don't try to sit up just yet." She gently smoothed Catrione's hair off her face, even as she glanced at Niona over her shoulder. "I told you we shouldn't wake her."

"She is cailleach, isn't she?" snapped Niona.

"What's happened?" asked Catrione. "Deirdre—did you find her? Did you find the young man?" Catrione fumbled for the words as Baeve wrapped her fingers around the goblet and helped her guide it to her lips. The warm spiced milk and honey, whipped into a foam, spilled down her throat and filled her mouth with satisfying sweetness. It helped her anchor her consciousness back into her body and her human mind. Speech returned, but language for all that she'd seen eluded her. She felt as if she'd been ripped out of the middle of a dream.

"Deirdre's been found, child." Baeve wrapped a shawl around Catrione's shoulders as she helped her upright.

"I hope you got some wisdom, Catrione." Niona turned on her heel and stalked out of the hall, followed by most of the others.

Catrione took another long drink. The milk and honey, strengthened with the druid's brew of distilled silver, was flowing into her veins now. Her vision was clearing, but the sense of being in more than one place was still strong. She tipped the goblet back and the contents spilled, running down her chin. She felt clumsy and weak as she handed Baeve the goblet, mopping up the mess with her shawl. Baeve scurried to help and Catrione said, "What else?"

"The ravens have returned, though not with any answers. Connla left Eaven Morna at least four or five nights ago. And according to the answer from Ardagh, she's not yet arrived."

"Maybe she's stopping here?"

Baeve shrugged. "Maybe. You should know, Catrione, the grove's dividing into two camps. There's one side that wants to wait for Connla and the other that believes we should act on whatever you may have learned."

"And Niona's on the wait-for-Connla side, no doubt?"

"No doubt." Baeve shut her mouth with a snap and a sniff.

She had to help Catrione dress, for Catrione's limbs felt fused and wooden, as if she'd forgotten how they moved. She also seemed to have forgotten how to think, for her thoughts felt clumsy, as if she couldn't connect them to words.

When Catrione was dressed, she had to cling to Baeve's arm. The courtyard was even more crowded than ever, it seemed, but people stopped and smiled when they saw her, pressed her hand and wished her well. "Where are the brothers and the sisters?" she asked, seeing no druids at all.

"Up there." Baeve pointed to the Tor, where it seemed every brother and sister in the grove was clustered around what looked like a gaping wound in the side.

"What're they doing up there?"

"That's another argument. Come, you'd better see for yourself."

Gripping Baeve's arm, Catrione started up the hill, the site triggering even more acute flashbacks of Deirdre in the Tor—Deirdre and that thing she'd birthed. As other hands reached for her, helping her, guiding her, gently encouraging her, she stumbled, not seeing the ground, only that dark, dank chamber. When at last she peered inside the tomblike entrance of the SunBirth Chamber, she understood why Baeve had side-stepped all her specific questions. Nothing, not even the memory of having witnessed it, could've prepared Catrione for the horror that lay beneath the shrouds. The honeyed milk boiled in her belly as Catrione pressed her hand against her mouth and nose. Baeve handed her a cloth soaked in peppermint oil. "Here," she said.

Silently, Athair Emnoch helped her down and into the chamber, sliding across mud and rocks and rubble. The thing that lay in the center of the floor looked more like a husk than anything that had once been a living human body. Deirdre's face had already crumbled against her skull, and her hair was flaked and dry. Her body had split from throat to groin, and what was left lay sprawled obscenely, straw-colored, flocked with rusty stains that Catrione realized were dried blood.

"Cailleach," the brother murmured. He touched her arm gently. "You must see this." He bent and gingerly pulled back the corner of a small hide that lay a few lengths from Deirdre. Something long and dark, like a shriveled snake, protruded from it, like a tail. As the druid lifted the hide, Catrione realized what the leathery thing was. It was the infant's umbilical cord.

Catrione clapped both hands across her mouth and the oil-soaked cloth stifled her gasp as she stared at the thing Deirdre'd birthed. The infant's body was a series of white segments, topped by an all too human-looking head. From just below its ears, two hands protruded from its shoulders. The bottom half divided into a double tail, each ending in a perfect little foot.

She turned aside, in search of fresh air, as the lines from the bark scrolls came back to her. *The child who can't be slain by the hand of woman, or of man…* Well, it hadn't been. The Great Mother had somehow conspired to send someone equipped with a hook for a hand.

"It's clear, don't you think, Catrione?" That was Niona, speaking over Baeve, who hovered about, wiping her face. Snake's memories tumbled around in her mind, visions that unfolded like the petals of a flower, overlapping on each other. She was there, and she was here. Nothing, not even crossing in and out of TirNa'lugh gave her such a feeling of being in two places and two times at once. It made her brain ache and swell.

"What's clear?" Catrione managed to ask. The sequence, at least, was coming back to her now. Sitting this close to Deirdre's remains, she could feel the echo of her last moments. Images and impressions, now coiled and stored somewhere in her Snake's awareness, flashed through her mind. The impression of a young man with a hook was the only one she had that made any sense at all. *He's the man you are to marry.*

"That this was the child who can't be killed by hand of woman or of man?" Niona crossed her arms over her chest.

Catrione sank down onto a rock. Was that what was clear? She wrinkled her brow, staring off into the distance.

"The khouri-keen and their crystals have disappeared." Athair Emnoch was speaking, even as the world reeled around her.

*Tiermuid has them.* "The young man…has no one tried to reach him?" Catrione asked.

"We should wait for the ArchDruid, don't you think, Cailleach?" asked Athair Emnoch. "If you don't mind my saying, you don't look well at all."

"I'm all right," she said automatically, even as she knew that wasn't quite the truth. "I don't—"

"What if he's druid?" cut in Niona, her voice sharp and shrill. "Do you really want to risk another thing like that?" With a sound that could've been a curse, she stalked down the hill, leaving Catrione's face burning as the wind blew harder out of the west.

Sunlight tickled the back of Morla's eyelids, and a soft breeze brushed across her face. She opened her eyes to a wide window filled with the upper branches of a leafy tree, white-washed walls and burning pain up and down her right leg. She heard a soft snore and looked over the edge of the bed to see Lochlan slumped on the floor underneath the window, his head propped on his arm. A dark haze of beard shadowed his chin and mud splattered his boots. She blinked and looked around, wincing as she shifted.

The linen beneath her head smelled of sun and thyme, the blanket that covered her well-woven and clean. Reed baskets, filled with folded towels and bandages, lined one wall. The walls were stone, the roof was low but white-washed. From the open casement, the tinkle of bells, a dog's sharp bark and shepherds' shouts as bleating animals were led to pasture filtered into the room. She tried to sit up, but a red-hot poker of pain shot up her entire leg. And then she remembered the goblins coming up and out of the water and something big and black swooping down and out of the trees, grabbing Bran away.

She fell back against her pillow as the door opened, and a dark-haired woman about the same age as Morla, though heavily pregnant, stepped into the room. She wore a tunic dyed a rich blue, and the plaid over it as well as the large copper brooch on her shoulder proclaimed her status as a chief. "You're awake," she said with a quick smile. "I'm Grania MaNessa. Welcome to my house. How'd you feel?"

"My leg hurts," Morla answered, grimacing as Grania eased the coverlets off, exposing her thigh.

"Let's have a look." Grania's mouth turned down as she gingerly peeled the top layer of linen away, and her brow furrowed. She glanced at Morla, and her eyes were grim. "I've a still-wife here—I'll get her now that you're awake."

"How long have I been asleep?"

"The better part of two days. Your husband—" Grania nodded at the sleeping Lochlan "—came in riding like the Great Hag of the Mountain herself was after you."

*He said we were married?* Morla's surprised hiss was swallowed by a gasp of real pain as Grania gently replaced the bandage. "I wish I had a druid, but they've all gone to Ardagh. Your knight—" she flashed another quick smile in Lochlan's direction "—Herne bless him—your knight's been scouring the countryside for the better part of two days. I think the only place you're likely to find a druid is at one of the bigger groves. The closest is the White Birch, but that's at least, three, maybe four days away."

Morla glanced at Lochlan as Grania continued, "I'll be right back." She shut the door behind her, and the latch's firm click startled him awake.

He opened his eyes and looked at her. A broad smile spread across his face. "Thank the goddess." He rose to his feet with an audible creak from his knees. He dusted off his trews, his fleeting grin fading into an expression of concern. "How's your leg?"

"It hurts," she replied. There was something in the way he was looking at her, in the way his hands hovered just above the edge of the bed that unsettled her, even as she became aware of a burning sensation, like tiny needles of fire, burrowing deep into her flesh. "It hurts a lot." She closed her eyes and tried to gather her thoughts. "What about Bran? Did we— Is he—"

"I'm not sure what happened to him."

Morla struggled to sit up despite the fire that shot down her thigh. Pain boiled in her bones, wormed like needles into her hip. "I don't really remember much about what happened. I remember sitting on the rock—I remember running back—" She broke off, trying to make sense of the scrambled images swirling through her mind. Bran had been there, and then he hadn't. But the goblins had been behind them— Bran was ahead of her. "What did you see?"

"I don't want to give you false hope… I saw him with you, running up the path. He was ahead of you, pulling you. He ran beneath an oak tree, and then he disappeared." Lochlan spread his hands. "There was no time to make sure, though. You and I got away with nothing but the clothes on our backs. But I'll swear on my own mother's grave, I saw Bran disappear before the goblins reached either of you."

"What about the others—the other Fiach—?"

Lochlan shook his head, dropped his eyes, and a shadow crossed his face. "There was no time."

The door opened, and a very tall woman with a raw-boned face and graying braids wound around her head stepped into the room. She had a tray of salves in one hand and a basket in the other, and she was followed by Grania.

"Good morning, Sir Aidan." Grania smiled almost girl-ishly as she looked at Lochlan. "This is our still-wife, Nuala."

Morla glanced at Lochlan, her question in her eyes. He glanced at her sideways and shook his head ever so slightly, even as he bowed to Grania. Morla understood she wasn't to say who she was. There were plots within plots in this world and she wondered for a moment why she'd not thanked her mother kindly and returned to Dalraida. Because they're all starving and she promised to send corn, thought Morla, and hoped Meeve had kept her word.

Lochlan turned his back, as the still-wife pushed the sheet off Morla's nearly naked body. But she forgot all about modesty, or any pretext of it, as the still-wife peeled back the bandages, and the pain that flamed through her leg went all the way to the roots of her hair and the soles of her feet. Tears came to her eyes, and she tasted blood as she bit her lip.

"I told you this is beyond me. It's got worse since she's lain here," Nuala said, shaking her head.

Morla dared a peek. Tiny pustules of contamination bubbled on her skin, streaking out from the deep center of the wound.

"She needs a druid and she needs the *uisce-argoid,* the silver water." The two women exchanged glances, and Morla felt a pang of real dread. This could kill her, she thought, and she looked at Lochlan, even as the still-wife addressed him. "She needs a druid as fast as you can get her to one, Sir Aidan. By the time you ride to the White Birch Grove and bring one here, she'll lose the leg. If you can take her there yourself, I say there's still a chance."

"To save my leg?" asked Morla.

"To save your life," Nuala answered flatly.

"But—" began Grania.

"I can't stop the poison." Nuala shook her head, then looked at Morla. "This may sting."

Stars exploded in front of Morla's eyes the moment the grassy-smelling liquid touched the suppurating flesh. Her spine went rigid, and her hands splayed and flexed. She gripped the sheets and felt a smooth, strong palm slide into hers, encouraging her with firm pressure. She gripped it reflexively, clung to it as the dark pain snaked through her, as the wound was cleaned and the bandages were changed. She opened her eyes and realized she'd been holding Lochlan's hand. The still-wife daubed at the beads of sweat pearled across Morla's forehead and upper lip, even as the ointment dulled the stinging pain.

"There, now, lass, just rest. I'll bring up some broth," said Nuala. "Are you hungry, lady?"

Morla stared at the ceiling. The pain throbbed through her in waves, dulling her appetite. "No," she answered after considering whether she was hungry or not. "I'm…I'm thirsty."

She saw Nuala exchange another significant look with Grania, who said, "I'll see about a wagon, Sir Aidan." She picked up the basket of soiled bandages and left.

Nuala lingered, fussing over her ointments. Lochlan asked, "Why's she not hungry?"

"That's what happens." Nuala shook her head grimly. "There's poison in goblin bites. It wastes you, even as it burns away your appetite. It's important you drink, lady." She picked up her tray. "I'll fetch the broth."

Lochlan waited until her footsteps faded down the hall, then said, "I suppose you're wondering what that's all about?"

"Unless there's more I can't remember," Morla replied, and the ghost of a grin flickered across his face. "What's going on? Why'd you tell that woman we're married? And why'd you tell her different names?"

"I told them we were married so I could stay in here with you without questions being asked. And your name's Moira."

"Moira?"

"I thought it close enough to Morla you'd answer to it."

"But why? Don't you trust Grania?"

He rubbed his hand across his face. "It's not Grania, though she's plenty cagey about which side of the fence she's sitting on. She's one of the ones Meeve's been supporting over the years, but you see Meeve's been supporting more than one claimant for the kingdom of Gar and has played them off each other when it suited her. There's not much love, apparently, between Meeve and Grania. Fortunately she doesn't seem to remember me behind this beard." He stalked to the window and peered out, thumbs hooked into his sword belt, then glanced at her over his shoulder. "Tell you the truth, I'll be glad to leave. I feel too vulnerable here, too exposed somehow. Sooner we get you to a druid, the better." He paused, looking distinctly uncomfortable, and as if there was something else he wanted to say, but he only shut his mouth and stared out the window for a moment. Then he turned swiftly on his heel and stalked to the door. "I'll let you rest, while I see to getting a wagon. This Grania's a tight-fisted one, but there's no way you can ride." With his hand on the latch, he turned and looked at her.

Their eyes met and in the depths of his, she saw something dark and painful.

"What's wrong?" she asked.

He shook his head and spread his hands. "Morla, I—" He hesitated, clearly struggling for words.

"None of what happened is your fault, Lochlan," she said. Pity welled up in her. He did consider himself responsible, she knew that without a doubt.

He sighed. "I doubt Meeve will see it that way. The sooner we find a druid, the better I'll feel."

"Me, too," she quipped. Their eyes met once more and this time, despite the pain and the worry and the fear, they smiled.

A single ray of moonlight pierced the leafy canopy of the tree directly outside the room where the young man lay, still and silent, on his pillow. The light fell directly on his forehead, into the space between his eyes. His eyes were closed, his one hand on his chest, the other arm lying bandaged beside him on top of the light-blue blanket. Catrione hesitated in the doorway. His damp, sun-streaked hair was fanned out on the linen pillow, his chiseled lips were the color of ripe peaches, and his fresh-shaved cheeks were nearly luminous as a sidhe's. Her ears and her face still burned with the quarrel she'd had with Niona.

Catrione watched the young man breathe. Druid-healing was the most sacred of all the druid rituals, and Niona characterized her wish to help the young man as something selfish. *But that's not true at all…after all, he's the man I am to marry,* thought Catrione. She sank beside him; he opened his eyes and turned his head to look at her. She was acutely aware she was naked under the linen shift, that beneath his thin cover, he was naked, too. A breeze brushed her cheeks and on it, she fancied she could smell the sea.

*Don't you ever wonder if someday a man will come...* Deirdre's words taunted her. She glanced over her shoulder. The still-wives had been called to keep order in the outer courtyard among the refugees, while the druids were up on the Tor, attempting to locate the khouri-keen.

The two of them were truly alone. Catrione stole over to the low cot and knelt beside it. She drew a deep breath, deliberately breathing him into her, drawing his essence deep into her lungs. She touched his arm and began to stroke his skin with long, gentle strokes, focusing on her fingertips, on the way the fine hair grew on his muscled forearm, the way the skin stretched over the curve of sinew and bone. It was like being gradually enveloped in a mist, or like allowing fog to enter her mind, insidious as ivy around an oak. It was like trying to wrap one's arms around someone with his head in a blanket. He was fighting her. The harder she tried to penetrate, the harder he fought against her. Like a swimmer coming to the surface, Catrione forced her awareness back into the chapterhouse.

The drums were pounding up on the Tor, the chanting a near continuous drone. The scent of burning cedar filtered through the heavy air. She reached over and shut the door, swinging the latch shut. In one swift motion, she pulled off her tunic and the blanket from his body. She straddled him, her hands flat on his chest, her body inches from his. Except for the bandaged stump, he was beautiful, she thought. His eyes opened, and she gasped.

"You're the one," he said as if he'd opened his eyes expecting to see a naked woman straddling him.

"Do you remember your name?"

"Cwynn," he said at once. His body lay motionless between her thighs. "What's yours?"

"I'm Catrione." She felt as much as saw his blue eyes flicker over her breasts, down her belly. She had never felt so self-conscious before a man.

"That thing is all I see." He shut his eyes with a groan and continued through gritted teeth. "As it died, it looked at me. I saw its eyes...I see them still. That's all I see."

"Cwynn, will you let me help you?" she asked. She leaned over him so that the tips of her nipples brushed his chest.

"What happened in there?" he whispered. "What was all that?"

"I can help you, if you let me." She ran her fingers over his head, over his face, touching his nose, his eyebrows, the tips of his ears. *And I hope you can help me.*

He closed his eyes, and his chin bobbed up and down in the barest of nods.

He thinks he's dreaming this, she realized. She stroked his hair, she touched his face, she ran one finger across his mouth, from right to left, the direction of banishment. She leaned down, so that her breasts touched the broad plane of his chest. "Cwynn, will you let me touch you, hold you, help you, heal you?"

Again, he gave that barest of nods.

She bent lower, kissed his eyelids, his earlobes, the vulnerable place beneath his chin where the blood beat visibly. She touched his nipples with the tip of her tongue, painted a backward swirl around his heart, his navel and finally, kneeling between his thighs, she paused. "Cwynn," she said, louder this time. The drummers picked up the beat. She took his phallus in her hands and stroked it up and down, gently, as it hardened and thickened. She touched the tip with the tip of her tongue, kissed the tiny opening. "Cwynn, may I take you in?"

This time the answer was a restless lifting of his hips, the clenching of his fist, a sigh. Catrione smiled and bent her head.

*He was riding, riding across the water-pocked sand, Shane hard at his heels and a white dog running along beside him. Eoch didn't seem to notice or care that the dog was there. Eoch! The name of the horse exploded into his mind, and he felt as if he'd suddenly cut through something that was constricting him. Suddenly, he was fighting off a goblin. There was someone else beside him, something that flashed, and the goblin was gone. The light shifted into a kind of golden green and a soft peach glow filled his mind. A cloaked silhouette moved across the glow, followed by the outline of a horse. Eoch! The shadow wanted his horse, he understood that now, but Eoch was his, raised from a foal. He looked down and the land had changed from spongy moss to a rocky, windswept road. In the distance he saw a glow and a dark hill rising starkly against an orange sunset. The shadow-figure jumped on Eoch and rode across the broad plain, directly toward the Tor.*

*Outrage roared through him, bringing a diamond-hard clarity that ripped across another layer of his memory. He re-membered charging across the plain as the moon rose, guided by Eoch's shape standing outlined on the Tor. It had taken nearly half the night, but he had made it, bursting into the dark, rock-lined cave in time to see a figure with an enormous writhing belly lying on the ground, legs splayed wide. Her skull was bald and mottled, her cheeks striated. Her body was covered in leathery skin that hung off her bones in folds. As Cwynn took a single step closer, she looked at him with eyes like a snake, and hissed.*

Drops of clear fluid, slippery as honey, oozed from his phallus. Catrione rose up, caught Cwynn's mouth up in hers, and positioned herself over him, nudging the tip into the opening between her legs. She sank down and the shaft plowed into her warm, wet flesh as she arched her back and groaned. "Show me his face," she breathed, though she thought she knew exactly who it was. "Let me see his face."

A moan split the hot air, followed by a long, keening echo. A shiver went down Cwynn's back as he looked around and saw what looked like thousands of stars glittering in the walls. Not crystals, he thought as they winked and moved—they were eyes, he realized and nausea rose in his gut. "I'll kill you, mortal," the figure roared.

He opened his eyes as the woman arched her back, her high, round breasts flushed, her honey-blond hair cascading down her back as her body shuddered. He felt her flesh contract around his and he shut his eyes as his seed boiled up from the base of his belly and the memories flooded into his mind.

## 13

Timias hauled himself out of Macha's lair, the pain burning in his groin nearly crippling him. Behind him, he heard the drumbeat begin to swell and the howling chant to rise. *AR-DAGH...AR-DAGH...AR-DAGH.* Even if the khouri-keen—the gremlins—hadn't removed all the crystals, the goblin horde was so grown in strength and size, Timias believed they might simply overwhelm the unsuspecting druids and overrun the very heart and center of druid power.

Assuming he lived long enough to know. He felt as if his guts might boil out either orifice as he scrambled through the tunnels, the pouch with the khouri-crystals clutched in one hand. He didn't want to be a goblin—he didn't want to live in a world where goblins ruled. He hesitated, torn between returning to the MotherWood, and ensuring that the gremlins had done his bidding, and going to the Forest House, to learn what had happened to Loriana.

He was sure that the head directly above Macha's throne had been Auberon's; the one beside it, Melisande's. *But I'd know if anything had happened to Loriana,* he told himself. *I'd feel it.* He remembered the way she'd looked at him as she'd thanked him for saving her life. And how had she responded when he said he didn't think the king expected him to ever return? *You came back in time to save my life.* There was a bond between them, a connection forged in those moments they'd fled the goblins. Of course there was. There had to be, and she couldn't be dead, couldn't be gone.

And suddenly, he knew with perfect clarity exactly what he had to do, if not how to do it. He had to find a way to make Faerie everything it should be—not just beautiful, but safe; not just healthy and whole, but secure. "There has to be a way," he muttered as he slipped through the Forest. Loriana, whether she accepted him as her Consort or not, deserved a place to live as fair as she was—after all, the world was called Faerie. It was meant to be fair, not overtaken by goblins. Of course there was a way—a way now. He hefted the pouch, reveling in its weight, imagining how much heavier it would be when it was filled with the crystals from Ardagh. Pleased with himself, he smiled. She would love him for what he alone could do.

The sun was up and it burned his goblin skin. The leathery surface dried and cracked, forcing him beneath the trees. He smelled the smoke almost immediately and under it, a bitter almost metallic odor. *I should make myself into a sidhe,* he thought, but he didn't want to stop. He scrambled as fast as he could through the trees, until the smell and the smoke nearly overwhelmed him and he was forced to stop on the edge of a clearing he realized had once been Loriana's bathing pool. Foul black water bubbled from the center, and dead creatures lined the water's edges. He sank down, and the ground beneath him burned. *This is what silver does,* he thought. He remembered the patch of silver poisoning he and Loriana had come upon. Could all this have spread from that, or had more silver somehow gotten into Faerie? Warily he backed up and realized that a thread of corruption ran all through the Forest, directly, like a path, to the Forest House, where the smoke was black and billowing.

Choking, he fought his way through the smoke and the trees to where the Forest House lay desecrated, the great trees that formed the walls and the supporting framework mostly smoldering black columns of ash. A few sidhe moved within the wreckage, stumbling blindly from side to side, place to place, and he realized they were looking for the wounded, or for bodies. Then one looked up, a warrior with smudges on his face and deep shadows beneath his eyes. He squinted into the trees, directly at Timias. "Goblin!" he cried, raising his spear, and Timias backed away into a piece of the hedges that were supposed to form the first line of defense around the Forest House. He stepped into them, heedless of the razor-sharp thorns, into what felt like mushy mud that stung like bees. He looked down and in the flickering light radiating from the ruins of the Forest House, he saw the bottom of the hedges were black, and that the earth below each plant was a soupy dark mess. *Silver,* he thought as he dodged onto firmer ground. *That's silver and it's rotted out the trees—rotting out the hedges.* He turned to look at the trees in the immediate vicinity and saw telltale lines of black encroaching up from the ground.

The shouts coming from what remained of the Forest

House as he scurried away told him that some of the Court, at least, had survived. He heard voices calling for the captain of the Queen's Guard. *The Queen's Guard!* Loriana must've survived—she had to have survived because otherwise, there'd be no Queen's Guard. So he had a little time, at least, to come up with a plan that would save Faerie, that would keep Faerie free of both goblins and silver.

Some sort of border or boundary, he mused, had to be created, something that would keep silver out, the gremlins in and the goblins contained. But how to make such a thing, let alone maintain it? All the magic in all four races would never be enough....

A line from the rotting bark scrolls the druids kept ran unbidden through his mind. *Four globes has the Hag—one for each Element.* There was even a druid symbol meaning balance—a large circle with four smaller half circles evenly spaced around it. It was meant to be the Hag's Cauldron, balanced on her globes, the still-maid, Sora, had so charmingly explained, her big eyes earnest and blue. Four elements...four races...four globes. The druids assumed that the gremlins, the khouri-keen, were the Earth elementals, the sidhe, the race born of Air. Mortals, they believed, were expressions of Water, and goblins, Fire. But the gremlins had been made when something larger had been shattered.

*The globes,* he thought. The Hag's globes—were there really four? Or were there only three? The druids really didn't know—they didn't know lots of things, but made assumptions based on what they saw unfolding around them. *As above, so below,* they liked to recite incessantly, when questioned. *As within, so without.*

But not one of them had ever been Below. Something was holding him in goblin form, he realized, and he suspected it was the khouri-crystals, which only seemed to reinforce his theory of how their magic would work in Faerie. It would help to be in goblin form, though, to pass Below. He had no doubt it was there…he could feel it the whole time he'd been in the MotherWood, calling him, seductive as a young sidhe, tempting as a live mortal. He flicked his tongue over his maw and decided to heed its subtle invitation at last.

*It's Tiermuid…Tiermuid… Tiermuid is the child who can't be killed…who was sidhe and mortal and goblin all at once… who was everything and nothing.* Catrione came reeling back to herself with a start as the implications of his many names and true nature and the fact he controlled the crystals and the khouri-keen crashed on her like an avalanche. She was crouching on all fours above Cwynn and she knew exactly who he was—Meeve's son, Deirdre's brother and the man her father thought she should marry.

He was lying flat beneath her, their bellies sealed together with sweat, eyes wide, his soaked hair curling from his temples, fanned out across the pillow, his one hand twisted in the sheet. She pulled herself off and away and wrapped a blanket around her shoulders. She sat on the side of the bed, trembling, trying to make sense of all she'd seen.

The monster was dead, thanks to Cwynn. Tiermuid, Timias—whatever his name was—was gone back into Tir-Na'lugh, presumably. She tried to recall if any of the brothers had remarked publicly on any strangeness in Tiermuid and could remember nothing. Even Deirdre never once mentioned the possibility that he was anything other than he appeared to be.

"Ca-Catrione?" Cwynn touched her shoulder hesitantly. He was sitting up, the sheet pulled modestly up to his navel. "Catrione—is that your name?"

With effort, Catrione forced herself to focus on Cwynn. He sounded confused. This was the reason one never attempted the healing without other druids present. She imagined Niona's sneer. She pushed her hair off her face and tried to smile reassuringly. "Yes, that's right—you remember?" As he nodded, she continued, "Good. What else do you remember now? Do you remember the Tor?"

He sat up. "I—I think I remember it all." He looked up and around at the whitewashed walls, at the wide window. "This is—this is a druid-grove, right? And what you did, what we did, just now—that's what you druids do?"

She ignored him, her mind racing furiously, putting pieces and images together. The child who can't be killed by the hand of woman or of man...with the khouri-crystals and reason to hate the druids... What's he planning? she wondered, as she reached for her clothing. Cwynn gripped her arm.

"Please?" He shook her arm and she realized he'd asked her questions. "I don't understand what's going on here, but I believe my children, my family, my village—"

"I know." She turned and put one hand on his bare shoulder. His skin was soft, smooth, the muscles firm beneath. "I know what you believe. I know what you're afraid of." She pulled her tunic over her head, then sat back down. "I know your people on Far Nearing need a druid,

Cwynn...." Her voice trailed off as more visions exploded
before her eyes, revealing more connections, more pieces of
the pattern she felt unfolding all around her. "Connla of
Mochmorna, the Ard-Cailleach, the ArchDruid of all Brynhyvar, called all the druids to Ardagh." *Tiermuid... Timias...
Tetzu...mortal...goblin...sidhe... He was all of them, and none
of them. And he had the crystals.* She felt as if the air had been
punched from her lungs. He had the crystals. He had the
source of druid power, and he had a reason to hate them all.
Not only had he been banished and lost Deirdre, he probably
blamed them for the monstrous child—in fact, she was sure
of it. The glimpse of his face as he'd rushed at Cwynn convinced her. She had to warn the druids—she had to warn
them all. An attack could come at any time, in any way.

"What is it?" he was asking. "Catrione, are you all right?"

She pressed her hands against her head, trying to wrap
her mind around every possibility at once. What was he
planning? Where had he gone?

"Cailleach Catrione?" A tap on the door brought
Catrione to her feet. She opened the door enough to see
Bride in the corridor, holding a candle. "Cailleach Catrione,
are you there? Please come. You're wanted—needed—in
the hall."

Catrione glanced over her shoulder at Cwynn. "Don't tell
me it's more messages from my father?"

"Oh, no, my dear." Bride coughed, then handed her the
candle and a basket containing a jug of hot water and clean
towels. "Take a moment—refresh yourself. This time it's
your father himself."

"Fengus-Da?" Catrione blurted. "He's here?" Father's

coming. A chill went down her back as she remembered that whisper in the wind.

"On his way to Ardagh. He made a special trip."

Catrione turned back to Cwynn. "I'll leave you now. I have to go and see—"

"Your father. The chief of Allovale… He's very powerful, isn't he? Almost as great as Meeve?"

"Greater, to hear him tell it," she said with a shake of her head as she finished dressing and left the room.

In the hall, Catrione peered into the shadows where the shapes of armed men clustered around the long tables, eating and drinking in the wavering rush light. "Fengus-Da? Is that really you?"

The barrel-chested warrior in black leather and a solid homespun cloak turned as Catrione entered the long dining area.

He squared his shoulders and hooked his thumbs in his sword belt. The sour look he regarded her with told her he was as glad to see her as spoiled cheese. "Can I ask what it is you're still doing here, when I sent a dozen men to bring you home?" was his only greeting.

In shock and disbelief, Catrione stared up into her father's dark face. A rough beard covered his jaw; he looked as if he'd been in the field a week and smelled as if he'd been there a month. "Can I ask what you're doing here at all, in the middle of the night?"

"I came to make sure my daughter was safe." His black eyes glittered, and he stank of old sweat and blood and something even more foul. She looked down and saw he had goblin spore on his boots and was tracking it all over the dining hall.

"You came to establish a position." Catrione was shaking inside, but she held herself steady. "Do you see what's on your boots? It's not safe to be riding the country at night—have you any idea what's happening—"

"Aye," he cut her off. "Do you? Meeve's been poisoned. Did you know that?"

Stunned, almost as if she'd been slapped or dumped with cold water, Catrione felt one more piece of the pattern click into place. She looked up at her father as if seeing him for the first time. Deep pockets of fatigue hung beneath his shadowed eyes, and for the first time she realized there was a difference in their expression. Like Niona, like the other druids, like all the other people around her, he was afraid. Her father, Fengus-Da, was afraid.

"She was betrayed," Fengus continued. "Her own cowherd—Briecru. Ever meet him? He killed my bull."

"But why?" Of all the news her father might've brought, this was the least expected. And yet…Catrione gazed out across the tops of the trees, to the fire still flickering on the Tor. It made sense. The queen was poisoned…no wonder the Land itself seemed sick.

"He made a bargain with those foreigners Meeve's so fond of. She thought she was making them dance to her tune—seems they were pulling the strings all along." He took a deep breath. "The poison was in her perfume, in some kind of oil. She knew she was sick…she just thought she was dying of whatever it was killed her mother."

"And why are you here?"

"You listen to me, girl, and you listen hard." His eyes pinned her as if she were a little girl caught disobeying.

"There's something stirring in the land, Catrione. These past months, the Lacquileans have been sneaking in, over our borders, through the mountains, a few at a time, waiting for a signal to rise when we're all looking the other way. And now—" He looked out over the land. "And now one of her own's betrayed her. I'm married to the land as much as Meeve is, at least in Allovale, and I don't like what I feel."

*Neither do I.* Catrione stared up at her father, trying to decide how much to tell him, trying to decide how much he could understand. *As above, so below. As within, so without.* Tiermuid's plot would affect everything, in the way the ripples of a stone thrown into the center of a pond affects the weeds along its edge. "Everything's affected, Fengus-Da. Everything—goblins getting loose—"

"Catrione, I'll wager anything those attacks aren't really caused by goblins. But now I know you're safe, and Tully has matters in hand here, I'll be leaving in the morning. I'd rather meet Meeve on my own terms, in my own way, than have to parade through her druids at Ardagh."

"So you do mean to intercept her."

"But not to make war. To make peace."

"Marrying me to Meeve's son isn't to be part of it, Fengus-Da. You can keep me out of any peace you mean to make."

"So you found out about that, did you?" He had the grace to look sheepish.

"I got it out of one of Tully's knights. What're you thinking? Was there ever a doubt in your mind I'm druid and mean to stay one?"

"It wasn't my idea."

"It wasn't?" She blinked.

"No, of course not. It was Meeve's—seems she's got a son everyone forgot about, in some goddess-forsaken place—"

"Out on Far Nearing."

"Oh, you found out about that, too, did you?"

Catrione shook her head. "If you should meet ArchDruid Connla on the way to Ardagh, please tell her—" Catrione broke off. "I'll give you a message in the morning, all right? You take it, and if you see the ArchDruid or any druid, in fact, warn them—"

"Catrione." He touched her cheek, patting it as he used to do, when she was small and demanding. "Times are changing. Are you sure—"

In disbelief she stared at him. "Of course, I am, Fengus-Da. This is my life. I've never doubted it." Maybe not never, she amended to herself.

"Would you understand me, Catrione, if I told you I found that troubling?" He shook his head. "I didn't come to upset you. Of course I'll take your message."

"She left Mochmorna nearly a sennight ago but according to the ravens we had from Ardagh, she's not there yet. It's likely you'll meet her—what's wrong?"

Fengus's brow was puckered, his mouth grim. "You say she set out from Mochmorna?"

"Aye?"

"When we were tracking my bull across the country, we came upon a group of travelers. They'd been slaughtered to look like goblins had been at them, but we could tell it wasn't goblins. What we could also tell is that they came from Eaven Morna."

"Are you telling me you think Connla's dead?" She felt

cold all over. *The child who can't be killed by hand of woman, hand of man, sows seeds of chaos through the land....*

"A poison is eating it's way across the land, Catrione. Meeve's not the only one married to the land, you know. I may not be druid in the way you are, but I can feel things, too."

"Garrison your men in the dining hall." She drew a deep breath, then put a hand on his arm. She was too tired to argue with him further. If he wanted to traipse across the country, it was his business. "Maybe you don't believe in goblins, but I do." *And worse things, even,* she thought, *but you wouldn't believe me if I tried to tell you.*

"I'll leave some men behind to garrison the house. You can't stop me—they'll camp outside the walls. I'm an old man—grant me the privilege of knowing my daughter is safe." He leaned down and kissed her cheek awkwardly.

She watched him join his men. He limped a little and he looked old. Her encounter with Cwynn, her journey into TirNa'lugh had invigorated her and she knew she would not sleep. *There's no use waiting,* she thought. *You know what Timias is, and you know what he's likely to do.* But how to stop this child who couldn't be slain? How to stop this thing that wasn't like anything else?

A low wind sighed in the trees as she crossed the crowded courtyard, threading her way through clustered camps of refugees. *The trees,* she thought. *Maybe there's something I missed. Maybe there's something I can understand now.*

She did not go to her dormitory. Instead she went to the still-house, where the rushlights still burned fitfully in iron sockets beside the door. She slipped inside and headed for the small chamber behind the still-room where the Mem'brances were kept.

There was fire and there was motion and they came together in a bolt of agony every time the wooden cart jounced over the rutted road. Morla clenched her jaw and twined her fists in the itchy wool blankets on which she lay and tried to remember a time before the pain.

"Drink this."

Lochlan's voice was ragged as the road, and the haggard look on his face made her want to weep. "Where are we?"

He gently eased a hand behind her head as he held a small flask to her lips. "Here. You have to have drink. Remember what the still wife said? Drink."

"What is it?"

"The still wife sent it—said it would help."

He coaxed two or three sips into her. Then she turned her head away, for the stuff was roiling in her stomach and the nausea only made the pain in her leg worse somehow. "I can't. I'm not thirsty and it's making me sick."

"She said it was important that you drink."

"I can't."

"You have to try, Morla." His eyes bore into hers.

"I'll try. Just—just let it settle, all right?"

A fleeting frown darkened his face, but he put the flask down beside her and eased out of the wagon. "I thought we'd stop the night here. It's the last druid-house before we enter the high country."

"Where're the druids?" She pushed herself up on her elbows and managed to peer out over the side of the wagon.

Lochlan shook his head. "I guess they all went to Ardagh. Connla was angry when she left Eaven Morna—who knows what she's got brewing? Every house we passed was empty."

"And you think Connla called them all to Ardagh? Every last one?"

"It looks that way."

"Any more sign of blight?"

Lochlan paused. "It must not've spread this far. Maybe that's a good sign. Aren't things supposed to be healthier around Ardagh? The ground more fertile, the cows give richer milk, all that?"

"I wouldn't know," she replied, then tried another sip. She fell back against the pillow as the liquid fought its way down. "I can't remember the last time I went to Ardagh."

"Good girl, have some more. I'm going to have a look around. See if I can find the still-house." He hesitated, his hands hovering over her, then turned and stalked away.

A soft breeze rustled the branches above her head and she realized the pain had diminished another notch or two. Nuala's brew was working. With a sigh, she pushed herself up and managed to swallow another two sips before he was back.

"There's a pool here." He jerked a thumb over his shoulder. "A healing pool. We should see if it helps you."

"All right." She took a deep breath, then forced herself to gulp a whole mouthful of the brew. Nausea rose in her gorge, and she pressed her lips together and clenched her fists so hard her nails bit into her flesh.

He unlocked the side and stood next to her. "Put your

arms around my neck," he said as he slipped his arms beneath her.

A white hot brand blazed up her spine as he lifted her, and she bit her lip so hard she tasted blood.

"It's not far," he murmured. "Easy now. Hold on tight."

But the pain and the motion and the brew was more than she could bear and she found herself vomiting watery white mucus streaked with brownish bile down his back. She made a choking noise and burst into tears, but he only shook his head and murmured, "Enough, now, it's all right—we're almost there."

Her vision condensed to a pinprick and she felt her head loll back against his shoulder and she thought she felt him shift her weight ever so slightly, so that she nestled in the hollow of his chest. A memory of warm sun and the scent of mountain thyme flashed through her mind. Images, so long suppressed she'd thought them forgotten, swirled through her mind like lengths of rainbow-colored ribbons against a black velvet sky.

*The full moon coincided with Beltane that year—the grandmothers all predicted a bumper crop of babies. "Who will you choose?" he asked her as they sat, chewing on willow stalks, watching the brook bubble over the stones.*

*She shrugged, looking at him sideways. She liked him in a different way than she liked anyone else and she had always hesitated to join the ranks of all the other girls in the keep, who threw themselves at the young men, spurred on by Meeve's abandon. She didn't necessarily want him to know she admired the breadth of his shoulders, the color of his eyes, the cleft in his chin.*

*"How 'bout Liam? Will you choose him?"*

*Liam had distinct buckteeth. She laughed.*

*"Dougal. He's a good lad—how 'bout him?"*

*Dougal was ten. She rolled her eyes, shaking her head as he named one after the other, each one more ridiculous until at last he said, "Well, then, I suppose you'll have to choose me."*

*That took her by surprise. "You?"*

*"I've named every unmated man in ten sheepfolds. There's no one left."*

*"You've named every cripple and child and old man, yes. There're plenty you haven't named—how about Colm? Or Niall? They're both unmated."*

*"Colm's a bit thick—he'll never keep up with you."*

*"I hear he's plenty thick." Morla snickered, then poked Lochlan in the ribs. "You want me to pick you?"*

*He met her eyes. "It'd be an honor."*

*"You never pick me—not even for bat-ball or pickle-stick."*

*"I wasn't sure you'd see that as an honor. You always get the maids to teasing me. It's hard to talk to girls when they're all laughing at me over something you've said."*

*She splashed him then, with a hard little kick. "That's not the reason at all, you liar. You know I'm better than you are. You just don't like being stood up."*

*"I like being stood up just fine under the right circumstances,"* he had replied, and before she knew what was happening, she was on her back, and he was kissing her.

Morla opened her eyes to the loud trickle of water and billowing clouds of steam. She was lying on her back on a reed mat beside a smooth stone pool. "Lochlan?"

"I'm here." He waded up out of the pool, his naked arms and chest breaking the water, his hair wet and streaming off his face. His chest was covered with subtle red and green and blue tattoos, all worked in intricate patterns around scars, forming a living record of his deeds. "Come, I think this might help. It's already taking my aches away." Involuntarily she cringed as he reached for her. "I don't mean to hurt you. I'll be careful."

He eased her into the water on the reed mat, and gently pushed aside the tunic. The pool was very quiet, the steam very warm. She floated, her head supported on his shoulder, sensing the weight of his body beneath the surface of the water. "Are you all right?" he breathed against her ear. Despite the pain, desire rippled through her.

She nodded, feeling the pain in a detached kind of way. The steam relaxed her, seeped into her pores, easing the relentless burning.

"I'm just going to put some water on the wound, all right? Just a few drops—"

He might as well have driven nails into her eyes. She bolted up and off the mat, flailing into the pool, the pain stretching her and contorting her. She plunged into the water, swallowing gulp after choking gulp as Lochlan dragged her up and out. Lifting her, he carried her out of the pool, sheets of water streaming off them both. "Great Mother, I'm sorry, Morla—"

"N-no," she choked out, coughing and spitting. "It helped. It hurt, but it helped." She looked around as he helped her sit, suddenly acutely conscious of the way the wet linen clung to her breasts. "Is there—is there a ledge...usually there's a ledge in these places where you sit—"

"Of course," he said. "Over there."

This time when he picked her up, she managed not to flinch. "It feels better as long as I keep it in the water," she said.

He turned around and quickly strode across the pool, and she noticed he was careful to keep his back to her. "Then I'll leave you here, for a few minutes. I want to get dry clothes—food—" He was still talking as he turned the corner and she saw the bulge in his trews and realized he'd noticed the way the wet linen clung to her breasts, as well.

The water was easing the ache all over, she noticed, as long as she kept the wound submerged and didn't move it much. It was helping, but it wasn't a cure. *She needs a druid for that.* Nuala's insistence had struck her as disinterest, but maybe it had more to do with the wound's severity. She slipped into a drowse again. The heat was reminding her of the hall that crowded Beltane evening, as the sun set and the fires rose ever higher. The mead and the whiskey had flowed like rivers. And her mother had drawn Lochlan out of the hall.

She opened her eyes with a start to see Lochlan bending over her. "There's a healing cave just over there with a place to sleep, a hearth, already stocked with salves and bandages and such. I'll start a fire in it, see what I can find in the way of food. The larder looked bare when I checked it. Are you all right?"

She nodded. The heat and the steam and the easing of the pain were all making her sleepy.

"Are you cold?" His gaze flickered down, then up.

"No," she replied, wondering why he'd ask that. "Not at all." She flicked a few drops of water in his direction.

"Keep that up and I'll dunk you again." He turned on his heel, and she glanced down. Her nipples were hard and erect.

She lay back against the smooth slope, fitting the back of her skull into the special depression carved out for just that purpose. The water crept up around her hips, lapping at her waist. With the ugly gash below the water, her skin was ivory in the purplish twilight. The wet fabric clung to her uncomfortably and she considered removing it. But there was nothing else within reach to cover herself, not even a towel.

She closed her eyes, listening to him moving about, smelled the smoke of the fire, heard the snap and sizzle of frying meat. Steam surged around her, cushioning as a cloud, and she relaxed once more into the memory of the last day they'd been friends.

He had kissed her, there, under the tree, reaching for her as naturally and as hungrily as a man who wasn't quite certain he'd been invited to the feast. She remembered how he'd rolled on top of her, pressing her back into the thyme, letting her feel the rock-hard ridge pushing against her own swelling mound. "You think about that, tomorrow, when you choose," he whispered in her ear. And then he'd gotten up and he'd run away.

She had not seen him again, except on the playing fields, from the stands. She had been so intent on him she had not seen Meeve watching them both. She was Meeve's oldest daughter. It was her right to choose second. It had not occurred to either Lochlan or Morla that Meeve would choose him. Morla remembered her mother's slow stroll down the long line of men, smiling, stopping here and there, to cup a groin or rub her hand up and down a biceps, smooth an errant curl, or pinch a smooth-shaven cheek. She stopped before Lochlan, her fingers dancing over his chest, turning as if to pass him by, then stopping. And now, so many years later, somehow Morla knew exactly what it was. His nipples had hardened. Meeve looked at him, enchanted. Morla watched, dumbfounded, as her mother took Lochlan's hand, cupped it around her breast, and spoke the ancient invitation. Morla blinked away the memory and looked up to see Lochlan had returned.

"I found something to eat. It's not much. Can you come, do you think?"

"If you help me." She raised her arms.

"I found some robes—they may not fit, but they're dry and clean, at least. You put one on and I'll dress that wound."

To his credit, he didn't flinch when it came time to put a bandage on, but she could see that the still-wife was right. The water had eased the burning, but the flesh was still oozing. As he gently turned her leg, he said, "There's water in a flask over there—it's got a silver tinge to it. I think it's the stuff the druids make. You know, the silver-water—what the bards call water of life?"

"You think that'll help?"

"I think it could cure it."

"Then get it—"

"Morla, you know how bad it was when the water hit the wound? This'd be ten times worse. The way it was explained to me, its like cauterizing a wound with a red-hot blade. I've experienced that. It's enough to make a man shit. I don't think I can do that to you."

Morla stared at him. "This is why Nuala said I needed a druid?"

"I'm sure of it—they're the only ones who distill the stuff, the only ones who can."

"Then why should we wait?"

Lochlan nodded at the low bed on which she lay. "Look, Morla—see those rings—those leather ties? That's to hold you in place. I know what it's like."

"You have to." She reached out and hit him with a weak fist. "I've borne a child—three days I was in labor—and then he was stuck for nearly three turns of the glass with his head half hanging out of my bottom. Get the water. I can't stand this pain anymore. Please. It's getting worse again already. I can't spend all night with my leg in the pool."

"What if—what if it makes you worse?"

"Then you leave me here and ride to Deirdre—" She broke off, grimacing. "Or cut my throat with one clean slice. You'd not let your horse suffer this way."

That seemed to decide him. He got to his feet, retrieved the flask. For a moment, he hesitated, and then set to work, tying her securely to the bed. When she was bound, arms and legs, he placed a small pad of dried cudwort between her teeth. "Bite down on this," he said. He poured the water from the flask onto the wound, and she gasped, arched her back and stiffened as the first drops seared all the way to the bone. The world turned red, then white, then finally, blessedly, black.

At some point, Bran realized that day and night had different meanings in Faerie. The rising and setting of the sun wasn't a marker of time passing, but more like a melody that repeated in simple tones that rose and fell according to a preordained pattern. He lay, watching the sky begin to darken, the colors and the shadows begin to shift. He turned his head and looked directly into Loriana's green eyes. There was an intensity in her expression that took his breath away, and he remembered that TirNa'lugh was considered a dangerous place and that even the oldest and most experienced of druids never went there alone. He remembered Morla and Lochlan and he knew they must be very worried. He remembered how he'd felt after the last time he'd been here, how sick and faint and weak, and he remembered what Lochlan said about the sidhe. "Maybe I should go home," he whispered. "You know, back to my own world. I can come another time, right?"

But Loriana sat up and looked around, frowning. From somewhere deep in the wood, he heard the shrieking of what sounded like hundreds of birds, and suddenly the highest branches of the trees began to shake and sway as if a great wind was blowing through. Bran felt no wind, only a great deep sadness.

"Is there something wrong?" he asked as Loriana pressed her hands to her mouth, and her eyes grew wide. She appeared to be listening to something, something he could only dimly perceive as a vibration. "What is it?" he whispered as above them the trees began to dip and sway even more violently. A huge flock of birds rose screaming and took off in a dark cloud toward the east.

"It's the trees," Loriana whispered. "The Forest House, my father's house—where we all live—" Her face crumpled. "The Forest House is burning."

## 14

From his hiding place, Timias in goblin guise watched the Hag pull her stick through her enormous iron cauldron. She muttered as she stirred, low words that he couldn't quite hear, but the sense of which made the ruff on the back of his neck stand up while his tail coiled and uncoiled up and down his legs as he rocked back and forth on the balls of his feet, trying to find a smooth place big enough on which to stand. But despite his cramped limbs, his cold flesh, his empty belly, his gaze was riveted not on the shrunken creature crouching over her cauldron, but on the three stones that supported it—three stones, not four.

One was black, one was white and one glowed a pale green, the color that wreathed the trees of Faerie every spring. It drew his attention, for the images flickering across the surface appeared to pulsate in a manner inconsistent with glints and shadows thrown by flames. Even from this distance, he could see shapes, recognize outlines that looked like trees, and shadows with arms and heads and legs moved across its surface like clouds across a sky. Murkier shadows moved within the pearl and the surface of the obsidian sparkled with red and orange glints. There was something about the way the light flashed and glimmered off the surface that fascinated his goblin nature. The way it moved, he thought, reminded him of the way the goblins danced in Macha's halls. His claws tightened around the pouch as his mind began to churn.

The Mem'brances of Trees spoke clearly of the Hag's four globes, that within each pulsed the spark that enlivened every expression of the element within both worlds. The gremlins proved that this was literally true. If he could get his hands on the one that represented the sidhe, coupled with the power inherent in the shattered globe… A new idea began to form, an idea so radical he felt his ruff rise on the back of his neck and his tail quivered in its coil. There was a way to make certain that the druids and their silver never came into Faerie again and he could use their own magic to do it. Their own magic, used in an entirely unexpected way. Provided of course, he could get the globe away from the Hag and escape with his life. As much as he hated his goblin skin, he had recognized its advantages in finding his way here. He would have to hope it would offer similar advantages in getting out.

Timias leaned closer, trying to see how tightly the globe was wedged under the cauldron and if it truly was one of only three supports, when the long claw on the end of his toe dislodged a pebble, sending a shower of debris cascading down the rocks.

The Hag stopped chanting and stirring. Her head came

up, and she looked around, sniffing audibly, the hairs on the end of her nose quivering like the gremlin's ears. "Child?" she whispered. "Child, is that you?"

*Is that you? She's been expecting me?* he wondered, startled. There was something in the Hag's voice that made him want to run to her, embrace her, wrap his arms around her and never let her go. But something else kept him rooted into place and he clutched the crystals harder, anchoring his awareness into them, so that he could draw upon their power in the way the druids did.

"You know I've been waiting for you for a long time." She paused and sighed. "A very long time, indeed."

There was something of Macha in her, only worse. He felt the voice under his skin, under his nails, in his spine and all the way through his limbs into the marrow of his bones where it began to burn, igniting a longing so great he had to bite his tongue to keep from gasping aloud.

"Don't be afraid, child. This is your home. This is where you belong, down here with me. Maybe that seems quite extraordinary to you, after all you've seen. But surely you feel it, too, don't you child? You can't really feel you belong up there, do you, child? Up there, in the world above?"

It was a hard word the way she said it, the syllables short as the thud of an ax. He felt them in his breastbone.

"You realize it, too, don't you, child?" Her breath steamed in the still air. "Didn't you ever feel you didn't quite…belong?"

Even with the energy of the crystals, Timias found the lure of her voice nearly irresistible. It wasn't just the voice, he thought. It was the tidal wave of emotion that was sweeping across and into him, flooding every pore, every empty, broken place with something that felt like liquid light. It probed his deepest, most intimate recesses, and he shook and shivered as she continued, low and wooing as the softest wind's caress: "It's because you don't."

How does she know that? he wondered, and almost immediately, the Hag chuckled as if she read his mind. "I can read your needs, child. I carried you in me—don't you realize that? Who'd you think your parents were, child? The sun and the moon? The rain and the wind? The earth and the sea? Well, you were right." She cackled again, and the sound echoed around the vaulted ceiling like the shrieks of a flock of crows even as the import of what she said finally shattered his resolve.

"Are you saying you're my mother?" *The child who can't be slain by hand of woman, hand of man, the child of Herne and the Hag.* Shock made him step into her view. "M-my mother was killed by goblins—"

"That was just a story the sidhe-king made up." The Hag turned and he saw her eyes were blank gray discs set in a face as mottled as a week-old corpse. She drooled when she smiled and held out her hand. "He could only tell you what he knew."

Revulsion raced through him and he took a step backward. No, he thought, this wasn't—couldn't be—happening. It wasn't possible. He was having some strange kind of dream, induced by the crystals, perhaps, or the gremlins or maybe even the druids.

"Maybe you think it's impossible." She chuckled, a sound that made his hair stand on end and he realized he had changed from goblin to some odd mixture of all three races—leathery skin and hair gray as a goblin's, a long beard like a mortal, but with a body tall and slim and supple as a sidhe. And a tail, a goblin tail that flickered and curled and coiled around his legs, betraying his every emotion. "The world wasn't meant to hold something like you. And now you're back, finally where you belong." The cauldron was starting to simmer faster and she smiled as she stirred.

"But I—but I want to stay there," he heard himself blurt.

He was not prepared for the wave of disappointment that swept through him. It took him aback, but hardened his resolve.

She drew back her black lips and hissed, and he saw the long yellow teeth at the back of her mouth. The knuckles of her hands whitened as she clutched her stick. It occurred to him that this creature was very powerful and therefore very dangerous and that she could force him to stay. But she wouldn't. He stared into her reddish eyes and realized that this hideous creature loved him. She bent over her cauldron, muttering. "Don't worry. I can't make you stay. I can't make anyone do anything. I can only…stir the pot. But—" she looked over her shoulder and her eyes glittered green "—you'll stay with me awhile, won't you? Now you've come, surely you won't just run." She chuckled again softly.

"I—I—" He hesitated. What he really wanted was the moonstone globe, but he wasn't quite sure how to get it away from her. "I'll stay awhile if you give me some answers."

"What do you want to know?" Her voice was once again low and silky, and the skin crawled on the back of his neck.

"Why did the sidhe-king raise me?"

"That was all your father's doing," the Hag answered. "I

had no part of it—I wanted you here, with me. But your father insisted. He thought you were beautiful. He thought you belonged in Faerie."

*I do belong in Faerie. I want to belong in Faerie and I want to stay there,* Timias thought. "So…does that mean Herne is my father? Just as the trees remember?"

"Oh, yes. That's all true."

"The trees say you have four globes. But I see only three."

She hissed and glanced at him over her shoulder, the hair on the end of her nose quivering. "I had a fourth globe, once. But it broke."

"What happened?"

"You're interested in the beginnings of things," the Hag answered. "That's good, that's very good. I wasn't expecting that."

"But you were expecting me? You knew I was coming?" Talking to her made his bones melt.

"All things find their way to me eventually," she whispered, her voice as lulling as the sound of the wind sighing in the trees of the Forest House on a summer afternoon. "But you're mine. You found your way more easily than most."

"That's why I can change? Even into goblin flesh?" Timias asked.

She shrugged and gave him that ghastly grimace. "You needn't worry about that anymore. You can stay here. With me."

"But I don't want to stay here," Timias said. He glanced around the cold dank space, jagged edges and slippery rocks, tried to imagine never going back to Faerie again, never seeing

Loriana again and decided he could never let that happen. Especially now, now when the answer was so very close.

"Look at the globes." Her voice was soft, wooing. "They're very beautiful—I've spent ages just watching them. Maybe you'd like to look at one up close? One's for the goblins, black as night. One's for the mortals, wet and white, and one of moonstone for the sidhe, who flit and sing and live in trees."

The singsong rhythm of her voice forced him to shake his head and bite his lip hard enough to draw blood just to clear his head.

"Tell me, what do you think of them?"

"They're beautiful," Timias agreed, hedging sideways.

"Which one do you like the best?"

"The moonstone," he answered without thinking.

"Ahh, that's my favorite, too." She gave him another of her ugly smiles and he cringed. If she tries to touch me, he thought, I will vomit. "Really?" Timias managed.

She cackled and drool spooled into the cauldron. "Come and have a closer look, child. Have a look in my brew—I'll let you see what we're stirring up next."

*Crystal smooth and crystal strong, you still all to me belong, add your smoothness to my hands, that they will do what will commands…that I may do what I command…* Silently he repeated the words as he crept closer, examining how the globes were set into the rocks that surrounded the fire pit. They were just wedged.

The Hag smiled and beckoned.

Warily, he crept closer. The images in all three spheres leaped and spun, enticing and teasing. In the moonstone, he thought he saw Loriana, her mouth open, tears in her eyes.

She was speaking to someone, pointing into the distance. Wisps of black smoke blew across her face. He stumbled a little, and cut his foot, and the Hag's eyes flared red as his blood trickled to the ground.

"Come, child, look in the brew."

A puff of steam belched up, and in it, he thought he saw a tree on fire, a living tree engulfed in flame. The thin wail of its agony penetrated to its core. He looked at the Hag and he saw she was weeping.

"Come, child. Just a few more steps."

The images in the moonstone tantalized him, the phantoms in the steam captivated him, as in disbelief, he staggered closer. *Faerie is burning? The Forest House is on fire?* Horrified, in spite of his fear, he sidled to the rim and found he had to lean far over to peer into the depths of the brew. Steam swirled, and a foul odor rose up, engulfing him so that he turned his head to one side and saw the Hag, the round edge of a curved knife flashing red as her eyes.

His tail snaked out, pushed her aside, and he dodged, stumbled and fell. The moonstone was within his reach. *Crystal smooth and crystal strong, make me fast and make me strong.* He grabbed the moonstone, and the cauldron rocked on its base. The Hag shrieked. Timias ran.

The entire cavern quaked. Bits of lichen tumbled off the roof like falling stars into the green water where phosphorescent shapes roiled in the translucent depths. Boulders shuddered and heaved, and the stink of burning skin rose as the Hag grabbed for her cauldron and reached out for him. Timias heard the hiss but didn't pause. He raced up and out of the chamber, his prize clutched close, her cries reverberating off the rocks.

\* \* \*

The smell of cooking oats teased Morla out of sleep. She opened her eyes and lay for a moment, blinking up at the scattered stars twinkling in the purple sky above her, trying to remember where she was and why she was lying on what felt like a woolen blanket over a board. She remembered the goblins. She remembered random faces, both familiar and strange, through a fog of bone-burning pain. The pain, she thought, groping for her leg. The pain was mostly gone, replaced by a dull itch. She started up, realized she was inside a wagon. When and where and how long ago had she fallen asleep?

"Good evening."

She turned her head to see Lochlan smiling at her as he stirred something in a black iron kettle. The kettle hung from a tripod over a rock-lined fire pit. Morla clung to the low sideboard and looked around, blinking and sniffing. She couldn't remember oats ever smelling so good. "I'm starved."

At that a smile stretched across his broad face and he let out a huge sigh. "That's a good sign, thank the goddess. How's your leg?"

"It itches worse than new wool."

"Even better. Here, have a bowl of oats. I found some dried apples—not much but—"

She shoveled the oats into her mouth, gobbling spoonful after spoonful as fast as she could swallow them. When the bowl was empty, she licked the spoon and held out the bowl. "More?"

He filled the bowl to the brim, handed it back to her, then picked up his own. "I'm glad to see you eat."

"I can't believe I'm so hungry—it feels as if I haven't eaten in a week."

"Three days."

She put the spoon down. "Three days?"

"You've been sleeping."

"How much longer—?"

"We'll be at Ardagh late tomorrow, maybe the day after."

"I thought we were going to Deirdre?"

"You remember the woman who took us in? Grania? Between her map and what I know of these roads, Ardagh's not much farther. Once I saw you were on the mend, I decided we'd make for Ardagh. What if we get to Deirdre, and find everyone's packed up and gone to Ardagh? Why not just go there ourselves?"

"Where are we now?"

"I'm not sure, to be honest. I think this was an old grove that's been abandoned. There're stone walls over there—and pits that look like they were cellars, with stone pillars that were holding something up. And plenty of old wood to burn."

Morla swallowed another bite, looking around nervously. Night was falling quickly; bats wheeled and screeched above their heads. She shivered. "Are you sure it's safe here?"

He raised his spear, and in the fading twilight, she saw a shimmer along the blade as he indicated the edge. "I took the liberty, a few groves back, of taking a few bits of their silver and melting it down. So far, though, I've seen nothing, heard nothing of goblins at all."

"You shouldn't have taken the silver—they say the trixies'll come after us."

He shrugged. "I think all the trixies were asleep. So far

nothing's happened." He ladled out a portion into another bowl, noticed her watching, and winked. "There's more, here, don't worry." He paused. "Do you remember anything of the healing?"

She hesitated, her spoon poised above the food. She had the impression of horrible pain, a pain that seared all the way to the marrow of her bones, and his hands, those same hands he so lightly cupped around his own bowl, holding her, soothing her. "Not much."

"That's good," he said. He shoveled a spoonful into his mouth.

There was so much she wanted to ask, so much she wanted to know, but the nutty scent of the oats forced her to swallow her own portion as quickly as she could. For a while, the only sound was the scraping of their spoons against the inside of the bowls. The more she ate, the more she remembered, for it seemed that with every spoonful more and more memories fell into place. But the details of the healing, except for Lochlan's hands wrapping the bindings that held her down, eluded her. From under her lashes, she glanced at him. He was looking at her, and she felt herself blush as their eyes met. To cover her discomfort, she blurted, "Bran's in TirNa'lugh, don't you think? He's all right there, right?"

He looked startled, but replied, "We'll know as soon as we find a druid, Morla, though it looks to me as if every druid in Brynhyvar has packed up and gone to Ardagh. That's another reason I want to get there ahead of Meeve. I'd rather she not know we lost her boy."

"You think she'll notice he's gone?"

"Morla, why're you so angry at Meeve?"

Their eyes met and Morla felt herself flush. A breeze ruffled her hair, cooled her warm cheeks and she put down her spoon. "How much meal did you put in that pot?"

He looked at her as if he thought she'd taken leave of her senses, but he answered her. "A few handfuls, I suppose. Four or five. I wasn't counting."

"Look on the ground. Did you drop any?"

"I suppose I dropped a grain or two—what does it matter? What's your point?"

"It matters a great deal if you're watching the supply dwindle down to nothing, and you're not sure where your next mouthful is coming from."

"Morla, surely you understand that was all for the ambassador—"

"We were starving in Dalraida. We were counting grains, one by one, in some places. Children, old women— even young men in their prime—for they were the ones who did without first. Blight hit us hard." It's not about you, she wanted to say. "You know what I remember most about my homecoming?" He had the grace to look embarrassed as she continued. "The food in her antechamber— I guess it was for the three of you? I walked past that food and I knew it would've fed a family in Dalraida for a week."

Lochlan was silent. "Why didn't you send to Eaven Morna for help?" he asked at last.

"Of course, I did. And each time, nothing." She paused, stared out over the darkening landscape. The sun was going down, the shadows were beginning to thicken. "I assumed times were hard all over Brynhyvar, I assumed Mother had enough mouths of her own to feed. After the third or fourth time, when nothing came, I stopped asking."

"But—" Lochlan broke off with a puckered frown "—Meeve's not like that—"

Morla shrugged. "What would you think, if you were me?"

Lochlan looked away. "I didn't realize it was as hard for you as it was in Dalraida. When you were asleep, you dreamed, and you said things."

Startled, Morla blinked. "I did? What did I say?"

"Nothing that made a lot of sense. But enough. You buried a lot of babies." He looked uncomfortable. "This troubles me, Morla, for in truth, it's not the way Meeve is. If she knew things were as bad as they were—"

"As they are. The only reason I agreed to go to Far Nearing was because she swore she'd send grain. I had to come myself to get even a promise of help from her. What would you think? If you were me?" she demanded again.

Lochlan sighed. "I can't tell you I'd think any differently, I suppose. But I can tell you that's not how Meeve sees it. She's well aware of how you've made her strong. Your mother's built her peace because she knew she could count on the peace of Dalraida. She never fails to speak of you with anything but the highest regard." He dipped his spoon into the oats.

"Words are easy to spend." Morla put the bowl down. She wasn't hungry anymore, but she wasn't quite so angry, either. "But why didn't Mother send help?"

Lochlan shook his head as he spooned down the last of his food. "I don't know, Morla. All I know is, it isn't her.

Words may well be easy to spend, but a reputation's not so easy to earn."

"They didn't even know me at the gates, Lochlan."

"You've not been back in ten years," he returned. "I wager they knew your name. How do you expect anyone to know you if you never come back?"

"I didn't think there was anything to come back to."

"Old Tamkin remembers you kindly."

She laughed, despite the emotions now swirling through her and felt tears spring to her eyes. "Old Tamkin hasn't remembered breakfast in twenty years." Their eyes met and she laughed out loud, as the tears spilled down her cheeks. She wanted to believe him, she wanted to think that the message had never been delivered, even though she knew better.

Lochlan set his bowl down. He hesitated just a moment and then stood up. "Let me have a look at your leg?"

Morla hesitated. Her last memories of the wound were of something black and festering. But beneath the loose linen bandage, all it did was itch. "All right." She placed her own bowl to one side, then pushed aside the blanket. Her linen under-tunic was slit almost to her hip. Gingerly, she peeled back the bandage, and gasped. In the purplish twilight, her skin was very white and very smooth, marred only by the puckered red line. "Great Mother, look at that." She looked up at him. "You were right."

He took a step back in mock disbelief. "Where's the druid to work the date?" He looked up at the sky. "Did you hear that, Mother? Did you hear that, Herne? She said I was right."

"Stop that," Morla said, swatting at him. "What's got into you?"

"Maybe I'm glad you're on the mend. We got the silver in it just in time."

Their eyes met again and she felt an almost audible, tangible sense of connection. If only he hadn't disappeared after Beltane, she thought. They might've talked about it, come to terms with it. She remembered the humiliation of asking for him, more than once, in the practice yards and among the other young men. At first she'd gotten shrugs, and then sympathetic looks that reeked of pity. The wound began to itch, distracting her. She flexed her hands into fists.

"What's wrong?" he asked immediately.

"It's hard not to scratch."

He gestured over his shoulder. "There's a spring over there—looks like another healing well. You want to try it? Might help the itch." He unlocked the latch that held the side of the wagon in place, then held out his hand. "Come on. A bath'll do you good. I've even got soapweed. That hair of yours looks like a rat's nest."

"A bath will do us both good," she snapped without thinking. "You reek like a cess-boy."

"Such thanks," he replied. "Come on, then."

She swung her legs over the side, and the ground tilted up to meet her as the world spun, a crazy kaleidoscope of black trunks and pebble-strewn grass. She clutched the side of the wagon, hanging on to the wooden planks. "I'm not sure I can walk," she managed.

Without a word he picked her up. She tensed, but her body had other ideas. With every step he took, she felt herself relax a little more. More was coming back to her, too—the gentleness with which he'd tended her, the truth of what had really happened after Beltane. It didn't matter how she felt about him, she realized with a pang. He was Meeve's. He wasn't just a lad fresh from prenticing, on his way to seek his place in the world. He was Sir Lochlan of Eaven Morna, the First Knight of all of Brynhyvar. If she had a part in her mother's peace, so did he. And only a consort or a king outranked him. It wasn't Beltane that changed it all between them. It was Meeve.

He set her gently down beside the spring. It bubbled up between the rocks into a moss-lined pool. She turned to face him and her breath stopped in her throat as their eyes met. The shadows were deeper now, the sky above them lilac pink, and the first stars flickered in the east. They were less than a handspan apart, she thought in some rational corner of her mind. Then his mouth came down on hers and she had no more rational thoughts.

He gathered her in his arms and through the linen of his shirt, she was sure she could feel his heart pounding against her breasts. The world tilted and spun again and she closed her eyes, giving herself up to his kiss for just a second, until the more rational, logical side intruded like a splash of icy water. She turned her head and pushed away. "Morla—" he began.

"Why'd you have nothing to do with me after Beltane?" The words burst out of her like runaway horses.

For a long moment he stared at her. "I was sent away. Didn't they tell you?"

"I asked after you—no one seemed to know. All I got were shrugs and looks. And pity that made me feel like a moon-mazed calf."

He reached for her hand, brought it to his lips, and the kiss he pressed into the palm seared her flesh and made her nipples hard. "I should've known—" He broke off and turned away.

"Tell me, Lochlan. Who sent you away? Why?" The warm water eased the itch, and now, tension was filling her body, tension from long-denied need.

"Meeve, I suppose, though I didn't realize it at the time. It was only later—when I came back and they told me you'd gone to Dalraida to be married that I realized what I'd done—"

"What you'd done?"

"I told your mother how I felt about you." He gave a little sigh, a little snort. "That's how young I was, how full of myself that Great Meeve herself had chosen me for Beltane-god. She found me acceptable as a god, I thought she'd find me acceptable as her son—at least for a year and a day— until you tired of me."

*I wouldn't tire of you,* she thought, not quite sure she was hearing correctly. "So what did she say?"

"Nothing then, of course. She kissed me and we went at it some more. And then…" He sighed and squared his shoulders. "The next morning I was called to see my company chief. He told me I'd been selected by the queen to perform a great service for her, and I was sent off to Humbria with a message of some kind. By the time I got back, you were gone to Dalraida, to be married, they said."

"But…" She stared at him through the drifting steam. The summer twilight was deepening, the shadows turning purple. Crickets sang. "But, why didn't you tell me—"

"How?" he asked, almost savagely. "What was I to do?

Ride to Dalraida and congratulate the groom? That was no Beltane marriage you made with him, Morla—it was sealed in blood and silver. And my chief made it clear the only reason I wasn't dead was because you knew nothing. That's when I learned you don't get in the way of Meeve's plans."

"She still has plans, Lochlan." Morla shifted, suddenly uneasy. Was this part of it? Meeve knew Lochlan's feelings all those years ago—now that Meeve was dying, was this her idea of how to make some sort of amends? She pulled her hand free. "She still has plans and we're still part of it."

"Don't you understand what I'm telling you, Morla? I love you. I loved you then. I love you now. I realized it when you were sick—when I thought you would die before I found a druid, and I thought I'd lose you before I could tell you, I…" He broke off, shaking his head, and stared out into the dark wood, where the dim glow of the fire pit provided the only beacon. He cupped her face in his big hand. "We'll go to Ardagh. We'll find Bran. And then at MidSummer, I'll ask Meeve to release me. After she hears about Bran, she may do that anyway. And then—" He broke off. A ghost of a smile flickered across his face. "And then that depends on you." He looked down, looked uncomfortable as only a man in the presence of a woman he wished to bed ever did. "What happens next depends on you."

The air was still—the only sound was the bubbling water, the beating of her pulse. She was shaking. "I thought you…" She shut her eyes. *I can't remember what I thought. All I remember is one moment my mother led you from the hall, and I never saw you again.*

"Think about it." Lochlan got to his feet, and from a pouch in his belt, withdrew a packet of soapweed. As she twisted around, disappointed, he bent and pressed the packet in her palm, and a quick kiss on her cheek. "I'll go tend the fire—you're in no state for this."

"No—" She held out her hand. "Don't—don't go."

"You should get in the water and have a proper bath." Standing, he was so tall, his voice seemed to drift down. "And I'm not sure I can be that close to you without your clothes and not touch you."

"Touch me. All over." She ran one hand down the front of his thigh, and she heard him groan.

He dropped to his knees and was beside her in the water before she had time to blink. He swept her up and she wrapped her arms around his sweaty, gritty neck, then pulled his face to hers. Their mouths came together. She twined her fingers in his hair, clung to him, feeling like the starving villagers of Dalraida suddenly set before a feast. Every sense was filled—she was enveloped by his scent and strength, his taste and touch and feel. She arched against him as his hand went up her back, rolling her tunic up and over her head.

"Anyone there?"

They both jumped. It was Meeve's voice that cut through the purple shadows, and as Morla gasped, her mother, followed by at least a dozen of the Fiachna and a train of supply wagons, rode into the clearing.

"Mother?" Morla blurted, and instinctively drew closer to Lochlan, a gesture that made Meeve raise her eyebrow.

"Morla and Lochlan? What a surprise. Perhaps my First Knight and my daughter would be pleased to tell me how it is we meet them here all alone?"

"And what exactly did you see happen to Bran?" Meeve paused in the act of filling her goblet. The thick rug muffled the sounds outside the tent, and the tent itself was even more sumptuous than Meeve's own chambers. It was a gift from the Lacquilean ambassador and Meeve, who loved rich fabrics and bright colors as much as she loved men and gold, took it everywhere and used it at every opportunity. Focused on Meeve's face, Lochlan could almost believe the two of them were alone at Eaven Morna, not camped in the midst of the Forest of Gar.

"I know it sounds unbelievable. But I saw him lifted up by an enormous black bird and I believe he was taken into TirNa'lugh by a sidhe, disguised. Connla suspected something like that could happen to Bran—that's why she put the ward on him. But she's gone now, and they must be free."

"So what makes you think he wasn't just grabbed by the goblins when you and Morla rode away?" Meeve's face was white, her eyes bore into his like twin blades.

"I saw the raven grab him." Lochlan leaned forward and ran his hand through his hair, feeling the sweat run down his sides. "As soon as we get to Ardagh, as soon as we get anywhere there's a druid, Majesty, I swear, I'll go and look for him myself. But—"

"Until then, I suppose there's not much we can do." Meeve passed him the flagon and nodded. "Aren't you going to ask me about the ambassador?"

Lochlan stifled a sigh of relief. "He was called back to his own country?"

"You could call it that. Or to whatever part of the Summerlands such double-dealers are sent. It was Fengus who found out. Briecru was in league with them—aye, our very own Briecru. They were poisoning me, Lochlan. I'm not sick at all." She raised the goblet, drained it and filled it again.

"How did Fengus find out?"

"Because Briecru thought he'd stir up trouble, and he decided to steal Fengus's bull—aye, the one he calls the Black Bull of Allovale, that one. Well, you can imagine how happy Fengus was about that. What Briecru wasn't counting on was that Fengus himself would go after the animal. And to make a long story short, it was Fengus who found Briecru waiting for the beast, with a lot of incriminating evidence, I suppose you'd call it. He sent Briecriu's head back in a sack with the unguent they'd been giving me all over his face. Well, I took one look, and I called the whole lot of them together—every Lacquilean under my roof, that is—and after they feasted, I had their skins peeled off their bodies and their heads cut off. I stuffed the skins with straw, and I sent them back." Meeve gulped back the rest of her wine and set the goblet down with a thump, even as she motioned for Lochlan to pour her more. "Then we left."

The flagon was empty. Lochlan reached for the wineskin. He could feel the anger emanating off Meeve like a living thing.

"I sent a messenger to Fengus. With three milch cows, my own best bull-calf and my thanks." She raised the goblet and tipped it to her lips with a smile. "I might have to marry him myself."

Lochlan raised a brow. Meeve spurned Fengus as regularly as the sun turned in the sky. Now she owed him her life, for exposing the traitor Briecru and his plot to poison Meeve with the perfumed salve. It was clear to Lochlan, however, that the poison was still in her. She was going to need Connla's help.

As if she'd read his mind, Meeve said, "Assuming Connla can save me."

"Surely at Ardagh, there's the skill—"

Meeve rose to her feet, shaking her head and Lochlan broke off in alarm. She paced back and forth, rubbing her hands up and down her arms. "My limbs have started to shake for no reason." She flexed her mouth in a grimace that he knew she meant to be a reassuring smile, but in the flickering light of the single lantern, he could see she was quivering from head to toe.

He jumped up. "What can I do—should I call for the still-wife?" He fumbled for a wrap and shook out its copious folds. "Come, let me hold you—"

"Sit back down." She waved her hand impatiently. "There's nothing you can do—I've found it's best to move, not to fight it." She spoke through clenched teeth. "It—it just has to work itself out."

"So this does beholden you to Fengus."

That was a safer topic than her health. She sank down beside him, her eyes fastened on the fire. "I really might have to marry him, you know."

*If you live long enough.* He sensed that the poison had been perilously close to doing unredeemable damage, if it hadn't already. But he stretched out his legs and replied in the same tone, "And a lucky man Fengus would be."

"I owe him quite a lot." Meeve glanced at him over her shoulder.

Again, Lochlan hesitated. Meeve and Fengus were old rivals, never able to agree about anything for very long, but equal enough in power that neither had succeeded yet in toppling the other. With one masterful stroke, however, Fengus, to Meeve's way of thinking, had gained the upper hand. But to point out that seemed foolhardy with Meeve in this mood. She was testing him. "His daughter's a druid."

"I'm not the only one who believes a druid's not a good thing to be, Lochlan. The druid-houses are emptying in droves, and it's not just blight. I know you cling to the old ways—"

"I'm alive because of the druids, Meeve. Don't you remember that time my arm went bad, and the poison started to grow—" He broke off, for she had turned to him and was staring at him with a face black as night. "You know it's true—you were there."

She wrapped her arms around her legs. He saw gooseflesh speckling her arms. The air inside the tent was humid—he was warm to the point of perspiration.

"Are you cold, Meeve?"

"I'm fine," she snapped. He saw a slight tremor roll through her, but she only tossed her head. The red-gold hair didn't bounce—it hung, dry as straw, and she gathered it up and thrust it over one shoulder. He saw her wipe a handful of strands on her thigh.

He glanced again at the mattress, with its sumptuous furs, its silken pillows. She might've dispatched the Lacquileans but she'd clearly seen no reason to get rid of their possessions. Despite her protests, he reached for a fur and slipped it over her shoulders. She said nothing, but she didn't shrug it off.

Meeve was muttering, as if to herself, "I hope I've done the right thing…there's nothing of me in Morla, after all."

"Are you joking?" Lochlan sat back. "Maybe she's not like you in looks, but she's the image of you on the inside. You don't see it, perhaps, but no one takes her land and her people more seriously than she. Didn't you notice how thin she was, Meeve? Do you realize her people are starving? She's denied herself that others might eat."

Meeve turned to look at him, the fur clutched close. "How do you know this?"

"She raved. When she was sick. And so I asked her." She had more than raved, thought Lochlan, remembering the broken mutterings that had gone on and on, like a torrent long held in check. And she blamed Meeve.

"I sent her grain, cattle, whatever she asked for—except a useless druid."

"I don't think it reached her, Meeve. Who was in charge of the stores? Who oversaw the coming and going of everything in Eaven Morna?"

In the orange light, Meeve's color changed from deathly pale to sickly orange. "Briecru had charge, of course. Briecru—that pox-ridden pig. I hope Fengus burned his filthy corpse—he wasn't fit for goblin fodder." She spoke low and quickly, her voice breathy, her eyes wild. "He robbed my own child." With a cry, Meeve stumbled to her feet, knocking over her wine goblet.

Lochlan jumped up beside her, steadying her. Beneath the

heavy fur, the queen's body felt perilously frail, the palsy ripping through her in great quaking waves. She struggled weakly. He ignored her feeble protests, swept her up in his arms, and carried her to the low bed. Gently, he placed her on it, then drew back. As the queen writhed, her whole body engulfed in spasms, he said, "I'll be right back—I'm going for help."

He dashed across the camp, to the tent where the queen's women slept. He wasn't surprised to see Morla still sitting beside the fire.

She looked up. "What is it?"

"Your mother," he said. "She's sick—she needs the still-wives—"

"Sir Lochlan?" A woman with a face like a dumpling peeked through the flap, blinking in the torchlight.

"The queen's sick and needs you, lady," he said. "Please, come now."

The woman disappeared, but within the tent, he heard urgent stirrings. Across the camp, he saw the watch turn to look in their direction.

Morla got to her feet slowly, leaning on a thick branch. "Is she dying?"

There was no time to answer, for the still-wives and the serving women flooded out of the tent like a gaggle of white-gowned geese. They flocked around Lochlan and bore him away, voices raised in urgent questions that they fired at him like blows. He felt, as much as saw, Morla watching from the fire. He could hear Meeve vomiting as he shoved back the tent flap. The women surged past him, and he had a glimpse of a shuddering Meeve hanging weakly over the side of the bed. Then the tent flap was yanked out of his hand and slapped across his face. He'd been dismissed.

Lochlan stood a moment, collecting his thoughts. He had a sense that the world was dangerously close to spinning out of control, when Morla touched his arm.

"Is she dying?"

Their eyes met, and he felt the air between them crackle, even as he saw the dark look in her eyes and heard her bitter tone. *You have to tell her that Meeve never meant to slight her,* he thought. "Come." He led her down the path a little ways, cupped her elbow beneath his arm. She swayed close to him, face turned up, and he ached to lean down and kiss her again.

As if she'd read his thoughts, she stiffened, opened her eyes, then pulled away. "Well?"

He glanced around the clearing. The forest was quiet, the night air heavy as a cloak, thick with pine and something else, something sweet and musky that he realized was her. "I think we have to get to Ardagh, as fast as possible. Your mother needs a druid."

"You want to leave now."

It was a statement, not a question and once again, he felt that uncanny sense of connection. It was like stepping into yesterday, he thought, and he wanted to grab her and hold her close and do all the things he'd missed his chance to do all those years before. But he didn't dare delay. "If you can ride."

"Are you sure you want to leave her?"

Lochlan glanced over her shoulder, and she turned to see what drew his attention. Was that movement in the trees, or just a breeze? Not even the ghost of a breeze teased his cheek. It was as if the whole world held its breath, waiting. Waiting for what, he wondered. The sun must set on the old day before the new day dawns…. "I don't think we've a choice, Morla. I know she needs a druid. I know I can get to Ardagh by noon tomorrow if I ride through the night. I don't want to leave you here. Do you think you can ride?"

"Won't you get there faster without me?"

"I'm not leaving you here."

She stared up at him, her eyes blazing. Behind them, he could hear the still-wives calling for water from the spring. "Did you mean what you said, before?"

Lochlan caught her hands in his, pressed both of them to his mouth. "I never meant anything more. Meeve's too sick to even comprehend what's going on, I'm afraid. It sounds to me like the whole underbelly of the country, from the Marraghmourns and into the uplands of Allovale and Gar, is riddled with foreign troops, waiting for some signal. Meeve—goddess bless her—might very well have provided just what they were waiting for. So the sooner we leave, the sooner a druid comes back, the sooner a druid finds Bran, and the sooner you and I strike an alliance with Fengus."

"Fengus? What're you talking about?"

Lochlan shook his head. "Meeve never expected Cwynn to marry Fengus's daughter—she saw it as an opening. This was all an elaborate scheme on her part."

"I knew that—"

"But did you know she expected you to marry Fengus?"

*Marry Fengus. Marry Fengus. Did you know she expected you to marry Fengus?* The question echoed through Morla's mind to the rhythm of the hooves as they pounded down the moonlit road. The night was well advanced before Lochlan pulled his horse to a walk and suggested that they stop. "You have to be tired, Morla. You need to rest."

"But what makes you so sure?" she blurted, as if he'd not spoken. "What makes you so sure she expected me to marry Fengus?"

Lochlan heaved a great sigh, reached across and covered her hand with his. "I can't tell you exactly what it is that makes me so certain, other than it fits the way her spider's mind works. Let's find a place to rest. Or maybe it's the way she's clearly been contemplating marrying him herself, at last." He spread out a saddle blanket on the ground and beckoned her to join him beneath a tree. Hesitantly, awkwardly, she settled herself, her leg held stiff and straight beside her. A deep ache had begun inside and she hoped that the ride hadn't affected the healing. "And then there's the fact that Fengus's daughter is a druid.... Did you know that?"

"But druids are known to leave their druid-houses. I've heard of more than one who's left the life and married—"

Lochlan shook her head. "I know Meeve. She never does anything that transparent. Look, Morla, you're a better risk. You've proven you can rule, even through difficult times, you bring not only substantial holdings in Mochmorna from Meeve, but what you have from your husband, as well as the respect of all Dalraida. Between that and Allovale…why do you think Meeve's considering marrying him?"

"Fengus is old enough to be my father…" Her voice

trailed off as she shifted on the rocky ground. "I don't even know Fengus—how does my mother expect—"

"You didn't know Fionn, either. She expects you to see things the way she does, I suppose. It all makes perfect sense to me, Morla."

"How?"

He unhooked his plaid, folded it and offered it to her. "Here. Use this as a pillow for that leg. I was afraid we came too far." He hesitated, then said, "It's like this, Morla. Meeve likes to get people to think her ideas are their ideas. She gets you and Fengus and Cwynn and whatever the girl's name is…all together in a room and you all make peace and drink toasts and Meeve smiles benignly. The girl refuses to leave off being a druid. Cwynn's clearly a bumpkin fresh off a fishing boat. So now what's the next logical thing that will cross Fengus's mind as he gazes around the room? Where do you think his eye's going to fall?" His voice was soft and lulling, and when he touched her cheek gently with the back of one hand, she jumped.

"But…" Morla startled back. "I don't want to marry Fengus. I'm of age, she can't force me—"

"No, of course she can't. But, Morla, she's going to put the good of Brynhyvar before you. What will you say to that?" He slipped his hand behind her head, caressing the tight muscles at the back of her neck and she relaxed almost involuntarily under his touch. "She's always been right before, you know, about what the land needs."

A slow heat was spreading through her limbs. It made her head feel too heavy for her neck, made it seem only natural she should nestle in the hollow of his shoulder, only right that he should tip her face up and back. Her eyes fluttered as his breath caught in his throat. "She wasn't right about what I needed." She gazed up at the star-speckled sky and listened to the rapid beating of his heart beneath his leather breastplate. "I don't want to marry Fengus," she heard herself say, almost to herself. She looked up at Lochlan and desire so acute it left her breathless stabbed through her, forcing her to blurt, "I want to marry you."

In one swift motion, they reached for each other, sliding into each other's arms with all the ease of old lovers, falling into each other. Her arms twined around his neck, he lifted her gently onto his lap, and her head fell back onto his shoulder as his mouth came down on hers. They stayed like that for the space of many heartbeats, Morla scarcely daring to breathe. There were enough words, she had not enough awareness to process the rush of all the emotions that crashed upon her and so she clung to him, drinking in his strength, until at last, Lochlan raised his head. His breathing was ragged, his heart beat like a drum against her now-naked breasts. "Let me—" He got to his feet. "Let me build us a bower, a little farther back. We're too close to the track here."

Unsteadily, she got to her feet, tugged her clothing into some rough semblance of order, and followed, carrying the plaid in one arm and holding fast to his hand with the other. He steered her to a space beneath the spreading branches of some kind of tree and gently pushed her down. "Just wait."

She could hear him moving in the dark, saw the vaguest outline of his shape in the gray moonlight filtering through the branches. She knew exactly what he was doing— weaving together the little lean-to, covered with branches and boughs, heaped with pine needles, that every boy was taught to build before his thirteenth year; the little lean-to every man made every year at Beltane, to be his Beltane bower. She heard a sharp knock and a muffled swear, followed by a gasp of pain. "Are you all right?" She peered into the dark.

To her relief, he was there at once, extending a hand. "Stubbed my toe. Watch out for that root. And that branch."

She slid her palm into his hand, marveling to herself how easily her fingers twined with his. For a split second she hesitated and suddenly she knew in her bones that this was not at all part of Meeve's plan for either one of them. The faintest echoes of the druid blood that ran so strongly in her twin stirred. To do this would have repercussions and ramifications.

"Morla?"

She heard ten years of longing compressed in the two syllables of her name, and understood. At Beltane, it was always the woman who led the man. Swiftly, she reached for his hand and pressed a hot kiss on the back, as she spoke the words the ritual required. "Lord Lochlan of Glenrae, First Knight of Mochmorna, the Fiachna of all Brynhyvar, will you take me to the green woods?"

The sound he made could've been a sob as he lifted her and crushed her to his chest, heedless of her injury. As his mouth came down on hers, he answered her with the ritual reply, "I have a bower waiting that I built just for you."

Morla was dreaming. She knew she was dreaming, because she was walking along the shore with Bran, hand in hand, the way they used to do when he was very small.

He seemed to waver, too, depending on the angle at which she looked at him—sometimes he seemed very young, and sometimes he seemed older, old as he'd look at her age, or even older. He was holding her hand and explaining something to her, very earnestly, stopping now and again to pick up a rock, or a shell or point out something along the far horizon. There was an odd intensity to the light, and no matter how far they walked, they didn't seem to reach the end of the beach. Finally she stopped. "What is this place, Bran? Why are we here and where are we going?"

"We're both going back now," he said. His eyes were very brown and very sad, and he fumbled at his neck where he wore a leather cord. "I wanted to tell you I was sorry I lost it."

"Lost what?"

"My shell. The one we found the day you went away. I wanted you to know how sorry I was to lose it. I always kept it close. Whenever I smelled it, it brought me back here. I was happiest here with you, Morla. I just wanted you to know." A wave washed over their feet and white gulls wheeled above the water. Bran's face had taken on a translucency—she could see the horizon through it.

"Bran?" she cried, reaching for his hand. But all she grabbed was insubstantial mist. He was fading away in front of her, dissolving like the foam that ran over her feet and between her toes.

Birdsong pierced Morla's dream, not the harsh screams of the gulls, but the trills and warbles and cheeps of the forest at MidSummer. She opened her eyes to see a gray mist seeping between the cracks of the rough lean-to, and the sound of birds twittering very close. It was very early morning and Lochlan was beside her. She fumbled for his hand, and for a long moment, lay beside him, breathing in the mingled scent of pine and sex and man. For the first time in many years, maybe since they'd placed her son in her arms, she was happy. She shut her eyes and drifted back into her dream.

The next time she opened her eyes she was looking up at the edge of a glinting blade, held to her throat by a soldier dressed in a cloak of Lacquilean indigo. She tried to sit up, fell back at the sting of the sword and heard Lochlan bellow, "No!"

As she was grabbed by at least half a dozen men, her arms were forced behind her and bound together with a leather cord. She tried to struggle, kicking, biting, but her efforts were in vain. Pain exploded across the back of her skull, and twinkling lights exploded in front of her before everything went black.

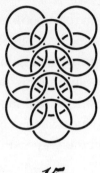

## 15

With the moonstone tight against his chest, Timias charged over the rocks, his tail propelling him down the tunnel. Beyond him, he heard the Hag shrieking. The roof and walls shook, and debris rained down on him as he scrambled through the falling rubble. One thought pounded through his mind, one thought ran over and over. *To Faerie. To Faerie and Above.*

Far away and far above, he saw a pinpoint of greenish light. *I can do this,* he told himself, even though the way appeared to be straight up. *I can do this.* He held up the pouch and stuffed the globe into it. The globe pushed against the crystals, and the pouch itself shifted and before his eyes grew larger. He smiled, grimly, gripped the pouch in his jaws, and began to climb up the sheer rock walls, aided by goblin instinct and his prehensile tail.

Initially it was painful and slow. His claws bled as he grasped for purchase, his shins and elbows and knees all scraped against the jagged walls. And then the crystals and the globe and his intention began to work their magic. The higher he climbed, the easier it was. The sheer walls began to angle, the rocks began to smooth. He got to his feet and straightened and found, to his delight, he was Timias again, and the green grass of Faerie was spilling over the lip.

He knotted the bag around his waist and stifled his impulse to laugh. Not yet, he told himself. Not yet. There was still Loriana to convince. There was still silver, of which Faerie must be rid. And there were still goblins that had to be controlled.

"CAW! CAW! CAW!" The most enormous raven he'd ever seen landed on the lowest limb of the tree, turned and looked at him as he came up over the rise of the land. "CAW! CAW! CAW!"

"Finnavar," Timias said. He spread his hands to show he was unarmed, except, he thought, except for the magic in the crystals and the globe.

"CAW! CAW! CAW!" Hatred burned in the bird's eyes, and her feathers gleamed blue-black.

He took a single step and she swooped at him, diving straight for his eyes. He threw up his arms and she flew in again, tearing at his flesh with talons and beak. The sudden ferocity of her attack took him by surprise and she battered away at him, forcing him to the ground, alternating plunging and feinting, avoiding his frantic kicks, his futile blows. Blood ran from his wounds. He flailed his arms and rolled around and around, trying to escape the battering beak.

The pouch on his waist loosened and he curled up in a ball around it, trying to protect it while she gouged at him with beak and talon. For a long moment, he lay, enduring the agony, soaking in the pain, waiting for the right moment to strike. In the one moment she paused to catch her breath, he was ready. In a single mighty move, Timias exploded, knocking Finnavar sideways into a tree. Stunned, she fell to the ground, shaking her head.

He seized her around the neck as she squawked and twisted, kicking at him with her taloned feet, trying to tilt her head enough to gouge him with her beak. She gouged at him with beak and talon, tearing at his flesh. He tightened his grip and she increased her efforts, all in vain. With a smile, he snapped her neck between his fingers and felt her body go limp.

An idea came to him. He snapped off one of her feet, and with her own talons, gutted her carcass. He flung the bloody carcass into the hole, and picked up the black-feathered skin. He stuffed the pouch, which was soaked in his own blood, into it. *Now,* he thought. *Now to find out.*

*By battle, blood and sacrifice, only then can the World be saved.* The lines from the Mem'brances of Trees ran through his mind unbidden, and he sank down onto the green grass of Faerie, breathing hard, too weak to set off, trying to decide what to do next. He had the globe, he had the crystals. So what would bind the two together… What would link the one to the other, while at the same time creating a boundary that would hold the druids out? What did he need to work a druid spell in Faerie, a spell that would forever hold against the druids, against the goblins, against silver. *And against you, ugly Hag,* he thought, seething with outrage. She'd wanted to kill him all along—no wonder she tried to make him believe she understood him, cared about him, loved him. It was all a trick to get him into her cauldron.

He picked up the carcass, slung it over his shoulder, still

musing. Druid magic was elemental magic, primarily, based on a combination of the four essential elements, and one each of three different things: medium, intent and outcome. His intent was clear. The crystals would add the element of Earth, just as the druids used them. He took a deep breath, pondering what else he needed and smelled the smoke.

Could the Forest House, surrounded as it was by hedges of thorns and walls of woven oak and ash, really be burning? Faintly on the wind, he heard the shrill, high screams, and knew if it were not the Forest House, some other part of the wood was indeed burning. *Loriana,* he thought with a pang. *Loriana.* Galvanized by fear, he took off through the trees, forgetting entirely he still had his tail.

"Catrione, we thought you should see this." Baeve's soft voice penetrated Catrione's reverie as she stared at the barks on the table spread out before her.

She turned to see the older woman hesitating in the doorway, carrying something dark and indistinct in the gloom. "What is it?"

"We found it under Deirdre—when they moved her remains, this was there. Sora saw it and gave it to me." She held out what appeared to be a thick piece of black fabric, folded in quarters, and Catrione noticed she was careful not to let the fabric touch her skin.

"What's wrong with it?"

"Feel it."

Perplexed, Catrione reached for the fabric and recoiled. "What is that thing? It feels like a slug."

"Yes, it scarcely bears touching. But that's not all." Baeve shook it out. "Watch what happens when I put it around myself."

With a swish, Baeve snapped the fabric open and pulled it over her shoulders. Instantly, she disappeared.

"Great Goddess," whispered Catrione. "What is that thing?"

Baeve spread it out on the table, and in the uncertain light, Catrione saw that it flowed like water across the surface, rippling out in long waves. "It's a blanket, or a cloak. There's a jagged edge—someone ripped a piece off."

"Or ripped it in half," murmured Catrione, fingering the frayed ends. She picked up the threaded edge and realized that amazingly, the fibers didn't so much end as blend into the shadows around the room. "Great Mother," she muttered. "Do you know what I think this thing is made of, Baeve?"

"Whatever it is, it's slippery as an eel. I don't like touching it. I can't imagine who could make such a thing."

"Deirdre made it," Catrione said. With the barest tips of her fingers, she smoothed the silky fabric. "I can read her signature all over it. She made it out of shadows…. Somehow she managed to find a way to give shadows weight and form and substance. But she didn't make it alone." It slipped off the table and disappeared into the puddle of darkness beneath the table. "Tiermuid helped her. They made it togeth—" She broke off and looked up at Baeve. "That's how the child was conceived. They weren't lovers. They weren't— What they were doing wasn't about love…" Catrione's voice trailed off. *By battle, blood and sacrifice…* Where'd she just seen that? That was how the Mem'brances said the changeling child was to be killed—by battle, blood and sacrifice. Deirdre had given up her life and Catrione hoped that counted for something.

She scrabbled through the barks. "I think I understand a little more, Baeve—"

"Excuse me." Cwynn stood in the doorway, wearing the tunic and trews they'd left for him. "I don't mean to be a bother, and it's obviously quite late, but—"

"What is it, son?" asked Baeve, kindly. "Is it your arm paining you? Can I bring you something to help you sleep?"

"Well, I just woke up, I feel. I'm not really tired. I was wondering if I could trouble you for something to eat?" He rolled his weight back and forth on the balls of his feet and Catrione had the distinct impression he'd far rather be on the deck of a boat.

"Of course you can," Baeve replied at once. "You wait here. I'll be back as quickly as I can."

Catrione sighed, and beckoned to Cwynn. "Come sit. You look like a cat trying to walk across hot coals."

"It's obviously late.…"

"I'm not sleepy, either," she admitted. Their eyes met and as he glanced away, she felt herself flush. What was wrong with her? she asked herself. She was no doe-eyed virgin— she'd lain with lots of men and women, too, to heal them. But there was something about this man that made her nervous. *Because he's the man you are to marry*, whispered the wicked voice in her head. "Please come sit."

He slid awkwardly onto the bench beside the wall, opposite Catrione, hugging the corner as if he might need to make a speedy exit. "I—uh, I suppose I should thank you, for what you did. Before, when we first come to, like, I was—well, I wasn't quite sure what to think."

"What do you think now?" she asked.

"I guess I'm starting to understand why my grandfather thought that druids cause a lot of trouble. At least I think I do."

"What do you mean?" Catrione wrinkled her brow.

"My grandfather would have no truck with them out on Far Nearing. Never said why, exactly. Before I left the midwife told me there's talk of banning the Beltane rites."

"Why?" Catrione sat upright. "Beltane's one of our most sacred nights. To stop the rites would—"

"End a lot of problems." Cwynn shrugged. "I sound like I'm not grateful. I'm sorry. I don't mean to sound that way. I just—"

"Didn't know what to expect."

"Right." He clasped his hand over his stump and in the rushlight, he looked young enough to be a child, face flushed, eyes sheepish. "So…you say your father's here."

"He was," Catrione nodded. "I've seen him. He's on his way to Meeve." She sighed and shook her head. "I hope this time he means what he says. This land has enough problems—we don't need Fengus-Da stirring up a war."

"He'll go to war if I don't marry you?"

"Of course not," laughed Catrione at the alarm on Cwynn's face. "Believe me, I don't want to marry you." It was her turn to realize that what she'd said sounded more hurtful than she meant it.

He moved his bandaged stump restlessly. "Listen, I knew right off— I don't want you to think I expected—"

"Cwynn." Catrione put her hand on his forearm, right

above the bandage. "It's nothing to do with your hand, or lack of it. I'm druid. We don't marry, not in the way of ordinary people."

"You do…what we did?"

"Yes," she replied. "With mortals. Mostly with the sidhe. Occasionally with each other."

"So nights like Beltane and MidSummer and Lammas are all just nights for everyone to have a chance to play like a druid, eh?"

She raised her eyebrows. "Well, not exactly."

"I'm sorry. I may be Meeve's son, but until day before yesterday, I didn't know it. There weren't many women in my grandfather's hall."

"I understand," she said gently, and she did, because as she sat here with him, in the soft orange dark, listening to the crickets chirp in the herb garden just outside, she remembered more of what he'd shown her—of violence and anger and envy. "So what did you think, when you found out?"

"Last thing I was expecting, really." He squirmed ever so slightly and she understood he didn't much like talking about himself.

"You realize Meeve has other children?" she asked.

"Oh, yes, Gran-da told me that right off. I was supposed to wait for them—two of them were coming to fetch me to Ardagh. But Gran-da didn't want me to wait."

"He was afraid your uncle would try to kill you." Catrione's visions had been detailed.

"Yes."

A silence fell between them and Catrione hesitated. "The woman in the Tor—well, that poor thing that was a woman—" She broke off as memories of Deirdre as she used to be, before the shadow of Tiermuid had fallen between them, cascaded through her mind. "She was a good friend of mine—a true sister, in many ways. Her name was Deirdre. She was your sister, Cwynn. She and Morla were twins."

He stared at her. "That was my sister?"

"I'm afraid it was."

Again, there was another silence. "How did…such a thing happen?" he asked at last. "Was that druid magic? Is there a possibility—" He nodded at Catrione.

"That we—? Oh, no." She shook her head. "Not at all. And no, that wasn't druid magic, not true druid magic. The father of the child wasn't a true druid—" He's not a true anything, she thought, remembering the images that had flooded her. "He's the person who tried to kill you." She nodded at the marks Tiermuid's fingers had left on Cwynn's throat.

Cwynn heaved a deep breath, just as Baeve appeared in the door. "The larder's looking very sparse, Cailleach. But I brought what I could get my hands on." She placed a napkin-covered tray between them. "You should eat, too, Catrione. You've not had much more than milk." With a flourish, she removed the napkin revealing two bowls of porridge heaped with cream and honey. "And there's that apple in your bag, son. I can cut it up for you, but in truth it was so pretty, I—I couldn't bring myself to do it."

"No," said Catrione. "No, don't dare cut up that apple."

"Why not?"

"That apple is from Summerlands. You see, Cwynn—" She paused and took a deep breath as Baeve gasped.

"For real, Catrione? For real?"

Catrione looked at Cwynn. "An old woman gave it to you, you said. You met her on the road? With the dog who guided us here?"

He nodded. "I did."

"Well, that explains it. The leaves on the apple are still fresh as though just picked." Baeve patted Catrione's shoulder. "You two eat. I'm going to my bed. These old bones are tired. Good night, dear." She bent and kissed Catrione's cheek, patted Cwynn on the forehead. "Sleep sweet, lad. You earned it."

As the old woman shuffled off, Catrione took a deep breath, wondering how much information Cwynn could possibly absorb.

Cwynn put his spoon down and raised his hand to his face. For a long moment, he sat, silent and staring into the palm of his hand. Then he ran his hand over his chin. He looked at her and his eyes were bleak. "I make my living from the sea. We have goats and pigs and chickens and such and I've seen my share of things not meant to live, things made by mistake. But I've never seen anything like that. What was that? What did that?"

Catrione sighed. So much to explain, so little time. "Have you ever heard the story of Seamus and Seanta of the Silver Hand?"

He stared at her blankly. "No."

"It's a song, a story, about a pair of twins, royal twins, who happen to save the world from the child who can't be slain by hand of woman, hand of man."

"Is that what that thing was? And I was able to kill it because of my hook?"

"No," Catrione said, "but the fact you did makes me think there's hope."

"Are you saying you believe this story is true? Isn't it just a story?"

"If you're asking is it true in the sense it happened before and can happen again? Yes. That's exactly what I'm saying."

He looked at her as if he thought she might be mazed. "I suppose, though, it doesn't really matter if the story is true or not." He shrugged. "She was my sister and he tried to kill me. If it's help you want to claim a head-price—"

"I want your help to kill him. It."

"Kill him?" Cwynn leaned across the table. "Are you sure a head-price won't do? It doesn't seem there's that many druids—"

"He's not a druid," she said. "Tiermuid, Timias—" *Tetzu*. She shook her head to clear it. "He's not even mortal, or goblin or sidhe. He's something else all together. Something that has to be sent down to the Hag and her cauldron as soon as possible, because he's not just killed your sister by getting her with that thing, he's stolen the khouri-crystals and the khouri-keen, as well. And he hates us for banishing him. I could see that in his eyes."

"So how do we find him?"

"You're willing to help?"

"You're willing to come to Far Nearing and make sure my boys are safe from goblins?"

It was Catrione's turn to hesitate, not from reluctance, but from surprise. "That seems a small enough exchange. I agree. You help me rid the world of Tiermuid, and I will gladly go to Far Nearing and make sure your boys are warded. All right?"

"So what do we do?"

"We go into Faerie. Whatever he's planning to do, he needs a druid to do it. He's either found one as willing as Deirdre or—and I hope this is the case—needs one. And you—we'll dip your new hook into silver. And you will slice his throat, when I get close enough."

"What's to keep him from seeing me?"

"This." Catrione reached under the table. "This is the object he and Deirdre made together. It's some strange blending of druid and sidhe magic. When you put it on, you disappear."

"How will we find him?"

"Leave that to me for now. In the meantime, let's eat and then there's a few things that need attending. So listen." She spooned the last of her porridge into her mouth and scraped the bowl clean. "I'll tell you the story of Seanta while you eat. We'll gather what we can here. And then we'll go to the forge. I can't manage a silver hand, but—" she broke off and nearly laughed aloud at the expression on his face "—I can surely manage something a bit better than that hook."

"It was silver, my Queen. Silver was the primary cause of the disaster. Rather than sinking immediately back into Shadow, some of the silver found its way onto the shore, almost as if it'd been thrown there, deliberately. From there, the poison seeped into the ground, burning the roots of the trees, the hedge walls, undermining all our defenses." The tall sidhe paused. His body was streaked with ash, his expression troubled, and he glanced at Bran with accusation in his tired eyes. "When the goblins came—" He broke off once more and raised his hands. "There were just too many."

Loriana stood on the edge of the charred and smoking ruins with tears in her eyes and streaked down her cheeks, Bran behind her, stunned into silence. The whirling and the sense of weightlessness in his head had eased, but he felt hollow and empty as he gazed at the grim scene.

Blackened trunks stood skeletal and bare against the smoke-clouded sky; cinders still glowed in piles within the open spaces. Foul black fluid oozed from the earth in places or seeped down the sides of trees or dripped from low-lying branches. A few brave sidhe darted amid the wreckage, searching out what few survivors there were.

"Most of the survivors have retreated to the Deep Forest, my lady. I have a horse here ready to take you to safety, but say the word."

"B-but, Ozymandian, we can't just leave—we have to do something," Loriana said. "What about the silver? Where's it coming from? Is it still in Faerie? We can't just let it stay here—we have to get rid of it."

"I agree, Your Majesty," Ozymandian replied. "That's what your father was attempting, when the goblins attacked. But none of us can actually touch the silver, and all our materials are just as useless."

"Maybe I can help you find it," Bran said. "Silver won't hurt me, right?"

"The poison's gone deep into Faerie," Ozymandian replied with a sniff and quirk of his lips.

"But if Bran finds it, he can throw it back," Loriana said. "He can throw it back into the deep part of the water, right?"

"What does that do?" Bran asked.

"It sends the silver back to Shadow," Loriana answered.

"It's dark," said Ozymandian.

"Bring torches," Loriana said. "So many trees have burned—there must be dead wood around somewhere. Come, Bran. We have to do this. We can't let the silver stay in Faerie."

"Hasn't this ever happened before?" asked Bran as he followed Loriana through the wood. The rot had seeped into the entire wood, he thought as he dodged slimy-looking pools and trees that oozed foul liquid.

She paused by the side of a pool that looked familiar. "This was the one…" he began as they both hesitated at the treeline. In places it was possible to see that the banks had once been white and sandy, and tiny-leaved thyme still clung to places along the low-lying rocks. "At the revel, the sacred spring—when they threw the coins into the pool—this is what happened?"

Loriana nodded. In the moonlight, her face was white, her hair gray and her eyes very old. She looked ancient, he thought, despite the smoothness of her skin, and he remembered that the sidhe lived many lifetimes compared to mortals. Behind them, five or six sidhe stepped out of the wood, carrying torches that snapped and smoked and lit the whole scene with an orange-red light out of a nightmare.

Ozymandian clapped one hand on his shoulder and pointed to the beach with the other. "See that, boy? Where the sand is black? There's a piece of silver in there, somewhere."

Bran gulped. The thought of sticking his hand into the reeking mess was the last thing he wanted to do; his head felt too heavy for his neck and the back of his throat stung. "You have a glove?"

Loriana only looked at him and the other sidhe made little noises of derision. "It won't hurt you."

He took a deep breath before the stink made him gag. "I guess it doesn't matter." With a long sigh, he bent beside the blackened sand. It wasn't painful, but it felt like plunging his arm into rotten flesh. His skin recoiled as he stretched out his fingers, feeling from side to side, through the gelatinous mess, up over his elbow, and finally, just as he thought his stomach would rebel and he would vomit before them all, he felt something hard and round and flat. He withdrew it and saw, in the flickering light, it was indeed a coin.

With a curse he threw it as hard as he could into the deep part of the pool. Loriana clapped and blew him a kiss. He hesitated just a moment, then stuck his hand once more into another reeking mess. All around him, sidhe were gathering, tall and slim and pale. They pointed and whispered, and he could feel the weight of all their eyes, the tug of all their voices as he worked, enmeshing him, entangling him, sucking him dry.

At last he'd retrieved all the coins but one, and thrown them all into the center of the pool. But the last was larger than the others, deeper, and he hesitated. His arms and shoulders ached and he was tired, so tired. Loriana leaned over him, kissing the back of his neck, infusing him with new strength. "Just one more," she whispered. "Please. You see what silver does. You see how dangerous it is. Even the tiniest piece can hurt us."

"All right," he said. He was forced to wade into the pit, up to his thighs, and then to his waist as he felt around with hands and feet, while she and the other sidhe watched from the safety of the trees. At last his big toe touched something. "I think I have it," he cried. He bent as low as he could, and finally, was forced to take a deep breath and submerge his head in order to reach down and grab the final coin out of the festering hole it was burning into Faerie.

He pulled himself up, covered in muck, but triumphant, holding the final coin aloft. He pulled his arm back to throw it as hard and as deep as he could, when a voice rasped from the other side of the pool, "Don't throw that coin, boy."

Bran looked up, incredulous, and a collective gasp went up from the sidhe. On the other side of the pool, a figure limped out from beneath the trees. He clung heavily to a stout branch of oak. His face was pockmarked with cuts and scratches, many of them deep, his hair was long and gray and wild as his beard. He scarcely looked like a sidhe at all and, in fact, was dressed in a long robe that appeared to be of mortal make. Every step appeared to pain him, and as he hobbled forward, Bran saw his footprints were stained with pale red blood.

But Loriana appeared to know him. "Timias?" she whispered. "Timias, is that you?"

"Yes, my queen," the newcomer panted. "Through blood and battle and sacrifice, my queen. I've come back."

"Timias, the Forest House has burned and the silver—"

"I know." He held up his hand. "I heard it in the trees. But don't worry. There's something we can do, after all." He hooked his thumbs in the belt he wore around his waist and straightened with effort. His eyes fell on Bran. "There's something we can do, indeed."

"What are you talking about?" asked Ozymandian. "Do you see what's happened here? The silver's rotted all the way in… How can we possibly hope to—"

Timias put his hand on the other sidhe's shoulder. "Just hear me out." He looked at Bran again.

*I should go home,* Bran thought. A chill went down his back as his eyes connected with Timias's and it occurred to him that while Timias definitely had the green eyes of a sidhe, there was something different and strange about him. He was the only one with a beard and gray hair. "I should go," Bran said.

"No!" cried Loriana. "Just stay a moment more." She held out her hand. "Come, let's hear what Timias can tell us."

"I've found a way to protect us—from goblins and silver both. We have to make a barrier so silver will never get in and the goblins will never get out."

"And just how do you intend to do that?" laughed Ozymandian, and the other sidhe followed suit. "Dig a trench and build a wall?"

"Not exactly," said Timias.

"Then how?"

Timias grimaced. "All I ask is a bit of the queen's time— and yours, as well, mortal."

"M-mine?" blurted Bran.

"Most of the Council survived," replied Ozymandian,

with a look that quelled Bran. "They should be consulted before any—"

"I'm not surprised the Council survived, my lord," interrupted Timias. "They always managed to find the highest trees. And now they've simply retreated deeper. What does the Council propose to do? What were they doing before?"

"Timias is right," Loriana said. She stepped between the two men and laid her hand on Timias's arm. To Bran's astonishment, he saw the sidhe's eyes soften. *Why, he loves her,* Bran realized with a start, and he found that interesting because the druids insisted that the sidhe were incapable of feeling real emotions, which was why they found mortals so intoxicatingly different.

But Loriana was continuing, with an authority in her tone he hadn't heard before. "I want to hear Lord Timias out. Not only did my father send him into Shadow, for the express purpose of learning druid magic, but he saved my life. I owe him that much, wouldn't you agree?"

Ozymandian glanced down. "Perhaps upon due consideration—"

"We can't wait any longer, Ozymandian. I can hear the trees screaming."

"You only fear what you don't know," Timias said. "Give me but a day, and by the time the sun has risen and set in Faerie, I promise you the goblins will be vanquished, the silver will be neutralized and the Forest House rebuilt."

Ozymandian snorted. "A day, my lord? Done." He shook his head. "My queen, when you are ready to remember the rest of us, we will be waiting in the Deep Forest." He turned on his heel and stalked back through the trees, calling for the others to follow.

*I should go,* Bran thought. But how could he leave now, he thought, especially if the silver coin had some part to play in this odd sidhe's grand plan? Loriana was looking at Timias as if she thought the sun might rise out of his brow, and he was looking down at her as if he expected to see stars in her eyes. As if he were communicating his plan with a look. "I think I should be getting back."

"We need you, boy," Timias said. He was smiling, his teeth gleaming white. They were very long teeth, Bran noticed, and pointed, almost like a goblin's, at the ends.

"We need you to hold the silver," Loriana said. "Please? Can't you please just stay here with us a little more?"

Bran hesitated. The still surface of the pool beckoned, and it occurred to him that he, like the coins, could dive into the deep water and find his way back into Shadow. But how could he abandon Faerie to the goblins and the silver? *I really should go.* "All right." He held out the coin. "What do you want me to do with this?"

"Just come with us, boy," said Timias. He reached for a torch. "Come and let me show you everything I've accomplished so far."

"Why do you keep looking over your shoulder?" asked Catrione as she stoked the fire in the forge. The smithy was deserted at this hour, the last sleepy apprentice chased away. Dawn was always the best time to cross into TirNa'lugh, but there was work to be done first. To his credit, Cwynn didn't question when she tapped on his window sill, lest the still-wives see. But even Niona's shrill harangue had gone silent, and not even a sister-druid had marked her silent passage in and out of the dormitory to fetch a few critical items, like silver daggers and her staff.

But all along the way, she'd noticed him whipping around, glancing left or right, clearly seeing something. "There's this white dog," he began, then paused at the look on her face. "You see him, too?"

Catrione hesitated. The white dog who'd guided him across the treacherous channel had resembled Bog, and she herself had glimpsed the plume of a white tail more than once or twice, disappearing around a corner or into an empty room. But the idea that Bog would come back from the Summerlands to help Cwynn—*though after all he is the man you are to marry*—unnerved her even more than the sense of connection she felt every time she looked into his eyes. "Come work these bellows—you can do it with one hand like this, see?" She handed him the tool, then withdrew from the pack of items she'd gathered the leather harness that he'd worn to hold his hook in place. "I had a dog like that. Deirdre—well, under the influence of that creature, she killed him."

"She killed your dog?" He looked at her with such horror, such disgust, she liked him just for that.

"You have to understand that that wasn't Deirdre, that person you saw in the Tor. She wasn't really like that, before."

"Before what?"

"Before she fell under Tiermuid's spell." Catrione tied her hair back. "She wasn't the only one—I think all us younger ones were affected, and maybe some of the older ones, too. It's just tells me whatever that creature is, it's no more natural than that thing it spawned."

She skipped her fingers over the hammers hanging on the walls, looking for something small and delicate.

"How is it you know how to do this? You don't look like a blacksmith to me."

"All druids have to pass an apprenticeship under a black-smith—just a year, unless, of course you have a particular gift for it. It's one of the foundations of elemental magic, you see—the turning of earth, or ore, into objects. Every druid needs at least a little experience in it."

"Ah." He raised his eyebrows but said nothing, his eyes fixed on the forge.

As the coals began to glow, she said, "Do you know what a pooka is?"

He shook his head.

She motioned for him to stop. "Let me see your arm again." As she unwrapped the long strips of linen, she said, "A pooka is an entity or an energy that for whatever reason binds itself to a soul. Sometimes it's an elemental energy, like a trixie. But most commonly, it's the spirit of an animal. It's like the soul makes a stop on the way to the Summerlands. They don't stay forever and some people attract them." She blinked away the tears that filled her eyes as she remembered Bog's still white body beside the cold hearth, and busied herself examining the harness and the small-pronged garden rake she'd had in mind to replace the hook. It was only a temporary solution—something more permanent, less clumsy, could be achieved given more time. But for right now, it would serve, not just as a limb, but as a weapon. "We'll coat the ends in silver," she said. "Let me see your arm."

Reluctantly, he held it out for her inspection. "It's not hurt—I didn't think it was. They just put a bandage on it, because it's not pretty."

Not pretty was an understatement. The jagged scar, the shiny red skin stretched tight over a broken knob of bone bore silent testimony to a terrible wound, a painful recovery, but also the means to a weapon even Tiermuid could not anticipate. "I think the first thing—"

"Excuse me." The raspy voice was like the scratch of a bat's wing, and at first, Catrione dismissed it merely as the scurrying of the mice in the rafters. "Excuse me."

Catrione peered beyond Cwynn and was startled to see a bent figure huddled in the doorway of the forge. Despite the temperate night, the old woman was wrapped in a motley collection of ragged shawls that quite possibly represented the sum total of her wardrobe. "Cailleach?" asked Catrione. "Is there something you require?" She was one of the refugees, of course, probably lost on her way to the latrine.

The old woman raised her head, and her outer layer of shawls fell away to reveal a small black cauldron, about the size of a large cat, cradled in her arms, almost like a child. She clutched it to her breast as if it were more precious than gold, arms quivering with the effort. "My cauldron…I was stirring my brew, you see…and someone came along and now my cauldron…"

"It needs a patch?" Catrione reached for the cauldron, but the old woman turned away, and a few drops of whatever it held splashed out, directly into her eyes. The hot liquid seared her, and she frantically wiped her eyes on her sleeve, blinking furiously. When she looked up, the forge was momentary blurry. Catrione blinked hard and her vision cleared. The night had gone absolutely silent and the flames in the two torches she'd lit above the anvil stood straight up.

"Are you all right?" Cwynn asked. "Here, this is clean water." He held out a wet rag, and she dabbed it at her eyes.

"Don't touch my cauldron." The old woman's chin was tucked so low against her sunken chest it made her look like an owl. She took a couple steps closer and the smell that rose from her was worse than a charnel pit.

The watch bawled midnight; from somewhere close by a woman moaned and a child cried. An owl hooted in the rafters. An acrid combination of the odors of old sweat and stale urine drifted from the folds of the old woman's garments. She smelled all too human to be anything but what she was.

Cwynn turned with his stump tucked inside his tunic. "So what happened to your cauldron, old mother?"

"Someone took my globestone. Once I had four, then I had three." Her striated face gleamed with tears but the smell that drifted off her clothing was enough to turn Catrione's stomach. "Now I've only two and I can't keep it all balanced with only two. I need a third. Please, you have to help me."

"She's talking about a set of stones, round stones, the old women use to balance their cauldrons and keep their food hot and their feet warm—oh, there's a thousand ways they use them," Catrione said. She sighed inwardly. The last thing she needed was a thief loose. She'd have thought her father would've at least seen his men kept some kind of order, but she hadn't asked him. "Good Cailleach," she began, choosing her words with care as pity warred with impatience. "King Fengus's men are here. Go find the captain of the watch—tell him Cailleach Catrione told you to seek him out, and ask—"

"Please," the old woman whined.

Cwynn dug Catrione in the ribs. "You can rig her something, right?"

Catrione turned and looked up at him. "Are you serious?"

"How's she supposed to eat?"

"She's supposed to eat with the others—"

"I can't stir the pot without losing half my brew at every turn," the old woman whimpered.

"We can't have that," said Cwynn before Catrione could either speak or move. He reached around her, took the cauldron out of the old woman's hands, and set it on a table. "Now then. What do you think, Cailleach? Is there something you can make to take the place of a globe?"

Catrione felt the hair go up on the back of her neck. The old woman pushed her black cap back, and Catrione could see the dirt crusted in her wrinkles, saw the bits of crusted saliva flaking on her lips. No, there was nothing of the OtherWorld about her at all. She clearly wasn't going away. Drool spooled down the old woman's chin and Catrione felt a chill of revulsion.

"Please," whined the old woman, even more loudly. "My brew's getting cold."

Catrione threw Cwynn a face. "This will slow us down—it has already."

"Can't you just do it? Figure out something?"

"Like what?"

"Oh—I don't know." He looked to the old woman. "How big's this globe-stone of yours, old mother? Big as my head? Bigger?"

Catrione turned to Cwynn, feeling as if a veil of unreality had suddenly descended on the forge and that she stood on one side of a thin membrane while he and the old woman stood on another. It was possible for her to hear them, see them, even smell them, but somehow she felt as if she'd stepped into some other place, separate and apart from the reality in which they stood. She stood, dumb, watching Cwynn's fingers weave through the air, his stump tucked into his shirt. Unbelievably, she saw him reach into his pack and hold out the apple from the Summerlands.

In the reddish light of the forge, it glowed. Catrione hissed as he handed it to the old woman with a smile and a flourish. His hand and stump sketched a design in the air before her; he pointed over her shoulder at the half-made tools on the table across the smithy. *What do you think you just did? We need that apple,* she wanted to scream, but somehow, she couldn't.

The old woman seemed to condense into a lump beside the door, and somehow Catrione found herself bending over the anvil, her hair tucked up, her sleeves rolled above her elbows, wearing a smith's long apron. She looked up at Cwynn with a scowl but he only smiled serenely back. As if from a great distance, she heard a voice chanting, "Wise the one who keeps me fed, he's the one who keeps his head."

And without feeling as if she were actually doing anything at all, Catrione watched herself tap and hammer, shape and form a three-legged contrivance, on which sat a rounded metal plate. Somehow she found time to adapt the garden rake to the harness, too, for to her amazement, Cwynn was already fitted with the contrivance. The tines of the rake gleamed silver as Cwynn handed over the tripod and the plate to the old woman, and Catrione wondered exactly when she'd melted silver and how, for there didn't seem to be any evidence of molten metal anywhere at all.

The old woman unfolded herself, pressing Cwynn's hand—and his new hook—to her face, kissing both flesh and metal. She fumbled inside her voluminous layers and pressed something into his hand, something wrapped in what looked like a dirty scrap of the roughest kind of linen. Catrione lifted the leather apron over her head, then dropped it as Cwynn gasped. "What's wrong?" she asked. The old woman, like the night itself, was gone. The sky was streaked with gray; she could hear the cocks crowing all over the compound. They would have just enough time to get away.

"Do you know that old woman?" His face was gray as the ash in the forge and Catrione realized she'd lost all sense of being behind a membrane. "Have you ever met her, ever seen her before tonight?"

"No, of course not. She's one of the refugees. Why? What did she give you?"

He held up a flat disk on a leather cord, a disk that gleamed a dull and unmistakable yellow. "This." He handed it to Catrione, and she turned it over in her hands, recognizing it as a druid-disk at once. "This is the thing I lost— the thing my grandfather gave to me, before I left Far Nearing."

"This very one? Are you sure?"

"Can't you read it? See what it says?"

"Hold that lantern close." Catrione squinted down at the spiraling lineages, at the stones, set at intervals she recognized. The hair on the back of her neck prickled and gooseflesh rose on her sweat-drenched arms. Deirdre had one just like it.

"It's what I said it is, isn't it?"

Frozen, Catrione nodded, even as her thoughts tumbled over each other, one after another, a twisting jumble she had no time to decipher. She pushed the disk back into his hand. "Don't lose it this time." She looked around the smithy. Her eyes were getting blurry, and she had to blink several times to clear them. It was getting close to dawn. "I think we should go now." She had to blink again as her vision clouded over once more.

"We should go that way." Cwynn pointed to the left of the forge.

"Why?" asked Catrione, astonished he should be so sure.

"I see that white dog again. And he's wagging his tail."

*16*

Morla woke up tied to a pole. A blinding pain throbbed in her right temple, and her limbs were cramped and constricted. She was lying on her side on a pile of the tanned skins of animals she didn't recognize. She was inside a large tent that reeked of the same cloying perfume that clung to Meeve. A girl, not much older than a child, was sitting on the other side of the tent, cross-legged on a low pile of cushions, stitching something large and silky. The girl startled when she saw Morla looking at her, gabbled something in a language Morla didn't recognize, jumped up and ran out of the tent.

Morla shut her eyes as a wave of nausea and dizziness rolled through her. Her tongue felt swollen and plastered to the top of her mouth, her lips dry and cracked. Wherever she was, at least she was alive. Lochlan was most likely dead. The memory of the way the warriors had converged on him, weapons drawn, flashed before her eyes. The tent flap opened behind her and a rush of warm fresh air helped clear her head momentarily. She heard a man's sharp voice, hurried responses. Boots stalked into her line of vision, and her head was picked up by the hair. She stared into the eyes of a dark-eyed, dark-haired, olive-skinned Lacquilean.

He regarded her with that same impersonal appraisal as the others she remembered at Eaven Morna—as if she were a dead thing, not a living creature. He looked over her head and shrugged. Behind her, Morla could hear other male voices.

"*Adiado.*" Even Morla recognized the tone of dismissal. The Lacquilean in front of her pulled her upright, but didn't untie her bonds, and another set of boots stalked around the pole. A lean-looking warrior stared down at her, hands on hips. He nodded at the other man.

"You say you're Meeve's daughter." The first speaker's Brynnish was nearly perfect, and it frightened her somehow that he could speak her own language so perfectly and she knew nothing of his.

She tried to speak, but her dry tongue stuck to the roof of her mouth.

The warrior nudged the first man and nodded at a pitcher. With a grimace, as if he begrudged it, he held the pitcher to her lips and let her drink. It was a vinegary sort of wine that made her choke and spilled down her chin. She wiped her face against her shoulder and turned back to face them both. "I'm Morla," she replied. "Morla of Dalraida."

"One of the twins." He rocked back on his heels, as if that answered the question.

"Who're you?"

He smiled at that, cocked his head a little, as if to say he hardly thought she was in the position to ask anything, then rose to his feet and addressed the warrior in their own tongue. She understood her mother's name, she understood the words *Ardagh* and *Eaven Morna*. But nothing else.

"You!" Morla twisted over her shoulder. "Who're you? Where am I? Where're you taking me?"

Both men only looked at each other, ducked outside and let the tent flap fall behind them, leaving Morla alone in the suffocating tent. Her belly rumbled and the pressure in her bladder felt near to bursting. She let her head fall back against the pole, closed her eyes and tried to marshal her thoughts into some semblance of order. They were still in Brynhyvar, she thought. And the one, was he at all familiar? She racked her brain, trying to remember his face, but she'd not spent much time beneath her mother's roof. And the ones she did remember…they all looked alike. They had some plan for her. And given what Lochlan had told her Meeve had done to the ambassador and his company…her thoughts dissolved into a wave of despair. The tent flap opened again, and the girl scampered back in, this time carrying a basket and a bucket of water.

She stole quickly into the room, bent down, untied Morla's hands and offered her a flask. Without any other thought, Morla ripped off the cork and chugged down the contents, then indicated her most immediate need. The girl pointed to a jug in the corner, then turned her back.

Morla stumbled when she tried to stand. Her legs were still tied, and when she tapped the girl on the shoulder, the girl shook her head, big brown eyes wide. Morla pointed to the jug. "How do you expect me—"

The girl slapped a hand across Morla's face, shook her head, and looked at the tent flap. Morla grimaced. The girl motioned Morla to stay still, then retrieved the jug, helped her to squat over it, then replaced it while Morla slumped back down. The girl held out the bucket and a towel. Morla washed her hands and face, then reached for the loaf of bread and heel of cheese the girl offered. Without thinking, she crammed one after the other into her mouth. "Who're you?" she muttered with her mouth full of bread and cheese.

"My name's Sabrys," the girl whispered back in flawless Brynnish. "You're in a camp, just to the west of Ardagh. My master intends to take you back to Lacquilea and give you to the Senex, to use as they will."

Morla stared. She hadn't really expected the girl to respond. "H-how do you know this?" She leaned down. "Where do you come from? How…how is it you know my lang—?"

"I come from a far-off place, on the edge of the Desert of Jebrew. I know this because I heard my master and the captain talking. I know your language because I listen. My master is…was the ambassador's secretary. We were out of your mother's castle before the feast was even served."

"He doesn't know you know how to—"

Sabrys held up her hand. "Be quiet!"

"You have to help, Sabrys. You have to help me to escape."

The girl looked back at her as if she had grown another head. "I have to do no such thing. I won't let you starve, won't let you live in filth—this is my tent he means to keep you in, after all. But I can't help you escape. It'll be my head if that happens. And the master isn't kind." She dropped her eyes and sat back. "Finish, please. He'll be back."

Morla put the bread down. She wasn't hungry anymore. A sick sense of abandonment swept over her. Lochlan had murmured to a still-wife where they were going—she'd over-heard the brief exchange herself. So they wouldn't be missed, neither of them. The bower Lochlan had made was off the road, too. It was unlikely anyone would notice his body. Tears filled her eyes.

"Don't cry," whispered Sabrys. "It won't get you anything, believe me. Keep your eyes open, your mouth shut. And listen. That's how I survive."

Morla handed back the bread and cheese, but took another swig from the flask.

"You'll see." Sabrys got to her feet, tucked the food back into the basket, and placed the basket beside her cushions. She took the bucket. "I don't intend to wait on you. Once he's sure you won't run away, I'll show you how things are done. I heard the master say you're a queen's daughter. Just so we understand each other—so am I." Before Morla could react, Sabrys tied Morla's hands behind her back around the pole. "If anything, they go harder on you for it."

"I'm getting out of here," Morla said.

Sabrys shrugged and shook her head. "Don't show Master defiance. They mean to degrade you, in every way possible. Master will look for the least excuse." She picked up the bucket and left the tent, leaving Morla to contemplate whether taking her own life might be preferable.

"…seen him before, Chief, I'm sure of it."

"This is Meeve's plaid, isn't it, Chief?"

The voices coming from very far away roused Lochlan from his stupor. He opened his eyes and saw a man's boot

less than a handspan from his face. He drew a deep breath
and tried to get up. Pain flared through the back of his skull,
and he collapsed with a groan, hardly having moved at all.
But it was enough.

Another voice, high above, said: "Would you watch where
you're walking, you big oaf? You nearly stepped in the poor
fellow's face."

Hands reached for him, turned him over, and a flask was
put to his mouth. Sunlight stabbed his eyes and he blinked.
From far away, he thought he heard his horse screaming in
protest. A rough voice said something Lochlan couldn't hear
and a unshaven face peered down at him. "Is that you,
Fengus-Da?" Lochlan muttered. "No one's managed to kill
you yet?"

"Not yet, boy. Everyone's waiting for you to do it. Looks
like someone had quite a go at you." The burly chief
squatted down beside him, hawked, then spat over his
shoulder. "What're you doing out here, Lochlan? Where's
Meeve? Where's the rest of the Fiachna?"

The drink revived him enough to explain, without details,
what had happened. When Lochlan paused, Fengus stared
out over the hills. "So you never got a chance to see how
many there are?"

"We can track 'em, Chief," piped up one of Fengus's
younger knights.

"Can you ride, lad?" Fengus looked down at Lochlan.
"We can patch you up a bit, but you're not far from a druid
house—the White Birch Grove where m'daughter is. We
just left there— If you can't ride with us we can—"

Lochlan grabbed Fengus's sleeve. "And there's druids

there?" He struggled to sit up. "You say you been there, and there's no blight?"

Fengus stared down at him. "None that I saw. They're all half out of their silly heads for fear of goblins but no blight. And aye, there's druids. A whole gaggle of 'em, a dozen or more, at least."

"I'll go to Ardagh with you." Lochlan touched the back of his head gingerly. He could feel an enormous bump but no blood. "But, please, send one of your men back there. And tell them that Bran—Meeve's son, her youngest—has been taken into TirNa'lugh and they need to send druids after him—Connla put a ward on him herself—"

"Connla's dead," said Fengus. "At least that's what my daughter seemed to think." In a few terse sentences, Fengus described the slaughtered camp.

Lochlan stared as his horse was brought up. The animal snorted and threw its head back in greeting. Slowly he got to his feet, numb with the news. "Maybe that explains it, then," he muttered, thinking that at some point, the trixies seemed to have stopped bothering Bran. "He's there, then, I'm sure of it. Please, Fengus-Da, if you'd be a friend to Meeve, send a man back and ask the druids to fetch her son. He's her baby and—"

"In your charge."

"Exactly." Their eyes met in perfect understanding.

"All right, boy." Fengus clapped a hand on his shoulder. "You sure you're all right now?"

"Let's put it this way," Lochlan said as he grasped the bridle and the reins and hoisted himself painfully into the saddle. "I'll feel a lot better when I know both Morla and Bran are safe."

* * *

"They're coming." Sabrys scampered back into the tent, leaped into her place among the cushions and picked up her needle. "Remember what I told you—show no defiance."

Morla turned to see the two men who'd confronted her before, followed by a woman cloaked all in black from head to toe, and three other soldiers. She swallowed hard and felt a finger of fear run down her spine.

"Remove the clothing." The one Sabrys called "Master" repeated the command in his own tongue, and she knew the first time had been for her benefit, to kindle her fear, and to provoke, perhaps, her defiance.

But before she could even consider what she might do, one soldier simply untied her hands and the other her legs. They placed her spread-eagled in the center of the tent, and the third used his dagger to cut the clothes off her body. As the blade flashed over her breasts, dangerously near her nipples, heedlessly between her thighs, she went rigid.

The captain, the one who seemed to be the military commander, said something, and the third pulled the shreds of her tunic off the top of her body. For a long moment, they simply stared at her. Then the captain said something else, and the third soldier yanked her mouth open. The woman bent down, ran one cold finger around Morla's teeth and gums, then yanked out her tongue. She tried to twist her head away instinctively, but the soldier held her head between his two enormous hands as if it were a nut he was about to crack.

The examination continued, coldly, dispassionately. The woman prodded at Morla's breasts, examined the silvery lines of the stretch-marks. The captain said something to which the woman shrugged and nodded.

Morla closed her eyes. Their eyes were on her, worse than the woman's pinching, probing fingers that dug into her navel, pulled on the sparse hairs in her armpits, twisted into her ears. Morla balled her hands into fists and went rigid as she felt her legs lifted and spread, and the woman's merciless examination begin.

"Open your eyes." Her head was slammed back against the hard-packed earth. She opened her eyes to see Sabrys's master inches from her face. His narrow, high-cheeked face reminded her of the druid descriptions of the sidhe, but the stench he blasted with each breath made her gag. His black eyes shone beady in the dusty light. "This is just the beginning."

"Of what?" she managed, even as she tried to squirm desperately away from the old woman's probing fingers. She tried to close her eyes and turn away, to spare herself at least the indignity of all those cold hard eyes, but he slapped her until she turned her face up once again.

"Look at me, or I let them rape you."

At that her eyes flew open and he smiled as he stuffed a leather gag into her mouth. It tasted bitter, of old salt and sweat and something coppery and metallic—the taste of dried blood. "That's better." With a word, he signaled the soldiers to tie her arms and legs together. They did so with such brutal efficiency, she yelped around the gag as her limbs were yanked and twisted, held and bound. They dropped her into a heap, as if she were a piece of rotting meat.

Morla saw Sabrys sitting back, watching impassively, but her eyes shouted, I told you so.

*"Dasa, compiedreos."* Even Morla understood the dismissal in the tone, and braced herself for whatever was to come next. The breeze stirred by the tent flap raised gooseflesh on her naked skin, and Morla wondered if they meant to leave her naked. The soldiers and the old woman marched out, but the other men bent over her, turning her on her knees and her elbows, prodding at her rump. Abruptly they let her fall as shouts rang through the camp. The captain's head jerked up, but silence fell. He pointed down, said something, and Sabrys's master replied.

Without a look at either of the women, the two men left the tent.

"They're talking about where to put the brand," Sabrys said. Morla gasped around the gag and her eyes widened, but Sabrys continued, "All slaves are branded several times. There's the first one they stick on you as soon as they get you. And then each House, each Family, has its own... Some masters like to decorate their slaves, too. But you, they think its important to get you marked as a slave as soon as possible. They mean to shave your head and your body hair, and get a brand on you. They know you'll run. But I don't think they plan to do anything worse than that. They want to present you, unmarked, to the Senex, so that the people of the City may decide what should be done with you. Virgin—unmarked— sacrifice is considered particularly pleasing to the gods."

Morla went cold as ice as she rolled on her side, curling up protectively into a ball of quivering flesh. What Sabrys hinted at made suicide seem like a viable option—far better to choose the Summerlands than a life ended in torment. They'd left the tent flap open and the smell of something burning wafted in. She tried not to imagine what it would feel like to have a red-hot iron seared into her flesh.

"It's not too bad," Sabrys was saying. "The first one's the hardest, of course. But afterwards, at least you know what to expect."

Morla stared at the other girl. *She's trying to frighten me,* Morla thought. *She's trying to frighten me so she won't be so afraid. Say what you want.* Morla turned away, feverishly pushing against her bonds. The leather cords were strong, but leather could stretch. *I'm going to find some way to escape. And I will not give them what they want.*

But all her resolve was for nothing. The old woman came back carrying a small brazier, followed by the captain and the master. The captain carried a long black iron with a small flat V at its base. Morla's resolve disappeared, her palms began to sweat. The captain pushed her over on her stomach and held her down with one knee placed squarely on the small of her back, his booted leg along her spine. He picked up her feet. Morla struggled and squirmed, but the two men held her easily. He meant to brand her on the sole of her foot, she realized, horrified. She'd be crippled; it would be so much harder to run, so much harder to escape.

The master held her torso down, but ripped the gag off her face. He smiled down at her, gently smoothing her tangled hair off her face. "Go on," he whispered in his eerily perfect Brynnish. "Go right ahead and scream."

"Is that someone screaming?" Lochlan reined his horse up short, cocked his head and held up his hand. "Do you hear that?" Like a high thin thread, the sound twisted through the air above the sounds of the company halting. *It sounded like a woman,* he thought as his pulse began to race.

"Sounds like someone being eaten alive. Maybe it really is goblins, chief." One of Fengus's knight nudged his master's elbow.

"Goblins don't come out in the day," said a second.

"Fengus-Da!" The voice of Fengus's youngest squire, Donn, his voice high and eager cut through the rising speculation. "Fengus-Da, I've an old woman here. An old woman who says she's seen the riders."

Lochlan turned in his saddle. From the shadows, the boy led out an old crone, her head wrapped in a linen coif, her torso in a plaid so blackened by soot, its pattern was indiscernible. She marched up to Fengus. "Boy says you're the king." She squinted up at him, one clawlike hand across her furrowed brow, the other munching the reddest apple Lochlan had ever seen. The juice of it ran down her chin, and it occurred to him that the apple was completely out of season. She glanced up at him and winked.

Fengus harrumphed. "Not the king, old mother, not the High King." He glanced at Lochlan, who thought he could hear the echo of Fengus's thoughts. *Not yet.*

It reminded Lochlan that while it suited Fengus, he would be Meeve's loyal ally, united against a common enemy. But only while it suited him. A bitter wind swept out of the trees and ran down Lochlan's back and he shifted in the saddle. There was something about this old woman that made his skin crawl.

"You saw the riders go past here, old mother?" Fengus was saying.

"We didn't see nothing, mind you—Father and me was hidden in the hayracks with the pigs. But they came inside and I heard them talking about their prisoner, the Princess, they called her." She crunched another bite out of the apple and Lochlan felt his mouth water and his knees go weak. The fragrance was under his nose now, twining up and into his belly. It smelled familiar, somehow, but he couldn't quite place it.

"Which way and how many?" asked another knight.

"That way," she pointed. "And maybe a hundred or more—could've been thousands. That's what it sounded like."

*Surely not thousands,* thought Lochlan. But the old woman met his gaze again and this time he was sure she winked.

Fengus flapped his reins and pointed off, across the rolling green hills that opened up into the Vale of Ardagh.

"Is there a place," asked Lochlan, staring down at the apple. "A place where an army of any size could hide?"

"Oh, aye," the old woman nodded, licking at the juice that ran down her fingers. "Right over the ridge, there, you'll see a hill with a rock called the Hag's Head perched on the top. Just over that hill, is a valley not many dare enter. But foreigners they'd not care."

"Why, old woman?" demanded Fengus. "What's in the valley?"

"Just an old well they call the Hag's Well." She limped off, muttering.

Lochlan exchanged glances with the other knights. If the Lacquileans could go there, so could they.

Fengus beckoned to Donn. "See she gets something for her trouble. All right," he cried, raising his arm. "Let's go."

* * *

Morla lay in the center of the tent where they'd dragged her after the branding, staring up in a delirium of pain. They'd shaved her head and her body hair, too, afterward, but that part was nothing but a blur of the agony that rolled in constant waves from the soles of her feet to the top of her spine. Such pain could not be borne, should not be borne, she thought. Even the goblin pain was not so awful as this. But the goblin had thought of her as prey. This branded her a slave and barred her now forever from reigning in Meeve's place at Ardagh. Only the unmarked could be a High King or Queen.

"Roll over." Sabrys's tone was as unyielding as her expression, but she held a basin, a roll of bandages and what looked like a pot of salve. "It's not that bad. Really. By next week you won't even remember. The first is always the worst 'cause it makes you a slave. We all go through it. I understand. Now roll over." She toed Morla's shoulder.

With a groan, Morla rolled over. She was still naked, her pubis and her head scraped raw, but at least on her belly she could bite into the leather gag and let the tears run freely down her face as Sabrys daubed at her throbbing feet. White-hot pain lanced through her as Sabrys slapped on the salve. She went rigid, her eyes flew open and she almost swallowed the gag. Another scream escaped her ragged throat.

"You be quiet or I don't put a bandage on them. I don't even want to think what Master's going to do to you for that."

*I shall not live as a slave,* Morla thought. *I simply shall not live.* A bolt of pain stabbed up the other leg as Sabrys finished tying on the second bandage. "They are deep, I give you that." Her eyes met Morla's. "I told you Master would make you pay."

*Master will not own me,* Morla wanted to scream, but she turned her face away and shut her eyes. The night air was damp and oppressively humid. It was going to rain soon. She could smell the parched top layer of earth crying out for it, but here, beneath her cheek, wasn't going to get any of it. They were under the tent. She turned her cheek into the dry earth and let it feel her tears, let the wetness on her face fall into it. *Gracious goddess of the living land,* she thought. *Send me Herne to either free me or take me to the Summerlands. Whichever is your will, great goddess.* Only let me not live a slave. Send me Herne.

The thought was not even out of her head when there was a crashing and a whinnying very close by, and with a rip of fabric, the tent flap was yanked aside. "Princess Morla, are you here?" roared the enormous bearded figure. It could be Herne, Morla thought as she raised her head and blinked. Sabrys was getting up, shooing him away, grabbing a poker from the charcoal brazier. But Morla flailed her legs, kicked up the sand. The big man saw her, peered down at her and his expression turned from battle-lust to horror to pity. A single push square in her chest, and Sabrys went flying back into the brazier. As she rolled and screamed and smoked, the warrior bent down, wrapped Morla in his own plaid, and picked her up as if she were a child. He pulled the blanket down over her face, then ran with her out into the night.

She felt herself handed from one set of strong arms into another, and then hoisted up into yet a third. She flinched and tried not to cry as the side of a saddle bumped her heel. An enormous crack of thunder rumbled across the sky, and without warning, a blanket of rain began to fall. One arm held her tight, while with the other, she felt reins and a big body moving behind her. The horse leaped into the night, even as all around them, curtains of water fell. Morla pushed the blanket off her face and ripped the gag out of her mouth, spitting it into the dark night. Her rescuer was a man big in the chest and arms, his face covered by a lustrous black beard shot with strands of gray.

"Who're you?" she demanded, even as the horse galloped down the lightning-lit road.

"I'm Fengus," he answered with a flash of crooked teeth. Behind them, she could hear fighting. He held her firmly, gently, the way one might a nervous animal. He looked down at her, tucking the plaid gently around her cheek. "Don't fret now—the lads will see we get away. So you sleep now, and when you wake up, with any luck at all, this'll all be just a bad dream with a happy ending."

"Where're we going?" she asked suspiciously.

"To the White Birch Grove, where my daughter is. Just relax now. You'll be fine."

"To the druids?"

"Aye, the druids. Just rest."

"But there was another. Lochlan—"

"How do you think we found you?"

"He's alive?"

"He was," replied Fengus with a look over his shoulder. "Don't worry, lass. A warrior like that knows how to take care of himself." He pulled her against him, and his big arm around her made her feel safe. The rain sluicing down her feet had a numbing effect on the brand. The rhythm of the horse's steady gallop lulled her so that even as another question occurred to her, her head nodded and she fell back onto Fengus's shoulder and into a deep sleep. She didn't see his look of triumph as he bore her through the night.

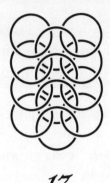

## 17

*I should go back. The trees need me. I can heal them. I have to heal the trees,* Bran thought as he stumbled after Loriana. *I should go home.* What was it Lochlan had said? *It's easy enough to get to TirNa'lugh—what's hard is finding your way home.* It seemed as if it had been a very long time since he'd been carried off by the raven and he wondered if that had been a dream and what had happened to the raven. He rubbed his head and realized that Loriana had come to a stop in the middle of the path. She was staring straight ahead at probably the last thing Bran expected to see in Faerie—the central tower of a keep.

It was made of pure white marble and shone in the sun. Arched windows set high above the tree line sparkled like diamonds, reflecting red and blue and green. It was the most beautiful tower Bran had ever seen. But when had the sun risen, he wondered? How had it come to be day? He remembered no dawn.

"What is this place?" Loriana breathed.

The strange sidhe leaned heavily on his stick and a crease

appeared in the furrow between his brows. He looked as if he were in the most horrible pain, and Bran wondered what ailed him. "In my time in Shadow, Loriana," he said softly, "I learned many things."

"You did this? You made this place? H-how?" She didn't take her eyes off the structure.

Bran blinked. Was the tower growing taller, even as they watched? Larger? Had the crenelated tops of a wall appeared, just above the row of oak trees just ahead?

"Magic," Timias answered, watching her face.

"What kind of magic is this?"

The tower was growing, Bran decided, and another tower had appeared behind it.

Timias hung on his staff, breathing heavily, even as sweat pearled across his forehead. Blood still trickled down the inside of his leg. He was wounded in some way, Bran realized.

"A better kind of magic than has been worked in either World, Loriana. And all for you." He reached out, tentatively, his hand hovered in the air just above her shoulder, but she was riveted by the towers, now three, sprouting up above the trees.

"The Forest House was vulnerable. The Queen of Faerie should have a house—a palace—that can stand against all threats, while becoming a beacon to all who dwell within her Court. And so I made you this, my queen, when I realized the Forest House was dying. I wanted to make you a place you'd be safe, Loriana—a house of light and stone." Timias was looking at Loriana with such naked need, Bran felt his own throat thicken, and he had to blink back tears.

"But…but how did you do this, Timias? How is such a thing possible?"

"It's the gremlins, Loriana," he replied. "The very creatures your father—and his Council—would spurn. See what they can do? This house can be even more magnificent than your father's ever was. Just tell them what you want, and they can make it so. Don't be frightened. Just come. And see."

I have to go home, Bran thought, but Timias's words were twining around him like ribbons, drawing him deeper and farther in TirNa'lugh, weighing on his flesh.

"You, too, Bran," Timias said. "We need that coin."

"Why do we need the silver, Timias?" asked Loriana.

"With just the amount of silver in this coin, my queen, we're going to create the barrier that will protect Faerie forever. You'll see."

"It'll have to be a very thin barrier," Bran blurted. "It's just a little coin."

Timias only smiled and pinched his cheek. "So clever. You're right. Let's go."

With a gentle tug on his hand, Loriana led him stumbling into the white-walled palace.

"I can't believe you gave her that apple." Catrione clutched Cwynn's arm. The brew was burning in her eyes in earnest, but Catrione ignored the pain and the moisture seeping down her face. They were headed across the quiet compound toward the wet meadow that surrounded the Tor. "Do you still see the dog?" she asked as she tripped over something in the long grass.

"He's just ahead," Cwynn replied. "Looks like he's headed around the Tor."

"Which way? Against the sun, or with it?"

"To the right, it seems—against it, I suppose."

"He's taking us to TirNa'lugh," Catrione muttered, satisfied. "Just go where he wants. But still I wish you hadn't given her the apple."

"Why not? It seemed like the right thing to do, and she was very grateful, she gave me back my disk. Catrione, are you all right?"

She felt the brush of his breath on the side of her face as he turned to look at her, but she kept her eyes tightly shut. "Whatever was in that cauldron burned my eyes," she said.

"Then let's turn back," he said at once. "Come on—"

"No, we don't dare," she replied. "You don't realize what Tiermuid stole. Those crystals aren't just the key to our magic, they're the whole foundation, the whole anchor, in this world. Without them—" She broke off, forced to wipe away a glob of jelly that had rolled down her cheek. She shut her eyes tightly, and more squeezed out. "Wait a minute."

"Are you sure you're all right?"

She ripped the hem off the bottom of her tunic and tied the strip of linen around her eyes. "There. Whatever got in them is making them weep so bad I can't see. Let's go."

"Catrione—"

"We have to do this, Cwynn. There's no telling what Tiermuid might do. He has the source of all our power, and with it—"

"Aren't there others? Don't you have more of these crystals?"

"Like attracts like," she answered. "He's got enough he

could send them out to gather more. Don't you see? He not only has the means to use our power, he has the reason to turn it against us. Do you still see the dog?"

"He's waiting for us up ahead. What's the apple got to do with it?"

"I hoped to use that apple to tempt the khouri-keen," she said grimly. "But never mind now. Just follow Bog."

It was curious, she thought, how acutely she could feel the border, how the edge felt sharp as a razor over her skin as if it had suddenly acquired a definition it had lacked before. Perhaps it was simply she was blindfolded, she told herself as Cwynn stopped short. "Where are we?" she asked. Abruptly, the pain in her eyes stopped. She untied the linen and looked around.

Angles and shadows and shifting forms of light greeted her eyes, and she blinked, but her vision didn't change. Cwynn was standing next to her, a glowing white shape against a dark gray backdrop. "Catrione?"

"I can't quite make anything out—"

"You can see?" He sounded dubious.

"Things are a little blurry, but I can make out forms and outlines and…" *Something else, as well, something for which she didn't know a word.* But there wasn't time to ponder it now. "My eyes don't hurt, and that's a good thing. Do you still see Bog?" Before Cwynn could answer, she saw him herself: a vaguely dog-shaped outline within a white-gold nimbus. "I see him!" she cried. "Look—there he is. Bog! Here I am!" She waved and without a doubt, she saw his feathery tail wag.

"Be careful," Cwynn said. He took her arm by the elbow.

"We're in some kind of cave, and he's leading us down a tunnel. It looks steep and very slippery."

"Just follow Bog," Catrione replied. From deep within the tunnel, she heard the khouri-keen screaming. At least, she thought it was the khouri-keen. The voices were high and shrill and piercing, and she couldn't so much hear them as see them; bright sparkling ribbons of harsh sound that darted like fireflies on the periphery of her vision. "Come. I think I hear the khouri-keen."

"We can do this by the time the sun sets today?" asked Loriana as she and Bran followed Timias into the keep.

*We have to do it by the time the sun sets today,* Bran thought. His hands and arms felt as if they were made of parchment and he could feel his muscles trembling beneath his skin. Beads of sweat crept down his face, trickled down his back and the air felt very dry down his throat. It burned his lungs and made him breathless.

Loriana stood perfectly still just inside the door. In the very center of the room, a small column, about waist high, apparently of the same marble as the walls, held a perfectly round stone that gleamed a soft green in the gloom. Dusty light filtered down from high above, and Bran looked up. The tower was roofed with a window and the sun shone down, washing the entire interior in a soft white glow. "What's that?"

"That's part of the magic," Timias replied. "Come. We have to go below."

He led the way to the rear of the chamber, where a circular flight of steps curved down into an underground cavern.

Bran swayed, dizzy, and fumbled for the wall. "I think I—" he tried. "I think I have to go home."

"You can't." Loriana shook his hand so hard his shoulder felt as if it would come out of the socket and he saw that she was much stronger than she appeared to be. He stumbled a little and his vision blurred. "Please, just a little more." She ran the tips of her fingers down his face, caressed the fine down on his cheek. "Please?" Her breath burned his earlobe as she stood on tiptoes, leaned against him. "Please, Bran of the soft brown beard. We'll sing about you forever."

"You will?" he whispered.

"Of course we will, Bran. Those who work magic great as this deserve to be remembered, don't you think?"

The entire room seemed to pulsate with that green and glowing light, and Bran felt his knees shake. The room began to spin and the stairs began to sway. As darkness closed around him, he felt himself begin to fall.

As if from very far away, he heard Loriana say, "Can we still use him in this state?"

"Of course we can," Timias answered as the world blinked out. "We only want his essence."

The slippery, uneven rocks prevented them from going faster than a careful walk. "I don't understand," Cwynn muttered. "Isn't there an easier path?"

"No," Catrione replied grimly. "I'm sure this is the easiest, and the safest, and the fastest. Bog led you to that creature. I believe he'll lead us to Tiermuid."

"And then what?"

"And then we kill him."

"How?"

"I'll distract him—you use the shadow cloak, sneak up behind him and sink the silver into him. You won't have to do more than touch him, I don't think." *Unless he's impervious to silver.* But nothing of Faerie is, she reassured herself. After all, that's how Seanta killed her monster, with her silver hand. It had to work.

She gripped Cwynn's forearm with renewed determination just as the color of the khouri-keen's cries changed.

"What's wrong?" he asked.

"They're saying something—they aren't just screaming," she said. "Their voices are different here, shriller, harder to understand. I think they're saying a name—or a phrase, over and over. Could it be—" she paused, listening carefully "—the Faerie-girl, the Faerie-girl?"

"I can't hear a thing."

"Most people can't. They might see flickers of movement, but that's usually all."

"Why are these things so important?" he asked as they set off.

"The khouri-keen are earth elementals. Remember I said druid magic was elemental magic? Druid magic is based on the element of water. Water's very powerful—unlike the other elements, for example, it exists in three forms. But it's fluid, and hard to shape. Like water, it has to be channeled or held in something in order to do anything. The khouri-keen are like the rock, under the soil. They're the foundation for almost all that we do."

"Almost all?"

"Except for the healing rites, the fertility rituals. Those

we work by the sun, the stars, the moon and the trees. But tree magic is slow magic. The khouri-keen are—"

"Easier?"

"In some ways. They're hard to control—but trees can't be controlled at all so—" She broke off and raised her head and as if from very far away, she heard a dog bark. "Bog?"

The cries of the khouri-keen shifted once more, and this time, she heard another name called unmistakably. *CONNLA...CONNLA...CONNLA.* Connla's dead, she thought. And the khouri-keen either didn't know it, or maybe had just found out. But then why were they now screaming, *BOY?*

*BOY...BOY...HE'S OURS... GIVE HIM TO KHOURI!* The screaming was deafening. They struggled down the tunnel, Catrione slipping and sliding ahead of Cwynn. "Hey, don't run off on me—"

"I think they have a human," Catrione said through clenched teeth. Her heart was beginning to pound. "I think they have a mortal—someone Connla put a ward on."

"What?" Cwynn staggered after her. "What are you talking about?"

"The sidhe are dangerous to mortals, Cwynn." She tried to think of how easiest to explain to someone who'd clearly been raised in near total ignorance. "We druids have as little to do with them as possible, and never by ourselves. Why do you think I wanted you to come with me? I can't do this alone. I might not get back."

"What happens if you don't get back?"

"You stay here, and this world—Faerie—milks you dry, if the goblins don't find you and the sidhe don't take your essence."

"What's an essence? A man's seed?"

"No, its something even more intimately a part of you than that. A man's seed is meant to go out of him, meant to create new life. The essence of a mortal is something deeper and richer, something that's in your bones, in your blood, in your mind. And the sidhe will take it if you let them, gorge themselves on it like the goblins on flesh. We druids give it to them in small doses, so it doesn't madden them, doesn't overwhelm them."

"But why have anything to do with them at all?"

"The sidhe have great magic, too. They breathe the magic in…they breathe the magic out. But they're even more dangerous than goblins, and believe me, twice as tricksie as any trixie."

"So they've got a boy?"

"A boy Connla the ArchDruid clearly didn't want them to have." Catrione slipped and slid and she felt Cwynn's arm go around her, steadying her. As she leaned into his strength, her mind began to spin. *Connla was coming from Eaven Morna… A boy from Eaven Morna… A boy Connla didn't want the sidhe to have… A boy from Eaven Morna.* What boy was there at Eaven Morna that the ArchDruid of all Brynhyvar would ward with trixies?

She gripped Cwynn's arm as the name came to her. Deirdre's little brother. Deirdre's little brother. "Bran," she whispered as she stopped short, nearly causing Cwynn to slide. "Great Mother, in all this time, I forgot about Bran."

"Who is Bran?"

"Bran's your brother." She stared ahead, where the dog had likewise stopped to scratch its ear. As she stared at Bog's familiar outline, she remembered the knight that had come from Eaven Morna, the day all this had started. "We had a message from Meeve, too, you see—I just wasn't connecting them."

"Catrione, what are you talking about?" He sounded anxious and impatient.

"I'll have to explain this as briefly as I can. The essence of druid magic isn't really in the khouri-keen—that's where the anchor is, the foundation. But the essence is in each druid. It's the same essence that the sidhe love in any mortal—but there's the power to do magic in a druid's. That's how Deirdre spun the cloak, that's how we make the silver-water that heals—"

"In other words, to work druid magic, you need a druid. Makes sense, I suppose."

"The way magic works—the way the Worlds are—there's echoes and reflections, images and shadows of people and things and places. TirNa'lugh's is our Shadowland, just as our World is theirs. Do you understand that?"

"Hmm. I'll have to think on that one."

"One of the things it means is that opposites have great power, as well as doubles. So twins, for example—most likely one will be druid and one won't. You have a sister, you know. Deirdre's twin. She's not druid at all. But Meeve had four children—two boys and two girls. The girls are twins— one's druid, one's not. The boys aren't, but they're the oldest and the youngest. One isn't a druid—"

"So Bran's a druid?"

"He's not a trained druid, of course. But Connla must've suspected something about him to have put a ward on him—every khouri here is screaming his name. So you see, not only does Tiermuid have the crystals and the khouri-keen, he's got a mortal—a powerful mortal. He's building up to a very great working indeed."

"How do you know that? How can you know that?"

"If you know how it all works, it falls into place. He's got all four Elements, an intention, a goal and I'll wager a medium, as well—those are easy to find. Mediums are anything through which energy can be directed, focused or held. So anything—a piece of wood, certain metals, anything that would absorb energy—" She broke off as through the ground, she felt a single throb rise and fall. "Did you feel that?" The throb came again.

"I felt it and I heard it. Do you have any idea what it is?"

"Goblin drums," Catrione said. "It was dawn, though, when we left… How could it possibly—"

"What's that have to do with anything?"

"The goblins won't come out in the sun."

"We're in TirNa'lugh, right? Maybe here it's different." He looked up. "Are they over us?"

"I can't really tell," Catrione said. "Come, let's go." They struggled on, and finally Cwynn halted. "Why're we stopping?" A cool wind stirred Catrione's hair, and she felt a sticky film coating her face.

"The dog stopped. I think we're there."

Light filtered down from the opening above, and in it, she saw Tiermuid standing in the center, before a rock, his form bent over a black cauldron that appeared to be made of feathers. On the back wall, a beautiful young sidhe dragged a limp mortal up a shallow set of winding steps. His arms were draped around her shoulders, and from one hand dangled what looked like something that exploded in a lacy shimmer of rainbow colors.

*That's the medium,* Catrione realized. *That's what holds the magic of this working. And it's not quite finished yet.* "If I can get that thing away from the boy," she breathed, assessing her chances of crossing the space without Tiermuid—*Tiermuid-Timias-Tetzu*—seeing her. But it was already too late. Not only had he seen her, he had recognized her. He was smiling.

Below her feet, she felt the earth rumble. *Run, run, the goblins come. There's not much time,* she thought. "Cwynn," she whispered. "Do you see the boy? And what he's holding? I've got to get up those steps and stop whatever they're doing. That's Bran. So you sneak up on Timias while he's distracted looking at me. I'll try to get as close to the steps as I can. And when you see me run—"

"Jump on him."

"Exactly." The sidhe was about halfway from the top and the boy looked as if he were practically dead weight. But they needed him, she realized. They needed him to hold the silver.

"He looks pretty far gone anyway, Catrione. I'm not saying we leave him, but he's so pale and white—"

"If he dies here, he doesn't go to the Summerlands," she hissed. "He goes to dance in Herne's Hunt. Would you want that for your brother?"

"No, I'd not want that for anyone," he said at once with a contriteness that made her like him. She felt him peck a quick kiss on her face. "Let's be quick. He doesn't look like he's got much time."

\* \* \*

"Catrione, what happened to your eyes?"

From across the floor, Timias saw her react to his question. She wasn't expecting his recognition, and he smiled.

"I know," she said with a laugh, head high. She spoke in that imperious tone he hated, the tone that told him she had been born the daughter of a chieftain and a queen, recognized druid from birth, honored and pampered and cherished by all. The only one he'd hated more than Catrione had been Deirdre. Catrione sidled around the edge of the rocks and something about the way she moved reminded him of himself in Macha's hall. He saw her turn her head fleetingly at the steps.

*She's trying to get up there, he thought. She'll stop Loriana and Bran if she can.* He sidestepped as she continued. "There's something different about my eyes, isn't there? I think the Hag changed them so I could see you for what you really are. Which is nothing, isn't that right? Tiermuid, Timias, Tetzu—which one are you really? You're none of them, are you? You're none of them and nothing. You're nothing but a changeling who trades one mask for another. You can't show your true face because you don't have one."

Enraged, he leaped. She ran. In mid-air, he felt a hand come down upon his shoulder, and he realized he'd been right all along. Someone had been there, and was wearing the cloak of shadows. Catrione's taunts had enraged him, and now he was face to face with this oaf of a mortal, who swung what looked like a silver-coated garden rake lashed to a primitive harness on the end of a blunted forearm. "I know you," cried Timias as they grappled back and forth at the bottom of the steps. He heard Loriana screaming, heard Catrione calling out for Bran. "Put it on the globe, Loriana," Timias screamed as the mortal swung his clumsy contrivance. *Don't fail me now,* he thought. *Don't fail me now, my queen.* Just a few more heartbeats, and the power of both silver and gremlins would be locked into Faerie, bound by fire, air and water, anchored in stone.

He heard a shrill scream, a boy's ragged cry, and he looked up as the rocks above shuddered and groaned. Gremlins rushed out, burrowing up and into the crevices, heeding his previous bidding to keep the great structure standing. Energy jolted through him and the mortal lost his footing and tumbled backward onto the floor. He rolled and clung to the floor as it tilted, shuddered and settled back into place. He got to his feet and rushed at Timias, who caught the mortal's upraised hand easily in his own and began to twist it with all the new-made magic coursing in his veins. As the bones began to crunch, he saw the mortal's eyes widen almost comically as he realized what had happened. Timias let the mortal's hand go.

The mortal realized his hook was now a flesh and blood hand, as much a part of him as the one he'd been born with, and his jaw dropped.

"Silver's not possible in Faerie anymore," hissed Timias, and he coiled himself, ready to strike, when Loriana cried from the top of the staircase:

"Don't kill him!"

"What?" Timias looked back at her, over his shoulder.

"The magic's done—the mortal threw the silver on top of the globe—but it didn't do what you said it would do,

Timias. It didn't fit over it—it melted, in a way. I let the druid take the boy. And you can't—you mustn't kill this one."

"Why not?"

The mortal scrabbled backward, and Timias saw the cloak of shadows float around his shoulders. *Clever Catrione*, he thought. She was the one who noticed everything. No wonder the Hag had rewarded her so well.

"Because," said Loriana, her expression soft, "he's the new High King. You have to let him live, Timias. He's my Consort. Don't you see?"

Thunderstruck, Timias swallowed hard, resisting the impulse to crumple to his knees. "A sidhe doesn't take a mortal as a consort, Loriana."

"But my heir is already conceived, Timias." Loriana looked at him over her shoulder and held out her hand, the other caressing her lower belly. "We made great magic, indeed. I think there's more than one swimming in me already. I can take who I choose. You said I'd be the greatest Queen ever seen in Faerie. And this mortal is the first of my Consorts. Don't you see, Timias? When one dies, I get a new one." She put her hands over her mouth and giggled.

"Oh, no, you don't." Cwynn scrambled to his feet and bolted up the steps after Catrione. "I'm going home!"

His footsteps faded. Timias looked at Loriana. "You let him go?"

"He'll be back, when they mate him to the land. Maybe I'll keep him for a while. Just because." She turned and began to walk up the winding steps, beckoning to Timias. "Just because I can. After all—" they reached the top of the steps, where the moonstone shimmered beneath the fine silver caul "—everything is different now. You were right, I can feel it." She threw her arms wide. "I can't wait." Timias watched as she bent over the caul, a knife twisting in his gut. How could this have happened? he wondered. She was supposed to choose him. He was her savior—he was the creator of the Caul that saved Faerie from goblins and mortals and the destructive power of silver. He was the builder of the new magic. She held out her hand to him. "What's wrong, Timias? You look very glum. You were right. Imagine what all the Council will say now? You've given us a place to live, a means to make a new world—you should be smiling. I almost feel I can fly."

"Then I am pleased, Most Glorious Majesty." He put his hand over his heart. He felt empty and drained and the wound beneath his tail itched. "But perhaps I, too, should go to the Deep Forest, await my time of changing—"

"No!" she cried, taking his hand. "I want you here with me, Timias. You created all this. You created this." She brought his hand to her belly and he felt, unmistakably, the flicker of life. One, no, two, he thought, and then was troubled to feel a third. He remembered Deirdre's child. No, he decided, he wouldn't think about that anymore. He twined her hand in his and raised it to his lips. "Now, Glorious Majesty, shall we decide how best to rid ourselves of the goblins before the sun completely fades?"

"I will rely on you, Timias," Loriana said. "I will rely on you to make the goblins go away." She stood on tiptoe and kissed his cheek, then strolled out of the room, humming a little to herself. She looked, he thought, like a cat who'd had a dish of cream.

For a long moment, he stared at the Caul, as it shimmered on the moonstone globe. The sky above had turned to violet, the goblin drums were beginning to beat. They were coming back, he knew, gorged on druid flesh, strong in a new way, just as the sidhe were. Only they didn't realize that the sidhe had the advantage. For a moment, he was tempted to rip the Caul off the moonstone, to let the goblins rampage and plunder, to let the trees of Faerie burn, the trees of Shadow fall to blight. But then it would all be nothing, and he would never see his dream of Faerie all powerful become reality. He glanced out the door into the courtyard, which was washed in lilac light and echoed with the sound of Loriana's singing. *She carries the future,* he thought, and that decided him.

If wise councilor she wanted, then wise councilor he would be. With a final look at the Caul, he strode purposefully from the chamber. Just over the threshold, he hesitated. He looked back inside the room. "Doors," he murmured. A set of brass-bound doors appeared immediately, almost before the final sound had faded from his lips. "Sealed." A click and the lock was cast. That would do for now, he decided. With a final glance, he strode away, to plan Macha's defeat.

*Run, run, the goblins come—run away from goblin drums— run away fast, run away run, run away, run away, run away run.* The old rhyme pounded through her brain, even as she stumbled, half carrying, half dragging Bran over the border and into a gray void that stank of blood and excrement. Catrione tripped and fell, hands extended to break her fall. She recoiled as they landed in something soft and squishy, something that reeked of the charnel pits. Had she somehow brought the boy into a goblin-hold?

As the horror of that possibility crashed over her, a bird cawed above her head, and she felt the rush of wings past her cheek and the scent of carrion on the breeze. She felt a rush of air overhead and looked up, seeing nothing but the gray blank, even as the harsh cries of crows filled her ears. She heard trees bending overhead, felt raindrops pelt her cheek. She raised her hands to her face and felt her eye sockets, felt empty scabbed pits. She really was blind.

"Cailleach?" It was Bran's voice, dry and hoarse. He sounded as if he'd not had anything to drink in days. Which, she realized, he probably hadn't.

"My name's Catrione," she said. "Your sister, Deirdre— she—she was my friend."

"She told me you were coming," he rasped.

"What do you mean?" she asked, feeling the splash of rain drops on her cheek. She was blind, and it was raining.

"She came to me. When I was down there, or over there, or wherever it was. She told me to hold on, that she was sending her best friend in all the world to get me and bring me home. She told me I just had to hang on a bit more."

Scarcely aware she did so, Catrione sank down, feeling the rocky earth beneath her fingers. The soil was chopped and hacked; it felt raw and newly turned. Her groping fingers came to something rubbery and gelatinous and she flinched again. She felt the sharp edge of something that felt like a dagger, then realized it was the broken head of a spear. She turned half to the right and felt a sword, the pommel still clutched in a rigor-stiff hand. "Bran, do you have any idea where we are?"

"No," he said, and she heard him gulp. "But this rain tastes good. It looks like there was a battle here. There's all kinds of stuff lying around—and bodies, too."

She took a deep breath and was nearly overcome by the smell. "Is it day? Night?"

"It's gray. I can't really tell."

"What kind of soldiers? Can you see what they're wearing?"

"I see a lot of purple-blue. I think our fellows beat the Lac-quileans. Looks like a lot of foreign bodies left lying where they fell."

The wind blew harder and Catrione tried to gather her scattered thoughts into some semblance of order. She had to do something, before both of them began to experience the aftereffects of so much time in TirNa'lugh. They'd escaped Tiermuid and the goblins only to find themselves lost and alone in the middle of what seemed like a battlefield, sur-rounded by the hacked-apart dead. The rain trickled down her neck, seeped down her back. She heard Bran gulping. "We can't stay here. Do you feel strong enough to walk?"

"I feel a little better. I'm so hungry, though, so weak. I feel…thin."

*You're not thin; you're practically transparent,* she thought. "We're not likely to find anything appetizing here unless we turn to crows. If you can lead me, maybe we can find a road." They had to reach a place of safety before the backlash hit them, but she didn't want to frighten him further. She was alarmed to feel how hot and dry his flesh, how sharp his bones. There was almost nothing left of him, she thought. He still might die, but at least if he died in this world, he'd go to the Summerlands and come back when he was ready, probably to face Tiermuid in some other guise again. The boy had a brave, bright spirit. He didn't deserve such a fate as an eternity in Herne's Hunt.

"Catrione, I think I see a dog—a white dog." Wispy as his voice was, Bran sounded excited and Catrione smiled inwardly. There was a chance, she thought. A chance they both might make it back. If they could reach a place of safety before the backlash hit them both, they might both make it through. "I wish you could see him. He's over there on that wagon, and he's wagging his tail. Hey, where'd he go? He was just right there!"

Catrione pushed her hair out of her face just as she felt a pointed nose nudge her thigh. "Bog?" Catrione whispered. "Bog, is that really you?" Another nudge, another lick and a flat head pushed up against the palm of her hand as tears filled her ruined eyes and leaked down her face. "I think we'll be all right, Bran." She smiled, despite the rain and the cold, and the scent of death rising all around. Despite knowing Cwynn might be lost forever. "Bog's come to take us home."

## 18

"I owe you my life, Fengus-da."

In the antechamber of her mother's sickroom, Morla paused, balancing her weight on the balls of her feet, chewing her lower lip. Ever since the battle, when Fengus, with a ragged army cobbled together mostly from refugees, had overcome the Lacquileans, Meeve had said those very words in Morla's hearing at least a dozen times. It was usually accompanied by a sidelong glance.

Morla was indeed grateful that Fengus had rescued her, but she felt no wish to spend any time at all in his company. She spent most of her time, in fact, in a chair by Lochlan's bed, where Lochlan clung to life by the slenderest of threads. A Lacquilean arrow had buried itself in his back as they'd fled the camp. Morla only cared whether or not Lochlan lived, though she knew exactly how Meeve expected her to repay Fengus.

"Come in, dear." Bride, the pigeon-breasted still-wife with a chin like a rabbit's stood in the doorway, smiling.

"They said my mother was asking for me?"

Bride nodded. As Morla limped past, the still-wife touched

her arm and said beneath her breath, "We don't think she has much longer."

Morla nodded. The poisoned perfume had done its work. Meeve's health continued to decline and in the days since the battle, had taken a precipitous turn for the worse. Now she lay, noticeably fading day by day, her pale flesh falling off her bones. In the bedroom door, she paused.

Fengus was sitting in the chair beside her mother's bed, hunched over, Meeve's pale hand sandwiched between both of his. He looked up, then down, when he saw Morla, and jumped to his feet awkwardly. Morla herself glanced down, for to make matters worse, Fengus seemed smitten with her. *But I love Lochlan,* she thought as she nodded a greeting to the king, then bent to kiss her mother's forehead. "Good morning, Mother."

The summer sun was less than kind as it streamed across the dying queen's face but Meeve seemed to crave the warmth. Soon she'll be in the Summerlands. And then what would happen was an open question. The victory over the Lacquileans had bought them a little time, Morla knew. But the Lacquileans weren't fools. They knew Meeve was dying. And once she was dead, they would be back. It was critical a strong leader took control and Fengus saw himself as that strong leader. As, apparently, did Meeve, who smiled up at Morla and took her hand. "Good morning, daughter. I see you're walking better today. Have you looked in on Bran?"

Morla nodded as she perched gingerly on the edge of Meeve's bed. "He's better, they say. He's stopped eating so much." She turned her back to Fengus and smiled at her mother.

"Well," said Fengus. "I'll leave you two alone. Good morning, Morla. Perhaps I'll see you later."

"Perhaps."

With a brief bow he was gone, and Meeve raised an eyebrow as she shifted restlessly on the pillows, her mouth pinched in her skeletal face. "You might be nicer to him, Morla. He did save your life."

"I don't want to encourage him."

"I owe my throne to Fengus," Meeve said. "And you owe him your life."

"Then let the druids set a head-price, Mother, and let him have it. Twice, three times, as far as I care. Mother, I know what you want. But I don't intend to marry Fengus. I love Lochlan. I always have. And now that I'm branded, I can't be High Queen."

Meeve drew a deep breath and pressed her lips together so tightly they nearly disappeared. She shook her head. "Stupid girl." She waved her hand. "After all this, after all you've seen in the last weeks—no, the last year—after everything that's happened how can you not see what threatens us? Have you a mind to send tribute to such a land—"

"I do see what threatens us. I understand we must stand united. I swear to you now so long as I draw breath in this body, I'll never make war with Fengus—unprovoked, I mean. But I don't want to marry him."

"You were happy with Fionn."

"But I love Lochlan."

Meeve's mouth twitched and she snorted softly. "All the women love Lochlan. Lochlan loves all the women. And besides…" Her voice trailed off. "From what they tell me, they expect him to be waiting for me in the Summerlands." The queen's bone-white face softened. "Morla, I understand you love Lochlan. But I think you have to accept what's happening. The Wheel's turning, his work is done, just like mine, obviously. And Fengus wants to marry you. You made quite an impression." She chuckled.

Morla opened her mouth, then shut it.

"You know, Morla," continued Meeve, "you're the only one left. Deirdre is dead, poor thing, Bran's mind may be gone and Cwynn's lost...."

It cut Morla to the quick to think that Bran could be gone forever. As Meeve stared out the window, Morla spoke over the drone of the bees. "Isn't there something the druids here can do about Bran, Mother? Some way to find his essence in Faerie? I know they said they'd try—"

"They have tried, Morla—they assure me they'll try again. I'm past the point I can force anyone to do anything." She lay back against the pillows, and then, just as suddenly as her strength seem to fade, she was back, her eyes as piercing as ever. "All I ever wanted was to leave this land settled and at peace. Now it seems I shall do neither." She plucked the sheet with one thin hand. "I understand Fengus is not your first choice. So does he, poor fellow. But he is chieftain-king of Allovale, Morla, what about a Beltane marriage? A year and a day—see how you like him? Maybe at the end you'll find he's not so bad?"

"I don't want—"

"Don't you understand it's not about what you want?" Meeve shot upright, eyes flashing fire. "Maybe that's what's the problem—you're not married to the Land as I am, as Fengus is. You were Fionn's spouse, not the Land's. Maybe you can't really understand what's at stake." Meeve sank back, a fine sheen of sweat on her cheeks, but her eyes still burned.

"I'll think about it, Mother," Morla answered. "I make no promises."

She expected her mother to protest, to continue, but to Morla's surprise, Meeve only sighed. She turned her face into the sunlight, and closed her papery lids. "I'm tired, Morla. I have to rest. Keep an eye out for your brother—your brother Cwynn. Goddess only knows what he'll think of all this. If he's wise, he'll head straight back to Far Nearing."

*What a strange thing for Mother to say.* She wanted to ask what Meeve meant, but Meeve turned on her side, and curled up like a child, her palm pillowed on her cheek. "Rest well," was all she said.

Meeve spoke when her hand was on the latch. "Morla?"

"Yes, Mother?"

"I didn't know Briecru was stealing the food I was sending you. I didn't realize you were starving. I thought you were being selfish."

"I know, Mother. Lochlan told me."

But the only answer was silence. Morla looked back. Meeve was still, and she wondered if her mother had really spoken. With a heavy feeling in her chest, Morla made her way out to the garden. She sank down beside the fountain, where the speckled fish darted under the lilies. Meeve's political instincts were unerring—a union between a princess of Mochmorna and a king of Allovale would indeed be a clear signal to the scattered lairds and chieftains that Brynhyvar should unite. But, oh, at what a cost? She gazed across the fountain, to the window she knew was Lochlan's. The window was open, the white linen curtains waved gently in the breeze. Cream-white roses twined around the frame. She felt no connection to anything that seemed to require such a sacrifice but her mother. It would be one thing if Lochlan were dead, she knew. But he wasn't. He clung to life, just as she clung to the hope of their love.

"Morla?"

Fengus's rough voice startled her out of her reverie. She turned, startled, and gasped, for he appeared to be a big black shadow blotting out the sun.

"I'm sorry. I was looking in on Catrione and saw you sitting here. Thought I'd come and say good morning—I didn't mean to frighten you." He bowed and took a step back.

*You should be nicer to him.* "How is Catrione?"

The look he gave her as he answered was one of doglike gratitude. "She…" His expression darkened. "The same. She comes and goes, in and out. One moment I think she knows me, the next, she babbles and gibbers. They tell me this is the way it is after an experience like hers. Young Bran—he was too out of it, I suppose, while it was all going on. He can't tell us a thing."

Morla was silent. "So no one knows what happened?"

Fengus shook his head. "Not till she comes out of it and can tell us. But even if she comes out, she may not be able to tell us. Apparently she didn't go in prepared the way they're supposed to. And she didn't have another druid with her—she was with some lad who was discovered here one night under very strange circumstances." He ran a hand through his grizzled hair. Morla felt a wave of real compassion. Whatever else he was, the man appeared to genuinely care about his daughter.

"I hope she recovers, too," Morla said softly.

Fengus took a deep breath, then said, "Morla, I'm a plain-speaking man, not like your mother, meaning her no disrespect, you understand. But I lack her wit and her way with words. So I'll come right out and tell you what I've been thinking, what your mother's been thinking—"

"I know she wants me to marry you."

"She told you that?"

"She didn't have to."

There was a long silence. Fengus squared his shoulders and lowered his head. "I can see what you think of that idea."

Morla felt herself flush, felt the warmth spread across her scalp.

"I know I'm old enough to be your father. But my last Beltane bride was less than twenty, so you've no need to fear that I cannot perform my obligations. The land needs us, Morla. We can't let those foreigners take Brynhyvar. Your mother, goddess save me, is right. Between the two of us, we'll bring the other lairds together. It will be a good thing, Morla. You'll see. I'll never be unkind. There'll always be a home for you and your brother."

Morla looked down at her knotted, white-knuckled hands. *You should be nicer to him.* He saved your life. "I—I am—I'm not unaware of the great honor you do me, Fengus-da, by asking me to be your wife, nor am I unaware of my responsibilities as my mother's heir. I told my mother I'd think about it. I'll tell you the same thing."

Fengus nodded. "All right, Morla. But Lughnasa's coming. I'd like to take a bride then. I think your mother would like to see a wedding, too." He bowed and strode away, his shoulders thrust aggressively forward. He was a man who was used to getting his way by one means or another, and Meeve had frustrated him for twenty years. Now he saw an acceptable ending in sight. Morla didn't feel so much wooed as pursued. She gathered herself up and hobbled out of the garden, into the quiet corridor and down to Lochlan's room.

In the doorway, she met Bride making her rounds. The woman met the question on her face with the same soft smile. "No change, I'm afraid, my dear. No change yet."

Morla limped inside the room. For weeks now, Lochlan had lain, gripped by fever, shaken by chills, locked inside some dark place no one could go. Twice the druid women had attempted to call him out of it, but both times, they'd back away, shaking their heads, saying his body was not yet strong enough. Increasingly, discussions about his recovery were prefaced by "if" rather than "when." That he'd survived this long was deemed miraculous, and Morla knew some of the druids believed he would cross to the Summerlands with Meeve, her champion and protector into death.

*But he's not Meeve's champion.* She sank down on the chair beside him and leaned forward, hands on her chin, watching his drawn profile. The window was open, and a soft breeze blew through it, ruffling the white linen curtains, ruffling the long curls around his face. She touched his cheek with the back of her hand. Stubble darkened his jaw. She traced his lips with her finger, kissed his cheek. What would he say to do? she wondered. Marry Fengus? Beltane marriages could be entered into at any of the four high festivals of the year, though Beltane was the traditional time. She could agree to that, perhaps. A Beltane marriage, begun at

Lughnasa, for a year and a day. But what if he came to and heard she'd married Fengus? What would he think?

*That you'd done what was right for the land.* The voice sounded suspiciously like Meeve's. *When you marry the land, you'll understand.* Bees buzzed outside the window in the roses that twined around the frame and the sweet scent filled the sickroom. Her heels throbbed. Maybe there was something in what Meeve was trying to tell her. She remembered the looks on the faces of the hungry people of Dalraida. A marriage alliance to Fengus—if it strengthened the land—wasn't that worth it?

But where did that leave Lochlan?

*All the women love Lochlan. Lochlan loves all the women.* Again, Meeve's voice echoed in her head, stinging as the memory of the brand. In all ten years, he'd never sent her a message, never found a reason to ride north. A Beltane marriage had a limit, after all—a year and a day wasn't forever. She drew a deep breath and clasped her hands, then leaned over and pressed a kiss on Lochlan's lips. "I love you, Lochlan. If you can, come back to me. But if you can't, these three things I bid you keep…" Her throat filled and tears ran down her face. She leaned closer and kissed his jaw, then his ear, and whispered, "The memory of merry days and quiet nights, quiet days and merry nights, of honor unstained by word or deed—" her voice broke "—and all the love I bear for thee." She kissed him once more on his unresponsive mouth, then stumbled, blinded by tears, out of the room and down the corridor to learn that Meeve had crossed to the Summerlands at last.

* * *

Cwynn heard the gulls crying and smelled the powdery sand beneath his cheek before he opened his eyes to see he was lying on the beach just below his grandfather's keep. It was just before dawn and already the birds were fighting over the refuse washed up by the tide. He was lying in it, he realized, and his clothing, what remained of it, was soaking wet. He had seashells and sand in his hair and under his fingernails—all ten of his fingernails. He sat up with a start.

*Catrione,* he thought with an unexpected pang. And Bran—his brother—what happened to him? Bran had been so close to death, he'd been surprised when Catrione managed to make him move. But he'd been too busy fighting the sidhe to know if they'd really got away. He felt around his neck. The flat gold disk was there, just as he remembered before he'd gone into TirNa'lugh. "Let me not go back there again," he muttered and a soft breeze ruffled his hair. But he had his hand back and he had his disk back. He looked up at his grandfather's keep. White smoke belched from the kitchen chimneys. He was ravenously hungry, he realized, his stomach felt shrunken, almost as if it clung to his spine. His tongue felt shriveled in his mouth. How'd I get here? he wondered. His last memory was of bolting up the steps and out the door, through a greenwood and toward home. *HOME*—he remembered how the word had reverberated through his mind, pounding like goblin drums in his bones. *Home…Home…Home.* No wonder he'd found himself here. He must've washed up on the tide.

He felt weak and worn as he tried to get to his feet and he stumbled a few times, collapsing into the powdery sand.

Catrione and Bran had gone up the steps before he had, he remembered, trying to recall details, and he'd seen no sign of them—not that he'd paused to look. What was the name of that grove, he thought—the one he'd gone to, the one where he'd killed that *HORRIBLE MONSTROUS THING?*

The image of it blazed up out of nowhere, searing itself back into his brain, just as it had before Catrione had erased it. The inhuman creature rose up once more, renewed, expanded its segmented body writhing, eyes shining with hate. *"You killed me,"* it hissed silently. *"Now it's my turn to kill you."*

With a cry, Cwynn collapsed onto the sand, clawing at his eyes with both hands. He heard the creature laughing. *That's what it wants,* he thought, and with every ounce of willpower he possessed, he scrabbled deep into the sand, burying his arms to the armpits. But the creature didn't stop. It danced and capered and gibbered through his head. Maddened, Cwynn twisted and contorted on the sand, bellowing like a bull as a pale sun rose. His cries roused the keep and the village, and from somewhere far away, he heard voices calling, knew that people reached him, touched him, tried to help him. He felt himself lifted and carried, and put into a wide bed. A soft hand covered his head, a firm palm lay over his heart. As if from far away, he heard Argael call his name.

*It won't let me come back to you,* Cwynn tried to say, over and over again but the creature only howled and spit poison or small needles into his mind that stung and made him shake and sweat and cling to the ropes that bound him to the bed. *It won't let me come back.* Again and again he tried to break free, fighting it with all his might, but the thing was strong and clever and had an unending repertoire of torments.

"Come back, Cwynn. Come back to us. We need you, Cwynn. We need you." Another voice was breaking through the cacophony, this one clearer and brighter. "Please come back, Cwynn. Come back and live with your boys. Come back and be with me."

It was Ariene's voice, reaching out through the mists, through the fog. For the first time, since the thing had come back, its face flickered and Cwynn realized he didn't have to see it. He could look through it, he realized, as if it weren't there.

"Please, Cwynn, please come back, we need you. The boys need you. Don't go to the Summerlands yet."

"I don't want to go to the Summerlands." He opened his eyes and looked through the creature, and the remnants of the apparition dissolved into nothingness. Ariene's face appeared, looking down at him, and he saw he was in his grandfather's room, lying in his grandfather's bed on sweat-soaked linen, his arms and legs tied spread-eagled to the posts. At least a week's growth of beard sprouted from his chin. He was naked and so was she, and a small puddle of semen lay in the shallow bowl of his belly. She wiped the corner of her mouth, and he realized what she'd done to bring him back. He looked deep into her blue eyes and felt the same kind of peace he felt when he looked out across the sea. "I want to stay here. With you."

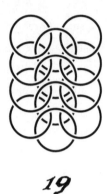

## 19

Sunlight burned Catrione's cheek, waking her with a start. She tried to open her eyes and realized her eyelids were held closed by a bandage. *I don't remember hurting my eyes,* she thought. And then she remembered the drops from the Hag's cauldron. She drew a deep breath and smelled lavender, soap and sun-warm wood. Her last memory was of collapsing into her father's arms. She lay flat on her back and wondered where she was.

"Catrione? Are you back with us, dearie?" Baeve's voice spoke from somewhere above her and to the right. Catrione turned in the direction of the sound and realized she could perceive Baeve—not as person, but as swirling colors and patterns of light against a midnight background. A chill went through her as she looked around the room. She remembered how everything appeared in TirNa'lugh—all shapes and shadows and blazing colors. *What will you pay for the vision of the Hag?*

Catrione pushed herself up in the bed. She put out her hand and the older woman wrapped it in both of hers, her grip gentle and strong, comforting and kind, all at once. "Baeve?" Her voice was scratchy and hoarse, her throat dry. "Is that you? How long—how long have I been here?"

"It's me, Catrione. You've been in and out a long time. It's nearly Lughnasa."

"MidSummer's passed?"

"Weeks ago." She released Catrione's hand with a gentle pat. "Here, dear, drink some water."

A goblet was brought to her lips, and Catrione swallowed. "What about Bran?"

"Bran's fine, dear. He doesn't remember much but he's making the brothers mad with his questions. He's taken to following Athair Emnoch around like a puppy. He'll be fine. It was good Meeve had a chance to see him."

"And my father? Is he still here?"

"Oh, no, he left after Meeve's funeral."

"Meeve's gone." A pang went through Catrione. No wonder the world felt so different, somehow. It wasn't just the blindness, it wasn't just the strange patterns of color and shimmering light. No wonder she had such a sense something was missing. A great bright spirit had gone back to the Summerlands and the world was more the shadowy for it. She'd be back, Catrione knew, some day when the time was right and the world needed her again. But Meeve had wreaked her own kind of havoc. She had lessons to learn before she came back.

"The poison had done its work, I'm afraid. You knew she'd been poisoned by her own steward? By the time we got her, there wasn't much we could do, I'm afraid—or that we were allowed to do." Bride finished with a sour little laugh.

"Allowed to do? What do you mean?"

There was a long silence while Bride bustled around the room, moving back and forth, her footsteps sharp and angry. "Bride?" Catrione reached out and touched her arm, her movement as precise as a sighted person's, and Bride froze and looked at her more closely.

"Now that you're awake at last, your father hoped you'd be at Eaven Avellach by Lughnasa. If you leave in the next sennight, you can be there for the wedding."

"What wedding?" asked Catrione, momentarily diverted, just as she suspected Bride wanted her to be. "Fengus-da is getting married?"

"He was hoping you'd be able to officiate, though that might be too much to expect, yet. But, still—you might see—"

"Who's he marrying?" Catrione cut through the older woman's prattle.

"Meeve's daughter, of course. Deirdre's twin." Bride was on her knees beside the bed, transferring folded laundry into a chest. "Her name's Morla. She was married before, of course, and has a son in fostering. I know it's what Meeve wanted."

"You don't approve?" There was something the woman wasn't saying. Catrione could see a small figure eight, in ugly shades of muddy green and brownish yellow, swirl in the area of the woman's throat.

"My approval wasn't asked," Bride answered, and the colors flared clear for just an instant, as something of her true feelings slipped out. Then the colors darkened, the green almost to black, the yellow to jaundiced brown. "You should go, Catrione. Your father was beside himself with worry."

"What aren't you telling me, Bride?" Catrione sat up,

clasping her arms around her knees. "I can see there's something you're holding back."

Bride froze on her knees. Her spine went stiff, she turned her head over her shoulder. "Catrione." She paused, her voice heavy. "Catrione, I don't know what you remember, or what you realize, but your eyes—your eyes are gone, Catrione. There's no chance you'll regain your sight. I don't mean to be harsh. I just don't want to give false—"

"Oh, Bride." Catrione sighed. "That's not it, and you know it." She patted the side of the bed, then held out her hand. "Please—"

From somewhere down the hall, a door slammed and women's voices echoed. Bride cocked her head, went to the door, then shut it. She hurried over to the bed and knelt beside Catrione, picked up her hand, and gently pushed her back against the pillow. "That's Niona. Listen to me, Catrione. I don't have much time. Things are different now—things have changed. It's not just Meeve's passing—most of our kind are gone. The goblins attacked Ardagh—the night of the battle here, or thereabouts. Except for a few druids sprinkled here and there, we're the only grove left in all of Brynhyvar. Niona's in charge. And things are different." She pressed Catrione's hand, as if to imprint her words.

"Please—please, wait. There's so much I want to know—there's so much I want to ask you. What about Cwynn?"

"No sign of him, Catrione. I suggested we send to Far Nearing—wasn't that where he came from? But Niona would have none of that."

"Why not? He's Meeve's son—"

"Oh, child, you don't know the half of it." Baeve sighed and patted Catrione's shoulder. "Believe me, child, get yourself beneath your father's roof as soon as you can. Niona's making so many changes—" Bride stopped as footsteps marched up and down the corridor past Catrione's door.

"What kind of changes?"

The bed creaked, the mattress dipped, and the muddy light moved across a flat field of varying shades of gray as Baeve stood up. "Catrione, Niona's blaming you. It's better for everyone, I think, for you to go now you're awake…."

"Leave? Bride, you don't understand I—I'm not injured, I'm not disabled. I can see…I can see you, I can see the window…"

"Drink the water, child. I'll be back with some gruel. Sip it slowly, now. It'll be good for the baby."

"What baby?" Catrione bolted upright.

"The one you're carrying, dearie. The one with which you're nearly two months' gone. Rest now, child. I'll fetch you something to eat." Then she was gone.

The quick patter of Baeve's footsteps faded down the corridor. Catrione sank back against her pillows, the sheets clenched between her hands. Whatever had happened in TirNa'lugh, nothing in this world was better. The idea of a marriage between her father and a girl the same age as Deirdre made her vaguely ill. Or maybe that was just the result of the child she was carrying. She touched her stomach, but her abdomen was flat. But beneath her hand, she felt a throb, faint as an echo but definitely there. *Cwynn,* she thought. *Cwynn's the father.*

She remembered the bargain they had made before they went to TirNa'lugh. Before she went to Fengus-da, she had to keep her promise to Cwynn. He was a good father, she thought, or would've been. *But wouldn't I know if he, too, were in the Summerlands?* She could feel Deirdre's spirit, dark and maroon, she could even feel Meeve's, all gold and copper. She could feel Bog's, pure and crystal. But she couldn't feel Cwynn's.

Another day or so, and she'd be strong enough to go to Far Nearing to keep her promise and ensure the village was protected. But what kinds of changes was Bride talking about that were so upsetting she hesitated to tell Catrione?

She drank down the rest of the water and was suddenly overtaken by ravenous hunger. Her stomach growled, and she hoped Bride hurried back with food.

*Help me.* The voice caught her unaware, even as a faint muddy shimmer flickered out of the corner of one eye.

Catrione sat up and swung her legs over the side of the bed. "Is someone there?" she called aloud. "Baeve? Sora? Bride?" The only answer came from the droning bees in the roses around the window frame.

*Help me.*

Catrione whipped around, for the flicker seemed to come from the other side of the room now. She reached out and encountered the edge of the bedside table. She cocked her head, listening. "Who's there?"

*Help me.*

Faint and weak and far away, this time the voice was not accompanied by a shimmer or a spark. Catrione stood up slowly, clinging to the edge of the table, and then the nearest chair. She made it as far as the open window and paused.

*Help me.*

Catrione spun around, knocking her bare foot against

the leg of the chair. Pain rammed through her, and she bit back a curse. "I can't help you if I don't know where you are."

*Help me.*

Exasperated, Catrione felt and sensed her way around the room, to the corridor. She knew she was in the still-house, in the nursing wing. *There must be other patients about,* she thought. But this wasn't an ordinary cry for help, or otherwise, someone would've heard and responded. She could hear someone humming a few rooms away, could hear the soft swish of a broom, the rapid click of shears in the garden. There were people close enough to hear. She edged out of the room, one hand on the wall. Her senses felt stretched, her sight a bizarre mosaic of varying hues of gray, shot through with particles of light.

*Help me.*

Catrione paused, listening. Doors and windows were outlined in bright white lines of light, and she realized, with a start that what she was looking at was a negative image. *Show me where you are,* Catrione thought, projecting the question out through her mind, into the realm of the Hag's vision. To her right, one of the doorways suddenly exploded in pale lights that as quickly dissipated. Catrione jumped. Her heart was beating rapidly, her head was starting to spin. *I'm with child,* she thought. *I'm with child and I'm blind. Maybe I shouldn't have gotten out of bed.*

*Help me.*

The voice was stronger, closer, and Catrione peered around a glowing doorway, into a room where she could discern the rough outline of a man lying on a narrow bed. "Are you the one who's calling for help?" she whispered.

*Yes.*

Catrione glanced over her shoulder. The corridor in both directions was empty, even though she could sense presences all around. It was almost distracting, as if she could see things in not just three dimensions, but in four or five. She stole over to the bed, her bare feet making no sound on the floor. She placed one hand on his forehead, trying to make sense of all she perceived. It was like being in TirNa'lugh and the mortal world, all at once. Images swirled around her, coiling and uncoiling like a giant snake. The knight—for there was no doubt in her mind from what she saw he was a knight—was locked in some place deep inside his own mind, a place any of the druids should've been able to bring him out of.

Why would they withhold healing? Clearly the knight understood what he needed—he was asking for it, so loudly she could hear him. This had nothing to do with the Hag's vision… *Maybe it does and maybe it doesn't. How much do you really remember?*

*HELP ME.*

The tenor of the images changed, assumed an urgency, a deepening of color. He needed her, she thought, needed what she could do for him. The knight didn't understand why he was lost, didn't understand why he wasn't being helped. He knew what he needed.

Catrione felt a sense of deja vu come over her.

"What are you doing, Catrione?" Niona's voice took her entirely by surprise.

Catrione startled, heart in her throat and saw only a dark gray shimmer in the open doorway. "Niona?"

"Catrione, this isn't your bed. Come with me. Bride said you were awake."

Catrione felt her upper arm seized. She was pulled firmly into the corridor and propelled toward her room and in Niona's grip, she read no mercy. "Niona?" she asked. "What's wrong?"

"What's wrong?" The woman pushed her back and Catrione felt the bed behind her knees. Forced to sit, she stared up, wondering why she couldn't see anything of Niona but a shadow.

*She's afraid. She's afraid and gone into hiding.* "What's wrong?" Catrione whispered again. Suddenly she was afraid for herself, because Niona stood over her, black and menacing and somehow all-encompassing. Did the woman intend to kill her?

"You lie in some dream-driven stupor for a whole half quarter, and you dare ask what's wrong? Didn't Bride tell you? Meeve's dead, Ardagh destroyed, the charnel pits full to overflowing."

"Niona, what are you talking about?" Catrione wiped spittle off her cheek. She felt as if she'd awakened into a looking-glass world, that might bear some resemblance to the one she'd known but yet was nothing like it.

Niona stalked to the door. "Stay in here, Catrione, and stay away from that knight. I'll have no more of that sacrilegious coupling. That's what started all this. That's the first thing I've made sure will stop." Without another word, she slammed the door shut behind her, and Catrione heard the outside latch click shut.

*She locked me in.* For the space of a few heartbeats, the reality didn't register and then she had to clench her hands into fists to prevent herself from rushing to the door and demanding to be allowed free access. But something told her not to do that.

In a few minutes, the latch clicked up, the door opened, and Baeve, not Bride stepped into the room. She was carrying a tray from which Catrione could see slow spirals of white steam rise. She had something else, too, a flowing piece of something that looked like fabric, giving off the scent of the OtherWorld. She shut the door behind her, set the tray on the table beside the bed and enfolded Catrione in a warm embrace. "Oh, child," she murmured over and over. "Oh, child, thank the goddess you're home."

"It doesn't feel like home, Baeve." Catrione raised her head and stared at the stillwife. "What's happening to Niona?"

"She's turning into her fears, I suppose you could say. Though truth to tell, Catrione, things are so…so different. No khouri-keen, no goblins. At least none of the other trees have shown blight. But the land's reeling. You can feel it— the people are confused, Meeve's dead, at least six have claimed the High Crown—"

"And Niona's blaming me for all of it?"

Baeve's sudden silence was all the answer Catrione needed.

"We—Bride, Sora and I—we think you should go to Eaven Avellach. You'll have no peace here, and there, your father—well, whatever else he is, he loves you. He'll not let anything happen to you or your child."

"You think Niona would threaten my child?" Instinctively she placed both hands on her belly.

Again, Baeve hesitated. "Catrione, she blames you for not taking Deirdre's child sooner. She blames you for misusing your druid-skills, for sorcery and sacrilege. I made this posset with my own hands. I don't advise you to eat or drink anything anyone else brings—"

"B-but, Baeve." Catrione gripped the woman's hands and shook them. "Baeve, I've seen things, I've done things—I'm not really blind, I know I don't have eyes, but I've another kind of sight I can see you—I swear—"

"Hush!" Baeve pressed two fingers against her lips. "Hush. Catrione, I can tell you see me. I don't not believe you. But I know how Niona will take what you say and twist it, turn it. We—Bride, Sora and I—we're only still-wives. We can't outsay her. We're hoping more druids come, for she's got these twisted around her fingers…" She heaved a sigh. "That poor knight in the other room…Niona won't let us touch him, Catrione. She's given orders—"

"Why don't you defy her?"

"I'm defying her by sending you away."

"What about that young knight? Surely you can't mean to just let him—I can hear him, Baeve. I didn't go into his room because I thought it was mine and couldn't see. I heard him calling."

"No one else does."

"I'm telling you, Baeve, I'm different." Catrione paused. "And you know I'm right—maybe you can't hear him, but you know what I'm saying is true. Please. If you won't defy Niona, at least leave the door unlatched. It's not human to leave a man in that kind of pain."

There was a long silence broken only by a long sigh, the rustle of skirts. Finally Baeve cleared her throat. "Drink that posset. You make ready to leave, I'll leave your door unlatched."

* * *

"Hello, Catrione." Bran's voice took her by surprise as Catrione sat beside the window, listening to the bees drone. "I'm glad to see you're better." She heard the latch slip shut, felt the rush of air as he came to stand beside her, smelled his sweat. "I'm sorry about your eyes."

"It's all right, Bran, I can see." She turned her head to him. He was a blaze of rose and purple light. "It's a different way of seeing, but I can see."

He cleared his throat.

"What's wrong," she prompted.

"It's Lochlan," he said. "He needs help and—"

"It's all right, Bran." She put her hand on his shoulder and smiled. "I hear him, too. Tonight, I mean to help him."

"The other one—the other cailleach—she tried to help him, several times, but he wasn't ready to come back and so it didn't—"

"Ah." Catrione's brows rose. Niona was saving Lochlan for herself, perhaps? Or perhaps that's why she felt the sacred rites were no longer effective. "Well. That's interesting. But how do you know that?"

"He comes to me and tells me. But I told the brother, and he didn't do anything. I know that. Lochlan told me."

Catrione patted his hand and contemplated the information. "Bran, maybe you should come with me."

"With you? With you and Lochlan? Where?"

"I think, from what I'm sensing, that Lochlan will head to Allovale. But I have another errand—a druid errand. Maybe you'd like to come with me? It's no more than three or four days, I think. And then we'll go to Allovale ourselves."

"What kind of druid errand?"

"There's a village and a pair of little boys without a father. He asked me to check on them. It's a promise I need to keep."

"Of course, I'll come with you," he said at once. "I don't want to stay here. They're making me learn blacksmithing. I hate it."

"Every druid needs it," she replied. "But I don't think we should stay here, Bran. Something tells me our kind of druid isn't welcomed here much more."

"Where shall I meet you?" he asked. "Here?"

In the stables, she almost said. "No," she answered. "Come to Lochlan's room. Once I bring him back, he's likely to be very weak. I'll need your help to get him out. All right?"

"All right," he said. He got to his feet, then leaned down awkwardly and kissed her cheek. "Thank you. I'm very grateful that you saved me, Cailleach. My mother's very grateful, too."

"You see your mother, Bran?"

"Once in a while," he shrugged. "It's more I hear her voice—she always tells me to do what I don't want to do. She annoys me—I have to tell her to get out of my head." He paused. "That's what Morla used to say. She'd tell me to get out of her head. I didn't understand what she meant."

"But you do, now?" Catrione smiled. He would make a good druid when he learned discipline and self-control. *I had those things, and I wasn't a very good druid,* she thought. *Maybe I'll be a better druid now.*

"I do now." She heard him walk across the room.

"How will you know what time?" she asked, amused, as he lifted the latch.

"Lochlan says he'll tell me. He says I'll know."

"How?"

"I won't hear him like I do now." Then Bran was gone, in a flash of emerald brilliance that made Catrione smile for no reason at all.

She didn't need the knight's permission—she had it already—but in the moonlight, she paused. He was lying still on the bed, hands clasped just below his breastbone, eyes closed, mouth still. Only the even rising and falling of his chest and his rigid erection bulging beneath the sheet hinted that this man was anything but close to death or lost in sleep.

She saw the sheet as a translucent barrier, his body a coiled dark red flame. She felt the flesh between her legs quiver. *If I weren't pregnant already,* she thought, *we'd make a child tonight.* That's what had happened with Cwynn, she realized. All that energy—it had to go somewhere.

She felt a little dizzy. She went to the side of the bed and peeled the sheet back. *This is what the Hag sees, when she lies with her lover, Herne—all these beautiful colors and lines,* thought Catrione, and the need that went through her made her knees weak. She pulled off her tunic and moved his hands off his chest and felt the first flicker of pressure in his palms, heard his first sigh. "Lochlan, will you take me in?" she whispered.

His hips bucked from the bed and the tip of his phallus ensnared itself in the folds of her flesh. With a groan of pleasure, she slid down and back, pulling him deep inside her, pulling him up and back and out of the pale gray void.

## 20

A bloated orange moon hung low in the sky over the peaks around the sprawling keep of Eaven Avellach. Morla gripped the stone railing, squared her shoulders and took a deep breath. "I can't marry you, Fengus-da," she said. "I can't marry you—not even for a year and a day." No, no. That wasn't right. "Not even for a year and day" sounded weak. And "can't" sounded weak, as well. "I won't marry you, Fengus-da," she said aloud. "I won't."

If there was one thing she'd learned in the short time she'd been here at Eaven Avellach, Fengus took advantage of any sign of weakness, ruthlessly ready to exploit an opponent. He wasn't going to be happy to be told she'd changed her mind.

The preparations for the feast alone were staggering—he must've slaughtered a whole herd in preparation . Well, why not? he was counting on the fat herds of Mochmorna. Daily, more and more knights arrived in response to Fengus's decision to call for a tournament in which the winner would be crowned harvest king. Fengus was broadly suggesting Morla celebrate Lughnasa by being the harvest queen, a suggestion to which Morla hardly knew how to respond. She had to remind herself that this was a wedding—her wedding. But Morla felt herself in mourning.

Meeve's passing gave her an excuse to postpone and delay the ceremony, but Fengus's mother, old Fierce-eyed Fearne as she was called by everyone in the keep, including her son, seemed to know there was another reason. She watched Morla with black beady eyes that reminded Morla of the vultures perched on the trees above the corpses as they cleared them off the battlefield before the gates of the druid-house. Bald head and beaked nose, pointing down to her chin. Every day saw Fengus brooding on the walls, looking for some word of his daughter, but each day found him disappointed. Morla hoped for word from White Birch, too. She hoped for word of Lochlan. She hoped for word of Bran. She gazed out over the jagged peaks surrounding Eaven Avellach and felt herself even more a prisoner than ever. But she had given her word. She had made a promise. A year and a day. She could do that, she thought. A year and a day wasn't so long.

But just the thought of Fengus's gnarled hands on her body, of his bulk pressing her down, made her pulse race to the point of dizziness. *I just don't think I can bear to do this*, she thought, as she gazed out over the moon. *How can I give myself, heart and soul and body to a man I don't love, even for the sake of the land?* She'd done it once, and while her time with Fionn had not been unpleasant, still, she longed for the passion and the connection she'd shared, however fleetingly, with Lochlan. She squared her shoulders, lifted her chin, gazed at the moon, and declared, "I can't marry you, Fengus-da. I just can't."

"But will you at least come down to dinner?"

Shock made her knees weak. She spun around to face Fengus standing in the doorway of her antechamber. "Fe-Fengus, it's not—I didn't mean—well, I did mean…" she began, but he cut her off with a wave of his hand.

"If you're not happy here, Morla, you shouldn't stay. If that's how it is, that's how it is." Fengus's words sounded reasonable, but his mouth thinned as he spoke and the purple vein in his temple began to beat. Morla swallowed hard. He could push her, over the railing of the balcony, she thought, and for a split second, he looked as if he wanted to do that. "I'd never hold you prisoner. If you wish to leave, you can leave in the morning." His fists jerked closed.

Morla squared her shoulders. "If you'll just wait a moment, I'll come down with you."

"Thank you." He turned on his heel and shut the door carefully—too carefully—behind him.

Morla stared at the polished steel mirror, heart thumping. *You'd go further if you learned to be agreeable,* echoed Meeve's voice out of her memory. Well, she hadn't learned. Somehow she doubted Fengus was going to let her go tomorrow as easily as he agreed to tonight, in front of no one else. And it occurred to her that if she disappeared, or was found dead, as the result of an unfortunate accident, Fengus would have the perfect reason to claim most or all of Dalraida and Mochmorna. There'd been no word of her brother Cwynn. Deirdre was dead, Bran was a druid. If she turned up dead, Fengus would assert a bride claim and say her untimely death had deprived him of a wife, and he was entitled to some compensation to help heal his grief. And with no other immediate family to claim it—other than possibly Cwynn...her thoughts trailed off into a tangled knot of panic. She was alone, as alone as she'd been in that horrible camp.

She was being ridiculous, she decided. Fengus was simply upset, especially given the way he'd found out. He wasn't foolish enough to either hold her hostage, or worse, kill her. Everyone knew she was here. But only Fengus knew she wanted to leave. She did something with the remnants of her hair, covered her scalp with a coif...then tugged her kirtle into place.

The riding clothes she'd worn here had disappeared, taken, Fengus claimed, to allow his mother's women to fashion garments in her size. But the only garments Fearne's seamstresses seemed capable of producing were kirtles such as the old women themselves wore, and the long, confining tunics that went under them.

A cough from the antechamber brought her out of her reverie. She took another look at herself, pinched her cheeks and walked out to meet Fengus. He was squatting by the cold hearth, peering up the chimney. "Looks like a bird's roosting," he said. "Have to get that looked at before winter comes." He rose, dusting the soot off his hands. He wiped them on his thighs and indicated the door. "Shall we, my lady?"

"Fengus—I'm so sorry. I want to apologize—I never meant for you—"

"There's no need, my lady."

"But I think there is. It's not I'm not grateful. It's just—"

"You love the dead knight." He shrugged. "I understand. I knew that, before we left White Birch. I guess I—" He broke off, looked down. "I guess I thought you understood our marriage wasn't just between us—it was a symbol of something." He took a deep breath, then said, "But if it's not to be, it's not to be." He indicated the door. "Let's not keep them waiting. Tomorrow before you leave, we'll discuss how to explain the change in plans. But for tonight—" His mouth flexed in a smile that didn't reach his eyes, and he stood back to let her pass before him, then planted his hand squarely on the back of her cream-white kirtle. The outline of his sooty hand showed clearly. "Oh, my, look at that. I'm so sorry, my lady. I forgot myself. Would you like to change?"

She opened her mouth, put her hand on the door, unsure whether or not it was really an accident, when a young boy's high-pitched voice rang out from somewhere far below: "Fengus-da! Fengus-da! Tully's home—Tully's back—home from White Birch Grove!"

Fengus practically flew down the steps, Morla slowly following. Tully might be a blessing in disguise, for he might distract Fengus tonight, long enough, at least, for her to sneak out of the castle after he'd drunk himself into a stupor.

But at the bottom of the steps, she was amazed to see Fengus with his hands wrapped around Tully's throat, even while his knights worked to free the old man. "What do you mean, she's missing? How can she be missing? How could you have let her go?"

"We didn't let her go, chief," Tully answered when he could. Morla actually felt sorry for the old man. He had been extremely devoted to Fengus's daughter, she remembered, haunting the passage outside her room, bringing fresh flowers every day for her bedside table. "You don't understand all that happened… I can't explain it, none of the lads can, but they'll all swear to it. Just ask."

"What?" demanded Fengus. He shouldered away from the four men who held him back. "Don't tell me you were ambushed?"

The hall was getting crowded. Morla eased away from the bottom of the staircase, slipping next to a pair of serving maids who'd crept up from the kitchens.

"N-no," said Tully. He glanced around the room. "Are you sure you want me to speak here?"

A vein popped in Fengus's forehead and his cheeks turned nearly purple, as he bellowed: "Answer my question! That's my daughter you've lost!"

"I can't, Chief. I've got no answer."

With a roar, Fengus launched himself on Tully, dragging the old man to the ground, pummeling him. Six knights converged on top of them.

As the men rolled and struggled, a voice spoke directly into Morla's ear. "Old blowhard. Sure you want to marry him?"

Morla looked around surreptitiously. The two serving girls had scurried off, no one else was close to her. The crowd that gathered were comprised mostly of men, who closed around the fight in a tight-knit circle.

Something poked her back and she jumped. "Or was it some deathbed promise to Meeve?"

Morla's coif tumbled off her head, as if it had been pulled from behind, exposing the tight dark curls that clustered all over her head in silky ringlets.

"I like your hair," the same voice whispered.

But there was no one there. She picked up the coif and fled up the steps, certain she heard the rapid tap of boots behind her. She glanced over both shoulders, but saw no one.

She dashed into her room and would have slammed the door shut, but a hand—a big hand—inserted itself between the door and the frame and a boot appeared on the floor, preventing the door from closing. She stifled a scream, fumbled at her waist for her dinner knife and stumbled back as the door opened, and against all hope or reason, Lochlan stepped into the room.

He slammed the door behind him and slid the lock closed. For a long moment they stared at each other, and then in one smooth, near simultaneous motion, they reached for each other. His arms slid around her body, hers closed around his neck, her head fell into the hollow of his chest as if it had been made to fit. Her eyes filled as the most irrational joy flowed through her, and the tears spilled down her face as his mouth came down on hers. "I thought you were dying," she said when she could.

He wiped away the tears with his thumbs, and she saw his own eyes were wet. "Fengus's daughter—Catrione the druid—saved me. The others were just going to leave me to rot. I don't know why—my suspicion is Fengus paid them off." He took a single step toward her. "But I could not let you marry him, Morla, without coming to you myself—"

She cut him off, drawing his face to hers once more. For a long moment, they simply stood there, locked in a long kiss. When at last they separated, he grinned down at her. "Does that mean you don't really want to marry Fengus?"

"You know I don't want to marry Fengus. But tonight—just now—I— Oh, I am so stupid." She broke away, and explained what happened.

"How'd he take it?" asked Lochlan, an incredulous look on his face.

"Better than I thought."

"Hmm. Not well at all, then."

"What do you mean?"

"Morla, why'd you think Meeve would never agree to marry him?" Lochlan crossed to the door, opened it a crack, peered outside and turned back to her. "Listen. We might have an opportunity here to slip out while he's distracted. Are you willing?"

"But—but how? Just walk out?"

"Well, we could do that. Or, we could use this cloak Catrione was kind enough to let me borrow."

"What cloak? That cloak you're wearing?"

"Aye. In the shadows, it has special properties."

"Oh? Like what?" She took a few steps toward him, drawn by the need to simply touch him, to feel his skin under her fingers, to inhale his scent into her lungs.

As Fengus's bellowing rose even louder, Lochlan drew her close. "It's a magic cloak—it's how I got in here without being seen. Deirdre made it. Catrione thought maybe you should have it. At least long enough to get out of Eaven Avellach."

"You think Fengus won't let me go?"

"My dear Morla, we're going to have work on your tendency to blurt out the truth. I think at this point, Fengus would hold you captive—I heard talk of nothing but the wedding the whole way here. His pride's at stake along with his grab for the High Crown now that Meeve's gone. Marrying you is part of his plan." He broke off, and raised her chin with the tip of one finger. "But now that Meeve's gone—"

"Now that Meeve's gone, I don't intend to marry anyone but you." She threw her arms around him and pressed up close against him, as if to reassure herself he was real. "Assuming you can get us out of here."

He chuckled softly, pulled her close, and held her tightly for the space of just a couple heartbeats. Then he drew the cloak around himself and held it over her. "You have a bargain, lady. Assuming we make it out of here, first we marry, and then—" he cocked his head in the direction of the hall. "And then we'll do our best not to go to war."

The day was turning down to dusk and the golden light was nearly as incandescent as Faerie, when the salt tang in the air and the cries of seabirds overhead told Catrione she had reached Far Nearing at last. "I think we're here, Catrione," said Bran, above the cries of the seabirds. "Can you smell the sea?"

Catrione smiled and clucked to the horse, and he picked up the pace obligingly. To the end of her days, Catrione would feel guilty about the wrath she knew her father would inflict on poor Tully, but she had made a promise to Cwynn. He had given his life for hers. She would make certain that his grandfather's holdings, his sons and all who remembered him were safe. It was the least she could do. And then…

And then she supposed she would have to go back to Eaven Avellach, and see what peace might be brokered between her father and the other chieftains. Fengus wanted to be High King; he would see Meeve's death and his own heroic actions as reasons enough he should be chosen by the others. But he was a hothead, and he was about to be dangerously humiliated when Morla refused to marry him, assuming Lochlan arrived in time. The countryside she'd ridden across was rife with talk of his great contest of arms. A hundred hotheaded warriors, all flush with feasting and rewards, were very easy to mold into a formidable force, just in time to march across the harvested land. Not for nothing was autumn called the fighting time of the year.

But here, today, it was high summer, and the soft air caressed her cheek. Bran whooped and trotted through the flats. The breeze was ripe with salt and fish, the gulls shrieked above the rhythmic pounding of the water. On the beaches, Catrione could see the golden glimmers that were children digging in the shadows, and the more complex patterns of color and light that were the village women. They sat amidst the twisted shapes of the driftwood, mending nets, shucking shellfish and telling stories. Catrione could feel them stop and point and stare as she rode by, and a few even motioned for their children.

A query for the children of Cwynn MaMeeve, however, brought only questioning looks, and she had to rack her brain to remember his father's name. Even that brought head-scratches and frowns, until one of the old women hawked and spat and said, "She means Cermmus's boy, from up at the point." The old woman leaned out of her chair and pointed straight down the narrow causeway. "That way— you ride up to the gate and ask for Argael the midwife's house. She can tell you."

Catrione sketched a blessing over their heads and felt their eyes follow her the whole way up to the gates. The animal plowed through the bright, thick air, and Catrione felt her heart begin to beat. She had no idea how she'd be received, she thought, and it was obvious from the way Cwynn had acted, from his questions, that these people had little to do with druids. If they refused her help, she could still ward the village, perhaps not as effectively as if they'd all agreed to cooperate, but enough to prevent goblins from attacking.

At the gates, a woman rinsing laundry raised her head when Catrione asked her a question, and she put a hand over her brow to shield the long rays of the setting sun. "You're a druid." It was a flat statement, not a question and Catrione nodded. "And you're blind?"

"I've sight enough to bring me here," replied Catrione. "Please, can you tell me where the sons of Cwynn MaMeeve live?"

"Cwynn DaRuadan, as we call him here," the woman replied. "They're my grandsons. Ariene, their mother, is my daughter." She tossed the water into a gutter and picked up her board. "My name is Argael. Come. I'll take you." She looked at Bran. "You look like Cwynn as a lad."

Catrione dismounted and motioned for Bran to do the same. "This is Bran. He's Cwynn's brother. He's druid, as well."

"Ah," the midwife nodded. "They said his brother was coming for him. But no one ever showed up."

She wrapped the reins around her fist and led the big horse through the gates and up the roughly cobbled path that led between the buildings. To Catrione's eyes, the keep was comprised of huge slabs of light and shadow. The sunlight was intensely bright, reflecting off the white stone, off the sand, off the shells scattered in front of every house.

"Ariene!" Argael cried, as they approached a small cottage, set apart from the others. "Bring the boys. There's a druid—two druids here—come to see them."

From somewhere deep in the house, a younger woman called back, "They're down on the beach with Cwynn— they should be coming up for supper any time. You want me to fetch them?" The voice grew louder, and a silvery shimmer came through the door and out into the sun. An image sprang fully formed into Catrione's mind of a girl with long dark hair and a broad forehead, big eyes and full red lips. But the shimmer flushed an ugly shade of red as Catrione turned to greet her.

"Did you say Cwynn?" asked Catrione, even as some detached part of her noted Ariene's negative response. Her heart began to pound, her breathing slowed. Could he really have survived Tiermuid and made his way back here?

"She said Cwynn," put in Bran.

"Aye, this time of day he's on the beach, mending the nets. The boys like to—" Argael broke off and touched Catrione's arm. "Cailleach? Are you all right? You look a bit pale."

"We didn't think Cwynn was alive," said Bran. "Callie Catrione, come sit."

Catrione stumbled backwards, and the midwife caught her by the forearm. "Cailleach, sit. Here, you rest. Let me fetch you something to drink—we have a good sweet well, not one of those brackish ones. Just rest."

"How could he have got here?" Catrione muttered, more to herself than to Bran. "And all this time—we didn't know…" As if in a daze, she got to her feet. She heard Bran call her name, but she ignored him and followed the crunch of the pebbled path to the beach, where a tall man perched on a rock, with a wide swath of fabric across his knees.

A pair of dark-haired little boys of maybe two years dug in the sand at his feet. As she approached, the man looked up and dropped his mending with a little cry when he saw her. "Catrione?" he whispered harshly. "Catrione, by the Mother of us all, is it really you?" He ran to her, across the sand. The boys paused in their playing. They gaped, openmouthed as baby fish as Cwynn caught her hands. "I'm so glad to see you—I'm so glad to know you're—"

"Cwynn, what's this?" Catrione held up his hand, his whole right hand. "Your hand—you're whole—what happened to you? Did you kill him? Did you kill Tiermuid? And how did you get here?"

Cwynn turned his head and spoke over his shoulder. "Go on up to Mammy now, and tell Gammy there'll be extra for supper. Go, I'll be there in a trice." He waited until the boys went scampering up the path, then turned back to face Catrione. The soft air blowing off the water had just the hint of an edge in it, and it blew the tendrils around her face. Gently he pushed them back. "No. No, I didn't." He rammed his hands in his belt, looked down and shuffled his bare feet in the sand. "I don't really remember what I did. I remember we were fighting—I raised that silver-coated hook to kill him, and the next—" He broke off and turned toward the water "—I was lying on this beach, washed up on the tide. Ariene and her mother found me screaming my head off in some kind of fit—"

"Ah, the Afterward."

"You knew about this?"

"When you've been in TirNa'lugh too long, that's what happens. The effects wear off eventually."

"Argael told me I nearly died. I was in a mazed state for about a week."

"Sometimes that happens."

"Sometimes? I wished you warned me. But as it is, I woke up and, well, here I am, and now Ariene and me—we're trying to make a go of it, Catrione, for the boys' sake, you know?"

"A go of what?"

"A marriage, a Beltane marriage. We jumped the broom the new moon after MidSummer—that's a good time to begin new things, right? The boys—they're a handful, they need their father. And to tell you the truth, now I've got my hand back, well—I like to fish. You can be sure I'll be more careful from now on."

Catrione swallowed hard. The wind was getting stronger now, and the tide was coming in. She could hear it lapping around the jetties jutting out into the water. "Are you telling me—" She broke off, trying to collect her thoughts into some semblance of order. "Are you telling me you don't want to be High King?"

"That's what I'm telling you."

"Don't you understand? You can't just walk away from this. You've been healed, you've been made whole for a reason. Not so you can stay here and fish. You're whole now—did you know Morla was branded? She can't be High Queen, but you—you can become High King. That's why the Hag made you whole. Don't you know that? Can't you feel it?"

A wave washed over their feet and instinctively Catrione stepped back. But Cwynn stood his ground and when he spoke, his voice was so soft she had to strain to hear it. "The sidhe-girl, the Faerie queen, I think she was—she said the same thing. That's why he let me go, you see—when the magic—whatever it was, was done, my hand turned to flesh. And he was getting ready to kill me, but she stopped it. She said I was to be High King. So I don't think I want to be High King, Catrione. I want no part of Faerie. And it's beautiful here, I wish you could see it. The water's a clear, calm blue today, and the sky is just as blue. The sun's shining orange, the gulls are white against the black rocks—"

"I can see." She cut him off savagely. "There's going to be a kingmaking at Samhain. How can you say you will not come? Don't you see this is your destiny? How can you refuse it?"

"I guess I don't know it has to be my destiny." Cwynn heaved a long sigh and ran a hand through his hair. "Don't you see that?"

"What if there were a way to guarantee you wouldn't fall into Faerie, that the sidhe couldn't come and take you?"

"Like what?"

"Well, I don't know, but what if there were? What then?"

He opened his mouth, but before he could answer her, a shout rang out from the top of the path. "Supper!" cried Ariene. Catrione looked up to see a jagged crimson outline

with a gleaming pink child on each hip. Behind her stood
Bran, waving happily.

"How can you think I'd want to leave?" He took her hands
and brought them to his lips. "Is that Bran? It is? You can
both stay, then, as long as you like."

"I can't stay here, Cwynn—I've work to do, soon a child
to raise—" She broke off. "Your child, yes. Do you know how
precious this child is? Do you have any idea what this child
could mean to Brynhyvar? This child unites the blood of
Mochmorna and Allovale—"

"Then maybe you should stay and let me care for it.
Ariene will come around."

"No, she won't." Catrione stared at him, incredulous he
could even suggest such a thing. Nothing about Ariene suggested to Catrione her presence was welcome for any longer
than absolutely necessary. "No, she won't. You can't stay
here. You're the king, Cwynn, the rightful heir to Meeve. The
Hag herself made you whole. Don't you understand? You
owe her. She's coming back for you, whether you will it or
not. How could you think otherwise?"

He glanced up at the house. "You know, I caught the fish
myself this morning."

"You can't ignore this. It's not going away any more than
the child is." A sudden harsh gust whipped her hair around
her face, and with his new hand, he gently brushed it away
once more, tucking it tenderly behind her ear, a gesture that
inexplicably made her throat thicken.

As she brushed it away with an impatient sniff, he said,
"Remember the old woman who came to the forge?"

"How could I forget her?"

"When she thanked me, she asked me something. I thought it was strange. She asked me if I ever wanted to be a king."

"And what did you say?"

"Never once. That's when she chuckled and gave me the disk." For a long moment, he was quiet. Then he heaved a great sigh, and took her by the shoulders, and even though she couldn't see him, she could see the colors in his eyes, blue and green and gold, all swirling in a shimmering cloud of shifting light. "Maybe you're right. Maybe you're right, and I can't stay here forever. Maybe you're right, and I do owe the Hag something. Maybe I have to be king someday. But for right now—well, it's supper time and there's a fat fish frying and new bread and butter churned, and brambleberries my lads and I picked just this afternoon. And I'm hungry. Aren't you?"

Catrione stared out, in the direction of the coming night. The sun was setting, the night air was turning heavy and cold. She could hear the sea boiling over the rocks along the shore. The smell of the food, rich and tempting, made her mouth water as it drifted on the breeze from the houses up above. There would be time to argue more tomorrow. She tightened her fingers on her staff, and took the arm he offered her. "Yes," she said. "I am."

## AFTERWARDS

In the halls of the Goblin Queen, nothing stirred. The goblins lay in charred heaps, incinerated in the blaze of the new kind of light the sidhe unleashed upon them. The firepits smoked, the skulls of mortals tumbled from their high piles and rotted with their captors. But behind the throne, an enormous egg incubated, one of several hundreds kept alive by the smoldering corpses. Within the egg, the Goblin King opened his eyes, grew strong and began to dream.

Author's Note – A tale told of events occurring a thousand years before may differ from other versions. Some say the Silver Caul was created for other reasons, or even, by other hands. This was the account that made the most sense.

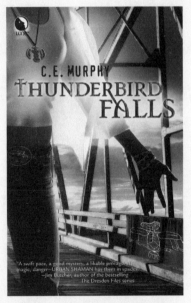

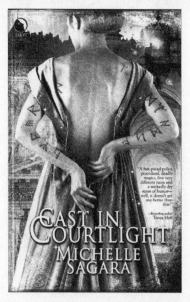